WARCRAFT®

WAR OF THE ANCIENTS
TRILOGY

BOOK ONE

THE WELL OF ETERNITY

RICHARD A. KNAAK

POCKET BOOKS
New York   London   Toronto   Sydney

This book is a work of fiction. Names, characters, places and incidents are products of the author's imagination or are used fictitiously. Any resemblance to actual events or locales or persons living or dead is entirely coincidental.

An *Original* Publication of POCKET BOOKS

 POCKET BOOKS, a division of Simon & Schuster, Inc.
1230 Avenue of the Americas, New York, NY 10020

Copyright © 2004 by Blizzard Entertainment. All rights reserved. Warcraft and Blizzard Entertainment are trademarks or registered trademarks of Blizzard Entertainment in the U.S. and/or other countries. All other trademarks are the property of their respective owners.

All rights reserved, including the right to reproduce this book or portions thereof in any form whatsoever. For information address Pocket Books, 1230 Avenue of the Americas, New York, NY 10020
ISBN 13: 978-0-7434-7119-0
ISBN 10:   0-7434-7119-9
First Pocket Books printing April 2004

20 19 18 17 16 15 14 13

POCKET and colophon are registered trademarks of Simon & Schuster, Inc.

Cover art by Bill Petras

Manufactured in the United States of America

For information regarding special discounts for bulk purchases, please contact Simon & Schuster Special Sales at 1-800-456-6798 or business@simonandschuster.com

A TERRIBLE HOWL ECHOED THROUGH THE PASS.

A massive, eight-legged lupine form dropped down on Rhonin. Had he been other than what he was, the wizard would have perished there, the meal of a savage, saber-toothed creature with four gleaming green eyes to go with its eight, clawed limbs. The monstrous wolf-creature brought him down, but Rhonin, having magicked his garments to better protect him from the elements, proved a hard nut to crack. The claws scraped at a cloak they should have readily tattered, only to have instead one nail snap off.

Gray fur standing on end, the beast howled its frustration. Rhonin took the opening, casting a simple but effective spell that had saved him in the past.

A cacophony of light burst before the creature's emerald orbs, both blinding and startling it. It ducked back, swatting uselessly at flashing patterns.

Dragging himself out of reach, Rhonin rose. There was no chance of flight; that would only serve to turn his back on the beast and his protective spell was already weakening. A few more slashes and the claws would be ripping the wizard to the bone.

Fire had worked against the ghoul on the island and Rhonin saw no reason why such a tried and true spell would not benefit him again. He muttered the words—

And suddenly they came out in reverse. Worse, Rhonin found himself moving backward, returning to the wild claws of the blinded beast.

Time had turned in on itself . . . but how?

For Martin Fajkus and my readers
throughout the world.

THE WELL OF ETERNITY

ONE

The tall, forbidding palace perched atop the very edge of the mountainous cliff, overlooking so precariously the vast, black body of water below that it appeared almost ready to plummet into the latter's dark depths. When first the vast, walled edifice had been constructed, using magic that melded both stone and forest into a single, cohesive form, it had been a wonder to touch the heart of any who saw it. Its towers were trees strengthened by rock, with jutting spires and high, open windows. The walls were volcanic stone raised up, then bound tightly by draping vines and giant roots. The main palace at the center had originally been created by the mystical binding of more than a hundred giant, ancient trees. Bent in together, they had formed the skeleton of the rounded center, over which the stone and vines had been set.

A wonder to touch the hearts of all when first it had been built, now it touched the fears of some. An unsettling aura enshrouded it, one heightened this stormy night. The few who peered at the ancient edifice now quickly averted their gaze.

Those who looked instead to the waters below it found no peace, either. The ebony lake was now in violent, unnatural turmoil. Churning waves as high as the palace rose and fell in the distance, crashing with a roar. Lightning played over its vast body, lightning gold, crimson, or the green of decay. Thunder rumbled like a thousand dragons and those who lived around its shores huddled close, uncertain as to what sort of storm might be unleashed.

On the walls surrounding the palace, ominous guards in forest-green armor and wielding lances and swords glared warily about. They watched not only beyond the walls for foolish trespassers, but on occasion surreptitiously glanced within . . . particularly at the main tower, where they sensed unpredictable energies at play.

And in that high tower, in a stone chamber sealed from the sight of those outside, tall, narrow figures in iridescent robes of turquoise, embroidered with stylized, silver images of nature, bent over a six-sided pattern written into the floor. At the center of the pattern, symbols in a language archaic even to the wielders flared with lives of their own.

Glittering, silver eyes with no pupils stared out from under the hoods as the night elves muttered the spell. Their dark, violet skin grew covered in sweat as the magic within the pattern amplified. All but one looked weary, ready to succumb to exhaustion. That one, overseeing the casting, watched the process not with silver orbs like the rest, but rather false black ones with streaks of ruby running horizontal along the centers. But despite the false eyes, he noted every detail, every inflection by the others. His long, narrow face, narrow even for an elf, wore an expression of hunger and anticipation as he silently drove them on.

One other watched all of this, drinking in every word and gesture. Seated on a luxurious chair of ivory and leather, her rich, silver hair framing her perfect features and the silken gown—as golden as her eyes—doing the same for her exquisite form, she was every inch the vision of a queen. She leaned back against the chair, sipping wine from a golden goblet. Her jeweled bracelets tinkled as her hand moved and the ruby in the tiara she wore glistened in the light of the sorcerous energies the others had summoned.

Now and then her gaze shifted ever so slightly to study the dark-eyed figure, her full lips pursing in something approaching suspicion. Yet, when once he suddenly glanced her way, as if sensing her observation, all suspicion vanished, replaced by a languid smile.

The chanting continued.

The black lake churned madly.

There had been a war and it had ended.

So, Krasus knew, history would eventually record what had happened. Almost lost in that recording would be the countless personal lives destroyed, the lands ravaged, and the near-destruction of the entire mortal world.

Even the memories of dragons are fleeting under such circumstances, the pale, gray-robed figure conceded to himself. He understood that very well, for although to most eyes he resembled a lanky, almost elven figure with hawklike features, silvering hair, and three long scars traveling down his right cheek, he was much more than that. To most, he was known as a wizard, but to a select few he was called *Korialstrasz*—a name only a dragon would wear.

Krasus had been born a dragon, a majestic red one, the youngest of the great Alexstrasza's consorts. She, the Aspect of Life, was his dearest companion . . . yet once again he dragged himself away from her to study the plights and futures of the short-lived races.

In the hidden, rock-hewn abode he had chosen for his new sanctum, Krasus looked over the world of Azeroth. The gleaming emerald crystal enabled him to see whatever land, whatever individual, he desired.

And everywhere that the dragon mage looked, he saw devastation.

It seemed as if it had only been a few years ago when the grotesque, green-skinned behemoths called orcs, who had invaded the world from beyond, were defeated. With their remaining numbers kept in encampments, Krasus had believed the world ready for peace. Yet, that peace had been short-lived. The Alliance—the human-led coalition that had been the forefront of the resistance—had immediately begun to crumble, its members vying for power over one another. Part of that had been the fault of dragons—or the *one* dragon, Deathwing—but much had simply been the greed and desire of humans, dwarves, and elves.

Yet, even that would have passed with little concern if not for the coming of the Burning Legion.

Today, Krasus surveyed distant Kalimdor, located on the far side of the sea. Even now, areas of it resembled a land after a terrible volcanic eruption. No life, no semblance of civilization, remained in those areas. It had not been any natural force, however, that had rent the land so. The Burning Legion had left *nothing* in its wake but death.

The fiery demons had come from a place beyond reality. Magic was what they sought, magic they devoured. Attacking in conjunction with their monstrous pawns, the Undead Scourge, they had thought to lay waste to the world. Yet, they had not counted on the most unlikely alliance of all . . .

The orcs, once also their puppets, had turned on them. They had joined the humans, elves, dwarves, and dragons to decimate the demonic warriors and ghoulish beasts and push the remnants back into the hellish beyond. Thousands had perished, but the alternative . . .

The dragon mage snorted. In truth, there had been *no* alternative.

Krasus waved long, tapering fingers over the orb, summoning a vision of the orcs. The view blurred momentarily, then revealed a mountainous, rocky area further inland. A harsh land, but one still full of life and capable of supporting the new colonists.

Already, several stone structures had risen in the main settlement, where the Warchief and one of the heroes of the war, Thrall, ruled. The high, rounded edifice that served as his quarters was crude by the standards of any other race, but orcs had a propensity toward basics. Extravagance to an orc was having a permanent place to live at all. They had been nomads or prisoners for so long that the concept of "home" had been all but lost.

Several of the massive, greenish figures tilled a field. Watching the tusked, brutish-looking workers, Krasus marveled at the concept of orc farmers. Thrall, however, was a highly unusual orc and he had readily grasped the ideas that would return stability to his people.

Stability was something the entire world needed badly. With another wave of his hand, the dragon mage dismissed Kalimdor, summoning now a much closer location—the once proud capital of his favored Dalaran. Ruled by the wizards of the Kirin Tor, the prime wielders of magic, it had been at the forefront of the Alliance's battle against the Burning Legion in Lordaeron and one of the first and most prized targets of the demons in turn.

Dalaran lay half in ruins. The once-proud spires had been all but shattered. The great libraries burned. Countless generations of knowledge had been lost . . . and with them countless lives. Even the council had suffered badly. Several of those Krasus had counted as friends or at least respected colleagues had been slain. The leadership was in disarray and he knew that he would have to step in to lend a hand.

Dalaran needed to speak with one voice, if only to keep what remained of the splintered Alliance intact.

Yet, despite the turmoil and tribulations still ahead, the dragon did have hope. The problems of the world were surmountable ones. No more fear of orcs, no more fear of demons. Azeroth would struggle, but in the end, Krasus not only thought it would survive, he fully believed it would thrive.

He dismissed the emerald crystal and rose. The Dragon Queen, his beloved Alexstrasza, would be awaiting him. She suspected his desire to return to help the mortal world and, of all dragons, she most understood. He would transform to his true self, bid her farewell—for a time—and depart before regrets held him back.

His sanctum he had chosen not only for its seclusion, but also for its massiveness. Stepping from the smaller chamber, Krasus entered a toothy cavern whose heights readily matched the now lost towers of Dalaran. An army could have bivouacked in the cavern and not filled it.

Just the right size for a dragon.

Krasus stretched his arms . . . and as he did, his tapering fingers lengthened further, becoming taloned. His back arched and from near the shoulders erupted twin growths that quickly transformed into fledgling wings. His long features stretched, turning reptilian.

Throughout all these lesser changes, Krasus's form expanded. He became four, five, even ten times the size of a man and continued to grow. Any semblance to a human or elf quickly faded.

From wizard, Krasus became Korialstrasz, dragon.

But—in the very midst of the transformation—a desperate voice suddenly filled his head.

Kor . . . strasz . . .

He faltered, all but reverting to his wizardly form. Krasus

blinked, then stared around the huge chamber as if seeking the source of the cry there.

Nothing. The dragon mage waited and waited, but the call did not repeat.

Shrugging it off to his own uncertainties, he commenced again with the transformation—

And again, the desperate voice cried *Korialstra* . . .

This time . . . he recognized it. Immediately, he responded in kind. *I hear you! What is it you need of me?*

There was no response, but Krasus sensed the desperation remaining. Focusing, he tried to reach out, establish a link with the one who so badly needed his aid—the one who should have needed no aid from any creature.

I am here! the dragon mage demanded. *Sense me! Give me some indication of what is wrong!*

He felt the barest touch in return, a faint hinting of some distress. Krasus concentrated every iota of his thoughts into the meager link, hoping . . . hoping . . .

The overpowering presence of a dragon whose magic dwarfed his own a thousandfold sent Krasus staggering. A sensation of centuries, of great age, engulfed him. Krasus felt as if Time itself now surrounded him in all its terrible majesty.

Not Time . . . not quite . . . but he who was the Aspect of Time.

The Dragon of the Ages . . . Nozdormu.

There were only four great dragons, four Great Aspects, of which his beloved Alexstrasza was Life. Mad Malygos was Magic and ethereal Ysera influenced Dreams. They, along with brooding Nozdormu, represented creation itself.

Krasus grimaced. In truth, there had been *five* Aspects. The fifth had once been called Neltharion . . . the Earth Warder. But long ago, in a time even Krasus could not recall clearly, Neltharion had betrayed his fellows. The Earth

Warder had turned on them and in the process had garnered a new, more appropriate title.

Deathwing. The Destroyer.

The very thought of Deathwing stirred Krasus from his astonishment. He absently touched the three scars on his cheek. Had Deathwing returned to plague the world again? Was that why the great Nozdormu would show such distress?

I hear you! Krasus mentally called back, now more than ever fearful of the reason for the call. *I hear you! Is it—is it the Destroyer?*

But in response, he was once again buffeted by an overwhelming series of astonishing images. The images burnt themselves into his head, making it impossible for Krasus to ever forget any.

In either form, Krasus, however adaptable and capable, was no match for the unbridled power of an Aspect. The force of the other dragon's mental might flung him back against the nearest wall, where the mage collapsed.

It took several minutes for Krasus to push himself up from the floor and even then his head spun. Fragmented thoughts not his own assailed his senses. It was all he could do for a time just to remain conscious.

Slowly, though, things stabilized enough for him to realize the scope of all that had just happened. Nozdormu, Lord of Time, had been desperately crying out for aid . . . *his* aid. He had turned specifically to the lesser dragon, not one of his compatriots.

But anything that would so distress an Aspect could only be a monumental threat to the rest of Azeroth. Why then choose a lone red dragon and not Alexstrasza or Ysera?

He tried once more to reach the great dragon, but his efforts only made his head swim again. Steadying himself, Krasus tried to decide what to do instead. One image in particular constantly demanded his attention, the image of a snow-swept mountain area in Kalimdor. Whatever Nozdormu had sought to explain to him had to do with that desolate region.

Krasus would have to investigate it, but he would need capable assistance, someone who could adapt readily. While Krasus prided himself on his own ability to adapt well, his species was, for the most part, obstinate and set in its ways. He needed someone who would listen, but who could also react instantly as unfolding events required. No, for such unpredictable effort, only one creature would serve. A human.

In particular, a human named Rhonin.

A wizard . . .

And in Kalimdor, on the steppes of the wild country, a grizzled, aged orc leaned close over a smoky fire. Mumbling words whose origins lay on another, long-lost world, the moss-green figure tossed some leaves upon the fire, increasing the already thick smoke. Fumes filled his humble wood and earth hut.

The bald, elderly orc leaned over and inhaled. His weary brown eyes were veined and his skin hung in sacks. His teeth were yellow, chipped, and one of his tusks had been broken off years before. He could scarcely rise without aid and when he walked, he did so stooped and slow.

Yet, even the hardiest warrior paid him fealty as shaman.

A bit of bone dust, a touch of tannar berries . . . all part of a tried and true tradition resurrected among the orcs. Kalthar's father had taught him all even during the dark years of the Horde, just as Kalthar's grandsire had taught his father before that.

And now, for the first time, the withered shaman found himself hoping he had been taught well.

Voices murmured in his head, the spirits of the world that

the orcs now called home. Normally, they whispered little things, life things, but now they murmured anxiously, warning . . . warning . . .

But of what? He had to know more.

Kalthar reached into a pouch at his waist, removing three dried, black leaves. They were almost all of what remained from a single plant brought with him from the orcs' ancient world. Kalthar had been warned not to use them unless he deemed it truly necessary. His father had never used them, nor his grandfather.

The shaman tossed them into the flames.

Instantly the smoke turned a thick, swirling blue. Not black, but blue. The orc's brow furrowed at this change of color, then he leaned forward again and inhaled as much as possible.

The world transformed, and with it the orc. He had become a bird, a huge avian soaring over the landscape. He flew over mountains without a care. With his eyes he saw the tiniest animals, the most distant rivers. A sense of exhilaration not felt since his youth almost overwhelmed Kalthar, but he fought it. To give in would risk him losing his sense of self. He might fly forever as a bird, never knowing what he had once been.

Even as he thought that, Kalthar suddenly noted a wrongness in the nature of the world, possibly the reason for the voices' concern. Something *was* that should not be. He veered in the direction that felt correct, growing more anxious as he drew nearer.

And just within the deepest part of the mountain range, the shaman discovered the source of his anxiety.

His learned mind knew that he envisioned a concept, not the actual thing. To Kalthar, it appeared as a water funnel—yet one that swallowed and disgorged simultaneously. But what emerged or sank into its depths were days and nights, months and years. The funnel seemed to be eating and emitting time itself.

The notion so staggered the shaman that he did not notice until almost too late that the funnel now sought to draw *him* in as well.

Immediately, Kalthar strained to free himself. He flapped his wings, pushed with his muscles. His mind reached out to his physical form, tugging hard at the gossamer link tying body to soul and trying to break the trance.

Still the funnel drew him forward.

In desperation, Kalthar called upon the spirit guides, prayed to them to strengthen him. They came as he knew they would, but at first they seemed to act too slow. The funnel filled his view, seemed ready to engulf him—

The world abruptly twisted around the shaman. The funnel, the mountains . . . everything turned about and about.

With a gasp, Kalthar awoke.

Exhausted beyond his years, he barely kept himself from falling face first into the fire. The voices that constantly murmured had faded away. The orc sat on the floor of his hut, trying to reassure himself that, yes, he now existed whole in the mortal world. The spirit guides had saved him, albeit barely in time.

But with that happy reassurance came the reminder of what he had witnessed in his vision . . . and what it meant.

"I must tell Thrall . . ." he muttered, forcing weary, aged legs up. "I must tell him quick . . . else we lose our home . . . our world . . . again . . ."

TWO

An ominous portent, Rhonin decided, vivid green eyes gazing at the results of his divining. *Any wizard would recognize it as so.*

"Are you certain?" Vereesa called from the other room. "Have you checked your reading?"

The red-haired mage nodded, then grimaced when he realized that of course the elf could not see him. He would have to tell her face to face. She deserved that. *I pray she is strong.*

Clad in dark blue pants and jacket, both gold-trimmed, Rhonin looked more like a politician than a mage these days, but the past few years had demanded as much diplomacy from him as magic. Diplomacy had never been an easy thing for him, who preferred to go charging into a situation. With his thick mane of hair and his short beard, he had a distinct leonine appearance that so well matched his temper when forced to parlay with pampered, arrogant ambassadors. His nose, broken long ago and never—by his own choice—properly fixed, further added to his fiery reputation.

"Rhonin . . . is there something you have not told me?"

He could leave her waiting no longer. She had to know the truth, however terrible it might be. "I'm coming, Vereesa."

Putting away his divining instruments, Rhonin took a deep breath, then rejoined the elf. Just within the entrance, though, he paused. All Rhonin could see was her face—a beautiful, perfect oval upon which had been artfully placed alluring, almond-shaped eyes of pure sky blue, a tiny, up-turned nose, and an enticing mouth seemingly always halfway to a smile. Framing that face was a rich head of silver-white hair that, had she been standing, would have hung nearly to the small of her back. She could have passed yet for a human if not for the long, tapering ears jutting from the hair, pointed ears marking her race.

"Well?" she asked, patiently.

"It's . . . it's to be twins."

Her face lit up, if anything becoming more perfect in his eyes. "Twins! How fortuitous! How wonderful! I was so certain!"

She adjusted her position on the wooden bed. The slim but curved elven ranger now lay several months pregnant. Gone were her breastplate and leather armor. Now she wore a silver gown that did not at all conceal the imminent birth.

They should have guessed from the quickness with which she had shown, but Rhonin had wanted to deny it. They had been wed only a few months when she had discovered her condition. Both were concerned then, for not only had their marriage been one so very rare in the annals of history, but no one had ever recorded a successful human-elven birth.

And now they expected not one child, but two.

"I don't think you understand, Vereesa. *Twins!* Twins from a mage and an elf!"

But her face continued to radiate pleasure and wonder. "Elves seldom give birth and we very, very rarely give birth to twins, my love! They will be destined for great things!"

Rhonin could not hide his sour expression. "I know. That's what worries me . . ."

He and Vereesa had lived through their own share of

"great things." Thrown together to penetrate the orc stronghold of Grim Batol during the last days of the war against the Horde, they had faced not just orcs, but dragons, goblins, trolls, and more. Afterward, they had journeyed from realm to realm, becoming ambassadors of sorts whose task it had been to remind the Alliance of the importance of remaining intact. That had not meant, however, that they had not risked their lives during that time, for the peace following that war had been unstable at best.

Then, without warning, had come the Burning Legion.

By that time, what had started as a partnership of two wary agents had become a binding of two unlikely souls. In the war against the murderous demons, the mage and the ranger had fought as much for each other as for their lands. More than once, they had thought one another dead and the pain felt had been unbearable to each.

Perhaps the pain of losing each other had seemed worse because of all those other loved ones who had already perished. Both Dalaran and Quel'Thalas had been razed by the Undead Scourge, thousands slaughtered by the decaying abominations serving the dread Lich King, who in turn served the cause of the Legion. Entire towns perished horribly and matters were made worse by the fact that many of the victims soon rose from the dead, their cursed mortal shells now added to the ranks of the Scourge.

What little that remained of Rhonin's family had perished early in the war. His mother had been long dead, but his father, brother, and two cousins had all been slain in the fall of the city of Andorhal. Fortunately, the desperate defenders, seeing no hope of rescue, had set the city ablaze. Even the Scourge could not raise warriors from ash.

He had not seen any of them—not even his father—since entering the ranks of wizardry, but Rhonin had discovered an emptiness in his heart when the news had arrived. The rift between himself and his kin—caused in great part because of his chosen calling—had vanished in that instant. All that had mattered at the time was that he had become the last of his family. He was all alone.

Alone until he realized that the feelings he had developed for the brave elven ranger at his side were reciprocated.

When the terrible struggle had finally played out, there had been only one logical path for the two of them. Despite the horrified voices emanating from both Vereesa's people and Rhonin's wizardly masters, the two had chosen to never be parted again. They had sealed a pact of marriage and tried to begin as normal a life as two such as they could possibly have in a world torn asunder.

Naturally, thought the mage bitterly, *peace for us wasn't meant to be.*

Vareesa pushed herself from the bed before he could help her. Even so near the time of birth, the elf moved with assured swiftness. The elf took hold of Rhonin by the shoulders.

"You wizards! Always seeing the dire! I thought my own people were so gloomy! My love, this will be a happy birth, a happy pair of children! We will make it so!"

He knew that she made sense. Neither would do anything that would risk the infants. When the two had realized her condition, they ceased their own efforts to help rebuild the shattered Alliance and settled in one of the most peaceful regions left, near enough to shattered Dalaran but not too near. They lived in a modest but not completely humble home and the people of the nearby town respected them.

Her confidence and hope still amazed him, considering her own losses. If Rhonin had felt a hole in his heart after losing family he had barely known anymore, Vereesa surely had felt a gaping chasm open in her own. Quel'Thalas, more legendary and surely more secure than even the magic-ruled Dalaran, had been utterly ravaged. Elven strongholds untouched by centuries had fallen in mere days, their once-proud people added to the Scourge as easily as the mere humans. Among the latter had been included several of Vereesa's own close-knit clan . . . and a few from her very family.

From her grandfather she had heard of his desperate battle to slay the ghoulish corpse of his own son, her uncle. From him she had also heard how her younger brother had been ripped apart by a hungering mob of undead led by their own elder brother, who later had been set afire and destroyed along with the rest of the Scourge by the surviving defenders. What had happened to her parents, no one yet knew, but they, too, were presumed dead.

And what Rhonin had not told her . . . might never dare tell her . . . was of the monstrous rumors he had heard concerning one of Vereesa's two sisters, Sylvanas.

Vereesa's other sister, the great Alleria, had been a hero during the Second War. But Sylvanas, she whom Rhonin's wife had sought to emulate her entire life, had, as Ranger General, led the battle against the betrayer—Arthas, prince of Lordaeron. Once the shining hope of his land, now the twisted servant of the Legion and the Scourge, he had ravaged his own kingdom, then led the undead horde against the elven capital of Silvermoon. Sylvanas had blocked his path at every juncture and for a time, it had seemed that she would actually defeat him. But where the shambling corpses, sinister gargoyles, and gruesome abominations had failed, the dark necromancy granted the traitorous noble had succeeded.

The official version had Sylvanas dying valiantly as she

prevented Arthas's minions from slaying Silvermoon's people. The elven leaders, even Vereesa's grandfather, claimed that the Ranger General's body had burned in the same fire that had devastated half the capital. Certainly there had been no trace left.

But while the story ended there for Vereesa, Rhonin, through sources in both the Kirin Tor and Quel'Thalas, had discovered word of Sylvanas that left him chilled. A surviving ranger, his mind half gone, had babbled of his general being captured, not killed. She had been horribly mutilated, then finally slain for the pleasure of Arthas. Finally, taking her body up in the dark temple he had raised in his madness, the prince had corrupted her soul and corpse, transforming her from heroic elf into a harbinger of evil . . . a haunting, mournful phantom called a banshee that still supposedly roamed the ruins of Quel'Thalas.

Rhonin had so far been unable to verify the rumors, but he felt certain that they had more than a grain of truth. He prayed that Vereesa would never hear the story.

So many tragedies . . . small wonder that Rhonin could not shake his uncertainty when it came to his new family.

He sighed. "Perhaps when they're born, I'll be better. I'm likely just nervous."

"Which should be the sign of a caring parent." Vereesa returned to the bed. "Besides, we are not alone in this. Jalia aids much."

Jalia was an elder, full-bodied woman who had given birth to six children and midwifed several times that number. Rhonin had been certain that a human would be leery of dealing with an elf—let alone an elf with a wizard for a husband—but Jalia had taken one look at Vereesa and her maternal instincts had taken over. Even though Rhonin did pay her well for her time, he very much suspected that the townswoman would have volunteered anyway, so much had she taken to his wife.

"I suppose you're right," he began. "I've just been—"

A voice . . . a very familiar voice . . . suddenly filled his head. A voice that could not be bringing him good tidings.

Rhonin . . . I have need of you.

"Krasus?" the mage blurted.

Vereesa sat up, all cheer vanishing. "Krasus? What about him?"

They both knew the master wizard, a member of the Kirin Tor. Krasus had been the one instrumental in bringing them together. He had also been the one who had not told them the entire truth about matters at the time, especially where he himself had been concerned.

Only through dire circumstance had they discovered that he was also the dragon Korialstrasz.

"It's . . . it's Krasus," was all Rhonin could say at the moment.

Rhonin . . . I have need of you . . .

I won't help you! the mage instantly responded. *I've done my share! You know I can't leave her now . . .*

"What does he want?" Vereesa demanded. Like the wizard, she knew that Krasus would only contact them if some terrible trouble had arisen.

"It doesn't matter! He'll have to find someone else!"

Before you reject me, let me show you . . . the voice declared. *Let me show both of you . . .*

Before Rhonin could protest, images filled his head. He relived Krasus's astonishment at being contacted by the Lord of Time, experienced the dragon mage's shock when the Aspect's desperation became evident. Everything Krasus had experienced, the wizard and his wife now shared.

Last of all, Krasus overwhelmed them with an image of

the place the other believed the source of Nozdormu's distress, a chill and forbidding chain of jagged mountains.

Kalimdor.

The entire vision lasted only a few seconds, but it left Rhonin exhausted. He heard a gasp from the bed. Turning, the wizard found Vereesa slumped back on the down pillow.

He started toward her, but she waved off his concern. "I am all right! Just . . . breathless. Give me a moment . . ."

For her Rhonin would give eternity, but for another he had not even a second to grant. Summoning the image of Krasus into his head, the wizard replied, *Take your quests to someone else! Those days are through for me! I've got far more important matters at stake!*

Krasus said nothing and Rhonin wondered if his response had sent his former patron searching for another pawn. He respected Krasus, even liked him, but the Rhonin the dragon mage sought no longer existed. Only his family concerned him now.

But to his surprise, the one he expected most to stand by him instead suddenly muttered, "You will have to go immediately, of course."

He stared at Vereesa. "I'm not going anywhere!"

She straightened again. "But you must. You saw what I saw. He does not summon you for some frivolous task! Krasus is extremely worried . . . and what worries *him* puts fear into *me.*"

"But I can't leave you now!" Rhonin fell down on one knee next to her. "I will not leave you, or them!"

A hint of her ranger past spread across Vareesa's face. Eyes narrowing dangerously at whatever mysterious force would separate them, she answered, "And the last thing I would wish would be for you to thrust yourself into danger! I do not desire to sacrifice my children's father, but what we have seen hints at a terrible threat to the world they will be born in! For that reason alone, it makes sense to go. Were I not in this condition, I would be right at your side, you know that."

"Of course I do."

"I tell myself that he is strong, Krasus is. Even stronger as Korialstrasz! I tell myself that I let you go only because you and he will be together. You know he would not ask if he did not think you capable."

That was true. Dragons respected few mortal creatures. That Krasus in either form looked to him for aid meant a great deal . . . and as an ally of the leviathan, Rhonin would be better protected than anyone.

What could go wrong?

Defeated, Rhonin nodded. "All right. I'll go. Can you handle matters until Jalia arrives?"

"With my bow, I have shot orcs dead at a hundred yards. I have battled trolls, demons, and more. I have nearly traveled the length and breadth of Azeroth . . . yes, my love, I think I can handle the situation until Jalia arrives."

He leaned down and kissed her. "Then I'd best let Krasus know I'll be coming. For a dragon, he's an impatient sort."

"He has taken the burden of the world upon his shoulders, Rhonin."

That still did not make the wizard overly sympathetic. An ageless dragon was far more capable of dealing with terrible crises than a mere mortal spellcaster about to become a father.

Fixing on an image of the dragon mage as he knew him best, Rhonin reached out to his former patron. *All right, Krasus. I'll help you. Where should we rendez—*

Darkness enveloped the wizard. Off in the distance, he heard Vereesa's faint voice call out his name. A sense of vertigo threatened Rhonin.

His boots suddenly clattered on hard rock. Every bone in

his body shook from the impact and it was all he could do to keep his legs from collapsing.

Rhonin stood in a massive cave clearly hollowed out by more than simply the whims of nature. The roof was almost a perfect oval and the walls had been scorched smooth. A dim illumination with no discernible source enabled him to see the lone, robed figure awaiting him in the center.

"So . . ." Rhonin managed. "I guess we rendezvous here."

Krasus stretched one long, gloved hand to the left. "There is a pack containing rations and water for you, just to your side. Take it and follow me."

"I barely had a chance to say good-bye to my wife . . ." grumbled Rhonin as he retrieved the large leather pack and looped it over his shoulders.

"You have my sympathies," the dragon mage responded, walking ahead already. "I have made arrangements to see to it that she is not without aid. She will be well while we are gone."

Listening to Krasus for just a few seconds reminded Rhonin how often the ancient figure made assumptions about him without even waiting for the young wizard's decisions. Krasus had already taken the matter of Rhonin's agreement as settled.

He followed the tall, narrow figure to the mouth of the vast cave. That Krasus had moved his lair since the war with the orcs Rhonin had known, but exactly where he had moved was another question. Now the human saw that the cavern overlooked a familiar set of mountains, ones not at all that far off from his own home. Unlike their counterparts in Kalimdor, these mountains had a majestic beauty to them, not a sense of dread.

"We're almost neighbors," he remarked dryly.

"A coincidence, but it made bringing you here possible. Had I sought you from the lair of my queen, the spellwork would have been much more depleting and I have every wish of retaining as much of my power as possible."

The tone with which he spoke drained Rhonin of all animosity. Never had he heard such concern from Krasus. "You spoke of Nozdormu, the Aspect of Time. Have you managed to contact him again?"

"No . . . and that is why we must take every precaution. In fact, we must not use magic to transport ourselves to the location. We will have to fly."

"But if we don't use magic, how can we possibly fly—"

Krasus spread his arms . . . and as he did, they transformed, becoming scaled and taloned. His body grew rapidly and wide, leathery wings formed. Krasus's narrow visage stretched, twisted, becoming reptilian.

"Of course," Rhonin muttered. "How silly of me."

Korialstrasz the dragon peered down at his tiny companion. "Climb atop, Rhonin. We must be off."

The wizard reluctantly obeyed, recalling from times past the best manner with which to seat himself. He slipped his feet under crimson scale, then crouched low behind the dragon's sinewy neck. His fingers clutched other scale. Although Rhonin understood that Korialstrasz would do his best to keep his charge from slipping off, the human did not want to take a chance. One never knew what even a dragon might encounter in the sky.

The great, webbed wings flapped once, twice, then suddenly dragon and rider rose high into the heavens. With each beat, miles fell away. Korialstrasz flew effortlessly along, and Rhonin could feel the giant's blood race. Although he spent much of his time in the guise of Krasus, the dragon clearly felt at home in the air.

Cold air assailed Rhonin's head, making the wizard wish he had at least been given the opportunity to change into his robes and travel cloak. He reached back, trying to draw his coat up—and discovered his garment now had a hood.

Glancing down, Rhonin found that he did indeed wear the dark blue travel cloak and robes over his shirt and pants. Without so much as a word, his companion had transformed his clothing to something more suitable.

The hood drawn over his head, Rhonin contemplated what lay ahead. What could distress the Lord of Time so much? The threat sounded both immediate and catastrophic . . . and surely much more than a mortal wizard could handle.

Yet, Korialstrasz had turned to him . . .

Rhonin hoped he would prove worthy, not only for the dragon's sake . . . but for the lives of the wizard's growing family.

Impossible as it seemed, somewhere along the way Rhonin fell asleep. Despite that, even then he did not tumble from his seat to certain death. Korialstrasz certainly had something to do with that, although to all appearances the dragon appeared to be flying blithely along.

The sun had nearly set. Rhonin was about to ask his companion if he intended to fly through the night when Korialstrasz began to descend. Peering down, the wizard at first sighted only water, surely the Great Sea. He did not recall red dragons being very aquatic. Did Korialstrasz intend to land like a duck upon the water?

A moment later, his question was answered as an ominous rock appeared in the distance. No . . . not a rock, but an island almost entirely bare of vegetation.

A feeling of dread swept over Rhonin, one he had felt before while crossing the sea toward the land of Khaz Modan. Then it had been with dwarven gryphon riders and the island they had flown over was Tol Barad, an accursed place overrun early on by the orcs. The island's inhabitants had been slaughtered, their home ravaged, and the wizard's highly attuned senses had felt their spirits crying out for vengeance.

Now he experienced the same kind of horrific, mournful cries again.

Rhonin shouted to the dragon, but either the wind swept away his voice or Korialstrasz chose not to hear him. The leathery wings adjusted, slowing their descent to a gentle decline.

They came to a halt atop a promontory overlooking a series of shadowed, ruined structures. Too small for a city, Rhonin assumed them to have once been a fort or perhaps even a walled estate. In either case, the buildings cast an ominous image that only reinforced the wizard's concerns.

"How soon will we be moving along?" he asked Korialstrasz, still hoping that the dragon only intended to rest a moment before moving on to Kalimdor.

"Not until sunrise. We must pass near the Maelstrom to reach Kalimdor, and we will need our full wits and strength about us for that. This is the only island I have seen for some time."

"What's it called?"

"That knowledge is not mine."

Korialstrasz settled down, allowing Rhonin to dismount. The wizard stepped just far enough from his companion to catch one last glimpse of the ruins before darkness enveloped them.

"Something tragic happened here," Korialstrasz suddenly commented.

"You sense it, too?"

"Yes . . . but what it was I cannot say. Still, we should be secure up here and I have no intention of transforming."

That comforted Rhonin some, but even still he chose to

remain as near to the dragon as possible. Despite a reputation for recklessness, the wizard was no fool. Nothing would entice him down into those ruins.

His gargantuan comrade almost immediately went to sleep, leaving a much more wound-up Rhonin to stare at the night sky. Vereesa's image filled his thoughts. The twins were due shortly and he hoped that he would not miss their coming because of this journey. Birth was a magic unto itself, one that Rhonin could never master.

Thinking of his family eased the mage's tensions and before he knew it, he drifted off to slumber. There, Vereesa and the as-yet-unborn twins continued to keep him loving company even though the children were never quite defined as male or female.

Vereesa faded into the background, leaving Rhonin with the twins. They called to him, beseeched him to come to them. In his dreams, Rhonin began running over a countryside, the children ever more distant shapes on the horizon. What started as a game became a hunt. The once-happy calls turned fearful. Rhonin's children needed him, but first he had to find them . . . and quickly.

"Papa! Papa!" came their voices.

"Where are you? Where are you?" The wizard pushed through a tangle of branches that only seemed to tangle more the harder he pushed. At last he broke through, only to find a towering castle.

And from above, the children called again. He saw their distant shapes reaching out to him. Rhonin cast a spell to make him rise up in the air, but as he did, the castle grew to match his efforts.

Frustrated, he willed himself up faster.

"Papa! Papa!" called the voices, now somewhat distorted by the wind.

At last he neared the tower window where the two waited. Their arms stretched, trying to cut the distance between Rhonin and them. His fingers came within a few scant inches of theirs . . .

And suddenly a huge form barreled into the castle, shaking it to its very base and sending both Rhonin and his children tumbling earthward. Rhonin sought desperately to save them, but a monstrous, leathery hand snatched him up and took him away.

"Wake up! Wake up!"

The wizard's head pounded. Everything around him began swirling. The hand lost its hold and once more he plummeted.

"Rhonin! Wherever you are! Awaken!"

Below him, two shadowy forms hurried to catch him . . . his children now trying to save *his* life. Rhonin smiled at the pair and they smiled back.

Smiled back with sharp, vicious teeth.

And just in time, Rhonin *did* awaken.

Instead of falling, he lay on his back. The stars above revealed that surrounding him now was a roofless ruin of a building. The dank smell of decay assailed his nostrils and a horrific, hissing sound beset his ears.

He lifted his head—and looked into a face out of nightmare.

If someone had taken a human skull, dipped it in soft, melting wax and let that wax drip free, that would have come close to describing the gut-wrenching vision at which Rhonin stared. Add to that needle-shaped teeth filling the mouth, along with red, soulless orbs that glared hungrily at the wizard, and the picture of hellish horror was made complete.

It moved toward him on legs much too long and reached out with bony arms that ended in three long, curved fingers that gouged into the already ravaged stone. Over its macabre form it wore the ripped remnants of a once-regal coat and pants. It was so thin that at first Rhonin did not think it had any flesh at all, but then he saw that an almost transparent layer of skin covered the ribs and other visible areas.

The wizard scrambled back just as the monstrosity grabbed at his foot. The slime-encrusted mouth opened, but instead of a hiss or a shriek, there came a childlike voice.

"Papa!"

The same voice in Rhonin's dream.

He shivered at such a sound coming from the ghoul, but at the same time the cry sent an urge through him. Again he felt as if his own children called to him, an impossibility.

An earth-shaking roar suddenly filled the ruined building, eradicating any urge to fling himself into the deadly talons of the fiend. Rhonin pointed at the creature, muttering.

A ring of fire burst to life around it. Now the pale monstrosity shrieked. It rose as high as its ungainly limbs would enable it, trying to climb over the flames.

"Rhonin!" Korialstrasz shouted from without. "Where are you?"

"Here! In here! A place no longer with a roof!"

As the mage replied, the gaunt creature suddenly leapt through the fire.

Flames licking its body in half a dozen places, it opened its maw far wider than should have been possible, wide enough to engulf Rhonin's head.

Before the wizard could cast another spell, a huge shadow blotted out the stars and a great paw caught the ghoulish beast square. With another shriek, the still-burning horror flew across the chamber, crashing into a wall with such force the stones caved in around it.

A breath of dragon fire finished what Rhonin's own spell had begun.

The stench almost overwhelmed the wizard. Holding one sleeve over his nose and mouth, he watched as Korialstrasz alighted.

"What—what was that thing?" Rhonin managed to gasp out.

Even in the dark, he could sense the leviathan's disgust. "I believe . . . I believe it was once one of those who called this home."

Rhonin eyed the charred form. "*That* was once human? How could that be?"

"You have seen the horrors unleashed by the Undead Scourge during the struggle against the Burning Legion. You need not ask."

"Is this their work?"

Korialstrasz exhaled. Clearly he had been as disturbed as Rhonin by this encounter. "No . . . this is much older . . . and even more unholy an act than the Lich King ever perpetrated."

"Kras—Korialstrasz, it entered my dreams! Manipulated them!"

"Yes, the others sought to do the same with me—"

"*Others?*" Rhonin glanced around, another spell already forming on his lips. He felt certain that the ruins swarmed with the fiends.

"We are safe . . . for the time being. Several are now less than what remains of yours and the rest have scattered into every crevice and gap in these ruins. I believe there are catacombs below and that they slumber there when not hunting victims."

"We can't stay here."

"No," agreed the dragon. "We cannot. We must move on to Kalimdor."

He lowered himself so that Rhonin could climb aboard,

then immediately flapped his wings. The pair rose into the dark sky.

"When we have succeeded with our mission, I will return here and end this abomination," Korialstrasz declared. In a softer tone, he added, "There are already too many abominations in this world."

Rhonin did not answer him, instead taking one last glance down. It might have been a trick of his eyes, but he thought that he saw more of the ghouls emerging now that the dragon had left. In fact, it seemed to him that they gathered by the dozens, all of them looking up hungrily . . . at the wizard.

He tore his gaze away, actually happy to be on the journey to Kalimdor. Surely after a night such as this, whatever awaited the pair could hardly be worse.

Surely . . .

THREE

Korialstrasz reached the shores of Kalimdor late in the day. He and Rhonin paused only to eat—the dragon imbibing in fare away from the wizard's sight—and then set off again for the vast mountain chain that covered much of the western regions of the land. Korialstrasz flew with more and more urgency as they neared their goal. He had not told Rhonin that every now and then he attempted to contact Nozdormu . . . attempted and failed. Soon, however, that would not matter, for they would know firsthand what had so distressed the Aspect of Time.

"That peak!" Rhonin shouted. Although he had slept again, he hardly felt fresh. Nightmares concerning the sinister island had haunted his dreams. "I recognize that peak!"

The dragon nodded. It was the final landmark before their destination. Had he not seen it at the same time as his rider, he would have nonetheless sensed the wrongness in the very fabric of reality . . . and that meant something terrible indeed awaited them.

Despite that certainty, the leviathan only picked up his pace. There was no other choice. Whatever lay ahead, the only ones who might stop it were him and the tiny human figure he carried.

* * *

But while the sharp eyes of man and dragon had sighted their destination, they failed to notice eyes that had sighted them in turn.

"A red dragon . . ." grumbled the first orc. "A red dragon with a rider . . ."

"One of us, Brox?" asked the second. "Another orc?"

Brox snorted at his companion. The other orc was young, too young to have been much use in the war against the Legion, and he certainly would not have remembered when it had been orcs, not humans, who had ridden such beasts. Gaskal only knew the stories, the legends. "Gaskal, you fool, the only way a dragon'd carry an orc these days would be in his belly!"

Gaskal shrugged, unconcerned. He looked every inch the proud orc warrior—tall and muscular with a rough, greenish hide and two good-sized tusks thrusting upward from his broad, lower jaw. He had the squat nose and thick, bushy brow of an orc and a mane of dark hair trailing down between his shoulders. In one meaty hand Gaskal hefted a huge war ax while with the other he clutched the strap of his goatskin backpack. Like Brox, he was clad in a thick, fur cloak under which he wore a leather kilt and sandals wrapped in cloth to preserve heat. A hardy race, orcs could survive any element, but high in the mountains even they required more warmth.

Brox, too, was a proud warrior, but time had beaten at him as no other enemy could. He stood several inches shorter than Gaskal, part of that due to a slight but permanent stoop. The veteran warrior's mane had thinned and started going gray. Scars and lines of age had ravaged his wide, bullish visage, and unlike his youthful companion, the constant expression of eagerness had given way to thoughtful distrust and weariness.

Hefting his well-worn war hammer, Brox trudged through the deep snow. "They're heading for the same place as us."

"How'd you know that?"

"Where else would they be going here?"

Finding no argument, Gaskal quieted, giving Brox the chance to think about the reason that had sent both of them to this desolate place.

He had not been there when the old shaman had come to Thrall seeking an immediate audience, but he had heard the details. Naturally, Thrall had acquiesced, for he very much followed the old ways and considered Kalthar a sage advisor. If Kalthar needed to see him immediately, it could only be for a very good reason.

Or a very bad one.

With the aid of two of Thrall's guards, withered Kalthar entered and took a seat before the towering Warchief. Out of respect for the elder, Thrall sat on the floor, enabling the eyes of both to meet at the same level. Across Thrall's folded legs lay the massive, square-headed Doomhammer, bane of the Horde's enemies for generations.

The new Warchief of the orcs was broad-shouldered, muscular, and, for his position, relatively young. No one doubted Thrall's ability to rule, however. He had taken the orcs from the internment camps and given them back their honor and pride. He had made the pact with the humans which brought about the chance for the Horde to begin life anew. The people already sang songs of him that would be passed down generation after generation.

Clad in thick, ebony plate armor etched in bronze—handed down to him along with the huge weapon by his predecessor, the legendary Orgrim Doomhammer—the greatest of warriors bent his head low and humbly asked, "How may I assist you who honor my presence, great one?"

"Only by listening," Kalthar returned. "And by *truly* listening."

The strong-jawed Warchief leaned forward, his startling and so very rare blue eyes—considered a portent of destiny by his people——narrowed in anticipation. In his journey from slave and gladiator to ruler, Thrall had studied the path of the shaman, even mastering some of the skills. He more than most understood that when Kalthar talked so, he did with good reason.

And so the shaman told Thrall of the vision of the funnel and how time seemed a plaything to it. He told him of the voices and their warnings, told him about the wrongness he had felt.

Told Thrall what he feared would happen if the situation was left unchecked.

When Kalthar finished, the Warchief leaned back. Around his throat he wore a single medallion upon which had been inscribed in gold an ax and hammer. His eyes revealed the quick wit and intelligence that marked him as a capable leader. When he moved, he moved not as a brutish orc might, but with a grace and poise more akin to a human or an elf.

"This smells of magic," he rumbled. "Big magic. Something for wizards . . . maybe."

"They may know already," returned Kalthar. "But we cannot afford to wait for them, great Warchief."

Thrall understood. "You would have me send someone to this place you saw?"

"It would seem most prudent. At least so we may know what we face."

The Warchief rubbed his chin. "I think I know who. A good warrior." He looked to the guards. "Brox! Get me Brox!"

And so Brox had been summoned and told his mission. Thrall respected Brox highly, for the older warrior had been a hero of the last war, the only survivor of a band of brave fighters holding a critical pass against the demons. With his war hammer Brox himself had caved in the skulls of more than a dozen of the fiery foes. His last comrade had died cleaved in two just as reinforcements had arrived to save the day. Scarred, covered in blood, and standing alone amid the carnage, Brox had appeared to the newcomers as a vision out of the old tales of his race. His name became almost as honored as that of Thrall.

But it was more than the veteran's name that garnered the respect of the Warchief and made him Thrall's choice. Thrall knew that Brox was like him, a warrior who fought with his head as well as his arm. The orc leader could not send an army into the mountains. He needed to trust the search to one or two skilled fighters who could then report their findings to him.

Gaskal was chosen to accompany Brox because of his swiftness and absolute obedience to orders. The younger orc was part of the new generation that would grow up in relative peace with the other races. Brox was glad to have the able fighter at his side.

The shaman had so perfectly described the route through the mountains that the pair were well ahead of the estimated time the trek should have taken. By Brox's reckoning, their goal lay just beyond the next ridge . . . exactly where the dragon and rider had vanished.

Brox's grip on his hammer tightened. The orcs had

agreed to peace, but he and Gaskal would fight if need be, even if it meant their certain deaths.

The older warrior forced away the grim smile that nearly played across his face at the last thought. Yes, he would be willing to fight to the death. What Thrall had not known when he summoned the war hero to him had been that Brox suffered from terrible guilt, guilt that had eaten at his soul since that day in the pass.

They had all perished, all but Brox, and he could not understand that. He felt guilty for being alive, for not dying valiantly with his comrades. To him, his still being alive was a matter of shame, of failure to give his all as they had done. Since that time, he had waited and hoped for some opportunity to redeem himself. Redeem himself . . . and die.

Now, perhaps, the fates had granted him that.

"Get a move on!" he ordered Gaskal. "We can reach 'em before they get settled in!" Now he allowed himself a wide grin, one that his companion would read as typical orc enthusiasm. "And if they give us any trouble . . . we'll make 'em think the entire Horde is on the rampage again!"

If the island upon which they had landed seemed a dire place, the mountain pass in which they now descended simply felt *wrong*. That was the best word Rhonin could use to describe the sensations flowing through him. Whatever they sought . . . it should not be. It was as if the very fabric of reality had made some terrible error . . .

The intensity of the feeling was such that the wizard, who had faced every conceivable nightmare, wanted the dragon to turn back. He said nothing, though, recalling how he had already revealed his uncertainties on the island. Korialstrasz might already regret summoning him.

The crimson behemoth arched his wings as he dropped

the final distance. His massive paws sank into the snow as he sought a stable landing area.

Rhonin clutched the dragon's neck tightly. He felt every vibration and hoped his grip would last. His pack bounced against his back, pummeling him.

At last, Korialstrasz came to a halt. The reptilian visage turned the wizard's way. "Are you well?"

"As well—as well as I could be!" gasped Rhonin. He had made dragon flights before, but not for so long.

Either Korialstrasz knew his passenger was still weary or the dragon himself also needed rest after such a monumental trek. "We shall remain here for a few hours. Gather our strength. I sense no change in the emanations I feel. We should have the time to recoup. It would be the wisest choice."

"I won't be arguing with you," Rhonin answered, sliding off.

The wind blew harshly through the mountains and the high peaks left much shadow, but with the aid of some magic and an overhang, the wizard managed to keep warm enough. While he tried to stretch the kinks out of his body, Korialstrasz strode along the pass, scouting the area. The behemoth vanished some distance ahead as the path curved.

Hood draping his head, Rhonin dozed. This time, his thoughts filled with good images . . . true images of Vereesa and the upcoming birth. The wizard smiled, thinking of his return.

He woke at the sound of approach. To Rhonin's surprise, it was not the dragon Korialstrasz who returned to him, but rather the cowled, robed figure of Krasus.

In response to the human's widening eyes, the dragon mage explained, "There are several unstable areas nearby. This form is less likely to cause them to collapse. I can always transform again should the need arise."

"Did you find anything?"

The not-quite-elven face pursed. "I sense the Aspect of Time. He is here and yet he is not. I am disturbed by that."

"Should we start—"

But before Rhonin could finish, a horrific yowl echoed harshly through the mountain chain. The sound set every nerve of the wizard on edge. Even Krasus looked perturbed.

"What was that?" asked Rhonin.

"I do not know." The dragon mage drew himself up. "We should move on. Our goal lies not far away."

"We're not flying?"

"I sense that what we seek lies within a narrow passage between the next mountains. A dragon would not fit, but two small travelers would."

With Krasus leading, the pair headed northeast. Rhonin's companion appeared unbothered by the cold, though the human had to enhance the protective spell on his clothes. Even then, he felt the chill of the land upon his face and fingers.

Before long, they came upon the beginning of the passage Krasus had mentioned. Rhonin saw now what the other meant. The passage was little more than a cramped corridor. Half a dozen men could walk side-by-side through it without feeling constricted, but a dragon attempting to enter would have barely been able to get its head in, much less its gargantuan body. The high, steep sides also created even thicker shadows, making Rhonin wonder if the two might need to create some sort of illumination along the way.

Krasus pressed on without hesitation, certain of their path. He moved faster and faster, almost as if possessed.

The wind howled even harder through the natural corridor, its intensity building as they journeyed. Only human, Rhonin had to struggle to keep pace with his former patron.

"Are we almost there?" he finally called.

"Soon. It lies only—" Krasus paused.

"What is it?"

The dragon mage focused inwardly, frowning. "It is not— it is not exactly where it should be anymore."

"It *moved?*"

"That would be my assumption."

"Is it supposed to do that?" the fiery-haired wizard asked, squinting down the dark path ahead.

"You are under the misconception that I know perfectly what to expect, Rhonin. I understand little more than you."

That did not at all please the human. "So what do you suggest we do?"

The eyes of the inhuman mage literally flared as he contemplated the question. "We go on. That is all we can do."

But only a short distance ahead, they came across a new obstacle of sorts, one that Krasus had been unable to foresee from high up in the air. The passage split off in two directions and while it was possible that they merged further on, the pair could not assume that.

Krasus eyed both paths. "They each run near to our goal, but I cannot sense which lies closer. We need to investigate both."

"Do we separate?"

"I would prefer not to, but we must. We will each journey five hundred paces in, then turn back and meet here. Hopefully we will then have a better sense of which to take."

Taking the corridor to the left, Rhonin followed Krasus's instructions. As he rapidly counted off paces, he soon determined that his choice had potential. Not only did it greatly widen ahead, but the wizard thought he sensed the disturbance better than ever. While Krasus's abilities were more acute than his, even a novice could sense the wrongness that now pervaded the region beyond.

But despite his confidence in his choice, Rhonin did not yet turn around. Curiosity drove him on. Surely a few steps more would hardly matter—

He had barely taken more than one, however, when he sensed something new, something quite disturbing. Rhonin paused, trying to detect what felt different about the anomaly.

It was moving, but there was more to his anxiety than that alone.

It was moving toward *him* . . . and rapidly.

He felt it before he saw it, felt as if all time compressed, then stretched, then compressed again. Rhonin felt old, young, and every moment of life in between. Overwhelmed, the wizard hesitated.

And the darkness before him gave way to a myriad flaring of colors, some of which he had never seen before. A continual explosion of elemental energy filled both empty air and solid rock, rising to fantastic heights. Rhonin's limited mind saw it best as a looming, fiery flower that bloomed, burnt away, and bloomed again . . . and with each blooming grew more and more imposing.

As it neared, he finally came to his senses. Whirling, the mage ran.

Sounds assailed his ears. Voices, music, thunder, birds, water . . . *everything.*

Despite his fears that it would overtake him, the phenomenal display fell behind. Rhonin did not stop running, fearing that at any moment it would surge forward and envelop him.

Krasus surely had to have sensed the latest shift. He had to be hurrying to meet Rhonin. Together, they would devise some way in which to—

A terrible howl echoed through the pass.

A massive, eight-legged lupine form dropped down on him.

Had he been other than what he was, the wizard would have perished there, the meal of a savage, saber-toothed creature with four gleaming green eyes to go with its eight clawed limbs. The monstrous wolf-creature brought him down, but Rhonin, having magicked his garments to better protect him from the elements, proved a hard nut to crack. The claws scraped at a cloak it should have readily tattered, only to have instead one nail snap off.

Gray fur standing on end, the beast howled its frustration. Rhonin took the opening, casting a simple but effective spell that had saved him in the past.

A cacophony of light burst before the creature's emerald orbs, both blinding and startling it. It ducked back, swatting uselessly at flashing patterns.

Dragging himself out of reach, Rhonin rose. There was no chance of flight; that would only serve to turn his back on the beast and his protective spell was already weakening. A few more slashes and the claws would be ripping the wizard to the bone.

Fire had worked against the ghoul on the island and Rhonin saw no reason why such a tried and true spell would not benefit him again. He muttered the words—

. . . Which, inexplicably, came out in reverse. Worse, Rhonin found himself moving backward, returning to the wild claws of the blinded beast.

Time had turned in on itself . . . but how?

The answer materialized from further in the passage. Krasus's anomaly had caught up.

Ghostly images fluttered by Rhonin. Knights riding into battle. A wedding scene. A storm over the sea. Orcs uttering war chants around a fire. Strange creatures locked in combat . . .

Suddenly he could move forward again. Rhonin darted out of the beast's reach, then turned to face it again. This time, he did not hesitate, casting his spell.

The flames burst forth in the form of a great hand, but as they neared the monstrous creature, they slowed . . . then stopped, frozen in time.

Swearing, Rhonin started another spell.

The eight-legged horror leapt around the frozen fire, howling as it charged the human.

Rhonin cast.

The earth beneath the abomination exploded, a storm of dirt rising up and covering the lupine creature. It howled again and, despite the intense forces against it, struggled toward the mage.

A crust formed over the legs and torso. The mouth shut tight as a layer of rock-solid earth sealed it. One by one, the inhuman orbs were covered by a film of dust.

Just a few feet from its victim, the creature stilled. To all appearances, it now seemed but a perfectly cast statue, not the actual monster itself.

At that moment, Krasus's voice filled Rhonin's head.

At last! the dragon mage called. *Rhonin . . . the disturbance is expanding! It's almost upon you!*

Distracted by the fearsome beast, the wizard had not glanced at the anomaly. When he did, his eyes widened.

It filled a space ten times higher and, no doubt, ten times wider than the pass. Solid rock meant nothing to it. The anomaly simply passed through it as if it did not exist. Yet, in its wake, the landscape changed. Some of the rock looked more weathered, while other portions appeared as if newly cooled from the titanic throes of birth. The worst transformations seemed to take place wherever the edges of the fiery flower touched.

Rhonin did not want to think what would happen to him if the thing touched him.

He started running again.

Its movement and growth have suddenly expanded much faster for reasons I do not understand, Krasus went on. *I fear I will not reach you in time! You must cast a spell of teleportation!*

My spellwork doesn't always work the way it should! he responded. *The anomaly's affecting it!*

We will stay linked! That should help strengthen your casting! I will guide you to me and we can regroup!

Rhonin did not care to teleport himself to places he had never seen, the inherent risk being that of ending up encased in a mountain, but with Krasus linked to him, the task would be a much simpler one.

He focused on Krasus, picturing the dragon mage. The spell began to form. Rhonin felt the world around him shift.

The fiery blossom suddenly expanded to nearly twice its previous dimensions.

Only too late did Rhonin realize why. It was reacting to the use of magic . . . his magic. He wanted to stop the spell, but it was already too late.

Krasus! Break the link! Break it before you're also—

The anomaly swallowed him.

Rhonin?

But Rhonin could not answer. He flailed around and around, tossed about like a leaf in a tornado. With each revolution he flew faster and faster. The sounds and sights again assailed him. He saw past, present, and future and understood each for what it was. He caught a glimpse of the petrified beast as it flew wildly past him into what could only be described as a whirlpool in time.

Other things flew by, random objects and even creatures. An entire ship, its sails tattered, its hull crushed in near the bow, soared by, vanishing. A tree on which still perched a flock of birds followed. In the distance, a kraken, fifty feet in length from tip of head to end of tentacle, reached out but failed to drag Rhonin along before vanishing with the rest.

From somewhere came Krasus's faint voice. *Rhonin . . .*

He answered, but there was no reply.

The whirlpool filled his gaze.

And as it sucked him in, Rhonin's last thoughts were of Vereesa and the children he would never know.

FOUR

He sensed the slow but steady growth of the leaves, the branches, and the roots. He sensed the timeless wisdom, the eternal thoughts within. Each giant had its own unique signature, as was true with any individual.

They are the guardians of the forest, came his mentor's voice. *They are as much its soul as I. They* are *the forest.* A pause. *Now . . . come back to us . . .*

Malfurion Stormrage's mind respectfully withdrew from the gargantuan trees, the eldest of the heavily wooded land. As he retreated, his own physical surroundings gradually reappeared, albeit murky at first. He blinked his silver, pupilless eyes twice, bringing everything back into focus. His breath came in ragged gasps, but his heart swelled with pride. Never before had he reached so far!

"You have learned well, young night elf," a voice like a bear's rumbled. "Better than even I could have expected . . ."

Sweat poured down Malfurion's violet countenance. His patron had insisted that he attempt this next monumental step at the height of day, his people's weakest point of time. Had it been at night, Malfurion felt certain that he would have been stronger, but as Cenarius pointed out again and again, that would have defeated the purpose. What his mentor taught him was not the sorcery of the night elves, but almost its exact opposite.

And in so many ways, Malfurion had already become the opposite of his people. Despite their tendencies toward flamboyant garments, for instance, Malfurion's own were very subdued. A cloth tunic, a simple leather jerkin and pants, knee-high boots . . . his parents, had they not perished by accident years before, would have surely died of shame.

His shoulder-length, dark green hair surrounded a narrow visage akin to a wolf's. Malfurion had become something of an outcast among his kind. He asked questions, suggested that old traditions were not necessarily the best, and even dared once mention that beloved Queen Azshara might not always have the concerns of her subjects foremost on her thoughts. Such actions left him with few associates and even fewer friends.

In fact, in Malfurion's mind, he could truly only count three as friends. First and foremost had to be his own twin, the equally troublesome Illidan. While Illidan did not shy away from the traditions and sorcery of the night elves as much as he, he had a tendency to question the governing authority of the elders, also a great crime.

"What did you see?" his brother, seated beside him on the grass, asked eagerly. Illidan would have been identical to Malfurion if not for his midnight blue hair and amber eyes. Children of the moon, nearly all night elves had eyes of silver. Those very few born with ones of amber were seen as destined for greatness.

But if greatness was to be Illidan's, he first had to curb both his temper and his impatience. He had come with his twin to study this new path that used the power of nature—their mentor termed it "druidism"—believing he would be the quicker student. Instead, he often miscast spells and failed to concentrate enough to maintain most trances. That he was fairly adept at traditional sorcery did not assuage Illidan. He had wanted to learn the ways of druidism because such unique skills would mark him as different, as nearing that potential everyone had spoken about since his birth.

"I saw . . ." How to explain it even to his brother? Malfurion's brow wrinkled. "I saw into the hearts of the trees, the souls. Not simply theirs, either. I saw . . . I think I saw into the souls of the entire forest!"

"How wonderful!" gasped a female voice at his other side.

Malfurion fought to keep his cheeks from darkening to black, the night elf equivalent of embarrassment. Of late, he had been finding himself more and more uncomfortable around his other companion . . . and yet he could not think of himself far from her, either.

With the brothers had come Tyrande Whisperwind, their greatest friend since childhood. They had grown up together, the three, inseparable in every way until the last year, when she had taken the robes of a novice priestess in the temple of Elune, the moon goddess. There she learned to become attuned to the spirit of the goddess, learned to use the gifts all priestesses were granted in order to let them spread the word of their mistress. She it had been who had encouraged Malfurion when he had chosen to turn from the sorcery of the night elves to another, earthier power. Tyrande saw druidism as a kindred force to the abilities her deity would grant her once she completed her own training.

But from a thin pale child who had more than once bested both brothers in races and hunting, Tyrande had become, since joining the temple, a slim yet well-curved beauty, her smooth skin now a soft, light violet and her dusky blue hair streaked with silver. The mousy face had grown fuller, much more feminine and appealing.

Perhaps too appealing.

"Hmmph!" added Illidan, not so impressed. "Was that all?"

"It is a good start," rumbled their tutor. The great shadow fell over all three young night elves, stifling even Illidan's rampant mouth.

Although over seven feet tall themselves, the trio were dwarfed by Cenarius, who stood well above ten. His upper torso was akin to that of Malfurion's race, although a hint of the emerald forest colored his dark skin and he had a much broader, more muscular build than either of his male students. Beyond the upper body any similarity ended. Cenarius was no simple night elf, after all. He was not even mortal.

Cenarius was a demigod.

His origins were known only to him, but he was as much a part of the great forest as it was of him. When the first night elves had appeared, Cenarius had already long existed. He claimed kinship with them, but never had he said in what way.

Those few who came to him for guidance left ever touched, ever changed. Others did not even leave, becoming so transformed by their teachings that they chose instead to join the demigod in the protection of his realm. Those were no longer elves, but woodland guardians physically altered forever.

A thick, moss-green mane flowing from his head, Cenarius eyed his pupils fondly with orbs of pure gold. He patted Malfurion gently on the shoulder with hands that ended in talons of gnarled, aged wood—talons still capable of ripping the night elf to shreds without effort—then backed away . . . on four strong legs.

The upper torso of the demigod might have resembled that of a night elf, but the lower portion was that of a huge, magnificent stag. Cenarius moved about effortlessly, as swift and nimble as any of the three. He had the speed of the wind, the strength of the trees. In him was reflected the life and health of the land. He was its child and father all in one.

And like a stag, he also had antlers—giant, glorious antlers that shaded his stern yet fatherly visage. Matched in prominence only by his lengthy, rich beard, the antlers were the final reminder that any blood link between demigod and night elf existed far, far in the past.

"You have all done well," he added in the voice that ever sounded of thunder. Leaves and twigs literally growing in his beard, his hair shook whenever the deity spoke. "Go now. Be among your own again for a time. It will do you some good."

All three rose, but Malfurion hesitated. Looking at his companions, he said, "You go on ahead. I'll meet you at the trail's end. I need to talk with Cenarius."

"We could wait," Tyrande replied.

"There's no need. I won't be long."

"Then, by all means," Illidan quickly interjected, taking Tyrande's arm. "We should let him be. Come, Tyrande."

She gave Malfurion one last lingering glance that made him turn away to conceal his emotions. He waited for the two to depart, then turned again to the demigod.

The descending sun created shadows in the forest that seemed to dance for the pleasure of Cenarius. The demigod smiled at the dancing shadows, the trees and other plants moving in time with them.

Malfurion went down on one knee, his gaze to the earth. "My shan'do," he began, calling Cenarius by the title that meant in the old tongue "honored teacher." "Forgive me for asking—"

"You should not act so before me, young one. Arise . . ."

The night elf reluctantly obeyed, but he kept his gaze down.

This made the demigod chuckle, a sound accented by the

sudden lively chirping of songbirds. Whenever Cenarius reacted, the world reacted in concert with him.

"You pay me even more homage than those who claim to
preach in my name. Your brother does not bend to me and
for all her respect of my power, Tyrande Whisperwind gives
herself only to Elune."

"You offered to teach me—us—" Malfurion responded,
"what no night elf has ever learned . . ." He still recalled the
day when he had approached the sacred wood. Legends
abounded about Cenarius, but Malfurion had wanted to
know the truth. However, when he had called out to the
demigod, he had not actually expected an answer.

He had also not expected Cenarius to offer to be his
teacher. Why the demigod would take on so—*mundane*—a
task was beyond Malfurion. Yet, here they were together.
They were more than deity and night elf, more than teacher
and student . . . they were also friends.

"No other night elf truly wishes to learn my ways,"
Cenarius replied. "Even those who has taken up the mantle
of the forest . . . none of them has truly followed the path I
now show you. You are the first with the possible aptitude,
the possible will, to truly *understand* how to wield the forces
inherent in all nature. And when I say 'you,' young elf, I
speak entirely in the singular."

This was not what Malfurion had remained to talk about
and so the words struck him hard. "But—but Tyrande and
Illidan—"

The demigod shook his head. "Of Tyrande, we have already spoken. She has promised herself to Elune and I will
not poach in the Moon Goddess's realm! Of your brother,
however, I can only say that there is much promise to
Illidan . . . but I believe that promise lies elsewhere."

"I—I don't know what to say . . ." And in truth,

Malfurion did not. To be told so suddenly that Illidan and he would not follow the same path, that Illidan even appeared to waste his efforts here . . . it was the first time that the twins would not share in their success. "No! Illidan will learn! He's just more headstrong! There's so much pressure upon him! His eyes—"

"Are a sign of some future mark upon the world, but he will not make it following my teachings." Cenarius gave Malfurion a gentle smile. "But you will try to teach him yourself, will you not? Perhaps you can succeed where I have failed?"

The night elf flushed. Of course his shan'do would read his thoughts on that subject. Yes, Malfurion intended to do what he could to push Illidan further along . . . but he knew that doing so would be a harder task. Learning from the demigod was one thing; learning from Malfurion would be another. It would show that Illidan was not first, but second.

"Now," added the forest lord quietly, as a small red bird alighted on his antlers and its paler mate did so on his arm. Such sights were common around Cenarius, but they ever left the elf marveling. "You came to ask of me something . . ."

"Yes. Great Cenarius . . . I've been troubled by a dream, a reoccurring one."

The golden eyes narrowed. "Only a dream? That is what troubles you?"

Malfurion grimaced. He had already berated himself several times for even thinking of distracting the demigod with his problem. Of what harm was a dream, even one that repeated itself? Everyone dreamed. "Yes . . . it comes to me every time I sleep and since I've been learning from you . . . it's grown stronger, more demanding."

He expected Cenarius to laugh at him, but instead the forest lord studied him closely. Malfurion felt the golden orbs— so much more arresting than even his brother's own—

burrow deep within him, reading the night elf inside and out.

At last, Cenarius leaned back. He nodded once to himself and in a more solemn voice said, "Yes, you are ready, I think."

"Ready for what?"

In response, Cenarius held up one hand. The red bird leapt down to the offered hand, its mate joining it there. The demigod stroked the backs of both once, whispered something to them, then let the pair fly off.

Cenarius looked down at the night elf. "Illidan and Tyrande will be informed that you are staying behind for a time. They have been told to leave without you."

"But why?"

The golden eyes flared. "Tell me of your dream."

Taking a deep breath, Malfurion began. The dream started as always, with the Well of Eternity as its focal point. At first the waters were calm, but then, from the center, a maelstrom rapidly formed . . . and from the depths of the maelstrom, creatures burst forth, some of them harmless, others malevolent. Many he did not even recognize, as if they came from other worlds, other times. They spread in every direction, fleeing beyond his sight.

Suddenly, the whirlpool vanished and Malfurion stood in the midst of Kalimdor . . . but a Kalimdor stripped of all life. A horrible evil had laid waste to the entire land, leaving not so much as a blade of grass or a tiny insect alive. The once-proud cities, the vast, lush woodlands . . . nothing had been spared.

Even more terrible, for as far as the eye could see, the scorched, cracked bones of night elves lay strewn everywhere. The skulls had been caved in. The stench of death was strong in the air. No one, not even the old, infirm, or young, had been spared.

Heat, horrific heat, had assailed Malfurion then. Turning, he had seen in the distance a vast fire, an inferno reaching into the heavens. It burned everything it touched, even the very wind. Where it moved, nothing . . . absolutely nothing . . . remained. Yet, as frightening as the scene had been, it was not that which had finally awakened the night elf in a cold sweat, but rather something he had sensed *about* the fire.

It had been *alive*. It knew the terrors it wrought, knew and *reveled* in them. Reveled . . . and hungered for more.

All humor had fled Cenarius's visage by the time Malfurion finished. His gaze flickered to his beloved forest and the creatures thriving within. "And this nightmare repeats itself with every slumber?"

"Every one. Without fail."

"I fear, then, that this is an omen. I sensed in you from our first encounter the makings of the gift of prescience—one of the reasons I chose to make myself known to you—but it is stronger than even I ever expected."

"But what does it mean?" the young night elf pleaded. "If you say this is an omen, I've got to know what it portends."

"And we shall try to discover that. I said, after all, that you are ready."

"Ready for what?"

Cenarius folded his arms. His tone grew more grave. "Ready to walk the *Emerald Dream*."

Nothing in the demigod's teachings so far had referred to this Emerald Dream, but the manner in which Cenarius spoke of it made Malfurion realize the importance of this next step. "What is it?"

"What is it not? The Emerald Dream is the world beyond the waking world. It is the world of the spirit, the world of the sleepers. It is the world as it might have been, if we sentient creatures had not come about to ruin it. In the Emerald

Dream, it is possible, with practice, to see anything, go anywhere. Your body will enter a trance and your dream form will fly from it to wherever you need to go."

"It sounds—"

"Dangerous? It is, young Malfurion. Even the well-trained, the experienced, can lose themselves in the Emerald Dream. You note I call it the *Emerald* Dream. That is the color of its mistress, Ysera, the Great Aspect. It is the realm of her and her dragon flight. She guards it well and allows only a few to enter it. My own dryads and keepers make use of the Emerald Dream in their duties, but sparingly."

"I've never heard of it," Malfurion admitted with a shake of his head.

"Likely because no night elf save those in my service has ever walked it . . . and they only when they were no longer of your race. You would be the first of your kind to truly take the path . . . if you so desire."

The idea both unnerved and excited Malfurion. It would be the next step in his studies and a way, perhaps, to make sense of his constant nightmare. Yet . . . Cenarius had made it clear that the Emerald Dream could also be deadly.

"What—what might happen? What might go wrong?"

"Even the experienced can lose their way back if they become distracted," the demigod replied. "Even I. You must remain focused at all times, know your goal. Otherwise . . . otherwise your body might sleep forever."

There was more, the night elf suspected, but Cenarius for some reason wanted him to learn on his own—if Malfurion chose to walk the Emerald Dream.

He decided he had no other recourse. "How do I start?"

Cenarius fondly touched the top of his student's head. "You are certain?"

"Very."

"Then simply sit as you have for your other lessons." When the slighter figure had obeyed, Cenarius lowered his own four-legged form to the earth. "I will guide you in this first time, then it is up to you. Lock your gaze in mine, night elf."

The demigod's golden orbs snared Malfurion's eyes. Even had he wanted to, it would have taken mammoth effort for him to pull his own gaze away. He felt himself drawn into Cenarius's mind, drawn into a world where all was possible.

A sense of lightness touched Malfurion.

Do you feel the songs of the stones, the dance of the wind, the laughter of the rushing water?

At first, Malfurion felt no such thing, but then he heard the slow, steady grinding, the shifting of earth. Belatedly, he realized that this was how the stones and rock spoke as, over the eons, they made their way from one point in the world to another.

After that, the others became more evident. Every part of nature had its own unique voice. The wind spun around in merry steps when pleased, or in violent bursts when the mood grew darker. The trees shook their crowns and the raging water of a nearby river chuckled as the fish within it darted up to spawn.

But in the background . . . Malfurion thought he sensed distant discord. He tried to focus on it, but failed.

You are not yet in the Emerald Dream. First, you must remove your earthly shell . . . the voice in his head instructed. *As you reach the state of sleep, you will slip your body off as you would a coat. Start from your heart and mind, for they are the links that most bind you to the mortal plane. See? This is how it is done . . .*

Malfurion touched at his heart with his thoughts, opening it like a door and willing his spirit free. He did the same with his mind, although the earthly, practical side of any living creature protested at this action.

Give way to your subconscious. Let it guide you. It knows of the realm of dreaming and is always happy to return there.

As Malfurion obeyed, the last barriers slipped away. He felt as if he had sloughed off his skin the way a snake might. A sense of exhilaration filled him and he almost forgot for what purpose he was doing this.

But Cenarius had warned him to remain focused and so the night elf fought the euphoria down.

Now . . . rise up.

Malfurion pushed himself up . . . but his body, legs still folded, remained where it was. His dream form floated a few feet off the ground, free of all restraints. Had he so desired, Malfurion knew that he could have flown to the stars themselves.

But the Emerald Dream lay in a different direction. *Turn again to your subconscious,* the demigod instructed. *It will show you the path, for that lies within, not without.*

And as he followed Cenarius's instructions, the night elf saw the world change further around him. A hazy quality enveloped everything. Images, endless images, overlapped one another, but with concentration Malfurion discovered that he could see each separately. He heard whispers and realized that they were the inner voices of dreamers throughout the world.

From here, you must take the path by yourself.

He felt his link to Cenarius all but fade. For the sake of Malfurion's concentration, the demigod had been forced to pull back. However, Cenarius remained a presence, ready to aid his student if the need arose.

As Malfurion moved forward, his world turned a brilliant, gemlike green. The haze increased and the whispers became more audible. A landscape vaguely seen beckoned to him.

He had become part of the Emerald Dream.

Following his instincts, Malfurion floated toward the

shifting dreamscape. As Cenarius said, it looked as the world would have looked had night elves and other creatures not come into being. There was a tranquillity to the Emerald Dream that made it tempting just to stay forever, but Malfurion refused to give in to that temptation. He had to know the truth about his dreams.

He had no idea at first where his subconscious was taking him, but somehow suspected it would lead him to the answers he desired. Malfurion flew over the empty paradise, marveling at all he saw.

But then, in the midst of his miraculous journey, he felt something amiss again. The faint discord he had sensed earlier increased. Malfurion tried to ignore it, but it gnawed at him like a starving rat. He finally veered his spirit form toward it.

Suddenly, ahead of him lay a huge, black lake. Malfurion frowned, certain that he recognized the foreboding body of water. Dark waves lapped its shores and an aura of power radiated from its center.

The Well of Eternity.

But if this was the Well, where was the city? Malfurion eyed the dreamscape where he knew the capital should have been, trying to summon an image of it. He had come here for a reason and now he believed that it had to do with the city. By itself, the Well of Eternity was an astonishing thing, but it was the source of power only. The discord the night elf felt originated from somewhere else.

He stared at the empty world, demanding to see the reality.

And without warning, Malfurion's dream self materialized over Zin-Azshari, the capital of the night elves. In the old tongue, Zin-Azshari translated into "The Glory of Azshara." So beloved had the queen been when she had made her ascension to the throne that the people had insisted on renaming the capital in her honor.

Thinking of his queen, Malfurion suddenly beheld the palace itself, a magnificent structure surrounded by a huge, well-guarded wall. He frowned, knowing it well. This was, of course, the grand abode of his queen. Even though he had at times made mention of what he believed to be her faults, Malfurion actually admired her more than most thought. Overall, she had done much good for her people, but on occasion he believed Azshara simply lost her focus. As with many other night elves, he suspected any problem there had to do in part with the Highborne, who administered the realm in her name.

The wrongness grew worse the nearer he floated down toward the palace. Malfurion's eyes widened as he saw the reason. With the summoning of the vision of Zin-Azshari, he had also summoned a more immediate image of the Well. The black lake now swirled madly and what appeared to be monstrous strands of multicolored energy shot up from its depths. Powerful magic was being drawn from the Well into the highest tower, its only possible purpose the casting of a spell of impossible proportions.

The dark waters beyond the palace moved with such violence that to Malfurion they seemed to be boiling. The more those within the tower summoned the might of the Well, the more terrible the fury of the elements. Above, the storm-wracked heavens screamed and flashed. Some of the buildings near the edge of the Well threatened to be washed away.

What are they doing? Malfurion wondered, his own quest forgotten. *Why do they continue even during weakness of day?*

But "day" was only a term, now. Gone was the sun that dampened the night elves' abilities. Even though evening had not yet come, it was as black as night above Zin-Azshari . . . no, even blacker. This was not natural and certainly not safe. What could those within be toying with?

He drifted over the walls, past stone-faced guards ignorant of his presence. Malfurion floated to the palace itself, but when he sought to enter, certain that his dream form would pass through something so simple as stone, the night elf discovered an impenetrable barrier.

Someone had encased the palace in protective spells so intricate, so powerful, that he could not pierce them. This only made Malfurion more curious, more determined. He swooped around the structure, rising again toward the tower in question. There had to be a way in. He had to see what madness was going on inside.

With one hand, he reached out to the array of protective spells, seeking the point that bound them all together, the point by which they could also be unbound—

And suddenly pain unimaginable wracked Malfurion. He screamed silently, no sound able to voice his agony. The image of the palace, of Zin-Azshari, vanished. He found himself in an emerald void, caught within a storm of pure magic. The elemental powers threatened to rip his dream form into a thousand pieces and scatter them in every direction.

But in the midst of the monstrous chaos, he suddenly heard the faint calling of a familiar voice.

Malfurion . . . my child . . . come back to me . . . Malfurion . . . you must return . . .

Vaguely the night elf recognized Cenarius's desperate summons. He clung to it as a drowning person in the middle of the sea might cling to a tiny piece of driftwood. Malfurion felt the woodland deity's mind reach out to him, guide him in the proper direction.

The pain began to lessen, but Malfurion was exhausted beyond measure. A part of him simply wanted to drift among the dreamers, his soul never returning to his flesh.

Yet, he realized that to do so would mean his end and so he fought against the deadly desire.

And as the pain dwindled away, as Cenarius's touch grew stronger, Malfurion sensed his own link to his mortal form. Eagerly he followed it, moving faster and faster through the Emerald Dream . . .

With a gasp . . . the young night elf awoke.

Unable to stop himself, Malfurion tumbled into the grass. Mighty yet still gentle hands picked him back up to a sitting position. Water dribbled into his mouth.

He opened his eyes and beheld Cenarius's concerned visage. His mentor held Malfurion's own water sack.

"You have done what few others could do," the stag god murmured. "And in doing so, you almost lost yourself forever. What happened to you, Malfurion? You went even beyond my sight . . ."

"I . . . I sensed . . . something terrible . . ."

"The cause of your nightmares?"

The night elf shook his head. "No . . . I don't know . . . I . . . I found myself drawn to Zin-Azshari . . ." He tried to explain what he had witnessed, but the words seem so insufficient.

Cenarius looked even more disturbed than he, which worried Malfurion. "This does not bode well . . . no. You are certain it was the palace? It had to be Azshara and her Highborne?"

"I don't know if one or both . . . but I can't help feeling that the queen must be a part of it. Azshara is too strong-willed. Even Xavius can't control her . . . I think." The queen's counselor was an enigmatic figure, as distrusted as Azshara was loved.

"You must think about what you say, young Malfurion. You are suggesting that the ruler of the night elves, she whose name is heard in song each day, is involved in some spellwork that could be a threat not only to your kind, but the rest of the world. Do you understand what that means?"

The image of Zin-Azshari intermingled with the scene of devastation . . . and Malfurion found both compatible with each other. They might not be directly linked, but they shared something in common. What that was, though, he did not know yet.

"I understand one thing," he muttered, recalling the perfect, beautiful face of his queen and the cheers that accompanied even her briefest appearances. "I understand that I must find out the truth wherever that truth leads . . . even if in the end it costs me my very life . . ."

The shadowed form touched with his talon the small, golden sphere in his other scaled palm, bringing it to life. Within it, there materialized another, almost identical shadow. The light from the sphere did nothing to push back the darkness surrounding the figure, just as on the other end the sphere used by the second form also failed. The magic cast to preserve each one's identity was old and very strong.

"The Well is still in the midst of terrible throes," commented the one who had initiated contact.

"So it has been for some time," replied the second, tail flicking behind him. "The night elves play with powers they do not appreciate."

"Has there been an opinion formed on your end?"

The darkened head within the sphere shook once. "Nothing significant so far . . . but what can they possibly do save perhaps destroy themselves? It would not be the first time one of the ephemeral races did so and surely not the last."

The first nodded. "So it seems to us . . . and the others."

"All the others?" hissed the second, for the first time some true curiosity in his tone. "Even those of the Earth Warder's flight?"

"No . . . they keep their own counsel . . . as usual of late. They are little more than Neltharion's reflection."

"Unimportant, then. Like you, we shall continue to monitor the night elves' folly, but it is doubtful that it will amount to much more than the extinction of their kind. Should it prove to be more, we shall act if we are ordered to act by our lord, Malygos."

"The pact remains unbroken," responded the first. "We, too, shall act only if commanded by her majesty, the glorious Alexstrasza."

"This conversation is over, then." With that, the sphere went black. The second form had severed the link.

The other rose, dismissing the sphere. With a hiss, he shook his head at the ignorance of the lesser races. They constantly meddled in things beyond their capabilities and so often paid fatally for it. Their mistakes were their own to suffer, so long as the world as a whole did not suffer with them. If that happened, then the dragons would have to act.

"Foolish, foolish night elvesss . . ."

But in a place between worlds, in the midst of chaos incarnate, eyes of fire turned in sudden interest, the work of the Azshara's Highborne having also reached them.

Somewhere, the one who gazed realized, somewhere someone had called upon the power. Someone had drawn from the magic in the mistaken belief that they and they alone knew of it, knew how to wield it . . . but where?

He searched, almost had the source, then lost it. It was near, though, very near.

He would wait. Like the others, he had begun to grow

hungry again. Surely if he waited a little longer, he would sense exactly where among the worlds the casters were. He smelled their eagerness, their ambition. They would not be able to stop drawing from the magic. Soon . . . soon he would find the way through to their little world . . .

And he and the rest would *feed*.

FIVE

Brox had a bad, bad feeling about their mission.

"Where are they?" he muttered. "Where are they?" How did one hide a dragon, the orc wanted to know. The tracks were evident to a point, but then all he and Gaskal could find afterward were the footprints of a human, possibly two. Since the orcs were near enough to notice if a dragon launched itself into the air—and they had seen no such astonishing sight—then it only made sense that the leviathan had to be nearby.

"Maybe that way," suggested the younger warrior, his brow furrowed deep. "That pass."

"Too narrow," growled Brox. He sniffed the air. The scent of dragon filled his nostrils. Almost masked by it was the smell of human. Dragons and wizards.

Treaty or no treaty, this would be a good day to die . . . if Brox could just find his foes.

Kneeling down to study the tracks better, the veteran had to admit that Gaskal's suggestion made the most sense. The two sets of tracks led into the narrow pass while the dragon's simply *vanished*. Still, if the orcs confronted the other intruders, the beast would surely come.

Not giving his companion any sign as to his true intentions, the older warrior rose. "Let's go."

Weapons ready, they trotted into the pass. Brox snorted as he looked it over. Definitely too narrow for a dragon, even a half-grown one. Where *was* the beast?

They had only gone a short distance when from further in they heard the monstrous howl of a beast. The two orcs glanced at each other, but did not slow. No true warrior turned at the first sound of danger.

Deeper they went. The shadows played games, making it seem as if unnatural creatures lurked all around them. Brox's breathing grew heavier as he sought to keep pace with Gaskal. His ax weighed heavily in his hand.

A shout—a human shout—echoed from only a short distance ahead.

"Brox—" the younger orc began.

But at that moment, a monstrous vision filled their view, a fiery image like nothing either had ever seen.

It filled the pass, overflowing even into the rock. It did not seem alive, but nonetheless moved as if with purpose. Sounds—random, chaotic sounds—filled the orcs' ears and when Brox stared into the center, he felt as if he stared into Forever.

Orcs were not creatures subject to easy fear, but the monstrous and surely magical vision overwhelmed the two warriors. Brox and Gaskal froze before it, aware that simple weapons would hardly turn it aside.

Brox had desired a heroic death, not one such as this. There was no nobility in dying so. The thing looked capable of swallowing him as readily and without notice as it would a gnat.

And that made his decision for him. "Gaskal! Move! Run!"

Yet Brox himself failed to follow his own command. He turned to run, yes, but slipped like an awkward infant in the slick snow. The huge orc tumbled to the ground, striking his head. His weapon fell just out of reach.

Gaskal, unaware of what had happened to his comrade, had not fled back, but rather darted to the side, to a depression in one of the walls. There he planted himself inside, certain of the protection of the solid rock.

Still trying to clear his head, Brox realized Gaskal's mistake. Rising to his knees, he shouted, "Not there! Away!"

But the cacophony of sounds drowned out his warning. The fearsome anomaly moved forward . . . and Brox watched with horror as Gaskal was caught on its very edge.

A thousand screams escaped the stricken orc as Gaskal both aged and grew younger simultaneously. Gaskal's eyes bulged and his body rippled like liquid. He stretched and contracted . . .

And with a last ungodly cry, the younger orc shriveled within himself, contracting more and more . . . until he completely vanished.

"By the Horde . . ." Brox gasped, standing. He stared at the spot where Gaskal had stood, still somehow hoping that his companion would miraculously reappear unharmed.

Then it finally sank in that he was seconds from being engulfed by the same monstrosity.

Brox turned, instinctively seized his ax, and ran. He felt no shame in it. No orc could fight this. To die as Gaskal had died would be a futile gesture.

But as fast as the orc ran, the fiery vision moved faster. Nearly deafened by the countless sounds and voices, Brox gritted his teeth. He knew he could not outpace it, not now, but he continued to try . . .

He managed only two steps more before it swallowed him whole.

★   ★   ★

Every bone, every muscle, every nerve in Krasus's body screamed. It was the only reason the dragon mage finally stirred from the black abyss of unconsciousness.

What had happened? He still did not quite know. One minute, he had been trying to reach Rhonin—and then somehow despite not being near it he, too, had been swallowed by the anomaly. His mental link to the human wizard had literally dragged Krasus along.

Images flashed through his befuddled mind again. Landscapes, creatures, artifacts. Krasus had witnessed time in its ultimate aspect, all at once.

Aspect? That word summoned another dread vision, one he had thankfully forgotten until now. In the midst of the swirling chaos of time, Krasus had glimpsed a sight that left his heart and hope shattered.

There, in the center of the fury, he had seen Nozdormu, the great Aspect of Time . . . *trapped* like a fly in a web.

Nozdormu had been there in all his terrible glory, a vast dragon not of flesh, but of the golden sands of eternity. His glittering, gemlike eyes, eyes the color of the sun, had been open wide, but had not in turn seen the insignificant figure of Krasus. The great dragon had been in the throes of both battle and agony, ensnared yet also fighting to hold everything together—absolutely *everything.*

Nozdormu was both victim and savior. Trapped in all time, he also held it from falling apart. If not for the Aspect, the fabric of reality would have collapsed there and then. The world Krasus knew would have disappeared forever. It would never have even existed.

A new surge of pain tore through Krasus. He cried out in the ancient tongue of the dragons, momentarily losing his accustomed control. Yet, with the pain came the realization that he still lived. That knowledge caused him to fight, to force himself back to full consciousness . . .

He opened his eyes.

Trees greeted his gaze. Towering, lush trees with green canopies that nearly blotted out the sky. A forest in the bloom of life. Birds sang while other creatures rustled and scurried through the underbrush. Vaguely Krasus registered the setting sun and soft, drifting clouds.

So peaceful a landscape, the dragon mage almost wondered if he had after all died and gone to the beyond. Then, a not so heavenly sound, a muttered curse, caught his attention. Krasus looked to his left.

Rhonin rubbed the back of his head as he tried to force himself up slightly. The fiery-haired human had landed facedown only a few yards from his former mentor. The wizard spat out bits of dirt and grass, then blinked. By pure accident, he looked in Krasus's direction first.

"What—?" was all he managed.

Krasus tried to speak but all that came from his own mouth at first was a sick croak. He swallowed, then tried again. "I . . . do not know. Are you . . . are you injured in any way?"

Flexing his arms and legs, Rhonin grimaced. "Everything hurts . . . but . . . but nothing seems broken."

After a similar test, the dragon mage came to the same conclusion concerning himself. That they had arrived so intact astonished him . . . but then he recalled the magic of Nozdormu at work in the anomaly. Perhaps the Aspect of Time had noted them after all and done what he could to save the two.

But if that was the case . . .

Rhonin rolled onto his back. "Where are we?"

"I cannot say. I feel I should know it, but—" Krasus stopped as vertigo suddenly seized hold of him. He fell back onto the ground, closing his eyes until the feeling passed.

"Krasus? What happened?"

"Nothing truly . . . I believe. I am still not recovered from what happened. My weakness will go away." Yet, he noted that Rhonin already appeared much better, even sitting up and trying to stretch. Why would a frail human better survive the anomaly's turmoil than he?

With grim determination, Krasus also sat up. The vertigo sought to overwhelm him again, but the dragon mage fought it down. Trying to take his mind from his troubles, he looked around once more. Yes, he certainly sensed a familiarity about his surroundings. At some point, he had visited this region, but when?

When?

The simple question filled him with a sudden dread. *When . . .*

Nozdormu trapped in eternity . . . all time open to the anomaly . . .

The thick woods and the growing shadows created by the vanishing sun made it virtually impossible to see enough to identify the land. He would have to take to the air. Surely a short flight would be safe. The area seemed bereft of any settlement.

"Rhonin, remain here. I will scout from above, then return shortly."

"Is that wise?"

"I think it absolutely necessary." Without a further word, Krasus stretched out his arms and began transforming.

Or rather, he *tried* to transform. Instead, the dragon mage doubled over in agony and overwhelming weakness. His entire body felt turned inside out and he lost all sense of balance.

Strong arms caught him just as he fell. Rhonin carefully dragged him to a soft spot, then helped his companion down.

"Are you all right? You looked as if—"

Krasus cut him off. "Rhonin . . . I could not change. I could not change . . ."

The young wizard frowned, not comprehending. "You're still weak, Master Krasus. The trip through that thing—"

"Yet, you are standing. Take no offense from me, human, but what we passed through should have left you in a far worse state than mine."

The other nodded, understanding. "I just figured that you spent yourself trying to keep me alive."

"I am afraid to tell you that once we entered it, I could do no more for you than I could for myself. In fact, if not for Nozdormu—"

"Nozdormu?" Rhonin's eyes widened. "What's he got to do with our survival?"

"You did not see him?"

"No."

Exhaling, the dragon mage described what he had seen. As he did, Rhonin's expression grew increasingly grim.

"Impossible . . ." the human finally breathed.

"Terrifying," Krasus corrected him. "And now I must tell you also that, even if Nozdormu did save us from the raw forces of the anomaly, I fear he did not send us back to where we came from . . . or even *when.*"

"You think . . . you think we're in a different time?"

"Yes . . . but as to what period . . . I cannot say. I also cannot say how we will be able to get back to our own era."

Slumping back, Rhonin gazed into empty space. "Vereesa . . ."

"Have courage! I said I cannot say how we will be able to get back, but that does not mean that we will not try! Still, our first action must be to find sustenance and shelter . . . and some knowledge of the land. If we can place ourselves, we might be able to calculate where best to find the assistance we need. Now, help me up."

With the human's aid, Krasus stood. After a few tentative steps, he decreed himself well enough to walk. A short discussion on which direction to take ended with agreement to head north, toward some distant hills. There the two might be able to see far enough over the trees the next day to sight some village or town.

The sun fell below the horizon barely an hour into their trek, but the pair continued on. Fortunately, Rhonin had in one of his belt pouches some bits of travel food and a bush they passed supplied them with a few handfuls of edible if sour berries. In addition, the smaller, almost elven form Krasus wore required far less food than his true shape. Still, both were aware that come the next day they would have to find more substantial fare if they were to survive.

The thicker garments used for the mountains proved perfect to keep them warm once darkness reigned. Krasus's superior vision also enabled them to avoid some pitfalls in their path. Still, the going was slow and thirst began to take its toll on the pair.

Finally, a slight trickling sound to the west led them to a small stream. Rhonin and Krasus knelt gratefully and began to drink.

"Thank the Five," the dragon mage said as they drank. Rhonin nodded silently, too busy trying to swallow the entire stream.

After they had their fill, the two sat back. Krasus wanted to go on, but neither he nor the human clearly had the strength to do so. They would have to rest for the night here, then continue on at first light.

He suggested as much to Rhonin, who readily agreed. "I

don't think I could go another step," the wizard added. "But I think I can still create a fire if you like."

The idea of a fire enticed Krasus, but something inside him warned against it. "We shall be warm enough in our garments. I would prefer to err on the side of caution for now."

"You're probably right. We could be in the time of the Horde's first invasion for all we know."

That seemed a bit unlikely to Krasus considering the peacefulness of the woods, but the centuries had produced other dangers. Fortunately, their present location would keep them fairly secreted from most creatures passing near. A rising slope also gave them a natural wall to hide behind.

More out of exhaustion than agreement, they stayed where they were, literally falling asleep on the spot. Krasus's slumber, however, was a troubled one in which his dreams reflected events.

Again he saw Nozdormu struggling against that which was his very nature. He saw all time tangled, confused, and growing more unstable each moment the anomaly existed.

Krasus saw something else, too, a faint, fiery glare, almost like eyes, gazing hungrily on all it saw. The dragon mage frowned in his sleep as his subconscious tried to recollect why such an image would seem so terribly familiar . . .

But then the slight clink of metal against metal intruded, ripping apart his dreams and scattering the bits away just as Krasus was on the verge of remembering what the burning eyes represented.

Even as he stirred, Rhonin's hand clamped over his mouth. Early in his long, long life, such an affront would have made the dragon teach the mortal creature a painful lesson in manners, but now Krasus not only had more patience than in his youth, he also had more trust.

Sure enough, the clink of metal again sounded. So very

slight, but to the trained ears of either spellcaster, still like thunder.

Rhonin pointed upward. Krasus nodded. Both cautiously stood, trying to see over the slope. Hours had clearly passed since they had fallen asleep. The woods were silent save for the songs of a few insects. If not for the brief, unnatural sounds they had heard, Krasus would have thought nothing amiss.

Then a pair of large, almost monstrous shapes materialized beyond the slope. At first they were unrecognizable, but then Krasus's superior vision identified them as not two creatures, but rather *four*.

A pair of riders atop long, muscular panthers.

They were tall, very lean, but clearly warriors. They were clad in armor the color of the night and wore high, crested helms with nose guards. Krasus could not yet make out their faces, but they moved with a fluidity he did not see in most humans. Both the riders and their sleek, black mounts journeyed along as if little troubled by the darkness, which made the dragon mage quickly caution his companion.

"They will see you before you clearly see them," Krasus whispered. "What they are, I do not know, but they are not of your kind."

"There's more!" Rhonin returned. Despite his inferior vision, he had been gazing in just the right direction to catch another pair of riders approaching.

The four soldiers moved in almost complete silence. Only the occasional breath from an animal or metallic movement gave any sign of their presence. They looked to be involved in an intense hunt . . .

Krasus came to the dread conclusion that they were looking for Rhonin and him.

One of the foremost riders reined his monstrous, saber-toothed mount to a halt, then raised his hand to his face. A small flash of blue light briefly illuminated the area around him. In his gauntleted hand the rider held a small crystal, which he focused on the dark landscape. After a moment, he cupped the artifact with his other hand, dousing the light.

The use of the magical crystal only partly bothered Krasus. What little he had seen of the hunter's scowling, violet countenance worried him far more.

"*Night elves . . .*" he whispered.

The rider wielding the crystal instantly looked Krasus's way.

"They've seen us!" muttered Rhonin.

Cursing himself for a fool, Krasus pulled the wizard with him. "Into the deeper woods! It is our only hope!"

A single shout echoed through the night . . . and then the woods filled with riders. Their fearsome yet agile mounts leapt nimbly along, padded feet making no sound as the beasts moved. Like their masters, they had gleaming, silver eyes that enabled them to see their quarry well despite the darkness. The panthers roared lustily, eager to reach the prey.

Rhonin and Krasus slid down a hill and into a thicket. One rider raced past them, but another turned and continued pursuit. Behind them, more than a dozen other riders spread out through the area, intending to cut off their quarry.

The two reached the denser area, but the lead rider was nearly upon them. Turning about, Rhonin shouted a single word.

A blinding ball of pure force struck the night elf square in the chest, sending him flying back off his steed and into the trunk of a tree with a resounding crash.

The powerful assault only served to make the others more determined to catch them. Despite the harder going, the riders pushed their mounts on. Krasus glanced to the east and saw that others had already made their way around the duo.

Instinctively, he cast a spell of his own. Spoken in the language of pure magic, it should have created a wall of flame that would have kept their pursuers at bay. Instead, small bonfires burst to life in random locations, most of them useless as any defense. At best, they served only as momentary distractions to a handful of the riders. Most of the night elves did not even pay them any mind.

Worse, Krasus doubled over in renewed pain and weakness.

Rhonin came to the rescue again. He repeated a weaker variation of the dragon mage's spell, but where Krasus had received for his efforts lackluster results and physical agony, the human wizard garnered an unexpected bounty. The woods before their pursuers exploded with hungry, robust flames, driving the armored riders back in complete disarray.

Rhonin looked as startled at the results as the night elves, but managed to recover quicker. He came to Krasus's side and helped the stricken mage retreat from the scene.

"They will—" Krasus had to gasp for breath. "They will find a path around soon! They know this place well from the looks of it!"

"What did you call them?"

"They are night elves, Rhonin. You recall them?"

Both dragon mage and human had spent their part in the war against the Burning Legion near or in Dalaran, but tales had come from far off of the appearance of the night elves, the legendary race from which Vereesa's kind was descended. The night elves had appeared when disaster had seemed imminent and it was no understatement to say that the outcome might have been different if they had not joined the defenders.

"But if these are night elves, then aren't we allies?"

"You forget that we are not necessarily in the same time period. In fact, until their reappearance, it was thought by even the dragons that their kind had become extinct after the end of—" Krasus became very subdued, not at all certain he wanted to follow his thoughts to their logical conclusion.

Shouts erupted nearby. Three riders closed on them, curved swords raised. In the lead rode the one who wielded the blue crystal. Rhonin's flames illuminated his face, the handsomeness typical of any elf forever ruined by a severe scar running down the left side from near the eye to the lip.

Krasus tried to cast another spell, but it only served to send him to his knees. Rhonin guided him down, then faced the attackers.

"*Rytonus Zerak!*" he shouted.

The branches nearest the night elves suddenly clustered, forming a weblike barrier. One rider became tangled in them and slipped from his mount. A second reined his protesting panther to a halt behind the one caught.

Their leader sliced through the branches as if cutting air, his blade leaving a streak of red lightning in its deadly wake.

"Rhonin!" Krasus managed. "Flee! Leave!"

His former student had as little intention of obeying such a command as the dragon mage would have in his place. Rhonin reached into his belt pouch and from it drew what first looked like a band of glowing quicksilver. The quicksilver swiftly coalesced into a gleaming blade, a gift to Rhonin from an elven commander at the end of the war.

In the light of the wizard's blade, the haughty expression of the night elves' leader transformed into surprise. Nonetheless, he met Rhonin's sword with his own.

Crimson and silver sparks flared. Rhonin's entire body shook. The night elf nearly slipped from the saddle. The panther roared, but because of his rider could not reach their foe with his razor-sharp claws.

They traded blows again. A wizard Rhonin might be, but

he had learned over his life the value of being able to fight by hand. Vereesa had trained him so that even among seasoned warriors he could hold his own . . . and with the elven blade he stood a good chance of success against any one foe.

But not against many. Even as he kept both night elf and beast at bay, three more riders arrived, two manipulating a net. Krasus heard a sound from behind him and glanced over his shoulder to see three more coming, also bearing a huge net.

Try as he might, he could not get the words of power out. He, a dragon, was helpless.

Rhonin saw the first net and backed up. He held the sword ready in case the night elves tried to snare him. The leader urged his mount forward, keeping Rhonin's attention.

"B-behind you!" Krasus called, the weakness overcoming him again. "There's another—"

A booted foot kicked the weakened mage in the side of the head. Krasus retained consciousness, but could not focus.

Through bleary eyes, he watched as the dark forms of the night elves closed in on his companion. Rhonin fended off a pair of blades, chased back one of the huge cats . . . and then the net caught him from behind.

He managed to sever one section, but the second net fell over him, entangling Rhonin completely. Rhonin opened his mouth, but the lead rider moved up and struck him hard across the jaw with his gauntleted fist.

The human wizard dropped.

Enraged, Krasus managed to pull himself partway from his stupor. He muttered and pointed at the leader.

His spell worked this time, but went astray. A bolt of golden lightning struck not the target in question, but rather a tree near one of the other hunters. Three large limbs ripped free, collapsing on one rider and crushing both him and his mount.

The lead night elf glared in Krasus's direction. The

dragon mage tried futilely to protect himself as fists and boots pummeled him into submission . . . and finally unconsciousness.

He watched as his subordinates beat at the peculiar figure who had, more by chance than by skill, slain one of their own. Long after it was clear their victim had lost all sense, he let his warriors take out their frustration on the unmoving body. The panthers hissed and growled, smelling blood, and it was all the night elves could do to keep them from joining in the violence.

When he judged that they had reached the limits of safety, that any further beating would jeopardize the life of their prisoner, he gave the command to halt.

"Lord Xavius wants all alive," the scarred night elf snapped. "We don't want him disappointed, do we?"

The others straightened, fear abruptly appearing in their eyes. Well they might fear, he thought, for Lord Xavius had a tendency to reward carelessness with death . . . painful, lingering death.

And often he chose the willing hand of Varo'then to deal out that death.

"We were careful, Captain Varo'then," one of the soldiers quickly insisted. "They will both survive the journey . . ."

The captain nodded. It still amazed him how the queen's counselor had even detected the presence of these unusual strangers. All Xavius had said when he had summoned faithful Varo'then was that there had been some sort of odd manifestation and that he wanted the captain to investigate and bring back anyone unusual discovered in the vicinity. Varo'then, ever sharp-eyed, had noticed the slight furrowing of the lord's brow, the only hint that Xavius was more disturbed about this unknown "manifestation" than he hinted.

Varo'then eyed the prisoners as their bound bodies were

draped unceremoniously over one of the panthers. Whatever the counselor had expected, it surely did not include a pair such as this. The weak one who had managed the last spell looked vaguely like a night elf, but his skin was pale, almost white. The other one, obviously a younger and far more talented spellcaster . . . Varo'then did not know what to make of him. He was not unlike a night elf . . . but was clearly not. He looked like no creature the veteran soldier had ever seen.

"No matter. Lord Xavius will sort it all out," Varo'then murmured to himself. "Even if he has to tear them limb from limb or flay them alive to get the truth . . ."

And whichever course the counselor took, good, loyal Captain Varo'then would be there to lend his experienced hand.

SIX

It was a troubled Malfurion who returned to his home near the roaring falls just beyond the large night elven settlement of Suramar. He had chosen the site because of the tranquility and untransformed nature around the falls. Nowhere else did he feel so at peace, save perhaps in Cenarius's hidden grove.

A low-set, rounded domicile formed from both tree and earth, Malfurion's simple home was a far contrast from those of most night elves. Not for him was the gaudy array of colors that bespoke of his kind's tendency to try to outshine one another. The colors of his home were those of earth and life, the forest greens, the rich, fertile browns, and kindred shades. He tried to adapt to his surroundings, not force them to adapt to him as was his people's way.

Yet nothing about his home gave Malfurion any sense of comfort this night. Still fiercely clear in his mind were the thoughts and images he had experienced while walking the Emerald Dream. They had opened up doors in his imagination he wished desperately to shut again, but knew would be impossible.

"The visions you see in the Emerald Dream, they can mean many things," Cenarius had insisted, "no matter how true they might look. Even what we think is real—such as your view of Zin-Azshari—may not be so, for the dreamland plays its own games on our limited minds . . ."

Malfurion knew that the demigod had only been trying to assuage him, that what the night elf saw had been truth. He understood that Cenarius was actually as concerned about the reckless spellcasting taking place in the palace of Azshara as his student was.

The power that the Highborne had been summoning . . . what could it be for? Did they not sense how stressed the fabric of the world had grown near the Well? It was still unfathomable to him that the queen could condone such careless and possibly destructive work . . . and yet Malfurion could not shake the certainty that she was as much a part of it as any of her subordinates. Azshara was no simple figurehead; she truly ruled, even when it came to her arrogant Highborne.

He tried to return to his normal routine, hoping that would help him forget his troubles. There were but three rooms to the young night elf's home, yet another example of the simplicity of his life compared to that of others. In one stood his bed and the handful of books and scrolls he had gathered concerning nature and his recent studies. In another, toward the back, was the larder and a small, plain table where he prepared his meals.

Malfurion considered both rooms nothing more than necessities. The third, the communal room, was ever his favored place. Here where the light of the moon shone bright at night and the glistening waters of the falls could be seen, he sat in the center and meditated. Here, with a sip of the honey-nectar wine so favored by his kind, he looked over his work and tried to comprehend what Cenarius had taught him the lesson before. Here, by the short, ivory table where a meal could be spread out, he also visited with Tyrande and Illidan.

But there would be no Tyrande or Illidan this evening. Tyrande had returned to the temple of Elune to continue her own studies and Malfurion's twin, in what was another sign of their growing dissimilarities, now preferred the raucousness of Suramar to the serenity of the forest.

Malfurion leaned back, his face agleam in the light of the moon. He shut his eyes to think, hoping to calm his nerves—

No sooner had he done so, though, when something large moved across the field of moonlight, briefly putting Malfurion in total darkness.

The night elf's eyes snapped open just in time to catch a glimpse of a huge, ominous form. Malfurion immediately leapt to the door and flung it open.

But to his surprise, only the rushing waters of the nearby falls met his tense gaze.

He stepped outside, peered around. Surely no creature so large could move so fast. The bullish Tauren and ursine Furbolgs were not unknown to him, but while they matched in size the peculiar shadow, neither of the two races was known for swiftness. A few branches rustled in the wind and a night bird sang somewhere in the distance, but Malfurion could find no sign of his supposed intruder.

Simply your own nerves, he finally chided himself. *Your own uncertainties.*

Returning inside, Malfurion seated himself again, his mind already caught up once more in his troubles. Unlike his phantom intruder, he was certain that he had not imagined or misread anything concerning the palace and the Well. Somehow, Malfurion would have to learn more, more than the Emerald Dream could at present reveal to him.

And, he suspected, he would have to do it very, very quickly.

* * *

He had almost been caught. Like an infant barely able to walk, he had almost lumbered right into the creature's lair. Hardly a worthy display of the well-honed skills for which a veteran orc warrior was known.

Brox had not worried about his ability to defend himself had the creature caught him, but now was not the time to give in to his own desire to meet a glorious finish. Besides, from what he had seen of the lone figure, it would hardly have been a good match. Tall, but too spindly, too unprotected. Humans were much more interesting and worthy opponents . . .

Not for the first time his head throbbed. Brox put a hand to his temple, fighting the pain. A swirling confusion reigned in his mind. What had happened to him in the past several hours, the orc still could not say with complete certainty. Instead of being ripped apart like Gaskal as he had expected, he was catapulted into madness. Things beyond the comprehension of a simple warrior had materialized and vanished before his eyes and Brox recalled flying around in a swirl of chaotic forces, all while countless voices and sounds had assailed him almost to the point of deafness.

In the end, it had all proven too much. Brox had blacked out, certain he would never wake.

He had, of course, but it was not to find himself safely back in the mountains or still trapped in the insanity. Instead, Brox discovered himself in an almost tranquil landscape consisting of tall trees and bucolic rolling hills for as far as the eye could see. The sun was setting and the only sounds of life were the musical calls of birds.

Even had he been dropped into the midst of a horrendous battle rather than this quiet scene, Brox could have done nothing but lay where he was. It had taken the orc more than an hour to recover enough to just stand, much less travel. Fortunately, during that anxious waiting time,

Brox had discovered one miracle. His ax, which he thought lost, had been swallowed with him and deposited but a few yards from the orc. Not yet able to use his legs, Brox dragged himself to the weapon. He had not been able to wield it, but clutching its handle had given him some comfort while he waited for his strength to return.

The moment he was able to walk, Brox had quickly pushed on. It did not pay to stay in one place when in a strange land, no matter how peaceful it looked. Situations always changed even in the most peaceful places and, in his experience, generally not for the better.

The orc tried to understand what had happened to him. He had heard of wizards traveling by means of special spells from one location to another, but if this was such a spell, then the mage who had cast it surely had to be insane. Either that, or the incantation had gone awry, certainly a possibility.

Alone and lost, Brox's instincts took over. No matter what had happened so far, Thrall would want him to find out more about the inhabitants of this place and what their intentions might be. If they were responsible by accident or design for reaching out with magic to the orcs' new homeland, they posed a possible threat. Brox could die later; his first duty was to protect his people.

At least now he had some notion as to what race lived here. Brox had never seen or heard of a night elf before the war against the Burning Legion, but he could never forget their unique looks. Somehow, he had landed in some realm ruled by their kind, which at least opened to him the hope of returning home once he gathered what information he could. The night elves had fought alongside the orcs in Kalimdor; surely that meant that Brox had merely ended up on some obscure part of the continent. With a little reconnaissance he was certain that he would be able to figure out which direction the orc lands were and head to them.

Brox had no intention of simply going up to one of the night elves and asking the way. Even if these were the same creatures who had allied themselves with the orcs and humans, he could not be certain that those of this land would be friendly to an intruder now. Until he knew more, the wary orc intended to remain well out of sight.

Although Brox did not immediately encounter any more such dwellings, he did note a glow in the distance that likely originated from some larger settlement. After a moment's consideration, the orc hefted his weapon and pushed on toward it.

Barely had he made that decision, however, when shadows suddenly approached from the opposite direction. Pressing flat against a wide tree, Brox watched a pair of riders approach. His eyes narrowed in surprise when, instead of good horses, he saw that they raced along on swift, gigantic panthers. The orc gritted his teeth and readied himself in case either the riders or their beasts sensed him.

But the armored figures hurried past as if determined to be somewhere quickly. They appeared quite comfortable traveling in little light, which made the orc suddenly recall that night elves could see in darkness as well as he could see in day.

That did not bode well. Orcs had fair night vision, but not nearly as good as that of the night elves.

He hefted his ax. Perhaps he did not have the advantage in terms of sight, but Brox would match himself against any of the scrawny figures he had so far come across. Day or night, an ax in the hands of an orc warrior skilled in its use would make the same deep, fatal cut. Even the elaborate armor he noted on the riders would not long stand up to his beloved weapon.

With the riders out of view, Brox continued on cautiously. He needed to find out more about these particular night elves and the only way to do that was to spy on their settlement. There he might find out enough to know where in relation to home he now wandered. Then he could return to Thrall. Thrall would know what to make of all this. Thrall would deal with these night elves who dabbled in dangerous magic.

So very, very simple—

He blinked, so caught up in his thoughts that he only now saw standing before him the tall female figure clad in silver, moonlit robes.

She looked as startled as the orc felt . . . then her mouth opened and the night elf cried out.

Brox started to reach for her—his only intention that of smothering the scream—but before he could do anything, other cries arose and night elves began appearing from every direction.

A part of him desired to stand where he was and fight to the death, but the other part, that which served Thrall, reminded him that this would achieve nothing. He would have failed in his mission, failed his people.

With a snarl of outrage, he turned and fled back in the direction he had come.

Yet, now it seemed that from every huge tree trunk, from every rising mound, figures popped into sight—and each let out the alarm at the sight of the burly orc.

Horns blared. Brox swore, knowing what such a sound presaged. Sure enough, moments later, he heard feline growls and determined shouts.

Glancing over his shoulder, he saw his pursuers nearing. Unlike the pair he had hidden from earlier, most of the new riders were clad only in robes and breast plates, but that hardly erased them as a threat. Each was not only armed, but their mounts presented an even more dire danger. One swipe of a paw would slice the orc open, one bite of the saber-toothed jaws would rip off his head.

Brox wanted to take his ax and sweep across their ranks, chopping away at rider and mount alike and leaving a trail of blood and maimed bodies behind him. Yet, despite his desire to lay waste to those who threatened him, Thrall's teachings and commands held such violence in check. Brox growled and met the first riders with the flat of his ax head. He knocked one night elf from his mount, then, after dodging the cat's claws, turned to seize another rider by the leg. The orc threw the second night elf atop the first, knocking the air out of both.

A blade whistled by his head. Brox easily smashed the slim blade to fragments with his powerful ax. The night elf wisely retreated, the stump of his weapon still gripped tightly.

The orc took advantage of the gap created by the retreat to slip past his pursuers. Some of the night elves did not look at all eager to follow, which raised Brox's spirits. More than his own honor, Thrall's pride in his chosen warrior continued to keep Brox from turning and making a foolish last stand. He would not let his chief down.

But just as escape looked possible, another night elf materialized before him, this one dressed in shimmering robes of brilliant green with gold and ruby starbursts dotting the chest. A cowl obscured most of the night elf's long, narrow visage, but he seemed undaunted by the huge, brutish orc coming up on him.

Brox waved his ax and shouted, trying to scare off the night elf.

The hooded figure raised one hand to chest level, the index and middle fingers pointed toward the moonlit sky.

The orc recognized a spell being cast, but by that time it was already too late.

To his astonishment, a circular sliver of the moon fell from the sky, falling upon Brox like a soft, misty blanket. As it enshrouded him, the orc's arms grew heavy and his legs weak. He had to fight to keep his eyelids open.

The ax slipping from his limp grasp, Brox fell to his knees. Through the silvery haze, he now saw other similarly clad figures circling him. The hooded forms stood patiently, obviously watching the spell's work.

A sense of fury ignited Brox. With a low snarl, he managed to push himself up to his feet. This was not the glorious death he had wanted! The night elves intended that he fall at their feet like a helpless infant! He would not do it!

Fumbling fingers managed to seize the ax again. To his pleasure, he noted some of the hooded figures start. They had not expected such resistance.

But as he tried to raise his weapon, a second silvery veil settled over him. What strength Brox had summoned vanished again. When the ax fell this time, he knew he would be unable to retrieve it.

The orc took one wobbly step, then fell forward. Even then, Brox tried to crawl toward his foes, determined not to make their victory an easy one.

A third veil dropped over him . . . and Brox blacked out.

Three nights . . . three nights and still nothing to show for our efforts . . .

Xavius was not pleased.

Three of the Highborne sorcerers stepped back from the continual spellwork. They were immediately replaced by those who had managed to replenish their strength with some overdue rest. Xavius's false black eyes turned to the three who had just finished. One of them noticed the dark orbs gazing their direction and cringed. The Highborne might be the most glorious of the queen's servants, but Lord Xavius was the most glorious—and dangerous—of the Highborne.

"Tomorrow night . . . tomorrow night we shall increase the field of power tenfold," he declared, the crimson streaks in his eyes flaring.

Unable to meet his gaze, one of the other Highborne nonetheless dared say, "W-with all due respect, my Lord Xavius, that risks much! Such an additional increase may destabilize all we have already accomplished."

"And what is that, Peroth'arn?" Xavius loomed over the other robed figures, his shadow seeming to move of its own accord in the mad light of the spell. "What *have* we accomplished?"

"Why, we command more power than any night elf has ever commanded before!"

Xavius nodded, then frowned. "Yes, and with it, we can squash an insect with a mountain-sized hammer! You are a shortsighted fool, Peroth'arn! Consider yourself fortunate that your skill is demanded for this effort."

Clamping his mouth shut, the other night elf bowed his head gratefully.

The queen's counselor looked with disdain upon the rest of the Highborne. "What we seek to do, we need perfect manipulation of the Well to accomplish! We must have the ability to slay the insect without its even realizing the death until after the fact! We must have such precision, such a fine touch, that there will be no question as to the perfect execution of our final goal! We—"

"Preaching again, my darling Xavius?"

The melodic voice would have enchanted any of the other Highborne into killing themselves if it would please the speaker, but not so the onyx-eyed Xavius. With a careless gesture, he dismissed the weary spellcasters, then turned to the one person in the palace who did not rightly show him the respect he deserved.

She glittered as she entered, a vision of perfection that his magical orbs amplified. She was the glory of the night elves, their beloved mistress. When she breathed, she made the crowds breathless. When she touched the cheek of a favored warrior, he went out and willingly fought dragons and more, even if it meant his certain destruction.

The queen of the night elves was tall for a female, taller even than many males. Only Xavius truly towered above her. Yet, despite her height, she moved like the wind, silent grace with every step. No cat walked as silently as Azshara and none walked with as much confidence.

Her deep, violet skin was as smooth as the almost sheer silk garment she wore. Her hair, long, thick, lush, and moonlight silver, cascaded down around her shoulders and artfully curved backside. In contrast to her previous visit, when she had matched her garments to her eyes, she now wore a flowing gown the same wondrous color as her luxurious hair.

Even Xavius secretly desired her, but on his own terms. His ambitions drove him far more than her wiles ever could. Still, he found much use in her presence, just as he knew she found the same in his. They shared an ultimate objective, but with differing rewards for each waiting at the end.

When that goal was finally reached, Xavius would show Azshara who truly ruled.

"Light of the Moon," he began, expression obedient. "I preach only of your purity, your flawlessness! These others I simply remind of their duty—nay, of their *love*—for you. They should not therefore wish to fail . . ."

"For they would be failing you, as well, my darling counselor." Behind the stunning queen, two handmaidens carried the train of her long, translucent gown. They shifted the train to the side as Azshara seated herself on the special chair she had made the Highborne erect so that she could watch their efforts in comfort. "And I think they fear that more than they love me."

"Hardly, my mistress!"

The queen positioned herself to gaze upon the struggling spellcasters, her gown shifting to best display her perfect form.

Xavius remained unmoved by her maneuver. He would have her and whatever else he desired after they had succeeded in their great mission.

A sudden flash of blazing light drew the eyes of both to the work of the sorcerers. Hovering in the center of the circle created by the Highborne, a furious ball of energy continually remade itself. Its myriad displays had a hypnotic effect, in great part because they often seemed to be opening up a doorway into *elsewhere*. Xavius especially spent long hours staring into the night elves' creation, seeing with his artificial eyes what none of the others could.

Watching now, the counselor wrinkled his brow. He squinted, studying the endless depths within. For just the briefest of moments, he could have sworn that he had seen—

"I believe you are not listening to me, darling Xavius! Is that at all possible?"

He managed to recover. "As possible as living without breathing, Daughter of the Moon . . . but I admit I was distracted enough that I may not have understood clearly. You said again something about—"

A brief, throaty chuckle escaped Queen Azshara, but she did not contradict him. "What is there to understand? I simply restated that surely we must soon triumph! Soon we shall have the power and ability to cleanse our land of its imperfections, create of it the perfect paradise . . ."

"So it shall be, my queen. So it shall be. We are but a short time from the creation of a grand golden age. The realm—*your* realm—will be purified. The world will know everlasting glory!" Xavius allowed himself a slight smile. "And the blighted, impure races that in the past have prevented such a perfect age from issuing forth will *cease* to be."

Azshara rewarded his good words with a pleased smile of her own, then said, "I am glad to hear you say that it will be soon. I have had more supplicants today, lord counselor. They came in fear of the violence in and around the great Well. They asked me for guidance as to its cause and danger. Naturally, I referred their requests to you."

"As you rightly should have, mistress. I will assuage their fears long enough for our precious task to come to fruition. After that, it will be your pleasure to announce what has been done for the good of your people . . ."

"And they shall love me the more for it," Azshara murmured, her eyes narrowed as if imagining the grateful crowds.

"If they could possibly love you any more than they do already, my glorious queen."

Azshara accepted his compliment with a momentary lowering of her slitted eyes, then, with a smooth grace of which only she was capable, rose from the chair. Her attendants quickly manipulated the train of her gown so that it would not in the slightest hamper her movements. "I will make the wondrous announcement soon, Lord Xavius," she declared, turning away from the counselor. "See to it that all is ready when I do."

"It will consume my waking hours," he replied, bowing to her retreating form. "And be the dreams of my slumber."

But the moment she and her attendants had departed, a

deep frown crossed the counselor's cold visage. He signaled to one of the stone-faced guards ever standing duty at the entrance to the chamber.

"If I am not alerted before the next time her majesty decides to join us, it will be your head. Is that understood?"

"Yes, my lord," the guard returned, expression never wavering.

"I also expect to be notified of Captain Varo'then's arrival before her majesty. His task is nothing with which to sully her hands. Make certain that the captain—and whatever he brings with him—is led directly to me."

"Yes, my lord."

Dismissing the guard, Xavius returned to the task of overseeing the Highborne's spellwork.

A lattice of dancing magical energy now enshrouded the fiery sphere, which continued to remake itself. As Xavius watched, the sphere folded within, almost as if it attempted to devour itself.

"Fascinating . . ." he whispered. This close, the lord counselor could feel the intense emanations, the barely bound forces summoned up from the source of all the night elves' magical might. It had been Xavius who had first suspected that his kind had only so far skimmed the surface of the dark water's potential. The Well of Eternity was aptly named, for the more he studied it, the more he realized that its bounty was endless. The physical dimensions of the Well were only a trick of the limited mind . . . the true Well existed in a thousand dimensions, a thousand places, simultaneously.

And from every aspect of it, every variation of it, the Highborne would learn to draw whatever they pleased.

The potential staggered even him.

Energies and colors unseen even by the others danced

and fought before Xavius's magical eyes. They drew him in, their elemental power seductive. The lord counselor drank in the fantastic sight before him—

But from within, from deep beyond the physical world . . . he suddenly felt something stare back.

This time, the night elf knew he was not mistaken. Xavius sensed a presence, a distant presence. Yet, despite that incredible distance, the might he also sensed was staggering.

He tried to pull back, but it was already too late. Deep, so very deep within the captured energies of the Well, the mind of the counselor was suddenly dragged beyond the edge of reality, beyond eternity . . . until . . .

I have searched long for you . . . came the voice. It was life, death, creation, destruction . . . and power infinite.

Had he even desired to do so, Xavius would have been unable to wrench his eyes away from the abyss within. Other eyes now snared his tightly . . . the eyes of the lord counselor's new *god*.

And now you have come to me . . .

The waters bubbled as if boiling. Great waves rose and crashed down time and time again. Lightning flashed from both the heavens and the dark Well.

Then came the whispers.

The first of the night elves to hear them thought the sounds only the wild wind. They soon ignored them completely, more concerned with the possible devastation of their elegant homes.

A few more astute, more attuned to the Well's unearthly energies, heard them for what they were. Voices from the Well itself. But what the voices said, even the majority of those could not say.

It was the one or two who heard clearly who truly

feared . . . and yet did not speak of their fear to others, lest they be branded mad and cast out from their society. Thus, they failed to heed the only warning they would truly get.

The voices spoke of nothing but hunger. They hungered for everything. Life, energy, souls . . . they wanted through to the world, through to the night elves' pristine realm.

And once there, they would devour it . . .

SEVEN

Their captors had grown very apprehensive . . . and to Rhonin, that made them even more of a threat.

It had much to do with the new stretch of forest that they had just entered. This area felt different to Rhonin compared to the dark stretches they had so far crossed. Here their captors seemed not so much the lords of the land as they did undesired intruders.

Dawn fast approached. He and Krasus, who appeared to still be unconscious, had been bound and unceremoniously tossed onto the back of one of the animals. Each jostle by the huge panther threatened to crack the wizard's ribs, but he forced himself not to make any sound or movement that would reveal to the night elves that he was awake.

Yet, what did it matter if they knew? He had already tried several times to cast a spell, but for his attempts had gained only a skull-splitting headache. Around his throat had been placed a small emerald amulet, a simple-looking thing that was the source of his frustration. Whenever he tried to concentrate too hard on his spells, his thoughts grew all muddled and his temples throbbed. He could not even shake the amulet free. The night elves had secured it well. Krasus wore one also, but from him it seemed their captors had nothing to fear. Rhonin also noted what had happened each time his former mentor had tried to aid in the struggle. Krasus had even less mastery over his power than Rhonin, a disturbing notion.

"This isn't the path we took," snarled the scarred leader, whom the human had heard referred to as Varo'then. "This isn't the way it should be . . ."

"But we've followed it back exactly as we should've, my captain," replied one of the others. "There was no deviation—"

"Does that look like the spires of Zin-Azshari on the horizon?" Varo'then snapped. "I see nothing but more damned trees, Koltharius . . . and there's something I don't like about them, either! Somehow, even with our eyes keen and our path understood, we've headed elsewhere!"

"Should we turn back? Retrace our route?"

Rhonin could not see the captain's face, but he could imagine the frustrated expression. "No . . . no . . . not yet . . ."

Yet, while Varo'then was not yet ready to give up on the trail, the wizard was becoming concerned about it himself. With each step deeper into the thick, towering forest, he sensed some growing presence, a presence the likes of which Rhonin had never experienced before. In some ways, it reminded him of how he sensed Krasus whenever the dragon mage contacted him, but this was more . . . much more.

But what?

"The sun's nearly upon us," muttered another of the soldiers.

From what Rhonin had so far ascertained, while his captors could function in daylight, they did not like it. In some ways, it weakened them. They were creatures of magic— even if individually they might not wield much of it—but their magic had to do with the night. If he could just rid himself of the amulet once the sun had risen, Rhonin believed the odds would swing back in his favor.

Making certain that no one watched, he surreptitiously shook his head. The amulet swung back and forth, but would not slip off. Rhonin finally tried thrusting his head up, hoping that might dislodge the piece. He risked being noticed by his captors, but that was a chance he had to take.

In the gloom of predawn, a face stared out at him from the nearby foliage.

No . . . the face was *part* of the foliage. The leaves and twigs formed the features, even creating a lush beard. The eyes were berries and a gap between the greenery represented what looked like a mischievous mouth.

It vanished among the bushes as swiftly as it had appeared, making Rhonin wonder if he had simply imagined it. A trick of the coming light? Impossible! Not with so much detail.

And yet . . .

The scrape of a weapon being drawn from its sheath caught his attention. One by one the night elves readied themselves for some battle that they did not understand, but knew was coming. Even the fierce cats sensed trouble, for not only did they pick up their already swift pace, but their backs arched and they bared their savage teeth.

Varo'then suddenly pointed to his right. "That way! That way! Quickly!"

At that moment, the forest erupted with life.

Huge, foliage-thick branches swung down, obscuring the faces of the riders. Bushes leapt up, becoming short, nimble figures with silent, smiling faces of green. The forest floor seemed to snag the claws of every panther, sending more than one rider tumbling. The night elves shouted recklessly at one another, trying to organize themselves, instead only adding to the chaos.

A low moan echoed through the vicinity. Rhonin caught only a glance, but felt certain that he had seen a massive tree bend over and sweep away two of the night elves and their mounts with its thick, leafy crown.

Curses filled the forest as Varo'then tried to regain command of his party. Those elves who remained mounted sat in a jumble, attempting not only to cut at the things swarming around them, but also to keep their excited panthers under control. For all their size, the huge cats clearly did not like what they faced, often pulling back even when their riders insisted that they move forward.

Varo'then cried out something and suddenly harsh, violet tentacles of radiant energy darted out at various points in the forest. One struck an approaching bush sprite, instantly turning the creature into an inferno. Yet, despite its apparent horrible demise, the creature continued forward without pause, leaving a burning trail in its wake.

Almost immediately, the wind, which had been nearly nonexistent prior to this, howled and roared as if angered by the assault. It blew with such fury that dirt, broken tree limbs, and loose leaves flew up in vast numbers, filling the air and further obscuring the night elves' view. The flames snuffed out, their would-be victim as oblivious to this phenomenal rescue as it had been to its previous peril. A huge, flying branch struck down the night elf next to Varo'then.

"Regroup!" the scarred captain shouted. "Regroup and retreat! Hurry, blast you!"

A leafy hand covered Rhonin's mouth. He looked again into the same startling face. Behind him, he felt other hands grasping his legs.

With a rather unceremonious push, they sent the mage sliding forward.

The panther took notice of this and roared. More of the

small shrublike figures swarmed around the beast, harassing it. As the world rocked around him, Rhonin caught sight of Varo'then twisting back to see what was happening. The scowling elf swore as it registered that his prisoners were being stolen, but before he could raise a hand to stop them, more branches came down, both entangling the captain's arms and face and blinding him.

The bush creatures caught Rhonin well before he would have been in danger of striking the ground headfirst. Silently and efficiently, they carried him like a battering ram into the thick forest. Rhonin could only hope that Krasus, too, had been rescued, for he could see nothing but the leafy figure before him. Despite their sizes, his companions were obviously strong.

Then, to his dismay, a lone night elf atop a snarling panther cut off their path. The wizard recognized him as the one called Koltharius. He had a desperate look in his eyes, as if Rhonin's escape would mean the worst for him. From what little Rhonin had learned of the captain, he did not doubt that.

Wasting no words, the night elf urged his beast forward. The elves Rhonin knew, especially his own beloved Vereesa, were beings with the utmost respect for nature. Koltharius's kind, however, seemed not to care a whit for it; he slashed at the tree limbs and shrubbery slowing him with unbridled fury. Nothing would keep him from his prey.

Or so he might have thought. Huge, black birds abruptly dropped from the foliage above, surrounding and harassing the night elf mercilessly. Koltharius swung madly about, but severed not even a pinfeather from his avian attackers.

So engrossed was the night elf by this latest assault that he did not notice another danger rising up from the earth. The trees through which he needed to pass rose by more than two feet, as if stretching their roots.

Koltharius's mount, driven nearly to madness by the birds, did not pay enough attention to its course.

The typically nimble feline first stumbled, then tripped badly as its paws became more and more entangled. A mournful yowl escaped it as it flew sideways. Its rider tried to hold on, but that only served to worsen his situation.

The huge panther twisted, putting Koltharius between it and two massive tree trunks. Trapped, the night elf was crushed between them, his armor crumpling like paper under the tremendous force. His cat suffered little better, a terrible snapping sound at its neck accompanying the crash.

Rhonin's leafy companions moved on as if nothing had happened. For a few more minutes, the wizard continued to hear the struggles of his former captors, but then the sounds suddenly shifted away, as if Varo'then had finally led his bedraggled hunters to escape.

On and on the tiny creatures carried him. He saw a movement to his right and made out what looked to be the dragon mage's still form being brought along in like fashion. For the first time, though, Rhonin started to fear what his rescuers intended to do with the pair. Had they been taken from the night elves in order to face some more horrific fate?

The forest sprites slowed, finally halting at the edge of an open area. Despite the impossibility of the angle, the first hints of daylight already lit up the opening. Small, delicate songbirds twittered merrily. Myriad flowers of a hundred colors bloomed full and tall grass within waved gently, almost beckoningly, to the newcomers.

Again a leafy face filled his gaze. The open-gap smile widened and to his surprise Rhonin saw that a small, utterly white flower bloomed within.

A tiny puff of pollen shot forth, splattering the human's nose and mouth.

Rhonin coughed. His head swam. He felt the creatures move again, carrying him into the sunlight.

But before one ray could touch his face . . . the wizard passed out.

Despite Rhonin's belief otherwise, Krasus had not been unconscious most of the time. Weak, yes, almost willing to let the darkness take him, true, but the dragon mage had fought both his physical and mental debilitation and, if not a victor, he had at least suffered no defeat.

Krasus, too, had noticed watchers in the woods, but he immediately recognized them as servants of the forest. With senses still more attuned than those of his human companion, Krasus understood that the night elves had been *drawn* to this place purposely. Some force desired something of the armored figures and it took no leap of logic to assume that he and Rhonin were the prizes in question.

And so the dragon mage had kept perfectly still throughout the chaos. He had forced himself to do nothing when the party was attacked and the creatures of the forest stole him and Rhonin from under the elves' very eyes. Krasus sensed no malice in their rescuers, but that did not mean the pair might not come to harm later. He had remained secretly vigilant throughout the forest journey, hoping he would be of more aid than the last time.

But when they had reached the sunlit opening, he had miscalculated. The face had appeared too swiftly, breathed too unexpectedly upon him. Like Rhonin, Krasus had passed out.

Unlike Rhonin, he had slept only minutes.

He awakened to, of all things, a small red bird perched atop his robed knee. The gentle sight so startled the dragon mage that he gasped, sending the tiny avian fleeing to the branches above.

With great caution, Krasus surveyed his surroundings. To all apparent evidence, he and Rhonin lay in the midst of a mystical glade, an area of immense magic at least as ancient as the dragons. That the sun shone here so brilliantly, that the grass, flowers, and birds radiated such peace, was no accident. Here was the chosen sanctum of some being whom Krasus should have known—but could not in the least recall.

And that was a problem of which he had not spoken truthfully to his companion. Krasus's memories were riddled with gaps. He had recognized the night elves for what they were, but other things, many of them mundane, had completely vanished. When he tried to focus on them, the dragon mage found nothing but emptiness. He was as weak in his mind as he was in his body.

But why? Why had he suffered so much more than Rhonin? While a human mage of impressive abilities, Rhonin was still a fragile mortal. If anyone should have been battered and beaten by their madcap flight through time and space, it should have rightly been the lesser of the two travelers.

The moment he thought it, Krasus felt guilty. Whatever the reason for Rhonin surviving more, Krasus only shamed himself by wishing for a reversal of their fortunes. Rhonin had nearly sacrificed himself for his former mentor several times.

Despite his tremendous weakness and lingering pain, he pushed himself to his feet. Of the creatures who had brought them here, Krasus saw no sign. Likely they had returned to being a literal part of the forest, tending to its needs until next summoned to action by their lord. That these had been the simplest of the forest's guardians Krasus was well aware. The night elves were a relatively paltry threat.

But what did the power that ruled here want of two way-ward wanderers?

Rhonin still slumbered deep and, judging by his own re-action to the pollen, Krasus expected him to do so for quite some time. With no evident threat in sight, he dared leave the human sleeping, choosing now to investigate the bound-aries of their freedom.

The thick field of flowers surrounded the soft, open grass like a fence, with what appeared an equal number pointed outward and inward. Krasus approached the closest section, watching the flowers warily.

As he came within a foot of them, they turned to face him, opening fully.

Instantly the dragon mage stepped back . . . and watched as the plants resumed their normal appearance. A simple, soft wall of effective guardians. He and Rhonin were safe from any danger outside while at the same time they were kept from causing trouble for the forest.

In his present condition, Krasus did not even consider leaping over the flowers. Besides, he suspected that doing so would only unleash some other hidden sentry, possibly one not as gentle.

There remained only one recourse. To better conserve his strength, he sat down and folded his legs. Then, taking a deep breath, Krasus studied the surrounding glade one last time . . . and spoke to the air.

"I would talk with you."

The wind picked up his words and carried them into the forest, where they echoed again and again. The birds grew silent. The grass ceased waving.

Then came the wind again . . . and with it the reply.

"And so we shall talk . . ."

Krasus waited. In the distance, he heard the slight clatter

of hooves, as if some animal had chanced by at this important moment. He frowned as the clatter grew nearer, then noticed a shadowy form coming through the woods. A horned rider atop some monstrous steed?

But then, as it drew up to the flowery guardians and the sun, ever shining, caught it full, the dragon in mortal form could only gape like a mere human child at the imposing sight.

"I know you . . ." began Krasus. "I know of you . . ."

But the name, like so many other memories, would not come to him. He could not even say with any certainty whether he had faced this mythic being before and surely that said something for the scope of the holes in his mind.

"And I know something of you," said the towering figure with a torso akin to a night elf and a lower half like that of a stag. "But not nearly as much as I would like . . ."

On four strong legs, the master of the forest strode through the barrier of flowers, which gave way as loyal hounds would to their handler. Some of the flowers and grass even caressed the legs gently, lovingly.

"I am Cenarius . . ." he uttered to the slight figure sitting before him. "This is my realm."

Cenarius . . . Cenarius . . . legendary connotations fluttered through Krasus's tattered mind, a few taking root but most simply fading back to nothing. Cenarius. Spoken of by the elves and other forest dwellers. Not a god, but . . . almost. A demigod, then. As powerful in his own way as the great Aspects.

But there was more, so much more. Yet, strive as he might, the dragon mage could not summon any of it.

His efforts must have shown on his face, for Cenarius's stern visage grew more kindly. "You are not well, traveler. Perhaps you should rest more."

"No." Krasus forced himself up, standing tall and straight before the demigod. "No . . . I would speak now."

"As you like." The antlered deity tilted his bearded head to one side, studying his guest. "You are more than what you seem, traveler. I see hints of night elven but also sense far, far more. Almost you remind me of—but that's not likely." The huge figure indicated Rhonin. "And he is unlike any creature to be found within or without my domain."

"We've come a long distance and are, frankly, lost, great one. We know not where we are."

To the mage's surprise, this brought thundering laughter from the demigod. Cenarius's laughter made more flowers bloom, brought songbirds to the branches around the trio, and set into motion a soft spring breeze that touched Krasus's cheek like a lover.

"Then you *are* from far off! Where *else* could you be, my friend? Where else could you be but *Kalimdor!*"

Kalimdor. That, at least, made sense, for where else would one find night elves in numbers? Yet knowing where he and Rhonin had been deposited answered few other questions. "So I suspected, my lord, but—"

"I sensed an unsettling change in the world," Cenarius interrupted. "An imbalance, a shifting. I sought out its origin and location in secret . . . and while I did not find all I searched for . . . I was led to you two." He stepped past Krasus to once more study the slumbering Rhonin. "Two wanderers from nowhere. Two lost souls from nothing. You are both enigmas to me. I would rather you had not been in the first place."

"Yet you saved us from captivity—"

The forest lord gave a snort worthy of the most powerful stag. "The night elves grow more arrogant. They take what does not belong to them and trespass where they are not wanted. It is their assumption that everything falls under their domination. Although they did not quite intrude upon my realm, I chose to make them do so in order to teach them a lesson in humility and manners." He smiled grimly. "That . . . and they made it simpler for me by bringing what I desired directly here."

Krasus felt his legs buckling. The effort to keep on his feet was proving monumental. With determination, he stood his ground. "They, too, seemed to be aware of our sudden arrival."

"Zin-Azshari is not without its own abilities. It does, after all, overlook the Well itself."

The dragon mage rocked, but this time not because of weakness. In his last statement, Cenarius had said two words that set fear into Krasus's heart.

"Zin . . . Zin-Azshari?"

"Aye, mortal! The capital of the night elves' domain! Situated at the very shores of the Well of Eternity! You know not even that?"

Disregarding the weakness he revealed to the demigod, Krasus dropped to the ground, sitting in the grass and trying to drink in the staggering reality of the situation.

Zin-Azshari.

The Well of Eternity.

He knew them both, even as perforated as his memory had become. Some things were of such epic legend that it would have taken the complete eradicating of his mind for Krasus to have forgotten them.

Zin-Azshari and the Well of Eternity. The first, the center of an empire of magic, an empire ruled by the night elves. How foolish of him not to have realized that during their capture. Zin-Azshari had been the focal point of the world for a period of centuries.

The second, the Well, was the place of magic itself, the

endlessly deep reservoir of power spoken of in awed whispers by mages and sorcerers throughout the ages. It had served as the core of the night elves' sorcerous powers, letting them cast spells of which even dragons had learned respect.

But both were things of the past . . . the *far* past. Neither Zin-Azshari nor even the wondrous and sinister Well existed. They had long, long ago vanished in a catastrophe that— that—

And there Krasus's mind faltered again. Something horrible had happened that had destroyed the two, had ripped the very world asunder . . . and for the life of him he could not recall *what*.

"You are not yet recovered," Cenarius said with concern. "I should have left you to rest."

Still fighting to remember, the mage responded, "I will be . . . I will be all right by the time my friend awakens. We— we will leave as soon as we can and trouble you no longer."

The deity frowned. "Little one, you misunderstand. You are both puzzle and guest to me . . . and so long as you remain the former, you will also remain the latter." Cenarius turned from him, heading toward the guarding flowers. "I believe that you need sustenance. It shall be provided shortly. Rest well until then."

Cenarius did not wait for any protest nor did Krasus bother with one. When a being such as the forest lord insisted that they stay, Krasus understood that it would be *impossible* to argue otherwise. He and Rhonin were guests for as long as Cenarius desired . . . which with a demigod might be the rest of their lives.

Still, that did not worry Krasus so much as the thought that those lives could be very short indeed.

Both Zin-Azshari and the Well had been destroyed in

some monstrous catastrophe . . . and the more the dragon mage pondered it, the more he believed the time of that catastrophe was rapidly approaching.

"I warn you, my darling counselor, I adore surprises, but this one I expect to be quite, quite delicious."

Xavius but smiled as he led the queen by the hand into the chamber where the Highborne worked. He had come to her with as much graciousness as he could command, politely pleading with her to join him and see what his sorcerers had accomplished. The counselor knew that Azshara expected something quite miraculous and she would not be disappointed . . . even if it was *not* what the ruler of the night elves had in mind.

The guards knelt as they entered. Although their expressions were the same as always, like Xavius, they, too, had been touched. Everyone now in the chamber understood, save for Azshara.

For her, it would be only a moment more before the revelation.

She eyed the swirling maelstrom within the pattern, her tone dripping with disappointment. "It looks no different."

"You must see it up close, Light of a Thousand Moons. Then you'll understand what we have achieved . . ."

Azshara frowned. She had come without her attendants at his request and perhaps she now regretted that. Nevertheless, Azshara was queen and it behooved her to show that, even alone, she was in command of any situation.

With graceful strides, Azshara stepped up to the very edge of the pattern. She first eyed the work of the Highborne currently casting, then deigned to set her gaze upon the inferno within.

"It still strikes me as unchanged, dear Xavius. I expected more from—"

She let out a gasp and although the counselor could not see her expression completely, he made out enough to know that Azshara now understood.

And the voice he had heard before, the voice of his god, said for all to hear . . .

I am coming . . .

EIGHT

The Ritual of the High Moon had been completed and now Tyrande had time for herself. Elune expected dedication from her priestesses, but she did not demand that they give to her every waking moment. The Mother Moon was a kind, loving mistress, which had been what first drew the young night elf to her temple. In joining, Tyrande found some peace to her apprehension, to her inner conflicts.

But one conflict would not leave her heart. Times had altered matters between her, Malfurion, and Illidan. They were no longer youthful companions. The simplicities of their childhoods had given way to the complexities of adult relationships.

Her feelings for both of them had changed and she knew that they, too, felt differently about her. The competition between the brothers had always been a friendly one, but of late it had intensified in a manner Tyrande did not appreciate. Now it seemed that they battled each other, as if vying for some prize.

Tyrande understood—even if they did not—that *she* was the prize.

While the novice priestess felt flattered, she did not want either of them hurt. Yet, Tyrande would be the one who would hurt at least one brother, for she knew in her heart that when it came time to choose her life mate, it would be either Illidan or Malfurion.

Dressed in the silver, hooded gown of a novice priestess, Tyrande hurried silently through the high, marble halls of the temple. Above her, a magical fresco illustrated the heavens. A casual visitor might have even thought that no roof stood here, so perfect was the illusion. But only the grand chamber, where the rituals took place, was truly open to the sky. There, Elune visited in the form of moonbeams, gloriously touching her faithful as a mother did her beloved children.

Past the looming, sculpted images of the goddess's earthly incarnations—those who had served in the past as high priestess—Tyrande finally strode across the vast marble floor of the foyer. Here, in intricate mosaic work, the formation of the world by Elune and the other gods was depicted, the Mother Moon of course illustrated most dominantly. With few exceptions, the gods were vague forms with shadowed faces, no mere flesh creature worthy of envisioning their true images. Only the demigods, children and assistants to their superiors, had definite visages. One of those, of course, was Cenarius, said by many to be perhaps the child of the Moon and the Sun. Cenarius, of course, said nothing one way or another, but Tyrande liked to think that story the truth.

Outside, the cool night air soothed her some. Tyrande descended the white alabaster steps and joined the throngs. Many bowed their heads in deference to her position while others politely made a path for her. There were advantages to being even an initiate of Elune, but at the moment Tyrande wished that she could have simply been herself to the world.

Suramar was not so glorious as Zin-Azshari, but it had a presence all its own. Bright, flashy colors filled her gaze as she entered the main square, where merchants of all status plied their wares on the population. Dignitaries in rich,

diamond-sequined robes of sun red and fiery orange, their
noses upward and their eyes only on the path ahead, walked
alongside low-caste elves in more plain garments of green,
yellow, blue, or some mix of the colors. In the market, everyone made an appearance in order to show themselves off as
best they could.

Even the buildings acted as displays for their inhabitants,
every color of the rainbow represented in the view Tyrande
had. Some businesses had been painted in as many as seven
shades and most had dramatic images splashed across every
side. Torchlight illuminated most, the dancing flames considered a lively accent.

The few non-night elves whom the novice priestess had
met during her short life seemed to find her people garish,
even daring to say that Tyrande's race must be color-blind.
While her own tastes tended to be more conservative, albeit
not so much as Malfurion's, Tyrande felt that night elves
simply appreciated better the variety of patterns and shades
that existed in the world.

Near the center of the square, she noted a crowd gathered. Most gestured and pointed, some making comments
either of disgust or mockery. Curious, Tyrande went to see
what could be of such interest.

At first, the onlookers did not even notice her presence,
certainly a sign that whatever they watched must be a rare
marvel. She politely touched the nearest figure, who upon
recognition immediately stepped aside for her. By this
method, she managed to wend her way deep into the throng.

A cage just slightly shorter than her stood in the midst of
it all. Made of good strong iron bars, it evidently held a beast
of some strength, for it rattled harshly and now and then an
animalistic growl set the audience to renewed murmurs.

Those directly in front of her would not move, not even

when they discovered who had tapped them on the shoulder. Frustrated and curious, the slim night elf shifted position, attempting to see between one pair.

What she beheld made her gasp.

"What is it?" Tyrande blurted.

"No one knows, sister," replied what turned out to be a sentry standing duty. He wore the breast plate and robes of one of Suramar's Watch. "The Moon Guard had to spellcast it at least three times to bring it down."

Tyrande instinctively glanced around for one of the hooded, green-robed wizards, but saw none. Likely they had ensorcelled the cage, then left the secured creature in the hands of the Watch while they went to discuss what to do with it.

But *what* had they left?

It was no dwarf, although in some ways its build reminded her of one. Had it stood straight, it would have been about a foot shorter than a night elf, but at least twice as broad. Clearly the beast was a creature of brute strength, for never had she seen such musculature. It amazed Tyrande that even with spells cast upon the cage the prisoner had not simply bent the bars aside and escaped.

A high-caste onlooker suddenly prodded the stooped figure with his golden staff . . . which caused renewed fury within. The night elf barely pulled his stick out of reach of the thick, meaty paws. The creature's squat, round-jawed face contorted as it snarled its anger. It likely would have managed to snag the staff if not for the thick chains around its wrists, ankles, and neck. The heavy chains were not only the reason it stayed stooped, but also why it could never deal with the bars, even supposing it had the strength and resolve.

From horror and disgust, Tyrande's emotions shifted to pity. Both the temple and Cenarius had taught her respect for life, even that which seemed at first only monstrous. The green-hided creature wore primitive garments, which meant that it—or *he*, in most probability—had some semblance of intelligence. It was not right, then, that he be set up for show like some animal.

Two empty brown bowls indicated that the prisoner had at least been given some sustenance, but from his massive frame, the novice priestess suspected it was not nearly enough. She turned to the sentry. "He needs more food and water."

"I've been given no orders for such, sister," the sentry respectfully replied, his eyes ever on the crowd.

"That shouldn't require orders."

Tyrande was rewarded with a slight shrug. "The elders haven't decided what to do with it yet. Maybe they don't think it'll need any more food or drink, sister."

His suggestion repulsed her. Night elf justice could be very draconian. "If I bring some sustenance for him, will you attempt to stop me?"

Now the soldier looked uncomfortable. "You really shouldn't, sister. That beast's just as liable to tear your arm off and gnaw on that instead of whatever fare you bring. You would be wise to leave it alone."

"I shall take my chances."

"Sister—"

But before he could try to talk her out of it, Tyrande had already turned away. She headed directly for the nearest food merchant, seeking a jug of water and a bowl of soup. The creature in the cage looked fairly carnivorous, so she also decided upon a bit of fresh meat. The proprietor refused to charge her, a benefit of her calling, so she gave him the blessing she knew he wanted, then thanked him and returned to the square.

Apparently already bored, much of the crowd had dissipated by the time Tyrande reached the center. That, at least, made it easier for her to confront the prisoner. He glanced up as the novice priestess approached, at first clearly marking her as just one more jaded gawker. Only when he saw what Tyrande held did he take more interest.

He sat up as best he could considering to be his chains, deep-set eyes warily watching her under the thick, bushy brow. Tyrande judged him to be toward the latter half of his life, for his hair had grayed and his brutish visage bore the many marks and scars of a harsh existence.

Just beyond what she calculated to be his reach, the young night elf hesitated. Out of the corner of her eye, Tyrande noted the sentry taking cautious interest in her actions. She understood that he would use his spear to gut the creature if it made any attempt to harm her. Tyrande hoped it would not come to that. It would be the most terrible of ironies if her intent to aid a suffering being led to its death.

With grace and care, she knelt before the bars. "Do you understand me?"

He grunted, then finally nodded.

"I've brought you something." She held out the bowl of soup first.

The wary eyes, so different from her own, fixed upon the bowl. She could read the calculation in them. Once they flickered ever so briefly in the direction of the nearest guard. The right hand closed, then opened again.

Slowly, ever so slowly, he stretched forth the hand. As it neared her own, Tyrande saw how huge and thick it really was, massive enough to envelop both of hers without difficulty. She pictured the strength inherent in it and almost pulled the offering back.

Then with a gentleness that surprised her, the prisoner took the bowl from her grasp, placing it securely in front of him and eyeing her expectantly.

His acceptance made her smile, but he did not respond in kind. Slightly more at ease, Tyrande handed him next the meat, then, lastly, the jug of water.

When he had all three safely tucked near, the green-skinned behemoth began to eat. He swallowed the contents of the bowl in one huge gulp, some of the brownish liquid spilling over his jaw. The piece of meat followed, thick, jagged, yellow teeth ripping away at the raw flesh without hesitation. Tyrande swallowed, but did not otherwise show her discomfort at the prisoner's monstrous manners. Under such conditions, she might have acted little better than he.

A few onlookers watched this activity as they might have a minstrel act, but Tyrande ignored them. She waited patiently as he continued to devour his meal. Away went every bit of meat on the bone, which the creature then broke in two and sucked on the marrow with such gusto that the remainder of the crowd—their fine sensibilities disturbed by the animalistic sight—finally left.

As the last of them departed, he suddenly dropped the bone fragments and, with a startling deep chuckle, reached for the jug. Not once had his eyes strayed from the novice priestess for more than a second.

When the water was gone, he wiped his wide mouth with his arm and grunted, "Good."

To hear an actual word startled Tyrande even though she had assumed earlier that if he understood, then he could also speak. It made her smile again and even risk leaning against the bars, an act that at first brought anxiety to the sentries.

"Sister!" cried one of the guards. "You shouldn't be so near! He'll tear—"

"He'll do nothing," she quickly assured them. Glancing at the creature, she added, "Will you?"

He shook his head and drew his hands close to his chest as a sign. The sentries backed away, but remained watchful.

Ignoring them once more, Tyrande asked, "Do you want anything else? More food?"

"No."

She paused, then said, "My name is Tyrande. I am a priestess of Elune, the Mother Moon."

The figure in the cage seemed disinclined to continue the conversation, but when he saw that she was determined to wait him out, he finally responded, "Brox . . . Broxigar. Sworn servant to the Warchief Thrall, ruler of the orcs."

Tyrande tried to make sense of what he had said. That he was a warrior was obvious by his appearance. He served some leader, this Thrall. A name in some ways more curious than his own, for she understood its meaning and therefore understood the contrary nature of a ruler so titled.

And this Thrall was lord of the orcs, which Tyrande assumed must be what Brox was. The teachings of the temple were thorough, but never had she heard there or anywhere else of a race called the orcs. Certainly, if they were all like Brox, they would have been well remembered by the night elves.

She decided to delve deeper. "Where are you from, Brox? How did you get here?"

Immediately Tyrande realized that she had erred. The orc's eyes narrowed and he clamped his mouth shut. How foolish of her not to think that the Moon Guard had already questioned him . . . and without the courtesy that she had shown so far. Now he must have thought that she had been sent to learn by kindness what they had failed to gain by force and magic.

Clearly desiring an end to their meeting, Brox picked up

the bowl and held it toward her, his expression dark and untrusting.

Without warning, a flash of energy coursed into the cage from behind the novice, striking the orc's hand.

With a savage snarl, Brox seized his burnt fingers, holding them tight. He glared at Tyrande with such a murderous gaze that she could not help but rise and step back. The sentries immediately focused on the cage, their spears keeping Brox pinned to the back bars.

Strong hands seized her by the shoulders and a voice she knew well anxiously whispered, "Are you safe, Tyrande? That foul beast didn't hurt you, did he?"

"He had no plans to do me any harm!" she blurted, turning to face her supposed rescuer. "Illidan! How could you?"

The handsome night elf frowned, his arresting golden eyes losing some of their light. "I was only fearful for you! That beast is capable of—"

Tyrande cut him off. "In there, he is capable of very little . . . and he is no beast!"

"No?" Illidan leaned down to inspect Brox. The orc bared his teeth but did nothing that might otherwise antagonize the night elf. Malfurion's brother snorted in disdain. "Looks like no civilized creature to me . . ."

"He was merely trying to hand back the bowl. And if there had been any trouble, the guards were already standing by."

Illidan frowned. "I'm sorry, Tyrande. Maybe I overreacted. You must admit, though, that few others, even among your calling, would have taken the terrible risk you did! You might not know this, but they say that when he woke up, he almost throttled one of the Moon Guard!"

The novice priestess glanced at the stone-faced sentry, who reluctantly nodded. He had forgotten to mention that little tidbit to her. Still, Tyrande doubted it would have made a difference. Brox had been mistreated and she had felt the need to come to his aid.

"I appreciate your concern, Illidan, but again I tell you that I wasn't in any danger." Her gaze narrowed as she took in the orc's injury. The fingers were blackened and the pain in Brox's eyes was obvious, yet the orc did not cry out nor did he ask for any healing.

Abandoning Illidan, Tyrande knelt again by the cage. Without hesitation, she reached through the bars.

Illidan reached for her. "Tyrande!"

"Stay back! All of you!" Meeting the orc's baleful gaze, she whispered, "I know you didn't mean me any harm. I can mend that for you. Please. Just let me."

Brox growled, but in a manner that made her think he was not angry but simply weighing his options. Illidan still stood next to Tyrande, who realized that he would strike the orc again at the slightest hint of something gone awry.

"Illidan . . . I'm going to have to ask you to turn away for a moment."

"What? Tyrande—"

"For me, Illidan."

She could sense his pent-up fury. Nevertheless, he obeyed her request, spinning around and facing one of the buildings surrounding the square.

Tyrande eyed Brox again. His gaze had shifted to Illidan and for the briefest moment she read the satisfaction in them. Then the orc focused on her and gingerly offered up the maimed hand.

Taking it in her own, she studied the wound in shock. The flesh had been burned away in places on two fingers and a third was red and festering.

"What did you do to him?" she asked Illidan.

"Something I learned recently," was all he would say.

It had certainly not been something he had learned in the forest of Cenarius. This was an example of high night elven sorcery, a spell he had cast with scant concentration. It revealed how skilled Malfurion's brother could be when the subject excited him. He clearly enjoyed the manipulation of sorcery over that of the more slow-paced druidism.

Tyrande was not so certain she liked his choice.

"Mother Moon, hear my entreaties..." Ignoring the aghast expressions of the guards, she took the orc's fingers and kissed each ever so gently. Tyrande then whispered to Elune, asking the goddess to grant her the ability to ease Brox's burden, to render whole what Illidan had, in his rashness, ruined.

"Stretch your hand out as far as you can," she ordered the prisoner.

Watching the sentries, Brox moved forward, straining to thrust his brutish hand beyond the bars. Tyrande expected some sort of magical resistance, but nothing happened. She supposed that since the orc had done nothing to escape, the cage's spellwork had not reacted.

The novice priestess looked up into the sky, where the moon hovered just above. "Mother Moon . . . fill me with your purity, your grace, your love . . . grant me the power to heal this . . ."

As Tyrande repeated her plea, she heard a gasp from one of the guards. Illidan started to turn, but then evidently thought better than to possibly upset Tyrande further.

A stream of silver light . . . Elune's light . . . encompassed the young priestess. Tyrande radiated as if she were the Moon herself. She felt the glory of the goddess become a part of her.

Brox almost pulled away, startled by the wondrous display. To his credit, though, he placed his trust in her, letting her draw his hand as best she could into the glow.

And as the moonlight touched his fingers, the burnt flesh

healed, the gaps where bone showed through regrew, and the horrific injury that Illidan had caused utterly *vanished*.

It took but a few scant seconds to complete the task. The orc remained still, eyes as wide as a child's.

"Thank you, Mother Moon," Tyrande whispered, releasing Brox's hand.

The sentries each fell to one knee, bowing their heads to the acolyte. The orc drew his hand close, staring at each finger and waggling them in astonishment. He touched the skin, first tenderly, then with immense satisfaction when no pain jarred him. A grunt of pleasure escaped the brutish figure.

Brox suddenly began contorting his body in the cage. Tyrande feared that he had suffered some other injury only now revealed, but then the orc finished moving.

"I honor you, shaman," he uttered, now prostrating himself as best as his bonds allowed. "I am in your debt."

So deep was Brox's gratitude that Tyrande felt her cheeks darken in embarrassment. She rose and took a step back.

Illidan immediately turned and held her arm as if to steady her. "Are you all right?"

"I am . . . it . . ." How to explain what she felt when touched by Elune? "It is done," she finished, unable to respond properly.

The guards finally rose, their respect for her magnified. The foremost one reverently approached her. "Sister, might I have your blessing?"

"Of course!" The blessings of Elune were given freely, for the teachings of Mother Moon said that the more who were touched by her, the more who would understand the love and unity she represented and spread that understanding to others.

With her open palm, Tyrande touched each sentry on the heart, then the forehead, indicating the symbolic unity of thought and spirit. Each thanked her profusely.

Illidan took her arm again. "You need some recuperation, Tyrande. Come! I know a place—"

From the cage came Brox's gruff voice. "Shaman, may this lowly one, too, have your blessing?"

The guards started, but said nothing. If even a beast so politely requested a blessing by one of Elune's chosen, how could they argue?

They could not, but Illidan could. "You've done enough for that creature. You're practically wavering! Come—"

But she would not deny the orc. Pulling free from Illidan's grasp, Tyrande knelt again before Brox. She reached in without hesitation, touching the coarse, hairy hide and hard, deep-browed head.

"May Elune watch over you and yours . . ." the novice priestess whispered.

"May your ax arm be strong," he returned.

His peculiar response made her frown, but then she recalled what sort of life he must have lived. His wish for her was, in its own odd way, a wish for life and health.

"Thank you," she responded, smiling.

As Tyrande rose, Illidan once more interjected himself into the situation. "Now can we—"

All at once she felt weary. It was a good weariness, though, as if Tyrande had worked long and hard for her mistress and accomplished much in her name. She recalled suddenly how long it had been since she had slept. More than a day. Certainly the wisdom of Mother Moon dictated that she return to the temple and go to her bed.

"Please forgive me, Illidan," Tyrande murmured. "I find myself tired. I would like to return to my sisters. You understand, don't you?"

His eyes narrowed momentarily, then calmed. "Yes, that would probably be best. Shall I escort you back?"

"There's no need. I'd like to walk alone, anyway."

Illidan said nothing, only bowing slightly in deference to her decision.

She gave Brox one last smile. The orc nodded. Tyrande departed, feeling oddly refreshed in her mind despite her physical exhaustion. When it was possible, she would speak with the high priestess about Brox. Surely the temple would be able to do something for the outcast.

Moonlight shone on the novice priestess as she walked. More and more Tyrande felt as if she had experienced something this night that would forever change her. Surely her interaction with the orc had been the design of Elune.

She could hardly wait to talk to the high priestess . . .

Illidan watched Tyrande walk away without so much as a second glance at him. He knew her mind well enough to understand that she still dwelled in the moment of her service for her goddess. That drowned out any other influence, including him.

"Tyrande . . ." He had hoped to speak with her of his feelings, but that chance had been ruined. Illidan had waited for hours, watching the temple surreptitiously for her appearance. Knowing that it would not look good for him if he joined her the moment she stepped out, he had waited in the background, intent on pretending to just happen by.

Then she had discovered the creature the Moon Guard had captured and all his well-thought plans went awry. Now, not only had he lost his opportunity, but he had embarrassed himself in front of her, been made to look the villain . . . and all because of a *thing* like that!

Before he could stop himself, words tumbled silently out of his mouth and his right hand flexed tightly.

There was a shout from the direction of the cage. He quickly glanced toward it.

The cage flared brightly, but not with the silver light of the moon. Instead, a furious red aura surrounded the cell, as if trying to devour it . . . and its occupant.

The foul creature inside roared in obvious pain. The guards, meanwhile, moved about in clear confusion.

Illidan quickly muttered the counter words.

The aura faded away. The prisoner ceased his cries.

With no one watching him, the young night elf swiftly vanished from the scene. He had let his anger get the best of him and lashed out at the most obvious target. Illidan was grateful that the guards had not realized the truth, and that Tyrande had already left the square, missing his moment of rage.

He was also thankful for those of the Moon Guard who had cast the magical barriers surrounding the cage . . . for it was only those protective spells that had prevented the creature inside from being *slain*.

NINE

They were dying all around him.

Everywhere he looked, Brox saw his comrades dying. Garno, with whom he had grown up, who was practically a brother, fell next, his body hacked to pieces by the screaming blade of a towering, fiery form with a hellish, horned face full of jagged teeth. The demon itself was slain moments later by Brox, who leapt upon it and, with a cry that made even the fearsome creature hesitate, cleaved Garno's killer in two despite its blazing armor.

But the Legion kept coming and the orcs grew fewer. Barely a handful of defenders remained, yet every minute another perished in the onslaught.

Thrall had commanded that the way be blocked, that the Legion would not break through. Help was being gathered, but the Horde needed time. They needed Brox and his fellows.

But there were fewer and fewer. Duun suddenly dropped, his head bouncing along the blood-soaked ground several seconds before his torso collapsed in a heap. Fezhar already lay dead, his remains all but unrecognizable. He had been enveloped in a wave of unnatural green flame belched by one of the demons, flame that had not so much burnt his body, but *dissolved* it.

Again and again, Brox's sturdy ax laid waste to his horrific foes, never seemingly the same kind of creature twice. Yet, whenever he wiped the sweat from his brow and stared ahead, all he saw were more.

And more, and more . . .

Now, only he stood against them. Stood against a shrieking, hungry sea of monsters hell-bent on the destruction of everything.

And as they fell upon the lone survivor—*Brox awoke.*

The orc shivered in his cage, but not from cold. After more than a thousand repetitions, he would have thought himself immune to the terrors his subconscious resurrected. Yet, each time the nightmares came, they did so with new intensity, new pain.

New guilt.

Brox should have died then. He should have died with his comrades. They had given the ultimate sacrifice for the Horde, but he had survived, had lived on. It was not right.

I am a coward . . . he thought once more. *If I had fought harder, I'd be with them.*

But even though he had told this to Thrall, the Warchief had shook his head and said, "No one fought harder, my old friend. The scars are there, the scouts saw you battle as they approached. You did your comrades, your people, as good a service as those who perished . . ."

Brox had accepted Thrall's gratitude, but never the Horde leader's words.

Now here he was, penned up like a pig waiting to be slaughtered for these arrogant creatures. They stared at him as if he had grown two heads and marveled at his ugliness. Only the young female, the shaman, had shown him respect and care.

In her he sensed the power that his own people talked about, the old way of magic. She had healed the fiery wound that her friend had caused him with but a prayer to the moon. Truly she was gifted and Brox felt honored that he had been given her blessing.

Not that it would matter in the long run. The orc had no doubt that his captors would soon decide how to execute him. What they had learned from him so far would avail them nothing. He had refused to give them any definitive information concerning his people, especially their location. True, he did not quite know himself how to reach his home, but it was better to assume that anything said concerning that might be hint enough for the night elves. Unlike those night elves who had allied themselves with the orcs, these had only contempt for outsiders . . . and thus were a threat to the Horde.

Brox rolled over as best as his bonds allowed. Another night and he would likely be dead, but not in the manner of his choosing. There would be no glorious battle, no epic song by which to remember him . . .

"Great spirits," he muttered. "Hear this unworthy one. Grant me one last struggle, one last cause. Let me be worthy . . ."

Brox stared at the sky, continuing to pray silently. But unlike the young priestess, he doubted that whatever powers watched over the world would listen to a lowly creature such as him.

His fate was in the night elves' hands.

What brought Malfurion into Suramar, he could not quite say. For three nights he had sat alone in his home, meditating on all Cenarius had told him, on all he himself had witnessed in the Emerald Dream. Three nights and no answers to his growing concerns. He had no doubts that the spellwork continued in Zin-Azshari and that the situation would only grow more desperate the longer no one acted.

But no one else even seemed to *notice* any problem.

Perhaps, Malfurion finally decided, he had journeyed to Suramar simply to find some other voice, some other mind, with which to discuss his inner dilemma. For that he had chosen to seek out Tyrande, though, not his twin. She gave more care to her thoughts, whereas Illidan had a tendency to leap into action regardless of whether or not he had hatched any plan.

Yes, Tyrande would be good to talk with . . . and just to see.

Yet, as he headed in the direction of the temple of Elune, a large contingent of riders suddenly bore down from the other direction. Edging to the side of the street, Malfurion watched as several soldiers in gray-green armor rushed by on their sleek, well-groomed panthers. Held high near the front of the party was a square banner of rich purple with a black avian form at the center.

The banner of Lord Kur'talos Ravencrest.

The elven commander rode at the forefront, his mount larger, sleeker, and clearly the dominant female of the pack. Ravencrest himself was tall, lanky, and quite regal. He rode as if nothing would deter him from his duty, whatever that might be. A billowing cloak of gold trailed behind him and his high, red-crested helm was marked by the very symbol of his name.

Avian also best described his features, long, narrow, his nose a downward beak. His tufted beard and stern eyes gave him an appearance of both wisdom and might. Outside of the Highborne, Ravencrest was considered one of those with the most influence with the queen, who in the past had often taken his counsel.

Malfurion cursed himself for not having thought of Ravencrest before, but now was not a good opportunity to speak with the noble. Ravencrest and his elite guard rode along as if on some mission of tremendous urgency, which made Malfurion immediately wonder if his fears about Zin-Azshari had already materialized. Yet, if that had been the case, he doubted that the rest of the city would have remained so calm; the forces at play near the capital surely presaged a disaster of monumental proportions, quickly affecting even Suramar.

As the riders vanished, Malfurion moved on. So many people clustered into one area made the young night elf feel a bit claustrophobic after his lengthy period in the forest. Still, Malfurion fought down the sensation, knowing that soon he would see Tyrande. As anxious as she made him feel of late, she also calmed his spirit more than anything else could, even his meditations.

He knew he would have to see his brother, too, but the idea did not appeal to him so much this night. It was Tyrande he wanted to see, with whom he wanted to spend some time. Illidan would still be there for him later.

Vaguely Malfurion noted a number of people crowded around something in the square, but his desire to see Tyrande made him quickly ignore the scene. He hoped that she would be readily available and that he would not have to go asking one acolyte after another. While the initiates of Elune were not bothered by friends and relatives desiring to speak with one of them, for some reason Malfurion felt more anxious about it than usual. It had little to do with his concerns about Zin-Azshari, either, and more to do with the odd discomfort he now felt whenever he was near his child-hood friend.

As he entered the temple, a pair of guards surveyed him. Instead of robes, they wore gleaming, silver breast plates and kilts, the former marked by a crescent moon design at the center. Like all of Elune's initiates, they were females and well versed in the arts of defense and battle. Tyrande herself was a better archer than either Malfurion or Illidan. The peaceful teachings of the Mother Moon did not preclude her most loyal children learning to protect themselves.

"May we help you, brother?" the foremost guard asked politely. She and the other stood at attention, their spears ready to turn on him at a moment's warning.

"I come seeking the novice priestess, Tyrande. She and I are good friends. My name is—"

"Malfurion Stormrage," finished the second, nearer to his age. She smiled. "Tyrande shares novice chambers with myself and two others. I have seen you with her on occasion."

"Is it possible to speak with her?"

"If she is finished with her meditation, then she should be free this hour. I will have someone ask. You may wait in the Chamber of the Moon."

The Chamber of the Moon was the official title of the roofless center of the temple, where many of the great rituals took place. When not in use by the high priestess, the temple encouraged everyone to make use of its tranquil environment.

Malfurion felt the touch of the Mother Moon the moment he entered the rectangular chamber. A garden of night-blooming flowers bordered the room and in the center stood a small dais where the high priestess spoke. The circular stone path leading to the dais was a mosaic pattern outlining the yearly cycles of the moon. Malfurion had noted from his past few visits that no matter where the moon floated in the heavens, its soft light completely illuminated the chamber.

He strode to the center and sat on one of the stone benches used by initiates and faithful. Although eased much by his surroundings, Malfurion's patience quickly deteriorated as he waited for Tyrande. He also worried that she might be displeased by his sudden appearance. In the past, they had always met only after making prior arrangements. This was the first time that he had been so bold as to intrude without warning into her world.

"Malfurion . . ."

For a moment, all his concerns vanished as he looked up and saw Tyrande step into the moonlight. Her silver robes took on a mystical glow and in his eyes the Mother Moon could have looked no more glorious a sight. Tyrande's hair hung loose, draping her exquisite face and ending just above her decolletage. The nighttime illumination emphasized her eyes and when the novice priestess smiled, she herself seemed to light up the Chamber of the Moon.

As Tyrande walked toward him, Malfurion belatedly rose to meet her. He was certain that his cheeks flushed, but there was nothing he could do about it save hope that Tyrande did not notice.

"Is all well with you?" the novice asked with sudden concern. "Has something happened?"

"I'm fine. I hope I haven't intruded."

Her smile returned, more arresting than ever. "You could never intrude upon me, Malfurion. In fact, I'm very glad you've come. I wanted to see you, too."

If she had not noticed his darkening cheeks before, she certainly had to now. Nevertheless, Malfurion pressed on. "Tyrande, can we take a walk outside the temple?"

"If that makes you more comfortable, yes."

As they departed the chamber, he began, "You know how I said I've had some reoccurring dreams . . ."

"I remember."

"I spoke with Cenarius about them after you and Illidan

departed and we took measures to try to understand why they keep repeating."

Her tone grew concerned. "And did you discover anything?"

Malfurion nodded but held his tongue as they passed the two sentries and exited the temple. Not until the pair had started down the outer steps did he continue.

"I've progressed, Tyrande. Progressed far more than either you or Illidan realized. Cenarius showed me a path into the world of the mind itself . . . the Emerald Dream, he called it. But it was more than that. Through it . . . through it I was able to see the real world as I never had before . . ."

Tyrande's gaze shifted to the small crowd near the center of the square. "And what did you see?"

He turned Tyrande to face him, needing her to understand utterly what he had discovered. "I saw Zin-Azshari . . . and the Well over which it looks."

Leaving nothing out, Malfurion described the scene and the unsettling sensations he had experienced. He described his attempts to understand the truth and how his dream self had been repulsed after attempting to see exactly what had transpired with the Highborne and the queen.

Tyrande stared wordlessly at him, clearly as stunned as he had been by his ominous discovery. Finding her voice, she asked, "The queen? Azshara? Can you be certain?"

"Not entirely. I never actually saw much inside, but I can't imagine how such madness could go on without her knowledge. True, Lord Xavius has great influence over her, but even she would never stand by blindly. I have to think that she knows the risks they take . . . but I don't think any of them understand how terrible those risks are! The Well . . . if you could have felt what I had when I walked the Emerald Dream, Tyrande, you would've feared as much as I did."

She put a hand on his arm in an attempt to comfort him. "I don't question you, Malfurion, but we need to know more! To claim that Azshara would put her subjects in danger . . . you have to tread lightly on this."

"I thought to approach Lord Ravencrest on the subject. He, too, has influence with her."

"That might be wise . . ." Again her eyes moved to the center of the square.

Malfurion almost said something, but instead followed her gaze, wondering what could constantly drag her attention from his revelations. Most of those who had gathered had wandered away, finally revealing to him what he had paid no mind to earlier.

A guarded cage . . . and in it some creature not at all like a night elf.

"What is that?" he asked with a growing frown.

"What I wanted to talk with *you* about, Malfurion. His name is Broxigar . . . and he's unlike any being I've ever heard or seen. I know your tale is important, but I want you to meet him now, as a favor for me."

As Tyrande led him over, Malfurion noticed the guards become alert. To his surprise, after a moment of staring at his companion, they suddenly fell to one knee in homage.

"Welcome again, sister," uttered one. "You honor us with your presence."

Tyrande was clearly embarrassed by such respect. "Please! Please rise!" When they had obeyed, she asked, "What news on him?"

"Lord Ravencrest has assumed control of the situation," answered another guard. "Even now he is out inspecting the location of the capture in search of more evidence and possible incursions, but when he returns, it's said that he intends to interrogate the prisoner personally. That means that by tomorrow, it's likely the creature will be transported to the cells of Black Rook Hold." Black Rook Hold was the walled domain of Lord Ravencrest, a veritable fortress.

That the guard was so free with his information surprised Malfurion until he realized how awed the soldier was by Tyrande. True, she was an initiate of Elune, but something must have happened that made her of particular importance to these soldiers.

Tyrande looked perturbed by the revelation. "This interrogation . . . what will it entail?"

The guard could no longer look at her directly. "It entails whatever satisfies Lord Ravencrest, sister."

The priestess did not press further. Her hand, which had lightly rested on Malfurion's arm, momentarily squeezed tight.

"May we speak with him?"

"For only a moment, sister, but I must ask you to speak so that we can hear you. You understand."

"I do." Tyrande led Malfurion to the cell, where they both knelt.

Malfurion bit back a gasp of astonishment. Up close, the hulking figure inside truly amazed him. He had learned of many strange and unusual creatures during his time with Cenarius, but never had he been taught of such a being as this.

"Shaman . . ." it—*he*—muttered in a deep, rumbling . . . and *pained* voice.

Tyrande leaned closer, obviously concerned. "Broxigar . . . are you ill?"

"No, shaman . . . just remembering." He did not explain further.

"Broxigar, I've brought a friend with me. I'd like you to meet him. His name is Malfurion."

"If he's your friend, shaman, I'm honored."

Shifting nearer, Malfurion forced a smile. "Hello, Broxigar."

"Broxigar is an orc, Malfurion."

He nodded. "I've never heard of an orc before."

The chained figure snorted. "I know of night elves. You fought beside us against the Legion . . . but alliances fade in peace, it seems."

His words made no sense, yet they stirred within Malfurion a new anxiety. "How—how did you come to be here, Broxigar?"

"The shaman may call me Broxigar. To you . . . only Brox." He exhaled, then stared intently at Tyrande. "Shaman . . . you asked about me the last time and I wouldn't tell. I owe you, though. Now I tell you what I told these . . ." Brox made a derogatory gesture toward the nearby guards. ". . . and their masters, but you'll believe me no more than they did . . ."

The orc's tale began fantastic and grew even more so with each breath. He was careful not to speak of his people or where they lived, only that at the command of his Warchief, he and another had journeyed to the mountains to investigate an unsettling rumor. There they had found what the orc could only describe as a *hole* in the world . . . a hole that swallowed all matter as it moved relentlessly along.

It had swallowed Brox . . . and ripped his companion apart.

And Malfurion, listening, began to relive his own sense of dread. Each new revelation by the orc fueled that dread and more than once the night elf found himself thinking of the Well of Eternity and the power drawn from it by the Highborne. Certainly the magic of the Well could create such a horrific vortex . . .

But it could not be! Malfurion insisted to himself. *Surely, this could have nothing to do with Zin-Azshari! They aren't that mad!*

Are they?

But as Brox continued, as he spoke of the vortex and the things he had seen and heard as he tumbled through it, it became harder and harder for Malfurion to deny the possibility of *some* link. Worse, without knowing how it struck the night elf, the orc's expression mirrored what Malfurion had felt when his astral self had floated above the palace and the Well.

"A wrongness," the orc said. "A thing that should not be," he added at another stage. These and other descriptions struck Malfurion like well-honed daggers . . .

He did not even realize when Brox's tale ended, his mind swept up by the truth of it all. Tyrande had to squeeze his arm to regain his attention.

"Are you all right, Malfurion? You look as if chilled . . ."

"I—I'm fine." To Brox, he asked, "You told this—this story—to Lord Ravencrest?"

The orc looked uncertain, but the guard responded, "Aye, that's what he told, almost word for word!" The soldier gave a harsh bark of a laugh. "And Lord Ravencrest believed it as little as you now! Come the morrow, he'll pull the truth from this beast . . . and if he has friends nearby, they'll find us not so tempting a target, eh?"

So an invasion by orcs was all that Ravencrest suspected. Malfurion felt disappointed. He doubted that the elven commander would see the possible link between his encounter and Brox's tale. In fact, the more he thought of it, the more Malfurion doubted Ravencrest would believe him at all. Here Malfurion was, ready to tell the noble that their beloved queen might be involved in reckless spellwork with the potential to bring disaster upon her people. The young night elf barely believed it himself.

If only he had more proof.

The guard began shifting anxiously. "Sister . . . I'm afraid I must ask you and your companion to depart now. Our captain will be coming shortly. I really shouldn't have—"

"Quite all right. I understand."

As they started to rise, Brox moved to the front of the cell, one hand reaching toward Tyrande. "Shaman . . . one last blessing, if you could grant it."

"Of course . . ."

As she knelt again, Malfurion desperately pondered what he should do. Properly, any suspicions should have been reported to Lord Ravencrest, but somehow that seemed a futile act.

If only he could consult with Cenarius, but by then the orc might be—

Cenarius . . .

Malfurion glanced at Tyrande and Brox, a fateful decision coming to mind.

Bidding the orc farewell, Tyrande rose again. Malfurion took her by the arm and the two thanked the guard for their time. The young priestess's expression grew perturbed as they left, but Malfurion said nothing, his own thoughts still racing.

"There must be something that can be done," she finally whispered.

"What do you mean?"

"Tomorrow they will take him to Black Rook Hold. Once in there, he—" Tyrande faltered. "I've every respect for Lord Ravencrest, but . . ."

Malfurion only nodded.

"I spoke with Mother Dejahna, the high priestess, but she says there is nothing we can do but pray for his spirit. She commended me for my sympathy, but suggested I let matters take their course."

"Let them take their course . . ." Malfurion muttered, staring ahead. He gritted his teeth. It had to be done now. There could be no turning back, not if his fears had any merit. "Turn here," he suddenly commanded, steering her down a side avenue. "We need to see Illidan."

"Illidan? But why?"

Taking a deep breath and thinking of the orc and the Well, Malfurion simply replied, "Because we're going to let matters take their own course . . . with our guidance, that is."

Xavius stood before the fiery sphere, staring into the gaping hole in its midst in rapt attention. Deep, deep within, the eyes of his god stared back and the two communed.

I have heard your pleas . . . he said to the counselor. *And know your dreams . . . a world cleansed of the impure, the imperfect. I would grant your desire, you the first among my faithful . . .*

His gaze never wavering, Xavius knelt. The other Highborne continued working their sorcery, trying to expand upon what they had created.

"You will come to us, then?" the night elf responded, artificial eyes flaring in anticipation. "You will come to our world and make it so?"

The way is not yet open . . . it must be strengthened . . . for it must be able to withstand my glorious entrance . . .

The counselor nodded his understanding. So magnificent, so powerful a force as the god would be too much for the night elves' feeble portal to accept. The god's sheer presence would rip it asunder. It had to be made larger, stronger, and more permanent.

That his supposed deity could not perform this task himself, Xavius did not question. He was too caught up in the wonder of his new master.

"What can be done?" he pleaded. Try as they might, the Highborne sorcerers had reached the limits of their knowledge and skills, Xavius included.

I will send one of my lesser host to guide you . . . he may pass through to your world . . . with effort . . . but you must prepare yourselves for his coming . . .

Almost leaping to his feet, the night elven lord commanded, "Let no one stumble in his efforts! We are to be blessed with the presence of one of his favored!"

The Highborne redoubled their efforts, the chamber crackling with raw, fearsome energy drawn directly from the Well. Outside, the skies roared furiously and anyone looking upon the great black lake itself would have turned their gaze away in fear.

The fireball within the pattern swelled, the gap in the center opening like a wide, savage mouth. What sounded like a million voices wailing filled the chamber, music to Xavius's ears.

But then one of the Highborne faltered. Fearing the worst, Xavius pushed himself into the circle, adding his own might and skill to the effort. He would not fail his god! He would not!

Yet, at first it seemed he and the rest would. The portal strained but did not grow. Xavius concentrated the full force of his determination upon it, finally forcing the gap wider.

And then . . . a wondrous, blinding light forced the assembled Highborne *back*. Despite their astonishment, though, they somehow kept up their efforts.

From deep within, an odd-looking form coalesced. At first it stood no more than a few inches tall, but as it swiftly moved toward them, it grew . . . and grew . . . and *grew* . . .

The strain took its toll on more of the spellcasters. Two collapsed, one barely breathing. The others teetered, yet, once again, under Xavius's manic control, they regained power over the portal.

Suddenly, the eerie cries of hounds shook them all. Only the counselor, with his eyes unnatural, saw what first emerged from the gateway.

The beasts were the size of horses and had low-set horns that curled down and forward. Their scaly hides were colored a deathly crimson accented by savage splatterings of black and on their backs fluttered a crest of wild, shaggy brown fur. They were lean but muscular hunters, each three-toed paw ending in sharp claws more than half a foot long. Each creature had back legs slightly shorter than the front, but Xavius had no doubt as to the beasts' speed and agility. Even their slightest movements suggested hunters well skilled in bringing down their prey.

Atop their backs thrust two long, whiplike, leathery tentacles that ended in tiny sucker mouths. The tentacles swayed back and forth, seeming to focus with eagerness on the assembled sorcerers.

The face most resembled some peculiar cross between a wolf and a reptile. From the long, savage jaws jutted scores of tall, sharp teeth. The eyes were narrow and completely white, but filled with a sinister cunning that implied these were no mere animals.

Then, from behind them stepped the towering figure of their master.

He wore body armor of molten steel and in his huge, gauntleted hand he wielded a whip that flashed lightning whenever used. His chest and shoulders, so much wider than the rest of his torso, dwarfed those of even the mightiest warrior. Wherever the armor did not hide his form, pure flame radiated from his scaled, fleshless, and *unearthly* body.

Set deep in the broad shoulders, the flaming visage peered down at the night elves. That it most resembled a brooding skull with huge, curled horns did nothing to dissuade the Highborne that here was a heavenly messenger sent to aid them in their dream of a perfect paradise.

"Know that I am the servant of your god . . ." he hissed, the flames that were his eyes flashing hot whenever he spoke. "Come to help you open the way for his host and his most *glorious* self!"

One of the beasts howled, but a snap of the whip sent lightning crackling over the creature, instantly silencing it.

"I am the Houndmaster . . ." the massive, skeletal knight continued, fiery gaze fixing most upon the kneeling counselor. "I am *Hakkar* . . ."

TEN

At last, Rhonin awoke.

He did so with reluctance, for throughout his magical slumber, his mind had been filled with dreams. Most of those dreams had revolved around Vereesa and the coming twins, but, unlike the sinister keep, these were happy visions of a life he once thought to have.

Waking up only served to remind him that he might not live to see his family.

Rhonin opened his eyes to one familiar, if not so welcome, sight. Krasus leaned over him, mild concern in his expression. That only aggravated the human, for, in his mind, it was the dragon mage's fault that he was here.

At first, Rhonin wondered why his eyesight seemed a bit dim, but then he realized that he looked at Krasus not in the light of the sun, but rather by a very full moon. The moon illuminated the glade with an intensity that was not at all natural.

Curiosity growing, he started to rise . . . only to have his body scream from stiffness.

"Slowly, Rhonin. You have slept more than a day. Your body needs a minute or two to join you in waking."

"Where—?" The young wizard peered around. "I remember this glade . . . being carried toward it . . ."

"We have been the guests of its master since our arrival. We are not in any danger, Rhonin, but I must tell you immediately that we are also unable to depart."

Sitting up, Rhonin gazed at the area. He sensed some presence around them, but nothing that hinted they were trapped here. Still, he had never known Krasus to invent stories.

"What happens if we try to leave?"

His companion pointed at the rows of flowers. "They will stop us."

"They? The plants?"

"You may trust me on this, Rhonin."

While a part of him was tempted to see exactly what the flowers would do, Rhonin chose not to take any chances. Krasus said that they were not in any danger so long as they stayed where they were. However, now that both of them were conscious, perhaps they could devise some manner of escape.

His stomach rumbled. Rhonin recalled that he had slept a day and more without eating.

Before he could comment, Krasus handed him a bowl of fruit and a jug of water. The human devoured the fruit quickly and, although it did not satiate his hunger completely, at least his stomach no longer disturbed him.

"Our host has not delivered any sustenance since early in the day. I expect him shortly . . . especially as he likely already knows that you are awake."

"He does?" Not something Rhonin liked hearing. Their captor sounded too much in control. "Who is he?"

Krasus suddenly looked uncomfortable. "His name is Cenarius. Do you recall it?"

Cenarius . . . it struck a chord, albeit barely. Cenarius. Something from his studies, but not directly tied to magic. The name made him think of stories, myths, of a—

A woodland *god?*

Rhonin's gaze narrowed. "We're the guests of a forest deity?"

"A demigod, to be exact . . . which still makes him a force that even my kind respect."

"Cenarius . . ."

"You speak of me and I am here!" chortled a voice from everywhere. "I bid you welcome, one called Rhonin!"

Coalescing from the moonlight itself, a huge, inhuman figure half elf, half stag stepped forward. He towered even over the tall, lanky Krasus. Rhonin stared openly in awe at the antlers, the bearded visage, and the unsettling body.

"You slept long, young one, so I doubt that the food brought earlier was sufficient for your hunger." He gestured behind them. "There is more for the two of you now."

Rhonin glanced over his shoulder. Where the emptied bowl of fruit had sat there now stood another, this one filled high. In addition, a thick piece of meat, cooked just to the wizard's liking if the aroma indicated anything, lay on a wooden platter next to the bowl. Rhonin had no doubt that the jug had also been refilled.

"I thank you," he began, trying not to be distracted by the nearby meal. "But what I really wanted to do was ask—"

"The time for questions will be coming. For now, I'd be remiss if you did not eat."

Krasus took Rhonin by the arm. With a nod of his head, the wizard joined his former mentor and the pair ate their fill. Rhonin hesitated at first when it came to the meat, not because he did not want it, but because it surprised him that a forest dweller such as Cenarius would sacrifice a creature under his care for two strangers.

The demigod read his curiosity. "Each animal, each being, serves many purposes. They are all part of the cycle of the forest. That includes the necessity of food. You are like the bear or wolf, both of whom hunt freely in my domain. Nothing is wasted here. Everything returns to feed new growth. The deer upon which you now feed will be reborn to serve its role again, its sacrifice forgotten to it."

Rhonin frowned, not quite following Cenarius's explanation, but knowing better than to ask him to clarify it. The demigod saw both intruders as predators and had fed them accordingly. That was that.

When they were finished, the wizard felt much improved. He opened his mouth with the intention of pressing on the matter of their captivity, but Cenarius spoke first.

"You should not be here."

Neither Rhonin nor Krasus knew how to answer.

Cenarius paced the glade. "I've conversed with the others, discussed you at length, learned what they know . . . and we all agree that you are not meant to be here. You are out of place, but in what way, we've yet to determine."

"Perhaps I can explain," Krasus interjected. He still looked weak to Rhonin, but not so much as when they had first materialized in this time.

"Perhaps you can," agreed the young wizard.

The dragon mage glanced at his companion. Rhonin saw no reason to hold back the truth. Cenarius appeared to be the first being that they had come across who might be of assistance to them.

But the story that Krasus passed on to their host was not the one the human expected.

"We come from a land across the sea . . . far across, but that is unimportant. What is of significance is the reason why we ended here . . ."

In Krasus's revised tale, it was he, not Nozdormu, who had uncovered the rift. The dragon mage described it not as a tear in time, but as an anomaly that had upset the fabric of reality, potentially creating greater and greater catastrophe. He had summoned the one other spellcaster he trusted—Rhonin—and the pair had traveled to where Krasus had sensed the trouble.

"We journeyed to a chain of stark peaks in the bitter north of our land, there being where I sensed it strongest. We came across it and the monstrous things it spewed out at random. The wrongness of it struck us both hard, but when we sought to investigate closer . . . it moved, enveloping us. We were cast out of our land—"

"And into the domain of the night elves," the demigod completed.

"Yes," Krasus said with a nod. Rhonin added nothing and hoped his expression did not betray his companion. In addition to Krasus's omissions concerning their true origins, the wizard's former mentor left out one other item of possible interest to Cenarius.

He had made no mention of being a dragon.

Backing up a step, the woodland deity eyed both figures. Rhonin could not read his expression. Did he believe Krasus's altered story or did he suspect that his "guest" had not been completely forthcoming with him?

"This bears immediate discussion with the others," Cenarius finally declared, staring off into the distance. His gaze shifted back down to Rhonin and Krasus. "Your needs will be dealt with during my absence . . . and then we shall speak again."

Before either could say anything, the lord of the forest melted into moonlight, leaving them once more alone.

"That was futile," Rhonin growled.

"Perhaps. But I would like to know who these others are."

"More demigods like himself? Seems the most likely. Why didn't you tell him about your—"

The dragon mage gave him such a sharp glare that Rhonin faltered. In a much quieter tone, Krasus replied, "I am a dragon without strength, my young friend. You have no idea what that feels like. No matter who Cenarius is, I wish that to remain secret until I understand why I cannot recover."

"And the . . . rest of the story?"

Krasus looked away. "Rhonin . . . I mentioned to you that we might be in the past."

"I understand that."

"My memories are . . . are as scattered as my strength is depleted. I do not know why. However, one thing I have been able to recall based on what was told me during your induced slumber. I know now *when* we are."

Spirits rising, Rhonin blurted, "But that's good! It gives us an anchor of sorts! Now we can determine who best—"

"Please let me finish." Krasus's dour expression did not bode well. "There is a very good reason why I altered our story as much as I could. I suspected that Cenarius knew some of what was going on, especially about the anomaly. What I could not tell him are my suspicions as to what it might *presage.*"

The quieter and darker the elder mage's voice dropped, the more Rhonin grew concerned. "What?"

"I fear we have arrived just prior to the first coming of the *Burning Legion.*"

He could have said nothing more horrifying to Rhonin. Having lived—and nearly died more than once—battling the demonic horde and its allies, the young wizard still suffered monstrous nightmares. Only Vereesa understood the extent of those nightmares, she having fought through more than a few herself. It had taken both their growing love and the coming children to heal their hearts and souls and that after several months.

And now Rhonin had been thrust back into the night-mares.

Jumping to his feet, he said, "Then we've got to tell Cenarius, tell everyone we can! They'll—"

"They must not know . . . I fear it may already be too late to preserve matters as they once were." Also rising, Krasus stared down his long nose at his former pupil. "Rhonin . . . as it originally happened, the Legion was defeated after a terrible, bloody war, the precursor of things to come in our own time."

"Yes, of course, but—"

Evidently forgetting his own concerns about the possibility of Cenarius listening in, Krasus seized Rhonin by the shoulders. Despite the elder mage's weakness, his long fingers dug painfully into the human's flesh. "You still do not understand! Rhonin, by coming here, by simply being here . . . we may have altered that history! We may now be responsible for the Burning Legion this time becoming the *victor* in this first struggle . . . and that would mean not only the death of many innocents here, but the erasing of our own *time.*"

It had taken some convincing to make Illidan a part of Malfurion's sudden and very rash plan. Malfurion had little doubt that the deciding factor was not anything he had said . . . but rather Tyrande's own impassioned plea. Under her gaze, even Illidan had melted, readily agreeing to assist even though he clearly did not care for the prisoner one bit. Malfurion knew that something had happened between his brother and the orc, something that Tyrande had also been involved in, and she used that shared experience to bring Illidan to their side.

Now they had to succeed.

The four guards stood alert, each facing a different point on the compass. The sun was only minutes from rising and the square was empty of all save the soldiers and their charge. With most of the other night elves asleep, it was the perfect time to strike.

"I'll deal with the sentries," Illidan suggested, his left hand already balled into a fist.

Malfurion quickly took over. He did not question his brother's abilities, but he also wished no harm to come to the guards, who were only performing their duties. "No. I said I would take care of them. Give me a moment."

Shutting his eyes, he relaxed himself as Cenarius had shown him. Malfurion receded from the world, but at the same time, he saw it more clearly, more sharply. He knew exactly what he had to do.

At his suggestion to them, the necessary elements of nature joined to assist his needs. A cool, tender wind caressed the face of each guard with the gentleness of a loved one. With the wind came the tranquil scents of the flowers surrounding Suramar and the soothing call of a nearby night bird. The calmingly seductive combination enveloped each sentry, drawing them without their noticing into a peaceful, pleasant, and very deep lethargy that left them oblivious to the waking world.

Satisfied that all four were under his spell, Malfurion blinked, then whispered, "Come . . ."

Illidan hesitated, only following when Tyrande stepped out into the open after his brother. The three of them slowly made their way toward the cage and the soldiers. Despite the certainty that his spell held, Malfurion still half expected the four sentries to look their way at any moment. Yet even when he and his companions stood only a few yards away, the soldiers remained ignorant of their presence.

"It worked . . ." murmured Tyrande in wonder.

Stopping in front of the foremost guard, Illidan waved his

hand before the watchful eyes—all to no effect. "A nice trick, brother, but for how long?"

"I don't know. That's why we must hurry."

Tyrande knelt down by the cage, peering inside. "I think Broxigar is also caught by your spell, Malfurion."

Sure enough, the huge orc lay slumped against the back of his prison, his disinterested gaze looking past Tyrande. He made no move even when she quietly called out his name.

After a moment's consideration, Malfurion suggested, "Touch him softly on the arm and try his name again. Make certain that he sees you immediately so that you can signal for silence."

Illidan frowned. "He's sure to yell."

"The spell will hold, Illidan, but you must be ready to do your part when the time comes."

"*I'm* not the one who'll risk us," Malfurion's brother said with a sniff.

"Be still, both of you . . ." Reaching in, Tyrande cautiously touched the orc on his upper arm, at the same time calling out his name again.

Brox started. His eyes widened and his mouth opened in what would certainly be a very deafening cry.

But just as quickly he clamped his mouth shut, the only sound managing to escape being a slight grunt. The orc blinked several times, as if uncertain that the sight before him could possibly be real. Tyrande touched his hand, then, with a nod to the orc, looked into Brox's eyes again.

Looking to his brother, Malfurion muttered, "Now! Hurry!"

Illidan reached down, at the same time whispering under his breath. As he grasped the bars, his hands flared a bright yellow and the cage itself suddenly became framed in red energy. A slight hum arose.

Malfurion glanced anxiously at the sentries, but even this wondrous display passed unnoticed by them. He exhaled in relief, then watched as Illidan worked.

There were advantages to night elven sorcery and his brother had learned well how to wield it. The astonishing yellow glow surrounding his hands spread to the cage, rapidly enveloping the red. Sweat dripped from Illidan's forehead as he pressed his spell, but he did not falter in the least.

At last, Illidan released his hold and fell back. Malfurion caught his brother before the latter could stumble into one of the sentries. Illidan's hand continued to glow for a few seconds more. "You can open the cell now, Tyrande . . ."

Releasing Brox, she touched the door of the cage—which then immediately swung open almost of its own accord.

"The chains," Malfurion reminded Illidan.

"Of course, brother. I've not forgotten."

Squatting, Illidan reached for the orc's manacles. Brox, however, did not respond at first, eyes narrowing warily at the sight of the male night elf. Tyrande had to take his hands and guide them to her companion.

With more muttered words, Malfurion's brother touched each of the bonds at the lock. The manacles snapped open like small mouths eagerly waiting to be fed.

"No trouble whatsoever," Illidan remarked with an extremely pleased smile.

The orc emerged slowly, his body stiff due to the cramped conditions of his cell. He curtly nodded his gratitude to Illidan, but looked to Tyrande for guidance.

"Broxigar, listen carefully. I want you to go with Malfurion. He'll take you to a safe place. I'll see you there later."

This had been some cause of argument between Tyrande

and Malfurion, the former wanting to see the orc to safety herself. Malfurion—with Illidan's more-than-willing assistance—had finally convinced her that there would be trouble enough when Brox was discovered missing without Tyrande, who had been seen caring for him, also vanishing. It would not be hard for the Moon Guard to add the facts together.

"They'll make the connection quickly," Malfurion had insisted. "You were the only one to give him aid. That's why you need to stay here. They're less likely to think of me and even if they do, it's doubtful that they'll blame you, then. You are an initiate of Elune. That you know me is no crime with which they can label you."

Although Tyrande had given in, she still did not like Malfurion taking on all the responsibility himself. True, he had been the one who had come up with this startling course of action, but it was she who had instigated everything in the first place simply by introducing Malfurion to the imprisoned orc.

Now the young priestess also asked the orc to have faith in one he did not know well. Brox studied Malfurion, then glared again at Illidan. "That one be with?"

Illidan curled his lip. "I just saved your hide, beast—"

"Enough, Illidan! He's grateful!" To Brox, Tyrande answered, "Only Malfurion. He'll take you to a place where no one will be able to find you! Please! You can trust me!"

Taking her hand in his huge fists, the brutish figure fell to one knee. "I trust in you, shaman."

At that moment, Malfurion noticed one of the guards beginning to fidget.

"It's starting to wear away!" he hissed. "Illidan! Take Tyrande and leave! Brox! Come!"

With astonishing speed and grace, the massive orc leapt to his feet and followed after the night elf. Malfurion did not look behind him, praying that his druidic spell would hold long enough. For Tyrande and his brother he had little fear. Their destination was Illidan's quarters, only a short distance away. No one would suspect either of any duplicity.

For Malfurion and Brox, however, the matter was different. No one would mistake the orc for anything but what he was. The two had to escape the city as fast as possible.

But as they left the square and entered the winding streets of Suramar, the sound that Malfurion had feared most arose.

One of the guards had finally awakened. His shouts were quickly multiplied by those of his companions and, mere seconds later, the blare of a horn filled the air.

"This way!" he urged the orc. "I've mounts awaiting us!"

In truth, Malfurion need not have said anything, for the orc, despite his sturdy build, ran with at least as much swiftness as his rescuer. Had they been out in the wilderness, the night elf suspected Brox would have even outrun him.

Everywhere, horns sounded and voices cried out. Suramar had sprung to life . . . much too soon for Malfurion's taste.

At last, the night elf spotted the corner for which he had been waiting. "Here! They're just around here!"

But as they turned into the side street, Brox suddenly stumbled to a halt, the fearsome orc staring wide-eyed at the mounts Malfurion had secured.

The huge panthers were black, sinewy shadows. They snarled and hissed upon first sighting the newcomers, then calmed as Malfurion approached them. He patted each on the flank.

Brox shook his head. "We ride *these?*"

"Of course! Now hurry!"

The orc hesitated, but then nearby shouts urged him forward. Brox took the reins given to him and watched as Malfurion showed how to mount up.

It took the former captive three tries to climb atop the huge cat, then another minute to learn how to sit. Malfurion kept glancing behind them, fearful that at any moment the soldiers—or, worse, the Moon Guard—would arrive. He had not given any consideration to the fact that Brox might not know how to ride a night saber. What other beast could the orc have expected?

Adjusting his position one last time, Brox reluctantly nodded. Taking a deep breath, Malfurion urged his mount onward, Brox following as best he could.

In the space of but a few minutes, the night elf had forever changed his future. Such an audacious act might only serve to condemn him to Black Rook Hold, but Malfurion knew that he could not let this chance slip away. Somehow, Brox was linked to the disturbing work of the Highborne . . . and come what may, Malfurion had to find out how.

He had the horrible feeling that the fate of all Kalimdor hinged upon it.

Varo'then had little desire to face Lord Xavius, but that choice was not his. He had been commanded to appear before the counselor the moment his party arrived and commands given by Lord Xavius were to be obeyed with as much urgency as if they had been made by Queen Azshara herself . . . perhaps even more so.

The counselor would not like the captain's report. How to explain that they had somehow been led astray, then attacked by a forest? Varo'then hoped to use the late, unlamented Koltharius as a scapegoat, but doubted that his lord would accept such a pathetic offering. Varo'then had been in charge and to Lord Xavius that would be all that mattered.

He did not have to ask where the counselor could be found, for when was his master anywhere but the chamber where the spellwork took place? In truth, Captain Varo'then preferred blades to sorcery and the chamber was not his favorite place. True, he also wielded a bit of power himself, but what Lord Xavius and the queen had in mind overwhelmed even him.

The guards came to attention as he approached, but although they reacted with the respect he was due, something in their manner seemed different . . . almost unsettling.

Almost as if they knew exactly what awaited him better than he did.

The door swung open before him. Eyes down in respect, Captain Varo'then entered the Highborne sanctum—and a nightmarish beast filled his view.

"By Elune!" Acting instinctively, he drew his curved blade. The hellish creature howled, two menacing tentacles above its muscled form groping eagerly toward him. The captain doubted his chances against such a monstrosity, but he would fight it as best he could.

But then a hissing voice that chilled Varo'then's bones to the marrow uttered something in a language unknown. A fearsome whip snapped at the beast's hunched back.

Cringing, the demonic hound retreated, leaving Varo'then to gape at the one who had summoned it away.

"His name is Hakkar," Lord Xavius remarked pleasantly, appearing from the side. "The felbeasts are entirely under his control. The great one has sent him to help open the way . . ."

" 'G-great one,' my lord?"

To the captain's dismay, the counselor placed an almost

fatherly arm around his shoulder, guiding Varo'then to the fiery sphere over the pattern. Something about the sphere looked different, giving the night elf the horrible sensation that if he stood close enough, it would devour him body and soul.

"It's all right, my good captain. Nothing to fear . . ."

He was going to be punished for his failure. If so, at least Varo'then would make a declaration of his mistakes beforehand, so that he would not lose more face. "My Lord Xavius, the captives were lost! The forest turned against us—"

But the counselor only smiled. "You will be given the opportunity to redeem yourself in good time, captain. First, you must understand the glorious truth . . ."

"My lord, I don't—"

He got no further, his eyes snared.

"You understand now," Xavius remarked, his false eyes narrowed in satisfaction.

Varo'then sensed the god, sensed how the wondrous presence peeled away every layer that was the captain. The god within the fiery sphere looked into the deepest depths of Varo'then . . . and radiated a pleasure with what he found there.

You, too, will serve me well . . .

And Varo'then fell to one knee, honoring the one who honored him so.

"He will be coming to us soon, captain," Lord Xavius explained as the soldier rose. "But so magnificent is he that the way must be strengthened in order to accept his overwhelming presence! He has sent this noble guardian to open the path for others of his host, others who will in turn guide our efforts in strengthening the vortex . . . and bringing about the fruition of all of our dreams!"

Varo'then nodded, feeling both pleased and ashamed. "My lord, my failure to capture those strangers I found near the site of the disruption—"

He was interrupted by the hissing voice of Hakkar "Your failure isss moot. They will be taken . . . the great one isss mosssst interested in what Lord Xavius hasss told him about this—*disssruption*—and their posssible connection to it!"

"But how will you find them? That forest is the realm of the demigod, Cenarius! I'm sure it was him!"

"Cenarius is only a woodland deity," the counselor reminded him. "We have behind us now much, much more than that."

Turning from the night elves, Hakkar snapped his whip at an open area before him. As the sinewy weapon cracked, a greenish flash of lightning struck the stone floor.

In the lightning's wake, the area hit glowed brightly. The emerald flare increased rapidly in size and as it did, it began to coalesce.

The two felbeasts howled, their fearsome tentacles straining, but Hakkar kept them back.

A four-legged shape formed, growing larger and wider. It quickly took on an aspect already familiar to Captain Varo'then, which it verified with a bloodcurdling howl of its own.

The new hound shook itself once, then joined the others. As the mesmerized night elves watched, Hakkar repeated the step with his whip, summoning a fourth monstrous beast that lined up with the rest.

He then spun the lash around and around, creating a circular pattern that flared brighter and brighter until it created a *hole* in the air before him, a hole as tall as the fearsome figure and twice as wide.

Hakkar barked out a command in some dark tongue.

The hellish felbeasts leapt through the hole, vanishing. As the last disappeared, the hole itself dissipated.

"They know what they ssseek," Hakkar informed his stunned companions. "And they will find what they ssseek . . ." The fiery being wound up the whip, his dark gaze turning to the night elves' spellwork. "And now we shall begin our own tasssk . . ."

ELEVEN

It had taken Krasus an entire day to realize that he and Rhonin were being observed.

It had taken him a half day more to come to the conclusion that the observer had nothing to do with Cenarius.

Who it was with the ability to keep their presence hidden from the powerful demigod, the dragon mage could not say. One of Cenarius's counterparts? Not likely. The lord of the forest would surely be too familiar with their tricks or any of the servants they might send. The night elves? Krasus dismissed that possibility immediately, as he did the chance that any other mortal race could be responsible for the secretive watcher.

That left him with only one logical conclusion . . . that the one who spied upon Cenarius and his two "guests" was of Krasus's own people.

In his own time, the dragons sent out observers to keep track of those with the potential to change the world, either for good or ill. Humans, orcs—*every* race—had its spies. The dragons considered it a necessary evil; left to their own devices, the younger races had a tendency to create disaster. Even in this period of the past, there would be spies of some sort. He had no doubt that some kept a wary eye on Zin-Azshari . . . but, as was typical of Krasus's kind, they would do nothing until absolutely certain that catastrophe was imminent.

In this case, by then it would be too late.

From Cenarius he had kept his secrets secure, but from one of his own, even those of the past, Krasus decided he needed to tell what he knew. If anyone could avert the potential ruin his and Rhonin's presence might have already caused, it was the dragons . . . but only if they would listen.

He waited until the human had gone to sleep and the chances of Cenarius returning became remote. The needs of Krasus and Rhonin were attended to by silent, invisible spirits of the forest. Food materialized at appointed times and the refuse vanished once the pair were finished eating. Other matters of nature were handled in similar fashion. This allowed Cenarius to continue his mysterious discussions with his counterparts—which, with deities, could take days, weeks, months, or even longer—without worrying that the two would starve to death in his absence.

No matter what the cycle of the moon, the glade remained almost as lit as day. Once satisfied that Rhonin slept deeply enough, Krasus quietly rose and headed toward the barrier of flowers.

Even at night, they immediately fixed on him. Moving as close as he could without stirring them, the dragon mage peered out at the forest beyond, studying the dark trees. He knew better than any the secrets of stealth used by his kind, knew them better than even a demigod could. What Cenarius might have missed, Krasus would find.

At first, the trees all looked the same. He studied each in turn, then did so a second time, still with no results. His body cried out for rest, but Krasus refused to let his unnatural weakness take control. If he gave in once, he feared he would never recover.

His gaze suddenly stopped on a towering oak with a particularly thick trunk.

Eyeing it sharply, the weary spellcaster mentally shielded his thoughts, then focused on the tree.

I know you . . . I know what you are, watcher . . .

Nothing happened. No reply came. Briefly Krasus wondered if he had erred, but centuries of experience insisted otherwise.

He tried again. *I know you . . . cloaked as part of the tree, you watch us and the lord of the forest. You wonder who we are, why we are here.*

Krasus felt a presence stir, however slightly. The observer was uncomfortable with this sudden intrusion in his thoughts, and not yet willing to declare himself.

There is much that I can tell you that I could not tell the lord of the forest . . . but I would speak with more than the trunk of a tree . . .

You risk us both, a somewhat arrogant mind finally responded. *The demigod could be watching us in turn . . .*

The dragon mage hid his pleasure at garnering an answer. *You know as well as I that he is not here . . . and you can cloak us from the knowledge of any other onlookers . . .*

For a moment, nothing happened. Krasus wondered if he had pushed too far . . .

Part of the trunk suddenly tore away, assuming as it separated a humanoid figure of ridged bark. As the tall shape approached, the bark faded away, transforming to long, flowing garments and a slim face shadowed to obscurity by a spell with which Krasus himself was long familiar.

In robes the color of the tree, the all-but-faceless figure paused on the outer perimeter of the magical glade. Hidden eyes surveyed Krasus from head to foot and although the imprisoned mage could not read any expression, he was certain of the other's frustration.

"Who are you?" the watcher quietly asked.

"A kindred spirit, you might say."

This was met with some disbelief. "You do not know at all what you suggest . . ."

"I know exactly what I suggest," Krasus returned strongly. "I know it as well as I do that she who is called Alexstrasza is the Queen of Life, he who is called Nozdormu is Time itself, Ysera is She of the Dreaming, and Malygos is Magic incarnate . . ."

The figure digested the names, then, almost as an afterthought commented, "You did not mention one."

Biting back a gasp, Krasus nodded. "And Neltharion is the earth and rock itself, the Warder of the land."

"Such names are known by few outside my kind, but they *are* known by a few. By what name might I know you, that I should think you kindred?"

"I am known as . . . Korialstrasz."

The other leaned back. "I could not fail to know that name, not when it belongs to a consort of the Queen of Life, but something is amiss. I have observed everything since your capture and you act like none of my kind. Cenarius is powerful, very much so, but he should not so readily hold you as his hostage, not the one called Korialstrasz . . ."

"I have been injured badly." Krasus waved that away. "Time is of the essence! I must reach Alexstrasza and tell her what I know! Can you take me to her?"

"Just like that? You do have the arrogance of a dragon! Why should I risk for all dragons the umbrage of the woodland deity on your questionable identity alone? He will know from now on that he is observed and will act accordingly."

"Because the potential threat to the world—our world— is more important than an insult to the dignity of a demigod." Taking a deep breath, the dragon mage added, "And if you only will permit, I will reveal to you what I mean . . ."

"I do not know if I trust you," the darkened watcher said, cocking his head to one side. "But in your condition, I do not think I have much to fear from you, either. If you know how . . . then show me what colors your words with such anxiety."

Krasus refrained from any retort, despite his growing dislike for this other dragon. "If you are ready . . ."

"Do it."

Their minds touched . . . and Krasus unveiled the truth.

Under the rush of intense images, the other dragon stumbled back. The shadow spell around his face momentarily lost cohesion, revealing a peculiar reptilian and elven combination locked in an expression of total disbelief.

But the shadows returned as quickly as they had dissipated. Still obviously digesting what he had been shown, the watcher nonetheless recovered some of his composure. "This is all impossible . . ."

"Probable, I would say."

"These are pure figments of your creation!"

"Would that they were," Krasus remarked sadly. "You see now why I must speak with our queen?"

His counterpart shook his head. "What you are asking is—"

The two dragons froze, both sensing simultaneously the nearing presence of an overwhelming force.

Cenarius. The demigod had made an unexpected return.

Immediately the watcher began to retreat. Krasus, fearful that his one chance might be lost, reached out. "No. You cannot afford to ignore this! I must see Alexstrasza!"

His arm passed over the flowers. The blossoms reacted,

immediately opening wide and spraying him with their magical dust.

Krasus's world swam. He teetered forward, falling into their midst.

Strong arms suddenly caught him. He heard a quiet hiss of anxiety and knew that the other dragon had taken hold of him.

"I am a fool for doing thisss!" the other gasped.

Krasus gave silent thanks for the watcher's decision, until a sudden realization struck the collapsing mage. He tried to say something, but his mouth would not work.

And as he blacked out, his last thoughts were no longer of gratitude to the other dragon for finally taking him with him . . . but rather fury with himself for not having had the chance to make certain that *Rhonin* would be included in the escape.

The panthers darted through the thick forest, Brox's racing with such ferocity that it was all the hapless orc could do to keep seated. Although he was used to riding the huge wolves raised by his own people, the cat's movements differed in subtle ways that constantly left the orc anxious.

Just within sight ahead, the shadowed form of Malfurion bent low over his own beast, urging it this direction or that. Brox was glad that his rescuer had a path in mind, but he hoped that the arduous journey would not take too much longer.

Soon it would be sunrise. The orc had thought this a bad thing, for then they would be visible from a greater distance, but Malfurion had indicated that the coming of day was to their benefit. If the Moon Guard pursued them, the night elven sorcerers' powers would be weaker once the darkness faded.

Of course, there would still be soldiers with which to deal.

Behind him, Brox heard the growing sounds of pursuit. Horns, distant shouts, the occasional snarl of another panther. He had assumed that Malfurion had more of a plan than simply hoping to outpace the other riders, but apparently that was not the case. His rescuer was no warrior, simply a soul who had sought to do the right thing.

The black of night began to give way to gray, but a murky, foggy gray—a morning mist. The orc welcomed the unexpected mist, however temporary it would be, but hoped that his mount would not lose Malfurion's in it.

Vague shapes appeared and disappeared around him. Now and then, Brox thought he made out movement. His hand ached for his trusted ax, still in the custody of the night elves. Malfurion had provided him with no weapon, perhaps a wary precaution on the former's part.

The horns sounded again, this time much closer. The veteran warrior snarled.

Malfurion vanished into the fog. Brox straightened, trying to make out his companion and fearing that his own animal would now run off in an entirely different direction.

The panther suddenly twisted as it adjusted its path to avoid a massive rock. The orc, caught unaware, lost his balance.

With a grunt of dismay, Brox slipped off the fleet cat, tumbling onto the hard, uneven ground and rolling headlong into a thick bush.

Trained reflexes took command. Brox shifted into a crouch, coming up ready to remount. Unfortunately, his cat, oblivious to his misfortune, continued on, disappearing into the mist.

And the sounds of pursuit grew louder yet.

Immediately Brox sought out something, *anything*, that he could use as a weapon. He picked up a fallen branch, only to have it crumble in his beefy hands. The only rocks were either too small to be of use or so huge as to be unmanageable.

Something large rustled the shrubbery to his left.

The orc braced himself. If a soldier, he had a fair chance.

If one of the Moon Guard, the odds were distinctly stacked against Brox, but he would go down fighting.

A huge, panting, four-legged form burst from the fog-enshrouded forest.

Shock nearly did Brox in, for what leapt at him was no panther. It howled something like a wolf or dog, but only vaguely resembled either. At the shoulder, it stood about as tall as him and from its back stretched two foul, leathery tentacles. The mouth was filled with row upon row of savage fangs. Thick, greenish saliva dripped from its huge, hungry maw.

Monstrous memories filled his thoughts. He had seen such horrors, even if he himself had never fought one. They had run ahead of the other demons, pack upon pack of slavering, sinister monsters.

Felbeasts . . . the forerunners of the *Burning Legion*.

Brox awoke from his renewed nightmares just before the felbeast had him. He threw himself forward, under the huge creature. The felbeast tried to snag him with its claws, but momentum worked against it. The massive beast stumbled to a quick halt and looked back at its elusive prey.

The orc struck it on the nose with his fist.

For most races, such an assault would likely result in nothing save possibly the loss of the hand, but Brox was not only an orc, he was a swift and powerful one. Not only did he strike before the felbeast could react, but he did so with the full fury and might of the strongest of his kind.

The blow broke the demonic hound's nose. The beast stumbled and a bloodcurdling whine escaped it. Thick, dark green fluid dripped from its wound.

His hand pounding with pain, Brox kept his gaze on his adversary's own. One did not let any animal, especially one so hellish as this, see any sign of retreat or fear. Only by facing it did the orc have any chance, however minute, of survival.

Then, from out of the fog in which it had disappeared, Brox's mount came charging. The cat's cry made the felbeast turn, all interest in the orc forgotten. The two behemoths collided in a fury of claws and teeth.

Knowing that he could do nothing for the panther, Brox started to back away. However, he had managed only a few steps when the low, steady sound of heavy breathing from behind him filled his ears. With slow, very cautious movements, the orc glanced over his shoulder.

A short distance away, a second felbeast poised itself to leap on Brox.

With no other option, the frustrated warrior finally ran.

The second demon gave chase, howling as it threw itself toward its quarry. The two combatants ignored it, caught up in their own struggle. Already the panther had suffered two savage wounds on its torso. Brox gave silent thanks to the creature for even this momentary rescue, then concerned himself with trying to elude his other pursuer in the enshrouded forest.

Wherever the path narrowed most, the orc pushed himself through. The much larger felbeast had to go around the natural obstacles or, if it could, crash through them, allowing Brox to remain just out of reach. He despised the fact that he had to keep running, but without a weapon Brox knew his chances of defeating the monster were nonexistent.

A short distance away, the mournful call of a dying animal informed Brox that the panther had lost the battle and soon there would be *two* felbeasts out for the orc's blood.

Distracted by the cat's death cry, Brox did not watch his footing well enough. Suddenly a tree root seemed to rise just enough to catch his foot. He managed to keep from falling, but his lack of true balance sent him spinning wildly to the side. He grasped at a slim, leafless tree only a head taller than himself, but the entire trunk broke away in his grip, sending him colliding with a much larger, sturdier one.

Head aching, Brox could barely focus on the oncoming behemoth. The small tree still in his hand, he swung it around and jabbed with it like a lance.

The demon hound swatted at the makeshift weapon, tearing away the top third and leaving jagged splinters on the end. Eyes still blurry, the orc held tight to what remained, then charged the monster.

The damage done by the felbeast gave the makeshift lance a deadliness it had not had prior. Shoving with all his might, Brox buried the sharp, fragmented end deep into the gaping jaws.

With a muffled howl of agony, the demon tried to fall back, but Brox advanced, his entire body straining as he pushed the lance deeper yet.

One of the tentacles reached for him. The orc released one hand, snagged the oncoming threat, and pulled as hard as he could.

With a moist, tearing sound, the tentacle came free.

Now much splattered with its own foul fluids, the felbeast's front legs collapsed. Brox did not relinquish his hold on the tree, adjusting his position to match his adversary's increasingly desperate movements.

The rear legs crumpled. Tail twitching frantically, the fearsome beast pawed at the obstruction in its gullet. It finally managed to snap Brox's weapon in two, but the front portion remained lodged.

Aware that the felbeast might still recover, the orc searched frantically for something to replace his lost lance.

Instead, he found himself facing his first foe again.

The other felbeast had scars across its body and, in addition to the nose wound Brox had given it earlier, a chunk of flesh had been torn from the right shoulder. Still, despite its worsened condition, the beast looked more than healthy enough to finish off the exhausted orc.

Seizing a thick, broken branch, Brox brandished it like a sword. But he knew that his luck had come to an end. The limb was hardly strong enough to ward away the huge monstrosity.

Crouching, the felbeast tensed—

But as it jumped, the forest itself came alive in defense of Brox. The wild grass and weeds under the demonic creature sprouted madly, shooting up with such astonishing swiftness that they caught the felbeast just after it left the earth.

Limbs hopelessly entangled, the horrific creature snarled and snapped at the grass. Its twin tentacles stretched down, trying to touch the animated plant life that held it from its prey.

"Brox!"

Malfurion rode toward the orc, looking as weary as Brox felt. The night elf pulled up next to him and reached a hand down.

"I owe you again," rumbled the veteran warrior.

"You owe me nothing." Malfurion glanced at the trapped felbeast. "Especially since it looks as if that won't hold him for very long!"

True enough, wherever the macabre tentacles touched the grass and weeds, the plants withered. One front paw had already been freed and even as the felbeast worked on liberating the rest, it strained to reach Brox and the night elf.

"Magic . . ." muttered Brox, recalling similar sights. "It's devouring the magic . . ."

Face grim, Malfurion helped his companion aboard. The panther grunted, but did not otherwise protest the added weight. "Then, we'd better leave quickly."

A horn sounded, this time so near that Brox almost expected to see the trumpeter. The pursuit from Suramar had almost caught up.

Suddenly, Malfurion hesitated. "They'll ride right into that beast! If any of them are Moon Guard—"

"Magic can still slay a felbeast if there's enough of it, night elf . . . but if you wish to stay and fight the creature with them, I will stand at your side." That doing so would mean either his death or recapture, Brox did not add. He would not abandon Malfurion, who had already rescued him twice.

The morning fog had already begun to dissipate and vague figures could already be seen in the distance. Grip tightening on the reins, Malfurion abruptly turned the panther *away* from the felbeasts and the approaching riders. He said nothing to Brox, instead simply urging his mount to as quick a pace as it could set and leaving both threats behind.

Behind them, the demon freed another limb, its attention already seized by growing sounds heralding new prey . . .

Something stirred Rhonin from his slumber, something that made him very uneasy.

He made no immediate motion, instead his eyelids opening just enough to let him see a bit of the surrounding area. Glimpses of daylight enabled the wizard to make out the surrounding trees, the ominous line of flower sentinels, and the grass upon which he lay.

What Rhonin could not make out was any sign of Krasus.

He sat up, searching for the dragon mage. Surely Krasus had to be somewhere in the glade.

But after a thorough survey of the region, Krasus's disappearance could no longer be denied.

Wary, the wizard rose and went to the edge of the glade. The flowers turned to face him, each bloom opening wide. Rhonin was tempted to see how powerful they were, but suspected that a demigod would hardly place them here if they could not readily deal with a mere mortal.

Eyeing the woods, Rhonin quietly called, "Krasus?"

Nothing.

Staring at the trees just beyond his prison, the wizard frowned. Something did not look the same, but he could not say exactly what.

He stepped back, trying to think . . . and suddenly noticed that he was in shadow.

"Where is the other one?" Cenarius demanded, no hint of kindliness in his tone. Although clear, the sky suddenly rumbled and a harsh wind came out of nowhere to swat the human. "Where is your friend?"

Facing the towering demigod, Rhonin kept his expression neutral. "I don't know. I just woke up and he was gone."

The antlered figure's golden orbs flared and his frown sent chills down Rhonin's spine. "There are troubling signs in the world. Some of the others have only just now sensed intruders, creatures not of any natural origin, sniffing around, seeking something—or *someone.*" He studied the wizard very closely. "And they come so soon after you and your friend drop from nowhere . . ."

What these unnamed creatures might be, Rhonin could only suspect. If so, he and Krasus had even less time than they had imagined.

Seeing that his "guest" had nothing yet to say, Cenarius added, "Your friend could not have escaped without assistance, but he leaves you behind. Why is that?"

"I—"

"There were those among the others who insisted that I should have given you to them immediately, that they would have found out through more thorough means than I prefer the reasons for your being here and what it is about you that so interests the night elves. I had, up until now, convinced them otherwise in this matter."

Rhonin's highly attuned senses suddenly detected the presence of another powerful force, one which, in its own way, matched Cenarius.

"Now I see I must acquiesce to the majority," the lord of the forest finished reluctantly.

"We heard your call . . ." growled a deep, ponderous voice. "You admit you were wrong . . ."

The wizard tried to turn and see who now spoke, but his legs—his entire body—would not obey his commands.

Something more immense than the demigod moved up behind Rhonin.

Cenarius did not seem at all pleased by the other's comments. "I admit only that other steps must be taken."

"The truth will be known . . ." A heavy, *furred* hand with thick claws enveloped Rhonin's shoulder, gripping it painfully. ". . . and known *soon* . . ."

TWELVE

Y ou should stay in the temple!" Illidan insisted. "Malfurion thought that best and so do I!"

But Tyrande would not be swayed. "I have to know what's happening! You saw how many rode in pursuit! If they captured them—"

"They won't." He squinted, the blinding sun not at all to his liking. He could feel his powers waning, feel the rush of magic fading. Illidan did not like such sensations. He savored magic in all its forms. That had been one reason he had even tried to follow the druidic path—that, and the fact that what Cenarius supposedly taught would not be affected by night or day.

They stood dangerously near the square, a place Tyrande had insisted upon returning to once matters had quieted down. The Moon Guard and the soldiers had ridden off after Malfurion, leaving only a pair of the former to inspect the cage for clues. That they had done, finding nothing to trace the culprits, just as Illidan had expected. In truth, he considered himself at least as proficient as any of the honored sorcerers, if not more.

"I should ride after—"

Would she never give in? "You do that and you'll risk everyone! You want them to take that pet creature of yours to Black Rook Hold and Lord Ravencrest? For that matter, they might take us there as w—"

Illidan suddenly clamped his mouth shut. From the opposite end of the square now entered several armored riders . . . and in their lead, Lord Kur'talos Ravencrest himself.

It was too late to hide. As the night elven commander rode past, his dour gaze shifted first to Tyrande, then her companion.

At sight of Illidan, Ravencrest called a sudden halt.

"I know you, lad . . . Illidan Stormrage, isn't it?"

"Yes, my lord. We met once."

"And this?"

Tyrande bowed. "Tyrande Whisperwind, novice priestess of the temple of Elune . . ."

The mounted night elves respectfully made the sign of the moon. Ravencrest graciously acknowledged Tyrande, then turned his gaze once more to Illidan. "I recall our encounter. You were studying the arts, then." He rubbed his chin. "You are not yet a member of the Moon Guard, are you?"

That Ravencrest would ask the question in such a way indicated that he already knew the answer. Clearly after their initial meeting he had kept an eye on Illidan, something that made the younger night elf both proud and extremely uneasy. He had done nothing he knew of to warrant bringing himself to the commander's attention. "No, my lord."

"Then you are free of some of their restrictions, aren't you?" The restrictions to which the commander referred had to do with the oaths each sorcerer swore upon entering the fabled order. The Moon Guard was an entity unto its own and owed no loyalty to anyone save the queen . . . which meant that they were not at the beck and call of those such as Lord Ravencrest.

"I suppose I am."

"Good. Very good. I want you to ride with us, then."

Now both Tyrande and Illidan looked confused. Likely fearing for Illidan's safety, the young priestess said, "My Lord Ravencrest, we would be honored—"

She got no farther. The night elven lord raised a polite hand to silence her. "Not you, sister, although the blessing of the Mother Moon is always welcome. No, 'tis the lad alone with whom I speak now."

Trying not to show his increasing anxiety, Illidan asked, "But what would you have need of me for, my lord?"

"For the moment, investigation into the escape of the creature we had penned here! News came to me just moments ago of his escape. Assuming that he's not been captured already, I've some notions as to how to find him. I might need the aid of a bit of sorcery, though, and while the Moon Guard are capable, I prefer someone who listens to orders."

To refuse a request by a night elf as highly ranked as Ravencrest would have been suspicious, but joining him risked Malfurion. Tyrande glanced surreptitiously at Illidan, trying to read his thoughts. He, on the other hand, wished that she could tell him the best path to take.

In truth, there was only one choice. "I'd be honored to join you, my lord."

"Excellent! Rol'tharak! A mount for our young sorcerer friend here!"

The officer in question brought forth a spare night saber, almost as if Ravencrest had expected Illidan all the time. The animal crouched low so that its new rider could mount up.

"The sun is well upon us, my lord," Rol'tharak commented to Ravencrest as he handed down the reins of the beast to Malfurion's brother.

"We will make do . . . as will you, eh, sorcerer?"

Illidan understood very well the veiled message. His powers would be weaker in daylight, but the commander was still confident that he would be of use. The confidence which Ravencrest had in him made Illidan's head swell.

"I will not fail you, my lord."

"Splendid, lad!"

As he slipped atop the panther, Illidan gave Tyrande a quick glance, indicating that she should not worry about Malfurion and the orc. He would ride with Ravencrest and aid in whatever way he could so long as the pair would still make good their escape.

Tyrande's brief but grateful smile was all the reward he could have desired. Feeling quite good about himself, Illidan nodded to the commander that he was ready.

With a wave and a shout, Lord Ravencrest led the armed force on. Illidan leaned forward, determined to keep pace with the noble. Somehow he would please Ravencrest while at the same time keeping his altruistic brother from being sent to Black Rook Hold. Malfurion knew the forest lands well, which meant that he would likely stay ahead of the soldiers and Moon Guard, but in the awful chance that pursuit had caught up with Illidan's twin and Tyrande's creature, Illidan had to at least consider sacrificing Brox to save his brother. Tyrande would come to understand that. He would do what he could to avoid it, but blood came first . . .

As often happened, a morning fog draped over the landscape. The thick mist would break up soon, but it meant more hope for Malfurion. Illidan kept his gaze on the path ahead, wondering if it was the same one his brother had used. It might be that the Moon Guard had not even chosen the right direction, which meant that he and Lord Ravencrest now pursued a futile course of action.

But as they raced deeper and deeper into the wooded lands, the fog quickly gave way. The morning sun seemed as eager to drain Illidan of his power as it did to eat away the mist, but he gritted his teeth and tried not to think of what that might mean. If it came to some sort of show of sorcery, he had no intention of disappointing the noble. The hunt for the orc had become as much Illidan's excuse to make new connections within the hierarchy of the night elf world as it had anything to do with the escape of Brox.

But just as they reached the top of a ridge, something farther down made Illidan frown and Lord Ravencrest curse. The commander immediately slowed his mount, the rest following suit. Ahead appeared to be a number of peculiar mounds scattered along the trail. The night elves cautiously descended the other side of the ridge, Ravencrest and the soldiers keeping their weapons ready. Illidan suddenly prayed that he had not overestimated his daytime skills.

"By the Blessed Azshara's eyes!" muttered Ravencrest.

Illidan could say nothing. He could only gape at the carnage revealed as they drew near.

At least half a dozen night elves, including two of the Moon Guard, lay dead before the newcomers, their bodies torn to shreds and, in the case of the two sorcerers, seemingly *sucked dry* by some vampiric force. The two Moon Guard resembled nothing more than shriveled fruit left in the sun too long. Their emaciated forms were stretched in positions of the utmost agony and clearly they had struggled throughout their horrible ordeals.

Five night sabers also lay dead, some with their throats torn out, the others disemboweled. Of the remaining panthers, there was no sign.

"I was right!" Ravencrest snapped. "That green-hided creature was not alone! There must've been two dozen and more to do this . . . and with the Moon Guard along yet!"

Illidan paid him no mind, concerned more with what

might have befallen Malfurion. This could not be the work of either his brother or one orc. Did Lord Ravencrest have the right of it? Had Brox betrayed Malfurion, leading him to his savage comrades?

I should've slain the beast when I had the opportunity! His fist tightened and he felt his rage fuel his powers. Given a target, Illidan would have more than proved his sorcerous might to the noble.

Then one of the soldiers noticed something to the right of the carnage. "My lord! Come look! I've seen nothing like it!"

Steering their animals around, Illidan and Ravencrest stared wide-eyed at the beast the other night elf had found.

It was a creature out of nightmare, in some ways lupine in form, but monstrously distorted, as if some insane god had created it out of the depths of his madness. Even in death it lost no bit of its inherent horror.

"What do you make of it, sorcerer?"

For a moment, Illidan forgot that *he* was the fount of magical wisdom here. Shaking his head, he responded with all honesty, "I have no idea, Lord Ravencrest . . . no idea."

However terrifying the monster was, someone had dealt hard with it, jamming a makeshift spear down its gullet and likely choking it to death.

Again Illidan's thoughts turned to his brother, last known by him to be heading into this forest. Had Malfurion done this? It seemed unlikely. Did his twin instead lie nearby, torn apart as readily as the two Moon Guard?

"Very curious," Ravencrest muttered. He suddenly straightened, looking around. "Where are the rest of the first party?" he demanded to no one in particular. "There should be twice as many as we found!"

As if to answer that, a mournful horn blast arose from the

south, where the forest dropped abruptly, becoming more treacherous to traverse.

The commander pointed his blade in the direction of the horn blast. "That way . . . but be wary . . . there may be more of those monsters about!"

The party worked their way down, each member, Illidan included, watching the thickening forest with trepidation. The horn did not sound again, not at all a good sign.

Several yards down, they came across another night saber, its entire side opened up by savage claws, its back also broken by the two huge oaks into which it had crashed. Only a short distance away, another of the Moon Guard lay pressed against a massive rock, his emaciated body and his horrified expression chilling even the hardened soldiers of Lord Ravencrest.

"Steady . . ." the noble quietly ordered. "Keep order . . ."

Once more, the horn sounded feebly, this time much closer and directly ahead.

The newcomers wended their way toward it. Illidan had the horrible feeling that something watched him in particular, but whenever he looked around, he saw only the trees.

"Another one, my lord!" the night elf called Rol'tharak blurted, pointing just ahead.

Sure enough, a second hellish beast lay dead, its body sprawled as if even in dying it had sought another victim. In addition to a crushed nose and a shoulder torn apart, it had several strange, ropelike marks on its legs. What had slain it, however, were a number of well-aimed thrusts to its throat by night elven blades. One still remained embedded in the beast.

They found two more soldiers nearby, the highly trained warriors of the realm tossed about like rag dolls. Illidan's brow furrowed in puzzlement. If the night elves had managed to slay both monsters, then where were the survivors?

Moments later, they found what remained.

One soldier sat propped against a tree, his left arm torn free. A poor attempt had been made to bandage the immense wound. He stared without seeing at the new arrivals, the horn still in his one remaining hand. Blood covered his torso.

Next to him lay the other to survive—if to survive meant to have half of one's face ripped apart and one leg twisted under at an impossible angle. His breathing was ragged, his chest barely rising each time.

"You there!" Ravencrest bellowed to the one with the horn. "Look at me!"

The survivor blinked slowly, then forced his gaze to that of the noble.

"Is this it? Are there any more?"

The mauled fighter opened his mouth, but no sound escaped it.

"Rol'tharak! Look to his wounds! Give him water if he needs it!"

"Aye, my lord!"

"The rest of you fan out! Now!"

Illidan remained with Ravencrest, watching warily as the others established what they hoped would be a safe perimeter. That so many of their fellows, including three spellcasters, had been so easily massacred did nothing for morale.

"Speak up!" Ravencrest roared. "I command you! Who was responsible for this? The escaped prisoner?"

At this, the bloody soldier let out a wild laugh, startling Rol'tharak so much that he stepped back.

"N-never saw that one, m-my lord!" the maimed figure responded. "Probably all eaten up h-himself!"

"So it was those monsters, then? Those hounds?"

The stricken night elf nodded.

"What happened to the Moon Guard? Why didn't they stop the things? Surely even in the daytime—"

And again the wounded soldier laughed. "M-my lord! The sorcerers were the easiest of the p-prey . . ."

Through effort, the story came out. The soldiers and the Moon Guard had pursued the escaped creature and another, unidentified figure through the forest, following their tracks even through fog and the coming sun. They had not actually seen the pair, but had been certain that it would only be a matter of time before they caught up.

Then, unexpectedly, they had come across the first beast.

No one had ever seen anything like it. Even dead it had unnerved the night elves. Hargo'then, the lead sorcerer, had sensed something magical about it. He had commanded the rest to wait a few paces behind him while he rode up to investigate the corpse. No one had argued.

"An unnatural thing," Hargo'then had proclaimed as he had begun to dismount. "Tyr'kyn . . ." he had called to one of the other Moon Guard. "I want you to—"

That was when the second beast had fallen upon him.

"It came from out behind the nearest trees, m-my lord . . . and went directly for . . . for Hargo'then! S-slew his mount with one swipe of the c-claws and th-then . . ."

The sorcerer had no chance. Before the startled night elves could react, two horrific tentacles on the creature's back had thrust out, adhering themselves like leeches to Hargo'then's chest and forehead. The Moon Guard leader screamed as no night elf had ever heard one of their own scream and before their eyes he had suddenly shriveled into a dry, limp husk quickly discarded by the slavering, four-legged monstrosity.

Finally recovering from their shock, the other night elves belatedly charged the beast, seeking at least to avenge Hargo'then's death.

Too late they realized that they were also being hunted

from behind by a third beast. The attackers had become the attacked, caught between twin demonic forces.

The resulting carnage had been clear for the newcomers to see. The Moon Guard had perished swiftly, their weakened magical abilities actually making them much more attractive prey. The soldiers had fared little better, but at least their blades had some effect on the demons.

As the survivor finished his tale, he grew less coherent. By the time he reached the conclusion, where he and three others had banded together at this spot, it was all Lord Ravencrest and Illidan could do to understand his ramblings.

Rol'tharak looked up. "He's passed out again, my lord. I fear he may not be waking up again."

"See what you can do for him to ease his pain. Check that other one, too." The noble frowned. "I want another look at that first carcass. Sorcerer, attend me."

Illidan followed Ravencrest back along the trail. Two guards broke off from their duties to follow the pair. The other soldiers continued to survey the area, trying unsuccessfully to find any more survivors.

"What do you make of the story?" the veteran commander asked of Illidan. "Have you heard of such things?"

"Never, my lord . . . but I am not part of the Moon Guard and so not privy to all their arcane knowledge."

"For all the good their knowledge did them! Hargo'then was always too confident! Most of the Moon Guard are!"

Illidan gave a noncommittal noise.

"Here it is . . ."

The macabre beast looked as if it still sought to remove the wedge from its throat. Despite the open wounds it bore, the creature was bereft of any eager scavengers, even flies. Even the forest life seemed repelled by the dead intruder.

To the two soldiers, Ravencrest commanded, "Check the

path we took. See if the trail the first party and ours followed continues on. I still want that green-skinned brute . . . more than ever now!"

As the other two rode on, both Illidan and the noble dismounted, the latter also unsheathing his blade. The night sabers were not at all keen on remaining so near the carcass, so their riders led them to a thick tree a short distance away and tied the reins to it.

Once back at the corpse, Lord Ravencrest knelt down. "Simply horrid! In all my years, I've never faced such a thing so well designed for carnage . . ." He lifted a leathery tentacle. "Curious appendage. So this is what the other used to suck Hargo'then dry! What do you make of it?"

Trying not to back away from the foul limb thrust in his face, Illidan managed, "V-vampiric in nature, my lord. Some animals drink blood, but this one seeks magical energy." He looked around. "The other's been torn off."

"Yes, so it has. Likely by an animal . . ."

While the noble continued his gruesome examination, Illidan considered the monstrosity's death. The soldier reported that this first one had been dead already. To the young night elf's quick mind, that meant the only ones who could have slain it were Malfurion and Brox . . . and judging by the physical struggle that had taken place, Illidan would have placed his bet more on the powerful orc.

Off to the side, the cats grew increasingly virulent in their protests at being so near the creature. Illidan tried to shut out the sounds of their hissing, still concerned about his brother. They had sighted no other corpses save those of the first party and the second of the three beasts mentioned, but—

Head snapping up straight, Illidan said, "My Lord Ravencrest! We never found any sign of the—"

The snarls of the night sabers reached a new crescendo.

Illidan sensed something behind him.

He threw himself to the side, accidentally colliding with the unsuspecting noble. Both fell flat to the ground, the younger night elf sprawled haphazardly over the commander. Ravencrest's sword flew wildly, landing far beyond either's reach.

The huge, clawed form that had just leapt at Illidan went sailing over the carcass of its twin.

"What in the name of—" Ravencrest managed. The night sabers struggled to attack, but their reins held, keeping the cats from being any aid.

Recovering first, Illidan looked up to see the hellish creature turning to attempt a second strike. He had thought the dead one terrifying enough, but to see one alive and bearing down on him nearly made Illidan flee in utter panic.

But instead of leaping again, the canine horror suddenly lashed at Illidan with the two tentacles atop its back. Memories of the husks that had once been powerful members of the Moon Guard filled the night elf's mind.

Yet, as the gaping appendages sought his magic, sought his very body, self-preservation took over. Recalling how one tentacle on the dead beast had been ripped free, Illidan quickly devised a plan of attack.

He did not try to strike the monster directly, knowing how little that would probably help. It would simply suck up Illidan's spell and perhaps continue draining him directly. Instead, Illidan chose to cast his spell on Lord Ravencrest's lost blade, which lay out of his hellish foe's sight.

The animated sword rose swiftly in the air and began to spin, whirling faster and faster. Illidan directed it at the creature's back, aiming for the parasitic appendages.

With pinpoint accuracy, the whirling blade shot across the shoulders of the toothy behemoth, severing both tentacles as simply as it could have shaved a blade of grass.

With a maddened howl, the houndlike beast shook, thick, greenish fluids spilling over its shoulders and down its backside. It snarled, its unsettling gaze narrowing on the one who had hurt it so.

Emboldened by his success and less fearful now that the danger to his sorcery had been eliminated, Illidan directed Ravencrest's sword back again. As the monster leapt at him, the young night elf smiled darkly at it.

With a force magnified by his intense will, he buried the weapon in the creature's hard skull.

The monster's leap faltered. It stumbled awkwardly. A glazed look filled the horrific orbs. The massive beast took two hesitant steps toward Illidan . . . then crumpled in a limp heap.

An incredible exhaustion overcame the young night elf, but one mixed with a sense of extreme satisfaction and triumph. He had done with little hesitation what three of the Moon Guard had failed to do. That he had learned from their mistakes, Illidan did not care. He only knew that by himself he had taken on a demon and won handily.

"Well done!" A heavy slap on his back nearly sent him stumbling into his monstrous foe. As Illidan fought to maintain his balance, Lord Ravencrest stepped past him to admire his companion's work. "A splendid counterattack! Remove the greatest danger, then strike the death blow while the enemy tries to recoup! Splendid!"

The noble put one boot on a forelimb of the demon and struggled to remove his blade. From the trail rode the two guards and further behind Illidan, others shouted as realization of the threat finally sank in among the rest of the party.

"My lord!" shouted one of the two guards. "We heard—"

Rol'tharak rushed up. "Lord Ravencrest! You slew one of the beasts! Are you injured?"

Illidan expected Ravencrest to take credit—after all, the

noble's weapon still pierced the monster's head—but instead the elder night elf stretched forth his hand and indicated Malfurion's brother. "Nay! Here stands the one who, after risking himself to throw me from the creature's path, readily disposed of the danger with scarcely a concern for his own life! I saw right about you from the first, Illidan Stormrage! More capable than a dozen Moon Guard you are!"

Cheeks darkening, the young night elf accepted the accolades of the powerful commander. Years of hearing how he was expected to be a hero, a champion of his people, had set a heavy load on his shoulders. Yet, now, Illidan felt as if his destiny had finally revealed itself . . . and it had done so with the innate sorcery he had almost rejected for the slower, more subtle druidic spells Cenarius had been teaching.

I was a fool to reject my heritage, Illidan realized. *Malfurion's path was never meant to be mine. Even in daytime, night elven sorcery is mine to command . . .*

It heartened him, actually, for he had felt strange taking up the ways of his brother. What hero of legend had been recorded following the footsteps of another? Illidan had been meant to *lead*.

The soldiers—Lord Ravencrest's capable, veteran soldiers—eyed him with a new and healthy respect.

"Rol'tharak!" the noble called. "I feel luck is with me this day! I want you to lead half the warriors on after the trail! We may still find the prisoner and whoever released him! Go now!"

"Aye, my lord!" Rol'tharak summoned several soldiers, then, after all had mounted, led them in the direction Malfurion and Brox had likely gone.

Illidan scarcely thought of his brother, already assuming that the delay here had given Malfurion all the time he needed to lose his pursuers. He did think of Tyrande, however, who would not only be quite pleased by what she would see as his having delayed the hunters but also would be rightly impressed by the high praise Lord Ravencrest had bestowed upon him.

And it seemed that the noble had more to bestow upon the one he thought had saved his life. Striding up to Illidan, Ravencrest put one gauntleted hand on the other night elf's shoulder, then declared, "Illidan Stormrage, the Moon Guard may be ignorant of your prowess, but I am not. You are hereby marked as one of Black Rook Hold's own . . . and my personal sorcerer! As such, you'll be of a rank outside of the Moon Guard, equal to any of their own and unable to be commanded by any of their order! You will answer only to me and to your queen, the Light of Lights, Azshara!"

The rest of the night elves put their left hands to their chests and dipped their heads in homage at the mention of the queen.

"I am—honored—my lord . . ."

"Come! We ride back immediately! I want to gather a larger force to bring these carcasses to Black Rook Hold! This must be investigated thoroughly! If we're to be invaded by some hellish horde, we must learn everything we can, then alert her majesty!"

Caught up in his euphoria, Illidan paid scant attention to any mention of Azshara. Had he done so, he might have had at least some slight concern, for it was because of her that Malfurion had dared the wrath of his brother's new patron. She it was who Malfurion insisted was involved in madness that might prove catastrophic to the entire night elf race.

But for the moment, all Illidan could think was, *I have found my destiny at last . . .*

THIRTEEN

H*e's strong of mind, strong of soul, strong of body* . . . said
a powerful, aggressive voice in Rhonin's head.

An admirable quality . . . at other times . . . replied a
second, calmer voice otherwise identical to the first.

The truth will be known, the first insisted. *I've never failed to
make it so . . .*

Rhonin seemed to float outside his body, but where he
floated, the wizard could not say. He felt as if he hung between life and death, sleep and waking, darkness and
light . . . nothing seemed quite right or absolutely wrong.

No more! interjected a third voice somehow familiar to
him. *He has been through enough! Return him to me . . . for
now . . .*

And suddenly Rhonin awoke in the glade of Cenarius.

The sun hung high overhead, although whether that
meant it was noon or merely a trick of the enchanted area,
the human could not say. Rhonin tried to rise, but, as before,
his body would not obey him.

He heard movement and suddenly the sky filled with the
antlered aspect of the forest lord.

"You're resilient, Rhonin wizard," Cenarius rumbled.
"You surprised one who is usually little surprised . . . and,

more to the point, you held your secrets, however foolish that may be in the long run."

"Th-there's nothing . . . I can . . . tell you." It amazed Rhonin that his mouth even worked.

"That remains to be seen. We will know what happened to your companion and why you—who should not be here—are." The demigod's visage softened. "But for now, I would have you rest. That much you deserve."

He waved his hand over Rhonin's face . . . and the wizard slept.

Krasus himself would have liked to know the answer of exactly where he was. The cavern in which he now awakened stirred no memories. He could not sense the presence of any other creature, especially not one of his own kind, and that worried him. Had the watcher simply brought him here to be rid of him? Did he expect Krasus to die here?

The last was a very real danger. Pain and exhaustion continued to wrack the dragon mage's lanky frame. Krasus felt as if someone had ripped half of him away. His memory continued to fail him and he feared that all his maladies would only grow worse with time . . . time he did not have.

No! I will not give in to despair! Not me! Forcing himself to his feet, he peered around. For a human or orc, the cavern would have been all but black, yet Krasus could make out its interior almost as well as if the light of the sun shone within. He could see the huge, toothy stalactites and stalagmites, identify each crack and fissure along the walls, and note even the tiny, blind lizards darting in and around the smallest crevices.

Unfortunately, he could not make out any exit.

"I do not have time for these games!" he snapped at the empty air. His words echoed, seeming to grow more self-mocking with each repetition.

He was missing something. Surely he had been put in this place for a reason . . . but what?

Then Krasus recalled the ways of his kind, ways that could, for those not dragons, be very cruel, indeed. A grim smile played across his face.

Straightening, the cowled mage slowly turned in a circle, eyes never blinking once. At the same time, he began reciting a ritual greeting, speaking in a language older than the world. He repeated the greeting three times, emphasizing the nuances of it as only one who had learned it from the very source of that language could.

If this did not garner the attention of his captors, nothing would.

"It speaks the tongue of those who set the heavens and earth in place . . ." thundered someone. "Those who brought us into being."

"It must be one of us," said another. "For it can surely not be one of them . . ."

"More must be known."

And suddenly from the empty air they materialized around the tiny figure . . . four gargantuan red dragons seated around Krasus, their world-spanning wings folded in dignified fashion behind them. They eyed the mage as if he were a small but tasty morsel of food.

If they thought to shock his supposedly primitive senses, then once again they had failed.

"Definitely one of us," murmured a heavier male, so noted by his larger crest. He snorted, sending puffs of smoke Krasus's way.

"And that isss why I brought him," a smaller male bitterly remarked. "That . . . and hisss incessant whining . . ."

Perfectly at ease surrounded by the smoke, Krasus turned to the second male. "If you had the sense the creators gave you, you would have known me for what I am and the urgency of my warning immediately! We could have been spared the chaotic retreat from the realm of the forest lord."

"I am ssstill not certain that I did not make a missstake in bringing you here!"

"And where is here?"

All four dragons leaned their heads back in slight astonishment. One of the two females now spoke. "If you are one of us, little dragon, then you should know it as well as you know your nest . . ."

Krasus cursed his addled memory. This could be only one location. "Then I am in the home caverns? I am in the realm of beloved Alexstrasza, Queen of Life?"

"You did want to come here," reminded the smaller male.

"The question remains," interjected the second female, younger, sleeker than the rest. "Do you come any farther?"

"He comes as far as he desires," intruded a new voice. "If he can but answer me a simple question."

The four leviathans and Krasus turned to where a fifth and obviously much more mature dragon suddenly sat. In contrast to the two other males, this one had an impressive crest running from the top of his head to down past his shoulders. He outweighed the second-largest dragon by several tons and his claws alone were longer than the tiny figure standing in the midst of the behemoths.

But despite his immense form and clear dominance, his eyes were sharp and full of wisdom. He more than any of the others would decide the success of Krasus's journey.

"If you are one of us despite that guise you wear, you must know who I am," the dragon rumbled.

The mage struggled with his tattered memories. Of course he knew who this *was*, but the name would not come to him. His body tensed and his blood boiled as he fought the fog in his mind. Krasus knew that if he did not speak to this giant by name, he would forever be rejected, forever be unable to warn his kind of the possible danger his presence in this time represented.

And then, with titanic effort, the name he should have known almost as well as his own sprang from his lips. "You are *Tyranastrasz* . . . Tyran the Scholarly One . . . *consort* to Alexstrasza!"

His pride at recalling both the name and title of the crimson giant must have been noticeable, for Tyranastrasz let out a loud, almost human chuckle.

"You are indeed one of us, although I cannot place you yet! I have been given a name for you by the one who brought you, but clearly it is wrong, as, among us, a name is granted to one and one alone."

"There is no mistake," the dragon mage insisted. "And I can explain why."

Alexstrasza's consort shook his mighty head. A hint of smoke escaped his nostrils. "The explanation you have given, little one, has been relayed to us . . . and still it is found too astonishing to be true! What you say falls into the realm of the Timeless One, Nozdormu, but even he would not be so careless as to do as you have shown!"

"He is addled, plain and simple," said the watcher from the forest. "One of our own, I will grant, but injured by accident or device."

"Perhaps . . ." Tyranastrasz startled the other dragons then, lowering his head to the ground just before Krasus. "But by knowing me you have answered my question! You are of the flight and thus have the right and privilege to enter the innermost recesses of this lair! Come! I will take you to the one who will settle this matter for us all, the one who knows all her flight as she knows all her children! *She* will recognize you and, therefore, recognize the truth . . ."

"You will take me to Alexstrasza?"

"None other. Climb atop my neck, if you are able."

Even with his physical debilitation, Krasus readily managed to climb up. Not only did the thought of at last finding help spur him on . . . but so did the simple opportunity to see his beloved once more, even if it turned out she did not recognize him after all.

The huge dragon carried Krasus through long-worn tunnels and chambers that should have been easily recognizable but were not. Now and then, some hint of memory stirred, but never enough to satisfy the mage. Even when they came across other dragons, none looked at all familiar to Krasus, who once had known all those of the red flight.

He wished that he had been awake when the watcher had flown him here. The landscape surrounding the red flight's domain might have sparked his memories. Besides, what more glorious sight could exist than to see the dragons at the peak of their rule? To witness once more the tall, towering mountains, the hundreds of great gaps in every cliff side, each of the latter an entrance into Alexstrasza's realm. It had been countless centuries since that time and Krasus had always mourned its passing, mourned the passing of the Age of Dragons.

Perhaps once I have convinced her . . . she will let me see the land of dragons from without one last time . . . before she decides what to do with me.

Tyranastrasz's huge form moved effortlessly through the high, smooth tunnels. Krasus felt a twinge of jealousy, for here he was, about to speak with his beloved, and forced to do so in this meager, mortal body. He greatly loved the lesser races, enjoyed his time among them, but now, when he might be putting his very existence on the line, Krasus would have preferred his true shape.

A bright yet comforting glow suddenly appeared ahead of them. The reddish glow warmed Krasus inside and out as they neared and made him think of childhood, of learning to grow up in the sky as well as the earth. Fleeting memories of his life danced in his head and for the first time since his arrival in this time period, the dragon mage almost felt himself.

They came to the source of the magnificent glow, the mouth of a vast cave. Kneeling at the entrance, Tyranastrasz lowered his head and rumbled, "With your permission, my love, my life."

"Always," returned a voice both delicate and all-powerful. "Always for you."

Again Krasus felt a twinge of jealousy, but he knew that the one who spoke had loved him as much as she loved the leviathan on which he rode. The Queen of Life had so much love not only for her consorts, but for all her flight. In truth, she loved all creatures of the world, although that love would not stop her from destroying those that in some way threatened the rest.

And that was one thing he had purposely failed to mention to Rhonin. It had occurred early on to Krasus that one way to avoid any further damage to the timeline might be to remove those objects that were not where they were supposed to be.

To save history from going further awry, Alexstrasza might have to slay both him and the human wizard.

As he and Tyranastrasz entered, all thought of what might happen to him vanished as Krasus beheld the one who would forever command his heart and soul.

The wondrous glow which permeated every corner and crevice of the huge chamber radiated from the shimmering red dragon herself. Alexstrasza was the most monumental of her kind, twice the size of the titan upon which Krasus rode. Yet, despite that, an inherent gentleness could be sensed within the massive frame, and even as the mage watched, the Queen of Life delicately moved a fragile egg from the warmth of her body to a smoking vent, where she secured it safely.

She was surrounded by eggs, eggs and more. The eggs were her latest clutch, a bountiful one. Each stood only a foot in height—large by most standards, tiny when compared to the one who had laid them. Krasus counted three dozen. Only about half would hatch and only half of those would survive to adulthood, but that was the way of dragons—a harsh beginning heralding a life of glory and wonder.

Framing the image was an array of flowering plants that should not have been able to exist under such conditions and especially underground. There were wall-crawling creepers and sprawling carpets of purple phlox. Golden daylilies decorated the area of the nest and roses and orchids lined the area where Alexstrasza herself rested. Every plant bloomed strong, all fed by the glorious presence of the Queen of Life.

A crystal-clear stream flowed through the cavern, passing within reach of the female dragon's maw should she desire a sip at any time. The calm gurgle of the underground added to the tranquillity of the scene.

Krasus's mount lowered his head so that his tiny rider could dismount. Eyes never leaving Alexstrasza, the dragon mage stepped to the cavern floor, then went down on one knee.

"My queen . . ."

But she looked instead to the huge male who had brought Krasus here. "Tyranastrasz . . . would you leave us alone for a time?"

Wordlessly the other behemoth backed out of the chamber. The Queen of Life shifted her gaze to Krasus, but said nothing. He knelt there before her, waiting for some sign of recognition yet receiving none.

Unable to hold his silence any longer, Krasus gasped, "My queen, my world, can it be that you of all beings do not know me?"

She studied him through slitted lids before answering, "I know what I sense, and I know what I feel, and because of both I have taken the story you have told the others under serious consideration. I have already decided what must be done, but first, there is another who must be involved in this situation, for his august opinion is as dear to me as my own—ahh! He comes now!"

From another passage emerged an adult male only slightly smaller than Tyranastrasz. The newcomer moved ponderously, as if each step was a heavy labor. Long, with faded crimson scales and weary eyes, he at first appeared much older than Alexstrasza's consort—until the mage realized that it was not age that afflicted this dragon, but some unknown malady.

"You . . . summoned me, my Alexstrasza?"

And as Krasus heard the weakened giant speak, his world turned upside down again. He stumbled to his feet, backing away from the male in open dismay.

The Queen of Life was quick to notice his reaction even though her gaze for the most part remained on the newcomer. "I asked your presence here, yes. Forgive me if the effort strains you too much."

"There is . . . nothing I would not do for you, my love, my world."

She indicated the mage, who still stood as if struck by lightning. "This is—what do you call yourself?"

"Kor—Krasus, my queen. Krasus . . ."

"Krasus? Krasus it is, then . . ." Her tone hinted of amusement at his sudden choice of names at this moment. She turned again to the ill leviathan. "And this, Krasus, is one of my most beloved subjects, my most recent consort, and one to whom I already greatly look for guidance. Being one of us, you may have heard of him. His name is *Korialstrasz* . . ."

Along the winding forest path they rode, Malfurion finally coming to believe that they had lost any possible pursuit. He had chosen a route that led over rocks and other areas where the night saber's paws would leave few tracks, hoping that anyone following would soon ride off in the wrong direction. It meant taking more time than usual to reach the point where he always met Cenarius, but Malfurion had decided he needed to take that chance. He still did not know what the forest lord might think when he heard what his pupil had done.

As they neared the meeting place, Malfurion slowed his cat. In a bit more ragged fashion, Brox did the same.

"We stopping?" grunted the orc, looking around and seeing nothing but more trees. "Here?"

"Almost. Only a few minutes more. The oak should soon be in sight."

Despite being so near his goal, the night elf actually grew more tense. One time he thought he felt eyes watching them, but when he looked, he saw only the calm forest. The realization that his life had forever changed continued to shake him. If the Moon Guard identified him, he risked being shunned, the most dire punishment that could be inflicted upon a night elf other than death. His people would turn from him, forever marking him as dead even though he still breathed. No one would interact with him or even meet his gaze.

Not even Tyrande or Illidan.

He had only compounded his crimes by leaving the hunters to face the demonic creature, something Brox had called a "felbeast." If the felbeast had hurt or slain any of the pursuit party, it would leave Malfurion with no hope of ever mending his situation . . . and, to make matters worse, he would be responsible for the loss of innocent lives. Yet, what else could he have done? The only other choice would have involved turning Brox over to the Moon Guard . . . and eventually to Black Rook Hold.

The oak he sought suddenly appeared ahead, giving Malfurion the opportunity to dwell no more, for the time being, on his growing troubles. To anyone else, the tree would have simply been a tree, but to Malfurion, it was an ancient sentinel, one of those who had served Cenarius longer than most. This tree, tall, thick of trunk, and so very wrinkled of bark, had seen the rest of the forest grow over and over. It had outlasted countless others of its kind and witnessed thousands of generations of fleeting animal lives.

It knew Malfurion as he approached, the leaves of the wide crown audibly shaking despite a lack of wind. This was the ancient speech of all trees and the night elf felt honored that Cenarius had taught him early on how to understand some of it.

"Brox . . . I must ask a favor of you."

"I owe you much. Ask it."

Pointing at the oak, Malfurion said, "Dismount and go to that tree. Touch the palm of your hand to the trunk where you see that gnarled area of bark."

The orc clearly had no idea why this would be required of him, but as it had been Malfurion who had requested it, he immediately obeyed. Handing the reins to the night elf, Brox trudged over to the sentinel. The huge warrior peered closely at the trunk, then planted one meaty hand where Malfurion had indicated.

Twisting his head so as to look back at his companion, the orc rumbled, "What do I do n—"

He let out a snarl of surprise as his hand sank into the bark as if the latter had become mud. Brox almost pulled the appendage free, but Malfurion quickly ordered him to remain still.

"Do nothing at all! Simply stand there! It's learning of you! Your hand will tingle, but that's all!"

What he did not go on to explain was that the tingling meant that tiny root tendrils from within the guardian now penetrated the orc's flesh. The oak was learning of Brox by becoming, however briefly, a part of him. Plant and animal meshed together. The oak would forever recall Brox, no matter how many centuries might pass.

The vein in the orc's neck throbbed madly, a sign of his growing anxiety. To his credit, Brox stood as still as the oak, his eyes ever fixed on where his hand had vanished.

Suddenly he fell back a step, the appendage released as abruptly as it had been taken. Brox quickly flexed the hand, testing the fingers and possibly even counting them.

"The way is open to us now," Malfurion proclaimed.

With Brox mounted once more, the night elf led the way past the oak. As he rode by the sentinel, Malfurion sensed a subtle change in the air. Had they not been given permission, he and Brox could have ridden on forever and never found the glade. Only those Cenarius permitted to come to him would find the path beyond the sentinels.

The differences in their surroundings became more noticeable as the pair journeyed on. A refreshing breeze cooled both. Birds hopped about and sang from the trees surround-

ing them. The trees themselves shook merrily, greeting the
night elf—who could understand them—especially. A feeling
of comfort embraced both to the point that Malfurion even
caught a hint of a smile on the orc's rough visage.

A barrier of dense woods abruptly barred their way. Brox
looked to Malfurion, who indicated that they should now
dismount. After both had done so, Malfurion guided the orc
along a narrow foot trail not at first visible between the
trees. This they followed for several minutes before stepping
out into a richly lit open area filled with tall, soft grass and
high, brightly petaled flowers.

The glade of the forest lord.

But the figure encircled by a ring of flowers in the midst
of the glade could never have been mistaken for Cenarius.
Seated in the ring's center, he leapt up at sight of the pair, his
odd eyes especially lingering on Brox—as if he knew exactly
what the orc was.

"You . . ." the stranger muttered at the green-skinned
warrior. "You shouldn't be here . . ."

Brox mistook the thrust of his remark. "I come with him,
wizard . . . and need no permission of yours."

But the fire-haired figure—to what race he belonged,
Malfurion could not yet say—shook his head and started
toward the orc, only to hesitate at the edge of the ring.
With a curious glance at the flowers—which in turn
looked as if they now studied him—the hooded stranger
blurted, "This isn't your time! You shouldn't exist here
at all!"

He raised his hand in what seemed a menacing posture to
the night elf. Recalling Brox's use of the word "wizard,"
Malfurion quickly prepared a spell of his own, suspecting
that Cenarius's druidic teachings would avail him better in
this sacred place than the stranger's own magic.

Suddenly the sky thundered and the ever-present light breeze became an intense gale. Brox and Malfurion were pushed back a few feet and the wizard was almost thrust into the air, so hard was he forced away from the edge of the ring.

"There will be none of this in my sanctum!" declared the voice of Cenarius.

A short distance to the side of the flower barrier, the harsh wind picked up leaves, dirt, and other loose bits of the forest, throwing them around and creating a whirlwind. The small twister grew swiftly in size and intensity while the leaves and other pieces solidified into a towering figure.

And as the air quieted again, Cenarius stepped forward to survey Malfurion and the others.

"Of you I expect better," he quietly remarked to the night elf. "But these *are* strange times." He eyed Brox. "And growing stranger with each passing hour, it seems."

The orc growled defiantly at Cenarius. Malfurion quickly silenced him. "This is the lord of the forest, the demigod Cenarius . . . the one to whom I said I would bring you, Brox."

Brox eased somewhat, then pointed at the hooded wizard. "And that one? Is he another demigod?"

"He's part of a puzzle," Cenarius replied. "and you look to be another piece of the same one." To the figure in the ring, he added, "You recognized this newcomer, friend Rhonin."

The robed spellcaster said nothing.

The demigod shook his head in clear disappointment. "I mean you no harm, Rhonin, but too much has come about that I and the others find disturbing and out of place. You and your missing companion and now this one—"

"His name is Brox," Malfurion offered.

"This one called Brox," Cenarius amended. "Another being the likes of which even I have never seen. And how does Brox come to be here, my student? I suspect that there is a tale to tell, a disturbing one."

With a nod, the night elf immediately went into the story of his rescue of the orc, in the process laying any possible blame at his feet alone. Of Tyrande and Illidan, he scarcely even spoke.

But Cenarius, far older and wiser than his pupil, read much of the truth. "I said that the destinies of your brother and you would take different roads. I believe that fork has now come, whether you know it or not."

"I don't understand—"

"It is a talk for another time." The demigod suddenly stepped past Malfurion and Brox, staring into the forest. Around the glade, the crowns of the trees suddenly shook with great agitation. "And time is not something we have at the moment. You had better prepare yourselves . . . you included, friend Rhonin."

"Me?" blurted the wizard.

"What is it, shan'do?" Malfurion could sense the trees' fury.

The sunlit sky filled with thunder and the wind picked up again. A shadow fell over Cenarius's majestic countenance, a dark shadow that made even Malfurion wary of his teacher.

The forest lord stretched forth his arms, almost as if to embrace something that no one else could see. "We are about to be attacked . . . and I fear even I may not be able to protect all of you."

The lone felbeast had followed the trail as no other animal or rider could, smelling not the scent of its quarry, but rather the magic the latter commanded. As much as blood and flesh, the energy that was magic and sorcery was its sustenance . . . and like any of its kind, the felbeast was always ravenous.

Mortal creatures would not have noticed the magic of the oak sentinel, but the demon did. It seized upon this unmoving prey with eagerness, the dire tentacles quickly thrusting out and striking the thick trunk.

The oak did its best to combat this unexpected foe. Roots sought to entangle the paws, but the felbeast dodged them. Loose branches dropped from high above, battering the monster's thick hide futilely.

When that did not work, from the oak came a peculiar keening sound, one that picked up in intensity. It soon reached a level inaudible to most creatures.

But for the felbeast, the sound then became agony. The demon whined and tried to bury its head, but at the same time it refused to release its hold on the guardian. The two wills struggled . . .

In the end, the felbeast proved the stronger. Increasingly drained of its inherent magic, the oak withered more and more, finally dying as the Moon Guard had, slain in its duty after thousands of years of successfully protecting the way.

The felbeast shook its head, then sniffed the air before it. The tentacles eagerly stretched forth, but the demon kept its position. It had grown as it devoured the oak's ancient magic and now stood almost twice as tall as before.

Then, metamorphosis took place. A deep, black radiance surrounded the felbeast, completely enveloping the demon. Within it, the felbeast twisted in various directions, as if trying to escape from itself.

And the more it tried, the more it succeeded. One head, two heads, three, four . . . then five. Each head strained harder, pulling and pulling. The heads were followed by thick necks, brawny shoulders, then muscular torsos and legs.

Fueled by the rich magic of the ancient guardian, the one felbeast became a pack. The great effort momentarily weakened each of the demons, but within seconds they recouped. The knowledge that ahead lay more sustenance, more power, urged them on.

As one, the felbeasts charged toward the glade.

FOURTEEN

You are a true servant, the great one told Lord Xavius.
*Your rewards will be endless . . . all you desire I will grant
you . . . anything . . . anyone . . .*

Artificial eyes unblinking, the night elf knelt on one knee
before the fiery portal, drinking in the god's many glorious
promises. He was the most favored of the great one's new
minions, one to whom miraculous powers would be granted
once the way had been opened.

And the more the Highborne failed to accomplish the
last, the longer the god's arrival was delayed, the more the
counselor's frustration grew.

His frustration was shared by two others. One of those
was Queen Azshara, who longed as much as he for the day
when all the imperfect would be eradicated from the
world, leaving only the night elves—and only the best of
that race—to rule the paradise that would follow. She did
not know, of course, that, in his wisdom, the great one
would make her Xavius's consort, but the counselor expected any protests to fade once their wondrous god informed her.

The other frustrated with the utter lack of success was
the towering Hakkar. Ever flanked by two felbeasts, the
Houndmaster marched around the Highborne sorcerers,

pointing out the flaws in their casting and adding his own might whenever possible.

Yet even with the addition of his arcane knowledge, only now had they at last achieved some minor triumph. Now at last Hakkar and his pets no longer stood alone among the night elves. Now there were three others, horned giants with crimson visages that some found horrific but that Lord Xavius could only admire. At least nine feet tall, they loomed over the Highborne, who themselves were more than seven feet in height.

These were anointed champions of the god, celestial warriors whose only purpose was to do his bidding regardless of the cost to them. Each was roughly nine feet in height and although built oddly thin, the bronze-armored figures had no difficulty wielding the massive, oblong shields and flaming maces. They obeyed to the letter any command given them and treated the counselor with as much respect as they did Hakkar.

And soon there would be more. Even as Xavius stepped back, he saw the portal flash. It bloomed, growing to fill the pattern over which it hovered, swelling until—

Through it came another of the Fel Guard, as Hakkar called these worthy fighters. The moment he entered the mortal plane, the newcomer bowed his fearsome head toward the Houndmaster, then toward Xavius.

Hakkar signaled for the warrior to join his predecessors. Turning to Xavius, the Houndmaster indicated the four. "The great one fulfills his first promise to you, lord night elf! Command them! They are yoursss to do as you pleassse!"

Xavius knew exactly what to do with them. "As they have been a gift to me, so they will best serve as a gift for the queen! I shall make them honored bodyguards for Azshara!"

The Houndmaster nodded approvingly. They both knew

the value of pleasing the queen of the night elves, just as both knew the counselor's secret desire. "You'd do bessst to bring sssuch a present to her yourssself, lord night elf! The work will continue while you are gone, I will sssee to that!"

The notion of making the presentation himself greatly appealed to Xavius. With a bow to Hakkar, the counselor snapped his fingers and led the four gigantic warriors out of the tower chamber. He knew exactly where he would find Azshara at this time.

And as he departed, the Houndmaster, stony eyes flaring brightly, watched the night elf intently.

Although her lord counselor slept very little—almost not at all of late—as queen of the realm, Azshara had the right and privilege to rest as she pleased. After all, she had to be perfect in every way, especially where her beauty was concerned. Therefore, the ruler of the night elves generally slept through the entire day, avoiding completely the harsh, burning sunlight.

Thus, Azshara did not take well at first to the meek entrance of one of her attendants. The latter fell quickly onto both knees before the rounded edge of the queen's room-spanning, down bed, the young female almost hiding behind the gossamer curtains that encircled it.

With a languid hand, the Light of Lights indicated that her servant could speak.

"Mistress, forgive this humble one, but the lord counselor requests an audience with yourself, stating he has brought something of interest to you."

There was nothing which Azshara could imagine desiring at the moment that would make her leave her bed, not even for the counselor. Silver hair draping her pillows, she pursed her lips as she pondered whether or not to send Xavius on his way.

"Make him wait five minutes," she finally purred, already artfully positioning herself. Well aware of Xavius's tastes, the queen knew best how to use them to her advantage. The counselor might think himself superior to his monarch, but as a female, she was superior to any male. "Then grant him entrance."

The attendant did not question her mistress's decision. Azshara watched her depart through slitted eyes, then stretched gracefully, already planning her encounter with her chief advisor.

The young servant nervously returned . . . but only after Xavius had already been waiting for several minutes. Keeping her head low—and thus her expression all but hidden—she ushered the counselor through the thick, skillfully carved oak doors leading into the queen's personal chambers.

Only a handful of times had he dared see her in this, her most private sanctum. Xavius knew something of what to expect; Azshara would appear flawless and seductive, all without seeming to notice this herself. It was the game she played and played well, but he was prepared. He was her superior.

Sure enough, the queen of the night elves lay in repose, one arm behind her head, two silken-clad attendants kneeling nearby. A silver stand with an emerald flask of wine stood within reach of the queen and one half-filled goblet gave evidence to her having already sampled its rich bounty.

"My darling lord counselor," she breathed. "You must have something dreadfully important to say to me to request an audience at such an hour." The thin, glistening sheet framed her exquisite shape. "I've therefore tried to accommodate you as best I can."

Fist to his heart, he went down on one knee. Gazing at the white, marble floor, Lord Xavius replied, "Light of

Lights, Cherished Heart of the People, I am grateful for this time given me. I apologize for disturbing you now, but I have brought with me a most interesting gift, a gift truly worthy of the queen of the night elves, the queen of the world. If I may summon it?"

He glanced up and saw that he had her attention. Her veiled eyes failed to hide both her growing curiosity and anticipation. Azshara shifted on her bed, the sheet ever clinging just so to her torso.

"You pique my interest, my dear Xavius. I grant you the honor of presenting me with your gift."

Rising again, the tall counselor turned to the doors and snapped his fingers.

There was a gasp from the outer room and two more attendants rushed inside, fleeing to the comfort and protection of their mistress. Frowning, Azshara sat up, almost but not quite letting the sheet slip.

The four fearsome warriors marched two abreast into the queen's sanctum, so tall that they had to duck through the doorway to avoid scraping the top with their horns. They spread out as they entered, shields before their armored bodies and maces held high in salute.

Azshara leaned forward, utterly fascinated. "What are they?"

"They are *yours*, my queen! The protection of your life is their duty, their only reason to exist! Behold, your majesty, your new bodyguards!"

He saw that he had pleased her well. There would be more and more celestial warriors sent through by the great one, but these were the very first and they were to be *hers*. That made all the difference.

"How wonderful," she murmured, stretching one arm out to a servant. The young maiden immediately reached for

Azshara's gown. The other attendants created a wall, obscuring all but the queen's head from the view of Xavius and the Fel Guard. "How very fitting. Your gift is acceptable."

"I am pleased that *you* are pleased."

The servants stepped back. Now clad in a translucent, frost-colored gown, Queen Azshara rose from her bed. With calculated steps, she walked up to the towering figures and inspected each, her gown trailing along over the marble floor. For their part, the Fel Guard stood so motionless that they might have been mistaken for statuary.

"Are there more?"

"There will be, eventually."

She frowned. "So few after so long? How will the great one himself come through if we cannot manage more than a few of his host at a time?"

"We draw from the Well as best we can, oh glorious queen. There are contradictory currents, outside reactions, the influence of other spellcasters elsewhere—"

Like a child reaching out to touch a new toy, Azshara let her fingers just graze the blazing armor of one of her new bodyguards. There was a slight hiss. The queen pulled back her fingers, an oddly pleased expression crossing her perfect features. "Then why haven't you cut off the Well from such outside interference? It would make your task then much simpler."

Lord Xavius opened his mouth to explain why the intricacies of the Highborne spellwork would not permit such— then realized that he had no good answer. Theoretically, Azshara's suggestion had tremendous merit.

"Truly you are the queen," he finally commented.

Her golden eyes seized his own. "Of course I am, my darling counselor. There has only ever been, only ever will be . . . *one* Azshara."

He nodded wordlessly.

She strode back to the bed, seating herself delicately on the edge. "If there is nothing else?"

"Nothing . . . for now, my queen."

"Then, I think you must have more work to do now."

Dismissed, Lord Xavius bowed low to his monarch, then backed out of her chambers. He did not take any umbrage at her regal tone or attitude, did not even grow more than slightly annoyed at her mastery of the situation.

Cut off the Well from interference . . .

It could be done. If not by the Highborne alone, then with Hakkar's good guidance. Surely the Houndmaster would know best how to do it. With use of the Well limited only to those of the palace, the power the Highborne drew from it would be more easily manipulated, more easily transformed . . .

Small matter what havoc cutting off the Well would wreak upon the *rest* of their people.

"He is definitely one of us . . . somehow I know this as well as I know myself."

The words were perhaps the most ironic ever spoken in history, or so Krasus believed at that moment. They had, after all, been uttered by the dragon Korialstrasz, the newest of Alexstrasza's consorts.

And also Krasus's younger self.

Korialstrasz did not recognize himself, at least, not consciously. However, the fact that Alexstrasza had not informed him of the newcomer's true identity raised many questions.

One question possibly related to the others had to do with the male dragon's present condition. While it was true that Krasus's memory was full of holes, he doubted that he could have forgotten such an illness as his earlier incarnation seemed to be suffering at this moment. Korialstrasz looked far older, far more feeble than his age. He looked older than Tyran, who was centuries Korialstrasz's senior.

"What else do you say about him?" Alexstrasza asked her mate.

The other dragon squinted at Krasus. "He is older, very old, in fact." Korialstrasz tilted his head. "Something in his eyes . . . his eyes . . ."

"What about them?"

The huge male drew back. "Forgive me! My head is addled! I am not worthy of being in your presence at this time! I should withdraw . . ."

But she would not yet let him go. "Look at him, my mate. I ask you this one last thing; with what little you know, would you trust the word of this one?"

"I . . . yes, my Alexstrasza . . . I . . . would."

Suddenly, a curious thing happened to Krasus. As the dragons continued conversing about him, he began to feel stronger, stronger than he had ever felt since first arriving in the past. Not quite as strong as he should have been, but at least much closer to normal.

And it was not him alone. He also noted that, despite words to the contrary, his younger self also started looking more fit. A bit of color had returned to the scales and Korialstrasz moved with somewhat better ease than earlier. His words did not come out in gasps anymore.

Alexstrasza nodded in response to her consort's answer, then said, "So I wanted to hear. It tells me much that you feel so."

"Is there more that you wish of me? My strength is better; being with you, being of assistance to you, has clearly heartened me."

The smile that Krasus knew so well graced the dragon queen's reptilian countenance. "Always the poetic one, my loving Korialstrasz! Yes . . . I wish much more of you. I know it will be difficult, but I must request your presence when I bring this one before the other Aspects."

She succeeded in stunning both versions of Krasus. The young incarnation spoke first, echoing the older's surprise. "You would convene a gathering of the Five? Over this one? But why?"

"Because he has told a story that they must hear, a story I tell you now . . . and you may choose again afterward to answer whether you trust him or not."

So at last his earlier self would know the truth. Krasus readied himself for the other's shock.

But as he had startled Rhonin by relating a tale that left out not only part of the truth but also his very identity, so now did the dragon queen tell much the same. She spoke of the disruption and all else Krasus had told the watcher, but of the mage's true identity, Alexstrasza said nothing. To her consort, Krasus was merely another of the red flight, one whose mind had been torn asunder by the powerful forces that had assailed it.

Krasus himself made no attempt to reveal himself. This was Alexstrasza—his life, his love. Advisor to her he might be, but she still wielded the wisdom of an Aspect. If she felt that his younger self should remain ignorant . . . then who was he to disagree?

"An astonishing tale," Korialstrasz murmured, looking and sounding even better. "I would have trouble believing it from any mouth but your own, my queen . . ."

"So your trust of him has faded?"

The eyes of the younger self met the eyes of the older. Even if Korialstrasz did not recognize himself, he must have recognized still the kindred spirit. "No . . . no, my trust has not faded. If you think he should be brought before the others . . . I must acquiesce."

"Will you then fly with me?"

"But I am not one of the Five . . . I am merely me."

The Queen of Life laughed lightly, a musical sound coming as it did from a dragon. "And thus you are as worthy as any of us."

Korialstrasz was clearly flattered. "If I am as strong as I now feel, I will gladly fly at your side and stand before the other Aspects."

"Thank you . . . that is all I ask." She leaned forward and briefly nuzzled heads with him.

Krasus felt a peculiar jealousy. Here he was, watching himself be intimate with his mate, yet it was not him. He wished that for just one moment he could have changed places with Korialstrasz, that for just this one particular moment, he could be his true self again.

With a last lingering glance, the male turned and left the chamber. As the tip of Korialstrasz's tail vanished into the passage, the mage suddenly felt light-headed. The weakness returned in a rush, causing him to teeter.

He would have fallen, but suddenly a massive, scaled appendage wrapped softly around him—Alexstrasza's own tail come to his rescue.

"The two parts made whole . . . at least for a time."

"I don't—" His head swam.

"You felt much better in his presence, did you not?"

"Y-yes."

"Would I were Nozdormu at this moment. He would understand this more. I think . . . I think that in the earthly realm, no creature can coexist with himself. I believe you and he, being one, draw off the same life force. When you are far from each other, you are halved, but when you are so very near, as just before, the draining is not so terrible. You help each other."

Nestled safely, Krasus recovered enough to think over her words. "So that is why you requested him to come with."

"Your story must be told and it will be told better if he is near. As to your unspoken question—why I did not reveal to him the truth—that is because of what may have to be done to salvage matters."

Her tone grew grim as she said the last, verifying for Krasus his own suspicions. "You think it may come to the point where one of us must be removed from this period . . . even if that means *death*."

The leviathan nodded reluctantly. "I am afraid so, my love."

"I accept the choice. I knew it from the beginning."

"Then there is only one more matter to discuss before I reach out to the others . . . and that is what must be done with this other who came with you."

Although inside he asked Rhonin to forgive him, Krasus did not hesitate to reply. "If it must be done, he will share my fate. He, too, has those he cares about. He would give his life for them."

The Queen of Life nodded. "As I trusted your counsel when it came to you, so I trust your counsel when it comes to him. Should the other decide so, he will also be removed." The dragon's expression softened. "Know that I will be saddened by this forever."

"Take no blame unto yourself, my queen, my heart."

"I must contact the others. It would be best for you if you waited for me here. In this place you will find yourself not so weary."

"I am honored, my queen."

"Honored? You are my *consort*. I could do no less."

With her tail she guided him to an area of the nest near the stream. Krasus settled into a natural depression that acted for him like a huge chair.

As the dragon queen moved to the passage, she paused and, with a trace of remorse, added, "I hope you will be comfortable among the eggs."

"I will be careful not to touch any." Krasus understood the value of any egg.

"I am certain you will, my love . . . especially knowing that they are yours."

She left him wordless. As the crimson giant disappeared, Krasus glanced from one egg to another. As consort, he had, of course, bred with his mate. Many of his children had grown to adulthood, bringing pride to the flight.

He slammed his fist against the rock, ignoring the pain the foolish act sent through him. For all he had revealed to his beloved Alexstrasza, he had kept from her several important facts. Most immediate was the coming of the Burning Legion. Krasus feared that even his queen, wise as she was, would be tempted to play with history . . . and that might create a more horrifying disaster.

Yet, even worse than that, Krasus had been unable to tell her about the future of their own kind, a future in which only a few would survive . . . a future in which most of the hatchlings of this and successive clutches would perish before they ever had the opportunity to reach full maturity.

A future in which the Queen of Life herself would become a slave, her children the war dogs of a conquering race.

FIFTEEN

The felbeasts charged through the enchanted forest, their snouts raised high as the scent of magic increased. Their hunger and their mission urged them on, the huge hounds snarling their impatience.

But as one leapt over a fallen trunk, limbs from another tree nearby bent down and entangled its legs. A second felbeast racing along a path found its paws sinking into suddenly muddy earth. A third collided with a sprouting bush filled with razor-sharp brambles that pricked even the demon's hard flesh and brought it immense agony.

The forest came alive, defending itself and its master. The charge of the five monsters faltered . . . but did not fail. Huge claws tore at the tangling branches, ripping them from trunks. Another felbeast aided the one trapped in the mire, dragging its comrade to solid ground before moving on. Hunger and fury enabled the one caught in the sharp brambles to burrow through even though it meant bleeding cuts everywhere.

The hunters would not be denied their prey . . .

"Shan'do! What is it?"

The demigod glanced down at his pupil, no recriminations in his fiery gaze. "The hounds of which you spoke . . . they have followed you here."

"Followed? Impossible! There was only one left and it—"

Brox interrupted, his rumbling voice offering no comfort. "The felbeasts . . . they are dark magic. Where there was one . . . there can be more if they're able to feed well . . . this I saw . . ."

"A good friend and able guardian fell to one," Cenarius commented, attention once more on the thick woods ahead of them. "He bore within him magic most ancient, most powerful. It only served to make him more susceptible to their evil."

The orc nodded. "Then the one is now many." Brox instinctively reached behind his back, but his beloved war ax did not await him there. "I've nothing to fight with."

"You will be armed. Quickly find a fallen limb the length of your favored weapon. Malfurion, attend me."

Brox swiftly did as commanded. He brought to the demigod and the night elf a massive branch, which Cenarius then had him place before Malfurion.

"Kneel before it, my student. You, too, warrior. Malfurion, place your hands upon the branch, then let him place his palms atop your hands." When they had done this, the forest lord commanded, "Now, warrior, clear your mind of all but the weapon. Think *only* of it! Time is of the essence. Malfurion, you must open your mind and let his thoughts flow to yours. I will guide you more when that is done."

The night elf did as he was told. He cleared his thoughts as his shan'do had early on taught him, then reached out to link himself to the orc.

Instantly a primal force bullied its way into his mind. Malfurion almost rejected it, but then calmed. He accepted Brox's thoughts and let the image of what the warrior wanted take shape.

You see the weapon, my student? came Cenarius's voice. *You sense the feel of it, the lines of its forming?*

Malfurion did. He also felt the orc's relationship to the weapon, how it was more than simply a tool, but also a true extension of the warrior.

Guide your hands over the wood, ever keeping the image in your head. Follow the natural grain and turn it to the shape desired . . .

With Brox's hands atop his own, the night elf began running his fingers along the branch. As he did, he felt it soften at his touch, then shift in form.

And under his guidance materialized a thick-bladed ax composed entirely of oak. Malfurion watched it shape, felt the satisfaction of creating a good solid weapon like the one he had lost when captured by the night elves—

He tensed. Those were the *orc's* emotions, not his. Quickly thrusting them back, Malfurion concentrated on the final bits—curvature of the handle, the sharpness of the blade.

The task is done, interjected Cenarius. *Return to me . . .*

The night elf and the orc pulled away. For a brief moment, they stared into each other's eyes. Malfurion wondered if Brox had experienced some of his own thoughts, but the green-skinned creature gave no hint of such a thing happening.

Between them lay a smoothly polished re-creation of that which Brox desired, though even the night elf wondered how the weapon could last more than one or two strikes.

In answer, the forest lord extended his hands—and suddenly the ax lay across them. Cenarius studied the weapon with his golden eyes.

"Let it always swing true, always protect its master. Let it be wielded well for the cause of life and justice. Let it add to the strength of its master and, in turn, let him strengthen it."

And as he spoke, a blue radiance surrounded the ax. The light sank into the wood, adding a sheen to Malfurion's creation.

The demigod offered the ax to the orc. "It is yours. It will serve you well."

Eyes wide, the graying orc took the gift, then swung it back and forth, testing the quality. "The balance . . . perfect! The feel . . . like a part of my arm! But it will crack—"

"No," interjected the forest lord. "In addition to Malfurion's work, it now has my blessing. You'll find it stronger than any mortal-forged ax. You may trust me on that."

As for the night elf, he did not reach for a weapon nor did he desire one such as Brox now carried. Despite knowing that the demonic beasts fed off of magic and sorcery, he still understood that his chances were better with spells than with some weapon with which he had only moderate skill. He already had some ideas as to how to use his talent without it becoming the cause of his defeat.

And so the three faced the coming foe.

The nightmares of Rhonin's recent past had come back to haunt him, but now they did so in the flesh. Felbeasts, the harbingers of the Burning Legion, were already here in the mortal plane. Could the endless ranks of horned, fiery demon warriors be far behind?

Krasus had put into the red-haired wizard's mind the fear of what would happen if either interacted more with the past. What might seem a victory could spell the end of the future as they knew it. To best preserve the lives of those he loved, it behooved Rhonin to do nothing at all.

But as the first felbeast leapt into the glade, such noble notions instantly vanished from his thoughts.

Thunder crashed around the demigod as he stepped up to meet the felbeasts. His stomping hooves shook the ground and even caused the earth to crack open slightly. He swung his hands together and lightning flashed as they met.

And from those hands, Cenarius unleashed what seemed a miniature sun at the foremost demon. Perhaps the demigod only tested his adversary or somehow underestimated the resilience of it, for the felbeast thrust forth both tentacles and, instead of the sunburst striking dead its target . . . the demon's hungry appendages *absorbed* Cenarius's spell with ease.

The felbeast hesitated, shimmered . . . and suddenly, where there had been one, there were now two.

They leapt upon the stag lord, clawing at him and trying to drain him of his great magic. With one hand Cenarius held the first at bay, the demon wriggling madly and snapping at the arm that kept him high in the air. But the other clamped itself onto his shoulder, the tentacles seeking the demigod's flesh. The three combatants fell back in a frenzy of movement.

They never did that! Rhonin himself had not faced felbeasts, but he had studied their corpses and read all the information gathered about them. He had heard the few rare tales of the hounds multiplying themselves, but only after gorging on magic and even then the process had been said to be slow, difficult. *It must be the ancient magic that the demigod and the forest itself wield . . . it's so rich and powerful that the creatures are made even more terrible by it . . .*

He shivered, knowing that magic had always been his best tool. He could fight by hand, yes, but he had no weapon and doubted that Cenarius could give him one now. Besides, against these creatures, his skill with a sword would be more than lacking. Rhonin needed his magic.

When Cenarius had first brought Krasus and him to the ring, Rhonin had found himself unable to cast any spell. The forest lord had placed an enchantment on his mind, keeping the might of both his "guests" in check. However, Rhonin had felt that enchantment removed from him the second that Cenarius had realized the danger to them all. The demigod meant no true harm to the wizard; he had acted only out of concern for his forest and his world.

But even if he disobeyed Krasus's recommendation, Rhonin wondered just how much good having his powers back would do him. Surely the demons would be most eager for his magic, just as they had hungered for the magic of so many wizards sucked dry in the future war against the legion.

The felbeasts pressed their foes, in the process drawing nearer and nearer to Rhonin. His hands curled into fists and words of power stood ready on his tongue.

And yet . . . still he did nothing.

As Cenarius and the twin felbeasts met, two more charged at Brox. The huge warrior met the creatures head on with a war cry that made one demon falter slightly. The orc used that hesitation to his advantage, swinging hard at his adversary.

The enchanted ax buried itself deep in the forepaw of the felbeast, severing three clawed toes as easily as if the orc had cut through air. The foul greenish fluid that passed for blood in many of the demons spilled over the grass, burning the blades like acid.

The injured felbeast let out a yelp and stumbled to the side, but its comrade continued its charge, throwing itself upon the orc. Brox, trying to recover from his swing, barely saved himself by using the bottom end of the ax shaft. He drove the end into the chest of the leaping behemoth.

A monstrous gasp escaped the felbeast, but did little to slow its momentum. It fell upon Brox, nearly crushing him under its massive form.

As for the night elf, the monster he faced eagerly reached for him with its vampiric tentacles. Malfurion concentrated, trying to think as Cenarius would think, drawing upon what he had learned from the demigod about seeing nature as both his weapon and his comrade.

Recalling the demigod's own arrival, Malfurion created from the ever-present wind a roaring twister that immediately surrounded the monstrous felbeast. The sinewy, gaping tentacles swung wildly about, seeking the magic, but Malfurion's spell had accented only the inherent forces of the wind and so the demon found little upon which to drain.

With a wave of his right hand, the night elf then asked of the surrounding trees the gift of whatever spare leaves they had to offer. He sought the strongest only, but he needed them in great numbers and quickly.

And from the crowns of the towering guardians descended hundreds, whatever each could give. Malfurion immediately used another breeze to guide the leaves toward the whirlwind.

Within it, the felbeast pushed forward, relentlessly closing on its intended prey. The twister matched each determined step, ever keeping the demon at its center.

The leaves poured into the whirlwind, spinning around faster and faster and increasing in number rapidly. At first the felbeast paid them no mind, for what were a few bits of refuse in the wind to a powerful fiend, but then the first sharp edge of a leaf sliced across its muzzle, drawing blood.

The enraged demon batted at the offending leaf, only to have several more cut it successively on its paw, its legs, and its torso. The wind now a hundred times more intense, the sharp edges of each soaring leaf became like well-honed blades, cutting and slashing wherever they touched the felbeast. Greenish ooze spilled over the demon's body, drenching its hide and even obscuring its vision.

Cenarius and the beasts who had attacked him now fought far from the rest. The cries of the demons were well matched by the majestic roar of the forest lord. He seized the foreleg of the felbeast that had attached itself to him and with a single twist snapped the bone. The demon howled and its tentacles released their hold, flailing about in response to its pain.

Momentarily rid of one menace, Cenarius focused on the other. His countenance took on a dark wonder and his eyes blazed in fury. Suddenly, there burst from them a spark of light that enveloped the demon held at bay. The slavering creature's tentacles greedily sought that light, drinking it in eagerly and wanting even more.

But this was not a wizard or sorcerer from which it sought to siphon magic. Now surrounded by a fearsome blue aura, Cenarius pressed with his attack, feeding his foe and giving it what it desired . . . but much too quickly and in abundance so great that even the demon could not take it all in.

The felbeast swelled, blowing up like a quickly filled water sack. Briefly it seemed as if about to divide . . . but the forces already ingested by it were more than it could handle.

The monstrous hound *exploded*, gobbets of stench-ridden flesh raining down upon the glade.

Thus far, Rhonin had been fortunate. No felbeast had come for him. He remained at the center of the ring, hoping that its power would keep him from having to decide whether or not to use his own abilities.

Rhonin watched Brox fend off the creature that had nearly crushed the orc. The veteran warrior appeared to have his struggle well in hand despite two foes. But as he continued to observe Brox, a terrible notion filled the human mage. If he and Krasus could not be returned to their time, Rhonin had understood that it might be best if both were slain quickly, the sooner to prevent whatever further alterations they might make to history. What neither had counted on, however, was a single orc warrior also being thrown into this era.

And as he stared at Brox's back, Rhonin began to contemplate a different sort of spell. In the midst of the struggle, it might go unnoticed by the others and would eliminate another danger to the timeline. Krasus would have told him he was making the right decision, that, more than even the demons, Brox was a danger to the very existence of the world.

But his hand faltered, the spell forming in his mind pushed back into the darkest recesses. Rhonin felt ashamed. Brox's people had become valuable allies and this orc now fought to save not only himself but others, *including* the wizard.

Everything Krasus had said urged Rhonin to deal quickly with Brox and worry about the consequences later, but the more he watched the orc battle beside the night elf—another allied race in the future—the more Rhonin regretted his moment of insanity. What he had contemplated seemed to him as horrible as the atrocities perpetrated in his time by the Burning Legion.

But Rhonin could no longer stand and do nothing . . .

"I'm sorry, Krasus," he muttered, calling up a new spell. "I'm truly sorry."

Taking a deep breath, the hooded mage stared from under his brow at one of the felbeasts in combat with the orc. He recalled the incantations that had helped him against the Scourge and other inhuman servants of the Legion. It would have to be done in such a way that the felbeasts would have no time to draw away the power of his spell.

Far, far to his right, Cenarius had finally managed to peel off his remaining foe. With one forelimb dangling, the demon could not maintain its hold. Muscles straining, the demigod bent back, held the beast over his head, and, with a roar of triumph, threw it high over the tops of the trees and deep into the waiting forest.

Rhonin cast his spell.

He had hoped to send a withering blast at the felbeast in focus, at least wounding it enough for Brox to finish the task. What Rhonin achieved instead, however, was far beyond his hopes.

An invisible, thundering wall of power that caused the very air to ripple madly materialized before him, then raced like the wind toward his objective. It spread as it moved, covering in the blink of an eye the entire expanse of the glade.

Through Brox and the night elf it passed without even the slightest hint of acknowledgment, but for the three savage demons in its path the fury that Rhonin had unleashed gave no quarter. The felbeasts had no time to react, no time to bring their hungry tentacles into play. They were as gnats in a raging fire.

As the wall of force passed through them, the demons burned to ash. The spell ate away at them from nose on back, a cloud of dust particles scattering from each decimated felbeast as it crumbled. One managed to unleash a short-lived howl, but then the only sound after was the rush of the wind as it sent to the heavens what had once been the rampaging monsters.

Silence filled the glade.

Brox dropped his ax, his wide, tusked mouth open in sheer disbelief. Malfurion stared at his own hands, as if somehow they had been responsible, then turned in the direction of Cenarius, thinking the answer lay with the demigod.

Rhonin had to blink several times to convince himself that what he witnessed had not only been real, but of his own creation. Belatedly the wizard recalled the brief struggle against the armored night elves, a struggle in which Krasus had proven disturbingly weak and Rhonin had excelled in a manner he could never have thought possible of him.

But any pleasure at his astonishing victory vanished immediately as agony tore into him from his back. He felt himself being ripped apart from inside, as if his very soul was being drained away—

Drained away? Even despite his horrific ordeal, Rhonin understood all too well what had just happened. Another felbeast had come around unnoticed from the rear and, as was its way, sought a source of magic to attack.

Rhonin recalled what had happened to spellcasters caught by the demons. He recalled the terrifying husks that had been brought back to Dalaran for investigation.

And he was about to become yet another . . .

But although now down on one knee, Rhonin rebelled. With all the power at his command, surely he could escape this parasitic beast!

Escape . . . it became the driving thought in his pain-wracked mind. Escape . . . all Rhonin sought was to flee the agony, to go somewhere where he would be safe.

Through the haze of his distress, he vaguely heard the voices of the orc and the night elf. His fear for himself overlapped them. With what it had sucked from him, the felbeast would be more than a match for either.

Escape . . . that was all Rhonin sought. *Anywhere* . . .

Then the pain vanished, replaced by a heavy but comforting numbness that spread throughout his body like fire. Rhonin gratefully accepted the startling change, letting the numbness take hold and envelop him completely . . .

Swallow him whole.

Not for the first time, Tyrande slipped through the silent corridors of the huge temple—past the countless chambers of sleeping acolytes, the meditation rooms, and places of public worship—and headed to a window near the main entrance. The bright sun nearly blinded her, but she forced herself to search the empty square beyond, seeking what she would likely still miss.

No sooner had she peered out than a clank of metal warned her of an approaching guard. The stern visage of the other night elf softened a touch upon recognition.

"You again! Sister Tyrande . . . you should really stay in your quarters and get some sleep. You've hardly had any rest for days and now you put yourself at risk. Your friend will be all right. I'm certain of it."

The guard meant Illidan, for whom Tyrande also worried, but what the novice priestess really feared was that when Illidan did return, it would be with his brother and the hapless orc in tow. She did not think that Malfurion's twin would ever betray him, but if Lord Ravencrest captured the pair, what could Illidan do but go along with matters?

"I cannot help it. I'm just so restless, sister. Please forgive me."

The sentry smiled sympathetically. "I hope he realizes how much you care for him. The time for your choosing is fast approaching, isn't it?"

The other's words bothered Tyrande more than she revealed. Her thoughts and reactions since the three had freed Broxigar had more than hinted to her of her preference, but she could not yet come to believe it herself. No, her concern was just that of one childhood friend for another.

It had to be . . .

There came the harsh clank of metal upon metal and the hiss of night sabers. Tyrande immediately darted past the bemused guard, heading to the outer steps of Elune's temple.

Somewhat dust-laden, Lord Ravencrest's party rode into

the square. The cloaked noble himself seemed quite at ease, even very pleased about something, but many of his soldiers wore darker expressions and constantly looked at one another as if sharing some terrible secret.

Of either Malfurion or Broxigar, there was no sign.

All but hidden on the far side of Lord Ravencrest, Illidan rode tall and proud. He appeared the most satisfied of the group and if that pleasure had to do with keeping his twin from capture, then Tyrande could certainly not blame him.

Without realizing what she did, the young priestess stepped down to the street. Her presence caught the attention of Lord Ravencrest, who smiled graciously and pointed her out to Illidan. The bearded commander whispered something to Malfurion's brother, then raised his hand.

The soldiers came to a halt. Illidan and Ravencrest steered their mounts toward her.

"Well, if it isn't the most lovely of the Mother Moon's dedicated servants!" the commander declared. "How interesting to find you awaiting our return despite the late hour!" He glanced at Illidan, whose expression bordered on embarrassment. "Very interesting, don't you think?"

"Yes, my lord."

"We must make for Black Rook Hold, sister, but I think I can spare a precious moment for you two, eh?"

Tyrande felt her cheeks darken slightly as Ravencrest guided his panther back to the rest of the party. Illidan dismounted quickly, stepping up to her and taking her hands in his own.

"They're safe, Tyrande . . . and Lord Ravencrest has taken me under his wing! We fought a fearsome beast and I kept it from harming him! Destroyed it with my own power!"

"Malfurion escaped? You're certain of it?"

"Of course, of course," he returned excitedly, waving

away any further questions about his brother. "I've found my destiny at last, don't you understand? The Moon Guard's all but ignored me, but I slew a monster that killed three of theirs, including one of their senior sorcerers!"

She wanted to hear what he knew about Malfurion and the orc, but it was clear that Illidan was caught up in his own good fortune. Tyrande could appreciate that, having watched him work hard and fruitlessly to achieve the glorious future so many had predicted for him. "I'm so glad for you. I feared that you were frustrated some with the pace of Cenarius's teaching, but if you were able to protect Lord Ravencrest with it where his own soldiers could not, then—"

"You don't understand! I didn't use those slow, cumbersome spells that Malfurion's adored shan'do tried to show us time and again! I used good, traditional night elf sorcery . . . and in the daytime, yet! It was exhilarating!"

His quick renunciation of the druidic ways did not entirely surprise Tyrande. On the one hand, she was grateful that he had successfully come into his own at such a drastic moment. On the other, it was yet another sign of the growing differences between the twins.

And another consideration for her already-overwrought mind.

Behind Illidan, Lord Ravencrest politely cleared his throat.

Malfurion's brother grew more animated. "I have to go, Tyrande! I'm to be shown my place at the Hold and then help organize a larger party to retrieve the dead beasts and all the bodies!"

"Bodies?" It had registered on her that some of the Moon Guard had perished because of a monster, but now she realized that only Ravencrest's band would be returning. The one that preceded them out after Malfurion had been completely slaughtered.

The horror of it all made Tyrande shiver . . . especially the fact that Malfurion had also been out there.

"The other creatures wiped out the pursuit almost to a soldier, Tyrande, didn't you understand?" Illidan's voice grew almost gleeful. He paid no mind to the increasing dismay on her face. "The sorcerers perished immediately, no help at all to the rest. It took the fighters all but two lives to stop them and *I* killed one creature with just two quick spells!" His chest swelled. "And these were monsters that devoured magic, too!"

Again, the noble coughed. Illidan quickly pulled her hands to his lips, kissing them ever so lightly. Releasing Tyrande, he leapt back atop the night saber.

"I wanted to be worthy of you," Illidan suddenly murmured. "And soon, I will be."

That said, he turned the cat about and headed to the waiting commander. Ravencrest gave Illidan a companionable slap on the back, then looked over his shoulder at Tyrande. The noble nodded his head toward Malfurion's twin and winked.

As Tyrande watched, still dazed by all she had heard, the armed party rode off in the direction of Black Rook Hold. Illidan peered back one last time before he vanished from the square, his golden eyes intent upon his childhood friend. Tyrande had no trouble reading in them his desires.

Drawing her robe around her, she rushed back up into the temple. The same sentry who had spoken to her earlier met her just within.

"Forgive me, sister! I couldn't help hearing much of what was said. I grieve for the lives lost on the futile hunt, but I also wish to give my congratulations on the fine future for your friend! Lord Ravencrest surely must have the highest respect for him to so readily take him under his guidance! Truly it would be hard to find a better match, eh?"

"No . . . no, I suppose not." When she realized how she sounded, Tyrande quickly added, "Forgive me, sister, I believe my exhaustion is catching up with me. I think I should return to bed."

"Understandable, sister. At least you know that you'll be in store for some pleasant dreams . . ."

But as Tyrande hurried to her room, she suspected that her dreams would be anything but pleasant. True, she was happy with the news that Malfurion and Broxigar had made good their escape and that no one apparently had linked Malfurion to the matter. Tyrande was also glad that Illidan had finally found himself, something she had begun to fear would never come about. What bothered her now, though, was that Illidan appeared to have made a decision regarding the two of them while Tyrande herself had not yet done so. There was still Malfurion to consider in the equation, and still his emotions to define.

Of course, that all depended upon whether or not Malfurion continued to evade the wary eye of the Moon Guard and Lord Ravencrest. If either discovered the truth, it would very likely mean Black Rook Hold for him.

And from there, not even Illidan would be able to save his brother.

The trees, the foliage, nothing had stopped the felbeast's plummet earthward. Cast into the sky by the demigod, the demonic hound could not save itself.

But the capricious nature of chance did what nothing else could. Cenarius had tossed his evil foe as far as he could, assuming logically that the fall would finish his task. Had the felbeast landed on rock or earth or hard against the trunk of one of the mightier oaks, it would have been killed in an instant.

Where the forest lord had thrown it, however, proved to be a body of water, so deep that even at the velocity with which the felbeast dropped, it did not strike the bottom.

The journey to the surface almost did what the fall failed to do, but still the demon managed to haul itself ashore. One foreleg hanging useless, the felbeast moved to a shaded depression where it paused for several minutes to recover.

Once it had recuperated as best as its wounds would allow, the demon sniffed the air, searching for a particular scent. The moment the felbeast located what it sought, it grew alert. Pulling itself forward, the injured horror slowly but steadily began to wend its way toward the source. Even from this distance, it could smell the power emanating from the Well of Eternity. There it would find the magic it needed to heal, the magic with which it could even restore the limb that had been ruined.

The felbeasts were not exactly the simple creatures that even Brox and Rhonin, who knew of them from their own war, assumed them to be. No creature that served the lord of the Burning Legion was without some wit, save perhaps the rampaging goliaths called Infernals. The demon hounds were a part of their handler and what they learned, Hakkar learned.

And from this lone survivor, the Houndmaster would learn much about those who might stand in the way of the Legion's coming . . .

SIXTEEN

I t is time."

Both Alexstrasza's return and her declaration caught Krasus by surprise. The dragon mage had sunk so deep into his thoughts that the passage of minutes and hours had become meaningless. He truly had no idea whether or not he had waited long for her return.

"I am ready."

She bent down and took him up onto her neck. Moving gracefully through the ancient passages carved out over generations by the red dragon flight, Alexstrasza and Krasus soon arrived at a wind-tossed opening overlooking a vast cloud-enshrouded region. Here was the realm of the red dragons, a breathtaking vista of proud mountain peaks capped with permanent snow and wrapped in endless stretches of mist. Krasus understood full well how high his clan's mountain home had to be for most of the clouds to be *below it*. Vaguely his splintered memory now recalled the majesty of the land, the great valleys carved out by ice and time, the jagged, individual faces of each peak.

He suddenly teetered, the rarefied air not quite sufficient for his battered body. Alexstrasza used her wings to keep him from falling off.

"Perhaps this might not be the best thing for you," she suggested, her voice filled with concern.

But as abruptly as he had almost collapsed, Krasus now felt renewed strength course through him.

"I trust . . . I am not late."

Korialstrasz lumbered toward his mate, initially looking much the way the mage had felt moments before. Yet the male dragon, too, now moved as if given an unexpected boost of energy. His somewhat haggard expression vanished as he neared.

"You are not. Do you feel up to the journey?"

"Until this very moment, I thought perhaps I could not . . . but it seems that I am feeling better again." His gaze flickered from Alexstrasza to Krasus and back again, as if he suspected the reason for his startling recuperation but could not accept it.

The dragon queen transferred Krasus to her consort. As Krasus touched his younger self, he felt his own body recover even more. Direct contact with Korialstrasz almost made him feel whole again.

Almost.

"Are you settled?" the male dragon asked of him.

"I am."

Stepping forward, Alexstrasza spread her huge wings and dove out of the passage. She dipped low, then vanished into the clouds. Korialstrasz stepped to the edge of the precipice, giving his tiny passenger an even more astounding view of the vast, mountainous terrain, then leapt out into the sky.

At first they dropped several yards—entering the clouds in the process—but then Korialstrasz caught the wind and the pair soared up. Through the mists, Krasus saw that Alexstrasza already flew far ahead. However, her pace was slow enough that her consort quickly caught up with her.

"All is well?" she roared, her question posed to *both* companions.

Krasus nodded and Korialstrasz replied in the affirmative. The dragon queen focused ahead and said no more.

The sensations of flying, even on the back of another, exhilarated the mage. Having been born to this, it made his presence circumstances that much harder to accept. He was a *dragon!* One of the masters of the sky! He should not be condemned to such a paltry existence . . .

They flew past mountain after mountain, through thick cloud cover and above many other startling peaks. Krasus's mortal body grew chilled, but he scarcely noticed, so fascinated was he.

With the utmost elegance the two massive dragons skirted a savage-looking peak, then dipped down into a wide valley in the midst of the chain. Krasus strained to see anything other than the landscape, but failed. Yet, somehow he felt that they were very close to their goal.

"Keep your grip tight!" Korialstrasz called out.

Before Krasus could ask why, the level to which the dragons descended *rippled*. The air itself twisted and wriggled like the surface of pond after a stone had been tossed into it. At first Krasus feared that the anomaly which had brought him to this time had materialized again, but then he noted the eagerness with which his mount headed for the unsettling display.

Ahead, Alexstrasza calmly entered the titanic ripple—and vanished.

Ancient memories grudgingly arose from the black abyss of Krasus's mind, memories of other times when he, as a dragon, had willingly tossed himself into this very sight. Krasus braced himself, recalling sensations that would assail him when Korialstrasz followed the queen.

They entered.

A static charge covered every inch of the mage's body. His nerves tingled. Krasus felt as if he had become a part of the heavens themselves, a child of lightning and thunder. The urge to fly on his own became demanding. It was all he could do to keep himself from letting go of his mount and joining the clouds and the wind.

The sensation passed, evaporating so unexpectedly that Krasus had to grip Korialstrasz tighter just to maintain his balance. He blinked, feeling very earthbound, very mortal. The shift in perspective overwhelmed him so much that at first Krasus did not realize his surroundings had completely changed.

They hovered within a vast, monumental cavern, so expansive that even Alexstrasza appeared as little more than a gnat in comparison. Entire kingdoms could fit inside, kingdoms with rolling landscapes and farmed fields. Even then, there would have been space for much, much more.

But this was not simply a cavern of tremendous size, for there were other features—or rather lack thereof—that marked it as a place most distinct from all others. The walls were smooth yet curved, rubbed so perfectly that if one put a hand to the rock and ran it across or down, there would be no friction, no resistance. That continued all the way down to the bottom, where the floor itself was an immense, flat circle that, had it been measured, would have been geometrically flawless.

The floor was indeed the only flattened area, for as the walls rose high, they continued to curve inward, sloping toward one another and creating overall a sphere-shaped chamber whose appearance was further accented by the utter lack of any mineral growth. No stalactites hung menacingly above; no stalagmites thrust up from the ground below. There were no fissures, not even one tiny crack.

There were no flaws whatsoever in what Krasus finally re-called as the *Chamber of the Aspects*.

A chamber that had been ancient before even *they* had existed.

It was said that here the creators had shaped the world, molded it and grown it in this sacred place until it had been ready to be set into the cosmos. Even the great dragons could not completely argue the validity of that tale, for with no exit other than the magical one they had discovered by ac-cident centuries earlier, they could not even say for certain that they met in a location situated on the mortal plane. All attempts to penetrate the walls had met with complete fail-ure and the Aspects had long ago given up even trying.

To further add to the mystery of the astonishing cavern, a bright, golden illumination filled the Chamber of the Aspects, a comforting glow with no source. Krasus recalled that experimentation by his kind had never been able to prove whether that glow vanished when the chamber was empty or whether it was perpetual, but all who entered felt welcomed by it, as if it acted as a sentinel.

As Korialstrasz descended, it suddenly occurred to Krasus that, despite his splintered memories, he remembered this sacred place very distinctly. It said something about the Chamber of the Aspects—here were recollections he could never misplace, never let fade.

The two red leviathans alighted on the rock floor, peering around. Despite the great expanse, it became obvious that none of the others had arrived yet.

"You spoke to each?" asked Korialstrasz.

The Queen of Life shook her majestic head. "Only Ysera. She said she would contact the others."

"And I did what I could," responded an almost dreamy but certainly feminine voice.

Some distance beyond them, a faint emerald form coalesced from thin air. It never truly solidified, but Krasus noted enough details to identify it as a slim, ethereal dragon almost as tall as Alexstrasza. A permanent haze surrounded the half-seen figure, but still she was visible enough to mark the fact that her eyes remained closed at all times, even when she spoke.

The other dragons dipped their heads in honored greeting, Alexstrasza adding, "I am pleased that you came so swiftly, good Ysera."

She of the Dreaming, as Krasus also knew her, gave greetings in turn. Her face turned to the two who had come with her counterpart and although the lids did not open, Krasus felt her penetrating gaze. "I come because you are my sister, my friend. I come because you would not request a gathering if you did not have good reason."

"And the others?"

"Nozdormu is the only one I could not reach directly. You know his ways. I was forced to contact one who serves him, who said he would do what he could to let his master know . . . that is the best I could accomplish there."

Alexstrasza nodded gratefully, but was unable to hide her disappointment with this last news. "Then, even if the others attend, we cannot come to a final decision."

"The Timeless One may still join us."

Still perched atop his younger self's neck, Krasus took as ill news the lack of any contact with Nozdormu. He understood the complexities of the Timeless One's nature, how Nozdormu was past, present, future . . . all history. Of all the others, it had been Nozdormu whom Krasus had secretly hoped to see here, for he offered the hope that there might still be a chance to send the two wayward travelers back to their own period, ending the matter peacefully.

And without that hope, Krasus once again had to look to the one other option . . . that to preserve the timeline, the Aspects might have to eliminate Rhonin and him.

Suddenly from above there came a brilliant flash of red bolts, an electrical storm that descended with swift fury to the ground. Once there, it exploded in a display of awe-inspiring colors before spreading out and forming a huge shape.

And as the last bits burned away, in place of the brief but startling storm stood a tall, glistening dragon who seemed part crystal, part ice. For a dragon, his expression was one quite merry, as if he had enjoyed the spectacle he created even more than any who witnessed it.

"Welcome, Malygos," Alexstrasza said politely.

"Such a pleasure to see you, Queen of Life!" The gleaming behemoth laughed heartily. "And you, too, my fair dream!"

Ysera nodded silently, a hint of humor touching her own expression.

"How fares your realm?" the red queen asked.

"As wondrous as I would wish it! Filled with brightness, filled with colors, and filled with young!"

"Perhaps the creators should have made you Father of Life instead of Guardian of Magic, Malygos!"

"An interesting thought! Perhaps a matter to discuss some other day!" He laughed again.

"Are you not well?" Korialstrasz asked Krasus, who, upon seeing the newcomer, had stiffened in horror.

"I am fine. I was simply adjusting my seating." The tiny figure was thankful that Korialstrasz had not been able to see his expression. The more Krasus watched and listened to Malygos, the more he regretted his need to keep from even the Aspects the full truth concerning the future.

What would you say, Guardian of Magic, if you knew the fate awaiting you? Betrayal, madness, a realm frozen and empty of all save yourself . . .

Krasus could not recall all he knew of Malygos's future, but he recalled enough from the bits and pieces to understand and regret the tragedy—and yet once more he could not bring himself to warn the glittering leviathan.

"And is that the one to whom we owe this gathering?" asked Malygos, his gleaming gaze now upon Krasus.

"It is," Alexstrasza replied.

The Guardian of Magic sniffed the air. "He has the scent of us upon him, although that may also be due to his proximity to your consort. I cannot say for certain. I also detect old magic surrounding him. Is he bespelled?"

"We shall let him tell his own story," Alexstrasza replied, sparing Krasus from any interrogation. "Once the others have arrived."

"One is coming even now," Ysera sagely announced.

The ceiling above rippled, then shimmered. A huge, winged form materialized, then swooped down grandly, circling the vast cavern twice in the process. The other Aspects grew respectfully silent, each watching the massive figure draw near.

In size he rivaled the largest of them, a winged behemoth as black as night with a bearing as noble as any depiction ever made of a dragon. Narrow veins of actual silver and gold streaking from front to back accented his spine and sides, while gleaming flashes between the scales hinted at diamonds and other precious stones embedded naturally in his hide. The newcomer radiated a sense of primal power, the power of the world itself in all its most basic forms.

He landed just beyond the rest, his huge, webbed wings folding masterfully behind him. In a voice deep and full, the black dragon said, "You have called and I have come. It is always good to see my friend Alexstrasza . . ."

"And I welcome your presence, dear Neltharion."

Before, it had been all Krasus could do to keep from reacting to Malygos's presence. Now he fought to keep himself from shaking, from showing the slightest sign at all of how he felt about this latest arrival. Yet, while his earlier reaction came from his knowledge concerning the doomed future of the Guardian of Magic, now Krasus worried more for the future of *all* dragons . . . and the world itself, should it survive the Burning Legion.

Before him stood Neltharion.

Neltharion. The Earth Warder. Most respected of the Aspects and, in addition, the close friend of Krasus's beloved queen. Had Neltharion been of her own flight, he surely would have long been chosen as one of her mates. Outside of her consorts, the Earth Warder was the one whom Alexstrasza most often sought for consultation, for the brooding black had a sharp mind that saw all angles. Neltharion did nothing without considering the consequences and, as a young dragon, Krasus had in some ways emulated him.

But in the future to which the mage belonged, any thought of emulating Neltharion would have gone beyond the point of madness. Neltharion had rejected his role, rejected the protection the Aspects gave the mortal realm. He had instead turned to the belief that the lesser races were the root of all that was wrong with the world, that they should be removed . . . and those who would aid them should be removed as well.

Neltharion had come to envision a world where only dragons—specifically his own flight—ruled all. That growing obsession had led him to countless acts of an increasingly dark design, acts so horrible that eventually Neltharion became as terrible a danger to the world as the demons of the

Burning Legion. The other Aspects had finally banded together against him, but not before he had spilled much blood and caused wholesale destruction.

And in rejecting all he had once been, Neltharion had also rejected his own name. From his former counterparts had come the name by which he was known to *all* creatures, one that had become synonymous with evil itself.

Deathwing . . .

There before Krasus loomed Deathwing, the Destroyer, the Black Scourge. Yet, the dragon mage could do nothing to warn the others. In fact, although he knew the danger that Neltharion would eventually become, Krasus could not recall when and where the tragedy had begun. To foment distrust among the Aspects at this critical juncture risked even more of a disaster than what the Earth Warder's future held.

And yet . . .

"I was surprised when Ysera, not you, contacted me," the black rumbled. "You are well, Alexstrasza?"

"I am, Neltharion."

He eyed her companions. "And you, young Korialstrasz? You are not at your best, I think."

"An illness passing," the red male answered respectfully. "It is an honor to see you again, Earth Warder."

They conversed like friendly acquaintances and yet Krasus managed to recall that as Deathwing, Neltharion would barely recognize him. By the time of the orc wars, the black behemoth would have dwelled so long in his madness that past friendships would be forgotten. All that would matter would be whatever advanced his dark cause.

But here still was Neltharion the comrade. He peered over Korialstrasz's neck, noting the tiny, cowled figure. "And you are the one. You have a name?"

"Krasus!" the mage snapped. "Krasus!"

"A defiant little one!" Neltharion said with amusement. "I believe that he is definitely a dragon, as Ysera hinted."

"A dragon with a tale to tell," Alexstrasza added. She gazed up at the ceiling, specifically the spot from which she and the others had entered. "But I would prefer to give Nozdormu more time before we begin."

"Give the Timeless One more time?" Malygos laughed. "How droll! I will not let dour Nozdormu leave without pressing him on *that* jest!"

"Yes and you will press him *time* and *time* again with it, will you not?" returned Neltharion, a vast, toothy smile spreading across his reptilian countenance.

Malygos laughed further. He and Neltharion shuffled to one side, already deep in some conversation.

"Brothers they may not be in blood," commented Ysera, her closed eyes following the pair. "But they are truly brothers in nature."

Alexstrasza agreed. "It is good that Neltharion has Malygos to turn to. He has been quiet with me of late."

"I, too, sense a distance. He does not take the actions by these night elves with pleasure. He stated once that they have grandiose visions of becoming like the creators without the knowledge and wisdom of the latter."

"There may be something to what he has said," the Queen of Life returned, her eyes sweeping briefly over Krasus.

The mage grew increasingly uncomfortable under her study of him. Of them all, Alexstrasza deserved this other warning. It would be Deathwing's doing that she would be turned into a slave of the orcs, whose warhounds readily sacrificed her children to their brutal cause. Deathwing would then use the chaos of the last days of the orc wars to seek what he truly desired . . . the eggs of the Queen of Life to re-create his own decimated flight, all but slain because of his past mad plots.

What limit do I set? Krasus demanded of himself. *When must the line finally be crossed? I can say nothing about the orcs, nothing about the Earth Warder's betrayals, nothing about the Burning Legion . . . all I can do is state enough facts to possibly exterminate myself and Rhonin!*

In frustration, he glared at one of the causes of his dilemma. Neltharion spoke merrily with Malygos, the latter's back turned to the other waiting dragons. The huge black stretched his wings and nodded at some remark by his gleaming counterpart. Had they been humans, dwarves, or some other mortal race, the pair would have looked quite at home drinking ale in a tavern. The lesser races saw the dragons as either monstrous beasts or dignified founts of wisdom, when in truth their characters were in some ways as earthy as the tiny creatures over which they watched.

Neltharion's eyes flickered past Malygos, meeting, however briefly, Krasus's.

And in that moment of contact, Krasus realized that all he and the others had seen so far of the black at this gathering had been a charade.

The darkness had already descended upon the Earth Warder.

Not possible, not possible! Krasus insisted, barely able to keep his expression neutral. *Not now!* It was too soon, too delicate a point in time for the transformation of Neltharion to Deathwing to begin. The Aspects needed to be united, not only to join against the coming invasion, but to deal with the disruptions of time caused by Krasus and his former student. Surely he had been mistaken about the black leviathan. Surely Neltharion was still one of the fabled protectors of the mortal plane.

Krasus cursed his feeble memory. When *had* Neltharion turned to betrayal? When *had* he forever become the bane of all other living creatures? Was it meant to be now or had Neltharion worked with his comrades even though darkness had already claimed him?

The cowled mage could not help but stare at the Earth Warder. Despite his own oath, Krasus began to think that perhaps here he had to bend the rules. How could it do anything but good to unveil the villain in the Aspects' midst? How—

Once more Neltharion glanced his way . . . but this time the eyes did not leave Krasus's own.

And only then did Krasus discover that Neltharion in turn saw the recognition in him, only then did he realize that the black dragon understood that here was one who could reveal his terrible secret.

Krasus tried to look away, but his eyes were held fast. Too late he realized the cause of that. The Earth Warder, having seen that he had been found out, had acted quickly and decisively. He now held Krasus with his power as easily as he breathed.

I will not fall to him! Yet, despite his determination to escape, his will did not prove strong enough. Had he been better prepared, Krasus could have battled Neltharion's mind, but the unexpected discovery had left him wide open . . . and the black one had seized the opportunity.

You know me . . . but I do not know you.

The chilling voice filled his head. Krasus prayed that someone would notice what passed between the pair, but to all appearances, everything passed as normal. It astounded him that not even his beloved Alexstrasza recognized the terrible truth.

You would speak against me . . . make the others see me as you do . . . you would have them distrust their comrade of old . . . their brother . . .

The Earth Warder's words gave clear indication of how deep his madness had already become. Krasus sensed within Neltharion a raging paranoia and an adamant belief that no one but the black dragon understood what was good for the world. Anyone who seemed at all the slightest threat to him was, in Neltharion's eyes, the true evil.

You will not be allowed to spread any of your malicious false-hoods . . .

Krasus expected to be struck down there and then, but, to his surprise, all Neltharion did was turn his gaze away and resume his conversation with Malygos.

What games does he play? the dragon mage wondered. *First he threatens me, then seems to forget my presence!*

He watched the black leviathan carefully, but Neltharion seemed entirely oblivious to him.

"He is not coming," Ysera finally said.

"He may still appear," suggested Alexstrasza.

Glancing at them, Krasus realized that they referred to Nozdormu.

"No, I have been contacted by the one with whom I spoke. He cannot locate his master. The Timeless One is somewhere beyond the mortal plane."

Ysera's news boded further ill. Knowing what he did of Nozdormu, Krasus suspected that the reason that even the Timeless One's servants could not contact him was because of the anomaly. If, as Krasus believed, Nozdormu held Time together all by himself, he would have needed to summon every instant of his existence. Multiple Nozdormus would be battling Time . . . leaving no moment for this gathering.

Krasus's hopes dwindled further. Nozdormu lost and Neltharion mad . . .

"I agree, then," Alexstrasza said, responding to Ysera's assessment. "We shall go on without the full Five. There is no rule that we cannot at least discuss the matter after the story is told, even if a course of action cannot yet be taken."

Lowering his head, Korialstrasz allowed his rider to dismount. Keeping his expression guarded, Krasus stepped out among the gathered giants, trying not to look at the Earth Warder. Alexstrasza's eyes encouraged him, enough so that the dragon mage knew what he had to do.

"I am one of you," he announced in a voice as booming as any of the leviathans surrounding him. My true name is known to the Queen of Life, but for now I am simply Krasus!"

"He bellows well, this hatchling," Malygos jested.

Krasus faced him. "This is not a time for humor, especially for you, Guardian of Magic! This is a time when a balance is nigh upset! A terrible mistake, a distortion of reality, threatens everything . . . absolutely everything!"

"How dramatic," Neltharion commented almost absently.

It took everything in Krasus's power not to blurt out the truth about the Earth Warder. *Not yet . . .*

"You will hear my story," insisted Krasus. "You will hear it and understand . . . for there is a worse danger on the horizon, one which touches us as well. You see—"

But as the first words of his tale ushered forth from his mouth, Krasus's tongue seemed to catch everywhere. Instead of a coherent telling, babbled words of whimsy escaped him.

Most of the gathered dragons pulled their heads back, startled by his peculiar behavior. Krasus looked quickly to Alexstrasza, seeking her help, but her expression indicated an astonishment as strong as any.

The mage's head spun. Vertigo worse than any he had suffered so far seized him, made him unable to keep his balance. Nonsense words continued to spew from his lips, but even Krasus no longer knew what he tried to convey.

And as his legs buckled and the vertigo took full hold of him, Krasus heard within his head the deathly calm voice of Neltharion.

I did warn you . . .

SEVENTEEN

Darkness came and the world of the night elves awoke. Merchants opened their businesses while the faithful went to their prayers. The general populace lived their lives, feeling no different then on any other eve. The world was theirs to do with as they chose, whatever other, lesser races might believe.

But for some, tiny annoyances crept into their lives, minor deviations from their routines, their notions.

A senior master of the Moon Guard, his long silver hair bound behind him, absently raised one long, nailed finger toward a flask of wine at the opposite end of the room as he perused the star charts in preparation for a major casting by the order. Although he was among the eldest of the sorcerers, his skills had remained undiminished, a reason for his continued high position. Spellcasting was to him as much a part of his existence as breathing, a matter simply and naturally done, almost without thought.

The crash that jarred him from his plush chair and made him crumple the parchment nearly to shreds proved to be caused by the flask's swift and fatal descent to the floor. Wine and glass spilled over the rich emerald and orange carpet the sorcerer had only recently purchased.

With a hiss of fury, the spellcaster snapped his fingers at the disastrous spill. Bits of glass suddenly rose into the air as the wine itself puddled together and formed into the shape of the container that had held it. The glass then began to mold together over the wine . . .

But a second later . . . everything again spilled all over the carpet, creating a worse mess than before.

The aged sorcerer stared. With a grim expression, he snapped his fingers again.

This time, the glass and the wine performed as he desired, even the slightest hint of stain removed. Yet, they did so with some sluggishness, taking far longer than the Moon Guard master would have expected.

The aged night elf returned to his parchment and tried once more to concentrate on the coming event, but his gaze constantly shifted back to the bottle and its contents. He pointed a finger at the flask again—then, with a frown, pulled the finger back and purposely turned his chair *away* from the cause of his annoyance.

At the edges of every major settlement, armed sentinels patrolled and guarded the night elves from any possible foe. Lord Ravencrest and those like him ever watched the areas beyond the main boundaries of the realm, their belief that the dwarves and other races constantly coveted the night elves' rich world. They did not look inward—for who of their own people would ever threaten them?—but permitted every settlement to maintain its own security simply in order to comfort the general citizenry.

In Galhara, a great city some distance on the opposing side of the Well from Zin-Azshari, sorcerers began the nightly ritual of realigning the emerald crystals that lined its boundaries. In conjunction with each other, the crystals acted, among other things, as defense against general magical attack. They had not, to anyone's recollection, ever been utilized, but the people took great comfort in their presence.

Despite there being hundreds, it was no troublesome feat to set the crystal arrays. All drew their power directly from the Well of Eternity and the sorcerers merely had to use the stars to adjust the lines of force that ran from one to another. In truth, this mostly required a simple twist of the crystal on the tall, obsidian pole upon which each had been placed. Thus, the local spellcasters were able to do several in the space of only a few minutes.

But with more than half already realigned, the crystals began to dim, even darkened completely. The sorcerers of Galhara, while not as proficient as the Moon Guard, knew their tasks well enough to understand that what happened now should *not* be happening. They immediately began checking and rechecking the arrays, but found nothing wrong.

"They are not drawing properly from the Well," one younger spellcaster finally decided. "Something has tried to cut them off from its might!"

But no sooner had he said that than the crystals renewed their normal activities. His elder associates looked at him in bemusement, trying to recall if, when as new to their roles as he was, they had made such outrageous statements.

And life among the night elves went on . . .

"It hasss *failed!*" Hakkar roared. He nearly whipped the closest of the Highborne, but pulled his savage lash back at the last moment. Eyes deathly dark, he looked to Lord Xavius. "*We* have failed . . ."

The felbeasts at the Houndmaster's flanks echoed their handler's fury with sinister snarls.

Xavius was no less displeased. He eyed the work that both

the Highborne and Hakkar had wrought and saw in it hours of futility . . . and yet both he and the Houndmaster had seen the merits of the queen's suggestion.

They simply did not have the knowledge or power needed to make it happen.

That the efforts of the Highborne had still enabled more than a score of Fel Guard to join those already on the mortal plane did nothing to assuage them. Such numbers were only a slow dribble and did nothing to pave the way for the great one's coming.

"What can we do?" asked the night elf.

For the first time, he read uncertainty in the Houndmaster's haunting visage. The huge warrior turned his baleful gaze toward the portal, where others of the Highborne ever continued to try to make it stronger and larger. "We mussst asssk *him*."

The counselor swallowed, but before his monstrous counterpart could take the step, Lord Xavius pushed himself forward, falling down on one knee before the portal. He would not shirk from his failures, not to his god.

Yet, even before his knee touched the stone, Xavius heard the voice in his head.

Is the portal strengthened?

"Nay, great one . . . the work in that regard has not progressed as we hoped."

For just the hint of a moment, what almost seemed an insane fury threatened to overwhelm the night elf . . . but then the sensation passed. Certain that he had imagined it, Xavius awaited the god's next words.

You seek something . . . speak.

Lord Xavius explained the notion of sealing off the Well's power from all but the palace and the failure to make that come to pass. He kept his head low, humble before the power that made the combined might of all night elves look no more terrible than that of an insect.

I have already considered this . . . the god finally answered. The one I sent first has failed in his duty . . .

Behind Xavius, the Houndmaster let out a brief sound bordering on dismay.

Another will be sent to you . . . you must make certain that the portal is made ready for him . . .

"Another, my lord?"

I now send you one of my . . . one of the commanders of my host. He will see to it that what is needed will come to pass . . . and quickly.

The voice departed Xavius's head. He swayed for a moment, the departure as stunning to him as if someone had just cut off one of his arms. Another of the Highborne helped him to his feet.

Xavius looked at Hakkar, who did not seem at all happy despite what the counselor saw as the most wonderful of news. "He sends us one of his *commanders!* Do you know which one?"

The Houndmaster anxiously rolled up his whip. Beside him, the two felbeasts cringed. "Aye . . . I know which one, lord night elf."

"We must make ready! He will be coming immediately!"

Despite whatever disturbed him, Hakkar joined Xavius as the latter inserted himself among the casting Highborne. The pair added their knowledge and skill, amplifying as best they could the framework of energy that kept the portal ever open.

The burning sphere swelled, sparks of multicolored forces constantly shooting out from it. It pulsated, almost breathing. The portal stretched, a savage, roaring sound accompanying the physical change.

Sweat already poured down Xavius's face and body, but he did not care. The glory of what he sought gave him strength. Even more than the Houndmaster, he threw himself into making the spell not only hold, but expand to what was needed.

And as it grew to touch the ceiling, the portal suddenly disgorged a huge, dark figure at once so wonderful and terrible that it was all Xavius could do to keep from crying out in gratitude to the great one. Here now stood one of the celestial commanders, a figure before whom Hakkar seemed as unworthy as Xavius had felt before the Houndmaster.

"Elune save us!" one of the other sorcerers gasped. He pulled free, all but destroying the precious portal. Xavius barely seized control and, straining mightily, held it in place until the others could recover.

A huge, four-digited hand large enough to encompass the counselor's head stretched forth, pointing a taloned finger toward the careless spellcaster. A voice that was both the roar of a crashing wave and the ominous rumble of an erupting volcano uttered a single, unrecognizable word.

The night elf who had stumbled away screamed as his body twisted like a piece of wet cloth being drained of water. A grotesque procession of cracking sounds matched the faltering scream. Most of the other Highborne immediately looked away and Hakkar's felbeasts whined.

Black flames erupted all over the macabre sight, enveloping what was left of the unfortunate sorcerer. The flames ate away at him like a pack of starved wolves, swiftly devouring the victim until but seconds later only a slight pile of ash on the floor remained to mark his passing.

"There will be no more failure," the thundering voice stated.

If the Houndmaster and the Fel Guard had not amazed Lord Xavius enough, surely only the god himself could have awed the counselor more than this new arrival. The fearsome figure moved forward on four thick, muscular limbs reminiscent of a dragon, save that these ended in blocky feet with three massive, clawed toes. A magnificent, scaled tail swept the floor over and over, the movement very likely a sign of the celestial one's impatience. From the top of his head down his back to the very tip of his tail ran a wild mane of pure green flame. Huge leathery wings also stretched from his back but even despite their span, Xavius wondered if they could lift so gigantic and powerful a form.

His hide, where black armor did not cover it, was a dark gray-green. He stood twice as wide as Hakkar and at least sixteen feet high, if the counselor was any judge. The massive tusks sprouting from the sides of his upper jaw nearly scraped the ceiling and the other, daggerlike teeth measured as long as the night elf's hand.

Under a thick brow ridge that almost completely obscured his burning orbs, the chosen of the great one stared down at the lord counselor . . . and the Houndmaster, especially.

"You have disappointed him . . ." was all the winged commander declared.

"I—" Hakkar paused in his protest, hanging his head. "I have no excussse, Mannoroth."

Mannoroth tilted his head slightly, looking at the Houndmaster as if studying an unpleasant bit of refuse found on his dinner plate. "No . . . you do not."

The felbeast on Hakkar's right suddenly whined loudly. Black flames akin to those that had removed the negligent sorcerer enveloped the frightened hound. It rolled desperately on the floor, trying to douse flames that would not be doused. The fire spread over it, consuming it . . .

And when only a wisp of smoke marked where the felbeast had stood, Mannoroth said again to the Houndmaster. "There will be no more failure."

Fear filled Xavius, but a wondrous, glorious fear. Here was power incarnate, a being that sat at the right hand of the great one. Here was one who would know how to turn their defeat into victory.

The dark gaze turned on him. Mannoroth gave a short sniff with his blunt nose . . . then nodded. "The great one approves of your efforts, lord night elf."

He had been blessed! Xavius lowered himself further. "I give thanks!"

"The plan will be followed. We will cut off the place of power from the rest of this realm. Then the arrival of the host can begin in earnest."

"And the great one? He will come then?"

Mannoroth gave him a wide smile, one with which he could have swallowed the counselor whole. "Oh, yes, lord night elf! *Sargeras* himself will want to be here when the world is cleansed . . . he will want to be here very, very much . . ."

Grass filled Rhonin's mouth and nose.

At least, he assumed it was grass. It tasted like grass, although he had not had much experience in such dining. The smell reminded him of wild fields and more peaceful times . . . times with Vereesa.

With effort, he pushed himself up. Night had fallen and while the moon shone fairly brightly, it revealed little beyond the fact that he lay in a lightly wooded area. Rhonin listened, but heard no sound of civilization.

The sudden fear that he had been catapulted into yet another era briefly overwhelmed him, but then the wizard recalled just what had happened. His own spell had sent him here, his desperate attempt to escape the demon draining him of his magic—and in the process, his life.

But if in the same time, then *where* had he landed? His

surroundings gave no hint. He could be a few miles away or on the other side of the world.

And if the latter . . . could he return to Kalimdor? He hoped Krasus still lived somewhere, and only with his former mentor's aid did the wizard think that they might yet return home.

Staggering to his feet, Rhonin tried to decide which direction to go. Somehow he had to at least discover his whereabouts.

A noise in the woods behind him made the human whirl about. His hand came up in preparation for a spell.

A hulking figure emerged.

"No quarrel, wizard! Only Brox before you!"

Rhonin cautiously lowered his hand. The huge orc trudged forward, still clutching the ax Malfurion and the demigod had fashioned for him.

At the thought of the night elf, Rhonin looked around. "Are you alone?"

"Was until I saw you. You make a lot of noise, human. You move like a drunken infant."

Ignoring the jibe, the wizard looked past the orc. "I was thinking of Malfurion. He was also nearby when I cast the spell. If you were drawn into it, he might've been."

"Sound." Brox scratched his ugly head. "Saw no night elf. Saw no felbeast, either."

The human shivered. He certainly hoped that he had not included the demon in his escape. "Any idea where we might be?"

"Woods . . . forest."

Rhonin almost snapped at him for the useless answer, but realized that he could do no better. "I was planning to go that way," he said, pointing toward what he believed was east. "You have any better ideas?"

"Could wait until sunrise. Better able to see and night elves, they don't like sun."

While that made much sense, Rhonin did not feel comfortable waiting for daylight and told his companion so. Brox surprised him by nodding in agreement.

"Better to scout, wizard." He shrugged. "Your direction as good as any."

As they started off, a question occurred to Rhonin that he simply had to ask. "Brox . . . how did you get here? Not this exact location—I know that, of course—but how did you come to this realm?"

At first the orc only clamped his mouth shut, but then he finally told the wizard. Rhonin listened to the tale, careful to hide his emotions. The veteran and his ill-fated partner had been right behind Krasus and him and, like the others, had been caught by the anomaly.

"Do you understand what swallowed us?"

Brox shrugged. "Wizard's spell. Bad one. Sent us far from our home."

"Farther than you might know." Deciding that Brox had a right to the truth regardless of what Krasus might think, Rhonin told him what had happened.

To the wizard's surprise, Brox accepted his story quite readily. Only when Rhonin thought about the history of the orc's people did he realize why. The orcs had already journeyed through time and space from another world. A spell that would cast one into the past was hardly that much different.

"Can we return, human?"

"I don't know."

"You saw. The demons are here. The Legion is here."

"This is the first time they tried to invade our world. Most beyond Dalaran don't know that history anymore."

Brox gripped his ax tighter. "We'll fight them . . ."

"No . . . we can't." Rhonin explained Krasus's reasoning.

But while Brox had quickly accepted all else, he drew the line when it came to leaving the past alone. The matter was simple for the orc; here was a dangerous, foul enemy who would slaughter all in their path. Only cowards and fools let such horror happen and Brox said so more than once.

"We might change history by interfering," the wizard insisted, in his heart wanting to agree with the orc.

Brox snorted. "You fought."

His simple statement completely repudiated Rhonin's only argument. The wizard *had* fought already and by doing so had made a choice.

But was it the right one? Already the past had been altered, but to what degree?

They moved on in silence, Rhonin in battle with his inner demons and Brox keeping a wary eye out for physical ones. Nowhere did they see any hint of where they might have ended up. At one point Rhonin considered concentrating on the glade and trying to send them both back there. Then he remembered the felbeast and what it had almost done to him.

The woods thickened, eventually becoming a full forest. Rhonin silently cursed, his choice of directions now seeming a poor one. Brox gave no indication of his own opinion, simply chopping away with his enchanted ax whenever the path grew impossible. The ax sliced through everything with such ease that the wizard hoped that his companion would never accidentally cut him with it. Not even bone gave the blade any pause.

The moon vanished, the thick foliage of the surrounding trees completely obscuring the heavens. The path became impossible. After a few more minutes of fruitlessly fighting their way along, the pair decided to turn back. Again, the orc said nothing about Rhonin's choice.

But when they turned around, it was to find that the way they came had completely *vanished*.

Huge trees stood where once the path had been and dense undergrowth around the trunks gave further evidence that this surely was not the right direction. Yet, both orc and human eyed the trees with distrust.

"We came from through there. I know we did."

"Agreed." Raising the ax, Brox moved in on the mysterious trees. "And we go back that way, too."

But as he swung, huge, branchlike hands seized the weapon by the sides of the blade and pulled it up.

Unwilling to relinquish the ax, Brox hung by the handle, the orc's legs dangling as he sought to use his weight to wrest the weapon free.

Rhonin ran up. He tugged on the orc's feet with no success. Staring at the long, inhuman fingers, he began to mutter a spell.

Something struck him from behind. The wizard stumbled forward and would have soundly hit the tree before him if not for the fact that it *moved* aside at the last moment.

Momentum sent Rhonin flailing to the earth. However, instead of striking either harsh ground or one of the many gnarled roots around him, he landed atop something softer.

A body.

Rhonin gasped, assuming that he had come across a previous victim of the sinister trees. But as he pushed himself up, a brief glimmer of moonlight that somehow had penetrated the vast crowns above allowed him to see the face.

Malfurion . . .

The night elf suddenly moaned. His eyes flickered open and he saw the wizard.

"You—"

Further back, Brox shouted something. Both human and

night elf quickly looked that way. Rhonin raised a hand in preparation for attack, but Malfurion surprised him by seizing his wrist.

"No!" The dark-skinned figure sat up, quickly scanning the trees. He nodded to himself, then shouted, "Brox! Do not fight them! They mean no harm!"

"No harm?" growled the orc. "They want my ax!"

"You must do as I say! They are protectors!"

From the warrior came a reluctant groan. Rhonin looked at Malfurion for explanation, but received none. Instead, the night elf released the wizard's wrist, then pushed himself to his feet. With Rhonin trailing behind, Malfurion walked calmly toward the area where Brox battled.

They found the orc surrounded by ominous-looking trees. A cluster of branches hung above and in them was tangled Brox's ax. The orc panted from effort, his body still tense. He looked from his companions to his weapon and back again, as if still not certain he should not try to climb after it.

"Knew your voice," he grunted. "You better be right."

"I am."

As the wizard and the warrior watched, Malfurion stepped up to the tallest of the trees and said, "I give thanks to the brothers of the forest, the keepers of the wild. I know you watched over me until my friends could find me. They mean no harm; they just did not understand."

The leaves of the trees began to rustle even though Rhonin could feel no wind.

Nodding, the night elf continued, "We will trouble you no longer."

More rustling . . . then the branches entangling Brox's ax separated and the weapon slipped earthward.

They could have let the ax fall harmlessly to the ground, but the orc suddenly stepped forward. He reached up with one powerful hand and caught the ax handle perfectly. Yet, instead of waving the weapon at the trees, he knelt before them, the blade turned downward.

"I ask forgiveness."

Again, the crowns of the towering trees shook. Malfurion put a hand on the orc's broad shoulder. "They accept."

"You can really speak with them?" Rhonin finally asked.

"To a point."

"Then ask them where we are."

"I already have. Not at all that far from where we were, but far enough away. Actually, we're both fortunate and unfortunate."

"How so?"

The night elf smiled ruefully. "We're only a short distance from my home."

This was excellent news to the wizard, but not such good news to the night elf, he gathered. Nor did it seem good news to Brox, who cursed in his native tongue.

"What is it? What do the two of you know?"

"I was captured close to here, wizard," growled the brawny warrior. "Very close."

Recalling his own capture, Rhonin could see why Brox might be upset. "I'll take us from here, then. This time I know what to expect—"

Malfurion held up a hand in protest. "We were fortunate once, but here, you risk being sensed immediately by the Moon Guard. They have the skill to usurp your spell . . . in fact, they may have, at the very least, already sensed the first one."

"What do you suggest?"

"As we are near my home, we should make use of it. There are others who could be of assistance to us. My brother and Tyrande."

Brox embraced his suggestion. "The shaman . . . she will help." His tone darkened. "Your twin . . . yes."

Rhonin still worried about Krasus, but with no notion as to how to find his former mentor, the night elf's decision made the most sense. With Malfurion in the lead, the trio headed off. The path through the forest now proved startlingly easy, considering the trek through which the human and the orc had earlier suffered. The landscape seemed to go out of its way to make Malfurion's journey a comfortable one. Rhonin knew something of druids and for the first time marked Malfurion as of that calling.

"The demigod—Cenarius—he taught you to speak with the trees, to cast such spells?"

"Yes. I seem to be the first to truly understand them. Even my brother prefers the power of the Well to the ways of the forest."

At mention of the Well, a feeling of anticipation and hunger suddenly touched Rhonin. He fought the emotions down. The Well that his companion had mentioned could only be the Well of Eternity, the fabled fount of power. Were they that near? Was that why his own spellwork had become magnified?

To wield such power . . . and so readily . . .

"We're not much farther," Malfurion said a short while later. "I recognize that gnarled elder."

The "elder" he referred to was a twisted old tree that, to Rhonin at least, looked like little more than a dark shape. Something else, however, attracted the wizard's attention.

"Do I hear rushing water?"

The night elf sounded more cheerful. "It flows very near my home! Only a few more minutes and—"

But before he could finish, the forest filled with armored figures. Brox snarled and made ready with his ax. Rhonin readied a spell, certain that these were the same foul attackers who had first seized Krasus and him.

As for Malfurion, the night elf looked entirely perplexed at the sudden appearance of the attackers. He started to raise a hand toward them, then hesitated.

Malfurion's hesitation caused Rhonin in turn to pause. That proved a mistake, for in the next instant a red shroud of energy fell upon each. Rhonin felt his muscles freeze and his strength fade. He could not move, could not do anything but watch.

"An excellent piece of work, lad," proclaimed a commanding voice. " 'Tis the beastman we sought—and no doubt those who aided in his escape!"

Someone replied, but too low for Rhonin to make out the words. A band of riders, two bearing glowing emerald staffs, entered the circle of soldiers. At their head was a bearded night elf who had to be the one in charge. Next to him—

Rhonin's eyes widened, the only response left to him in his present condition. It hardly signified his astonishment upon recognizing the figure next to the commander.

The garments were different and the hair was bound back, but there was no mistaking that the dour face was an exact duplicate of Malfurion's.

EIGHTEEN

Mannoroth was pleased . . . and that pleased
Lord Xavius.

"It is good, then?" the night elf asked the
celestial commander. So much hinged on everything going
as planned.

Mannoroth nodded his heavy, tusked head. His wings
stretched and folded in satisfaction. "Yes . . . very good.
Sargeras will be pleased."

Sargeras. Again the celestial commander had uttered the
true name of the great one. Xavius's magical eyes burned
bright as he savored it. *Sargeras.*

"We will work the portal the moment that the spell is set
in place. First will come the host, then, when all is made
ready, my lord himself . . ."

Hakkar approached, the much subdued Houndmaster
falling on one knee before Mannoroth. "Forgive thisss inter-
ruption, but one of my huntersss hasss returned."

"Only *one?*"

"Ssso it ssseems."

"And what have you learned from it?" Mannoroth loomed
over his counterpart, making the Houndmaster seem
smaller and smaller.

"They found two with the ssscent of othernessss that the

lord night elf ssspoke of, plusss one of hisss *own* kind with them! But in the hunt they alssso fell afoul of a being of power . . . great power."

For the first time, Mannoroth displayed a slight hint of uncertainty. Xavius noted carefully the reaction, wondering what could disturb so wondrous a being. "Not—"

Hakkar quickly shook his head. "I think not. Perhapsss with a touch of their power. Perhapsss a guardian left behind."

The pair spoke of something significant, but what, the counselor could not say. Taking a risk, he interrupted. "Is there a description of this last creature?"

"Aye." Hakkar held out one hand, palm up.

Above his palm there suddenly burst to life a tiny image. It moved violently and often lost focus, but revealed by bits and pieces an almost full view of the one in question.

"Ssseen through the eyesss of the felbeassst. An antlered entity asss tall asss one of the Fel Guard."

Lord Xavius frowned. "The legend is true, then . . . the forest lord is real . . ."

"You know this creature?" Mannoroth demanded.

"Ancient myth speaks of the forest lord, the demigod Cenarius. He is said to be the child of the Mother Moon . . ."

"Nothing more, then." The tusked mouth twisted into a grim smile. "He will be dealt with." To Hakkar, he commanded, "Show the others."

The Houndmaster quickly obeyed, revealing a greenskinned brute of warrior, a young night elf, and an odd, firehaired figure clad in hooded garments.

"A curious trio," Xavius remarked.

Mannoroth nodded. "The warrior shows much promise . . . I would see more of his kind, learn their potential . . ."

"Such a beast? Surely not! He's more grotesque than a dwarf!"

The winged figure did not argue, instead recalling the last of the threesome. "A spindly creature but with wary eyes. A creature of magic, I think. Almost like a night elf—" He cut off Xavius's new protest. "—but not." Dismissing Hakkar's images, the huge, reptilian limbs maneuvered through the chamber as Mannoroth contemplated what he had learned.

"More felbeastsss could be sssent to find them," suggested the Houndmaster.

"But with Fel Guard behind. This time, the objective will be capture."

"Capture?" echoed both the counselor and the Houndmaster.

The deepset eyes narrowed more. "They must be studied, their weaknesses and strengths assessed in case there are others . . ."

"Can the Fel Guard be ssspared?"

"There will soon be many, many more. Lord night elf, are your Highborne prepared?"

Studying the sorcerers, Xavius bowed his head. "They are ready to do what they must to see the glorious fulfillment of our dream, the cleansing of the world of all that is—"

"The world will be cleansed, lord night elf, you may trust to that." Mannoroth glanced at Hakkar. "I leave the hunt to you, Houndmaster. Do not fail again."

Keeping low, Hakkar backed away.

"And now, lord night elf . . ." the towering being continued, gaze turning to the place of casting. "Let us begin the molding of your people's future . . ." Mannoroth's wings flexed as they always seemed to do when he contemplated something agreeable to him. "A future I promise you that they cannot possibly even imagine . . ."

Deathwing soared over the landscape, breathing fire everywhere. Screams came from every direction around Krasus, but he could not find any of those who pleaded for his aid. Trapped in his tiny mortal form, he scampered over the burning earth like a field rat, trying to keep from being engulfed while in vain he sought to help the dying.

Suddenly a dark shadow covered the area over which he ran and a thundering voice mocked, "Well, well! And what little morsel is this?"

Huge claws twice the size of the dragon mage encircled Krasus, trapping him. With no effort whatsoever, they dragged him into the sky . . . and turned him to face the malevolent visage of Deathwing.

"Why, it's only a bit of old dragon meat! Korialstrasz! You've been around the lesser races much too long! Their weakness has rubbed off on you!"

Krasus tried to cast a spell, but from his mouth emerged not words but tiny bats. Deathwing inhaled, drawing the bats mercilessly into the hot, gaping maw.

The black behemoth swallowed. "Not much of a treat! I doubt you'll be any better, but you're already going to waste so I might as well finish you off!" He raised the flailing figure above his gullet. "Besides, you're of no use to anyone, anyway!"

The claws released Krasus, but as he plummeted into Deathwing's mouth, things changed. Deathwing and the burning landscape vanished. Krasus suddenly floated in the midst of a horrendous sandstorm, spun around and around by its ever more turbulent forces.

A dragon's head formed in the midst of the storm. At first

Krasus thought that the black beast had followed him, determined not to let his snack escape. Then another head identical to the first appeared, followed by another and another until an endless horde filled Krasus's view.

"Korialstraaaasz . . ." they moaned simultaneously over and over. "Korialstraaasz . . ."

It occurred to Krasus then that the heads had a different shape to them from Deathwing's and that each had formed from the sandstorm itself.

Nozdormu?

"We . . . are ssstretched through all!" the Timeless One managed. "We . . . ssseee alll . . ."

Krasus waited, knowing that Nozdormu spoke as his efforts permitted him.

"All endsss lead to nothing! All endsss . . ."

Nothing? What did he mean? Did he indicate that all the mage had feared had come to pass, that the future had been eradicated?

". . . but one . . ."

One! Krasus seized hold of the tiny ray of hope. "Tell me! What path? What do I do?"

In answer, the dragon heads changed. The snouts shrank and the heads elongated, becoming more human—no! Not human—elven . . .

A night elf?

Was this someone he should fear or someone he should seek? He tried to ask Nozdormu, but then the storm grew wild, mad. The winds tore apart the faces, scattering the grains of sand everywhere. Krasus tried to protect his body as sand ripped at his flesh even through his garments.

He screamed.

*   *   *

And sat up a moment later, his mouth still open in a silent scream.

"My queen, he is with us again."

Gradually Krasus's mind returned to reality. The nightmare involving Deathwing and the subsequent vision of Nozdormu still wreaked havoc with his thoughts, but he was at last able to focus enough to realize that he lay in the egg chamber where he and Alexstrasza had first spoken. The Queen of Life herself looked down in grave concern at him. To his right, his younger self also watched with worry.

"Your spell has passed?" Alexstrasza quietly inquired.

This time, he was determined that she would know regardless of the consequences. Nozdormu's frightening words indicated that the path to the future already had all but shut. What more trouble, then, would it be if he told her of Neltharion's madness and the horror the black dragon would cause?

But once more, when Krasus tried to speak of the fiend, the vertigo nearly did him in. It was all he could do to keep conscious.

"Too soon," cautioned Alexstrasza. "You need more rest."

He needed much more than that. He needed the sinister and subtle spell which the Earth Warder had evidently cast upon him removed, but clearly none of the Aspects had even recognized his condition as one caused by sorcery. In all his incarnations, Deathwing had always been the most cunning of evils.

Unable to do anything about the black dragon, Krasus's mind drifted to the night elf whose features Nozdormu had attempted to show him. He recalled the ones who had attacked Rhonin and him, but none had looked at all like this new figure.

"How far are we from the land of the night elves?" Krasus asked . . . then touched his mouth in surprise when he realized that the words had come out with no trouble. Apparently Neltharion's handiwork only involved the dragon himself, not any other matter of importance.

"We can take you there soon enough," his mate replied. "But what of the matter of which you spoke?"

"This . . . this still concerns that matter, but my course has changed. I believe . . . I believe I have just been contacted by the Timeless One, who tried to tell me something."

His younger self found this too much. "You had nightmares, delusions! We heard you moan several times. It is doubtful that the Aspect of Time would reach out to you. Alexstrasza, perhaps, but not you."

"No," corrected the red queen. "I believe he may have the truth of it, Korialstrasz. If he says that Nozdormu touched his thoughts, I suspect he states fact."

"I bow to your wisdom, my love."

"I must go to the night elves," Krasus insisted. With Korialstrasz nearby and no intention of mentioning Neltharion's duplicity, his condition had improved much. "There is one I seek. I hope I am not already too late."

The female leviathan tilted her head to the side, her eyes seeking within Krasus's own. "Is all you told me before still truth? All of it?"

"It is . . . but I fear there is much more. The dragons—all dragons—will be needed for a struggle."

"But with Nozdormu absent, a consensus cannot be reached. The others will not agree to anything!"

"You must convince them to go against tradition!" He forced himself to his feet. "They could very well be all that stands between the world and oblivion!"

And with that, he told both all he could recall of the horror of the Burning Legion.

They listened to his tales of blood, of decimation, of

soulless evil. Even the two dragons shook as he regaled them with the atrocities. By the time he had finished, Krasus had told more than enough for them to see his fear.

But even then, Alexstrasza said, "They may still not decide. We have watched the world, but we leave its progress in the hands of the younger races. Even Neltharion, who is warder of the earth itself, prefers to leave it that way."

He so much desired to tell her of Neltharion, but even thinking that made his head swim. With a reluctant nod, Krasus said, "I know you will do what you must."

"And you must do what you will. Go to the night elves and seek your answer if you think it will help this situation." She looked up at her consort. After a moment's consideration, the queen added, "I ask that you go with him, Korialstrasz. Will you do it?"

The male lowered his head in respect. "If you ask, I am only too glad to oblige."

"I also ask that you follow his lead, my consort. Trust me when I say that he has wisdom which will be of value to you."

It was not entirely clear from his reptilian visage whether or not Korialstrasz believed the last, but he nodded to that, too.

"Night has fallen," Alexstrasza informed Krasus. "Will you wait until light?"

The dragon mage shook his head. "I have already waited far too long as it is."

The first to bear the clan designation of Ravencrest had looked upon the huge, granite formation atop the high and treacherous mount. He had remarked to his companion how its stocky formation resembled a piece from a chessboard, a rook colored black. That huge, dark birds constantly circled about the formation and even nested atop it was taken as a sign that this was a special place, a place of power.

For more than a generation—and the generations of night elves were longer than those of most races—servants of the Ravencrest line had continually carved out the clan stronghold, gradually building from solid rock a fortress like none seen among their kind. Black Rook Hold, as it quickly became known, was an ominous, uncolored place which spread its influence over much of the night elf realm, becoming second only to the palace. When conflict arose between the night elves and the dwarves, it was the power of Black Rook Hold that tipped the balance. Those of the clan of Ravencrest became the honored of the throne and the blood of both sides intermingled. If the Highborne who served Azshara were jealous of any others of their race, it had to be those of the ebony fortress.

Windows had been carved out on the top floors of the hold, but the only way to enter was by the twin iron gates located not at the base of the structure, but at the very bottom of the hill. The solid gates were sealed shut and well guarded. Only fools would have thought to enter there without permission.

But for the present Lord Ravencrest, those gates had opened readily. They had also opened for his three prisoners, one of whom knew the stories of Black Rook Hold and grew worried.

Malfurion had never thought that he would enter the dark hold, especially under such dire conditions. Worse, he could never have imagined his twin being the main reason for his having to do so. In the course of their journey he had learned that it was Illidan, somehow suddenly associated with Lord Ravencrest, who had detected Rhonin's spell. With Malfurion's brother to aid him, the night elven commander had ridden out with a full force, determined this time to capture any invaders.

He had been most pleased to see Brox . . . and quite puzzled to see Illidan's twin.

In a chamber lit by glittering emerald crystals positioned high in each of the five corners, Lord Ravencrest inspected his catch. The commander sat upon a chair carved from the same stone as his hold. The chair stood upon a dais, also stone, giving Ravencrest the ability to look down on the trio even while seated.

Armed soldiers lined the walls of the chamber while others surrounded Malfurion and his comrades. Ravencrest himself was flanked by his senior officers, each of whom stood with his helm in the crook of one arm. At the noble's immediate right waited Illidan.

Present also were two high-ranking members of the Moon Guard. They were a late addition to the proceedings, having arrived at Black Rook Hold just as the commander had brought his prisoners to the gates. The Moon Guard, too, had detected Rhonin's spell, but their spies had informed them of Ravencrest's party before there had been any chance to send out searchers of their own. The sorcerers were not at all pleased by the noble's actions nor were they pleased with Illidan's presence, he being an unsanctioned spellcaster in their eyes.

"Once again, my Lord Ravencrest," began the thinner, elder of the two Moon Guard, an officious figure by the name of Latosius. "I must request that these outsiders be turned over to us for proper questioning."

"You've already had the beastman and lost him. He was to come to me, anyway. This simply shortens the procedure." The noble eyed the three again. "There's more here than what we see on the surface. Illidan, I would hear from you."

Malfurion's brother looked slightly ill at ease, but he answered strongly, "Yes, my lord, he is my brother."

"That much is as obvious as night and day." He studied the captive twin. "I know something of you, lad, just as I know something of your brother. Your name is Malfurion, yes?"

"Yes, my lord."

"You rescued this creature?"

"I did."

The commander leaned forward. "And you've an excellent reason why? One that would excuse this heinous act?"

"I doubt you would believe me, my lord."

"Oh, I can come to believe many things, young one," Lord Ravencrest replied calmly, tugging lightly on his beard. "If they're spoken in honesty. Can you do that?"

"I—" What other choice did Malfurion have? Sooner or later, through one method or another, they would pluck the truth from him. "I'll try."

And so he told them of his studies under Cenarius, which immediately raised doubtful brows. He explained his reoccurring dreams and how the demigod had taught him to walk in the world of the subconscious. Most of all, Malfurion described the disconcerting forces that had drawn him to, of all places, Zin-Azshari, and the palace of the night elves' beloved queen.

They listened as he told of the Well itself and the turbulence that the sorcerers within the palace had stirred up. He painted for Ravencrest, the Moon Guard, and the others the vision of the tower and what he sensed went on inside.

The one thing he did not mention, assuming that from his story it would be obvious, was his fear that Queen Azshara sanctioned everything.

Ravencrest did not comment on his story, instead looking

to the Moon Guard. "Has your order noticed any such trouble?"

The elder sorcerer answered. "The Well is more turbulent than usual and that could be from misuse. We have not monitored any such activity from Zin-Azshari, but then, such an incredible fiction as this—"

"Yes, it is incredible." The bearded commander glanced up at Illidan. "What say you concerning your brother?"

"He's never been one for delusions, my lord." Illidan would not look at Malfurion. "As to whether it's the truth . . ."

"Indeed. Still, I wouldn't put it past Lord Xavius and the Highborne to instigate some devilment without her knowledge. They act as if the queen is their prized possession and no one else has a right to her."

Even by the Moon Guard, this was greeted with nods. The arrogance of the lord counselor and those surrounding Azshara in the palace was well known.

"If I may," Latosius interjected. "Once we've settled matters here, I will pass on word to the heads of our order. They will put into motion surveillance of the Highborne and their activities."

"I should be most interested in that. Young Malfurion, your story—on the assumption that it is for the most part truth—explains some of your actions, but how does that fit into the freeing of a prisoner of your people, a most serious crime?"

"I can perhaps answer that better," Rhonin suddenly said.

Malfurion was not so sure it was a good thing that the other outsider spoke. Night elves were not so tolerant of other races and although Rhonin had some vague resemblance to his kind, he still might as well have been a troll for all the good it would do him.

But Ravencrest appeared willing to listen, if nothing else. He waved a negligent hand toward the hooded wizard.

"In my land . . . a land not far from where he's from," explained Rhonin, nodding toward Brox. "A strange magical anomaly opened up. My people sent me and Brox's sent him. We both discovered it separately . . . and were drawn unwilling through it. He ended one place, I another."

"And how does this pertain to young Malfurion?"

"He believes . . . as I do . . . that this anomaly was caused by the spellwork mentioned."

"That would be some cause for alarm," commented the senior Moon Guard dubiously. "The green-skinned creature hardly seems what one would send to study a creation of sorcery or magic."

"My Warchief commanded I go," retorted Brox with a defiant snarl. "I went."

"I cannot speak for the orcs," Rhonin answered. "But I am certainly adept at such a study." His eyes, so different from those of the night elves, dared the Moon Guard to deny him.

After a pause, both sorcerers nodded their agreement. Malfurion realized that they did not know what exactly Rhonin was, but they recognized one versed in the arts. Indeed, it was likely for that reason that the wizard had been allowed to speak at all.

"Perhaps I'm growing old, but I'm inclined to believe much of all this." This admission from Lord Ravencrest drew some looks from his officers and sent a wave of relief through Malfurion. If the commander took their story to heart—

"We remain undecided," Latosius declared. "Such information cannot be taken on faith alone. There must still be an inner interrogation."

The noble's brow rose. "Did I say otherwise?"

He snapped his fingers and the guards seized Malfurion tightly by the arms, dragging him toward the dais.

"Now I would like to test the faith I've placed in my new sorcerer. Illidan, we must ascertain the absolute truth, however distasteful that might seem to you. I trust I can rely on you to prove to us that *all* your brother says is true?"

The pony-tailed night elf swallowed, then looked beyond Malfurion. "My brother's word I trust, but I can't say the same for the robed creature, my lord."

Illidan was trying to keep from having to use his powers on his brother by instead focusing on an outsider. While Malfurion appreciated that concern, he did not like the idea of Rhonin or Brox suffering in his place.

"Lord commander, this is absurd!" The senior sorcerer marched up to the dais, eyeing Illidan with contempt. "An unsanctioned spellcaster who is the brother of one of the prisoners? Any questioning will be suspect!" He turned on Malfurion, silver eyes narrowed menacingly at the younger night elf. "In accordance with the laws set down at the very dawn of our civilization, in matters magical it is the responsibility and right of the Moon Guard to oversee all such interrogations!"

He advanced, coming within arm's reach of the prisoner. Malfurion tried not to show his anxiety. Against the physical threats of Black Rook Hold, he hoped his druidic training would allow him to survive, but the delving of a sorcerer into his mind threatened him much more. Such a questioning could leave his body whole, but his brain so shattered that he might never recover.

Illidan leapt down from the dais. "My lord, I'll interrogate my brother."

Whatever his twin would do to him, Malfurion suspected that Illidan would be much more careful in his approach than the Moon Guard, who only wanted answers. Malfurion looked at Lord Ravencrest, hoping that the noble would accept Illidan's offer.

But the master of Black Rook Hold only leaned back against his chair, stating, "The laws shall be followed. He is yours, Moon Guard . . . but only if you do the questioning here and now."

"That is agreed."

"Consider, in your work, that he may be telling the truth."

It was the closest Malfurion guessed Ravencrest would come to trying to preserve Illidan's twin from harm. First and foremost the bearded commander was protector of the realm. If that cost the life or mind of one night elf, then the sacrifice had to be made.

"The truth will be known," was all the sorcerer would answer. To the guards, he commanded, "Hold his head straight."

One of the armored figures positioned Malfurion for the Moon Guard. The robed figure reached up and touched the struggling prisoner's temples with his index fingers.

A shock ran through Malfurion and he was certain that he screamed. His thoughts swirled around, old memories rising to the surface unbidden. Yet, each one was swiftly thrust back down as what felt like a clawed hand dug into his mind, seeking ever deeper . . .

Struggle not! commanded a harsh voice that had to be that of Latosius. *Release your secrets and it will go the better for you!*

Malfurion wanted to, but did not know how. He thought of what he had already told the gathering and tried to project that forward. Of Azshara's possible duplicity, Malfurion still resisted revealing. It would lessen his chances of ever being believed if that suspicion leaked free—

Then, just as suddenly as the intrusive probe had burrowed into his thoughts . . . it ceased. It did not withdraw, did not gradually fade away. It simply ceased.

Malfurion's legs buckled. He would have fallen if not for the guards holding him.

Gradually he became aware of shouts, some in disbelief, others in consternation. One of the voices most strident sounded like that of the elder Moon Guard.

"It's outrageous!" someone else cried out. "Surely not the queen!"

"Never!"

He had let slip his ultimate fear. Malfurion cursed his feeble mind. Barely had the questioning begun and he had already failed himself, failed Cenarius's teaching . . .

" 'Tis the Highborne! It has to be! This is Xavius's doing!" another voice insisted

"He has committed evil against his own kind!" agreed the First.

What were they talking about? Although Malfurion's head refused to clear, he still felt certain that something was not right about the shouted conversation. The speakers were too excited, reacting too adamantly to his beliefs. He was only one night elf and not even of high rank. Why would his vague suspicions throw them into growing panic?

"Let me see to him," a voice said. Malfurion felt the guards hand him over to a single person, who lowered him gently to the floor.

Hands touched the sides of his face, lifting it up. Through bleary eyes, Malfurion met the gaze of his brother.

"Why didn't you give in immediately?" Illidan muttered. "Two hours! Do you still have a mind left?"

"Two—hours?"

Noting the response, Illidan breathed easier. "Praise Elune! After you spouted that nonsense about the queen, that old fool was determined to rip everything out of your head regardless of the cost! If not for his spell failing suddenly, he probably would have left you an empty husk! They haven't forgiven the loss of their brethren and blame you for it!"

"H-his spell failed?" That hardly made sense. Malfurion's interrogator had been a most senior sorcerer.

"*All* of their spells have failed!" Illidan persisted. "After he lost control of the first, he tried another and when that didn't work, his companion attempted a third . . . with no success!"

Malfurion still did not understand. What his twin hinted at sounded as if both of the Moon Guard had lost their powers. "They can't cast?"

"No . . . and my own powers feel muted . . ." He leaned next to Malfurion's ear. "I think I have some control . . . but barely. It's as if we've been cut off from the Well!"

The commotion continued to grow. He heard Lord Ravencrest demand if the Moon Guard still maintained contact with their brethren, to which one of the sorcerers admitted that the ever-present link had been severed. The noble then asked of his own followers if any still retained their own skills, however slight.

No one answered in the affirmative.

"It's begun . . ." Malfurion whispered without thinking.

"Hmm?" His twin frowned. "What's that? What has?"

He looked past Illidan, recalling the violent forces carelessly summoned by those in the tower. He saw again the lack of regard for what such spellwork might do to those beyond the palace walls.

"I don't know . . ." Malfurion finally told his brother. "I wish by the Mother Moon I did . . . but I just don't." Beyond Illidan he saw the concerned countenances of Brox and Rhonin. Whether or not they understood as he did, both looked as if they shared his growing fear. "I only know that, whatever it may be . . . it's *begun.*"

All over the realm of the night elves, all over the continent of Kalimdor, thousands of others sensed the loss. The Well had been cut off from them. The power that they had so blithely wielded . . . was all but gone. A sense of alarm swiftly grew, for it was as if someone had reached up and just stolen the moon.

Those living nearest to the palace naturally turned to their queen, calling upon Azshara for guidance. They waited before the bolted gates, gathering in greater and greater numbers. Above, the sentries watched blank-faced, neither moving to open the gates nor calling down to calm the growing crowd.

Only after more than half the night had passed and most of the city had emptied out into the areas before the palace did the gates finally open. The people poured forward, relieved. They were certain that Azshara had finally come out in response to their pleas.

But what emerged from within the palace walls was not the queen, nor was it anything ever imagined in the night elf world.

And so fell the first victims of the Burning Legion.

NINETEEN

A wave of vertigo struck Krasus, the attack so unexpected that it nearly cost him his life. Only moments before, he had felt much his old self, that due in great part to his immediate proximity to Korialstrasz. The dragon now carried him swiftly toward the general direction of Cenarius's glade, although not near enough that the demigod might notice. A determination to find this one night elf Nozdormu had revealed to him had further fueled the mage—and that was why the sudden vertigo had caught him so off guard that he had nearly fallen from the dragon's neck.

Korialstrasz adjusted for him at the last moment, but Krasus's younger self also seemed oddly disoriented.

"Do you fare better?" the dragon roared to him.

"I am . . . recouping." Krasus peered into the night sky, trying to make sense of what had just happened. He searched his ragged memories, finally coming up with a possible answer. "My friend, do you know of the night elves' capital city?"

"Zin-Azshari? I am vaguely familiar with it."

"Veer toward there."

"But your quest—"

Krasus was adamant. "Do it now. I believe it is of the utmost importance that we go there."

His younger self grumbled something, but arced toward the direction of Zin-Azshari. Leaning forward, Krasus peered ahead, awaiting the first signs of the legendary city. If memory served him—and he could not be certain that it did—Zin-Azshari had been the culmination of the night elf civilization, a grand, sprawling metropolis the likes of which would never be seen again. However, the opulence of the ancient city was not what interested him. What concerned Krasus was his recollection of Zin-Azshari's nearness to the fabled Well of Eternity.

And it was the Well that now drew him. Although the origins of the Burning Legion's first entrance into the world was lost to him, Krasus still retained a sharp enough mind to make some fairly accurate assumptions. In this time period, the Well *was* power, and power was not only what the demons sought, but also what enabled them to reach the very realms that they destroyed.

Where more likely to find the portal through which the Burning Legion would *have* to arrive than in the immediate proximity of the greatest fount of sorcerous energy ever known?

They soared across the night sky, Korialstrasz flying mile after mile in the space of only minutes. Even still, hours passed, precious hours that Krasus suspected the world could not afford.

At last, the dragon called, "We will soon be in sight of Zin-Azshari! What do you hope to see?"

It was more what he hoped not to see, but Krasus could not explain that to his companion. "I do not know."

Ahead appeared lights, countless lights. He frowned. Of course the night elves would have illumination for some of their activities, but there seemed too many for a realm of nocturnal beings. Even a city as great in size as Zin-Azshari would not be so bright.

But as the duo neared, they saw that the illumination came not from torchlight or crystals—but from raging fires coursing throughout the night elven capital.

"The city is ablaze!" roared Korialstrasz. "What could have started such an inferno?"

"We need to descend," was all Krasus replied.

The red dragon dipped, dropping hundreds of feet. Now details became visible. Elaborate, colorful buildings burned, some of them already collapsing. Sculptured gardens and massive tree homes had become pyres.

And scattered throughout the streets lay the bodies of the dead.

They had been brutally slaughtered, with no compassion given for the elderly, the infirm, or the young. Many had died in clusters while others had clearly been hunted down one by one. In addition to the populace of Zin-Azshari, a variety of animals, especially the great night sabers, lay dead as well, their demises no less foul.

"There has been war here!" snarled the winged leviathan. "No—not war! This is genocide!"

"This is the work of the Burning Legion," Krasus muttered to himself.

Korialstrasz veered toward the city center. Curiously, the damage lessened as they neared what looked to be the palace. In fact, certain walled sections of the center appeared completely untouched.

"What do you know of these sections?" Krasus asked his mount.

"Little, but I believe that those linked by walls to the queen's palace belong to what are referred to as the

'Highborne.' They are considered the most esteemed of the night elves, all somehow involved directly in service to her majesty, Azshara."

"Circle once around them."

Korialstrasz did. Studying the vicinity, Krasus had his suspicions verified. None of the quarter that housed the regal Highborne had been touched in the slightest by the monstrous disaster.

"There is movement to the northwest, Krasus!"

"Fly there! Quickly!"

He need not have encouraged his companion, for Korialstrasz clearly sought the answers as much as he. Not at all surprising, considering that they were one and the same.

Krasus now saw what the dragon's superior vision had already noted. A wave of movement, almost like locusts, pouring through the city. Korialstrasz descended further, enabling the pair to identify individuals.

And for Krasus, it was the return of evil.

The Burning Legion marched relentlessly through Zin-Azshari, leaving nothing untouched in their wake. Buildings fell before their might. There were the tall, brutal Fel Guard with their maces and shields. Mindless Infernals battering their way through stone walls or any other physical opposition. Near them hovered huge, winged figures with blazing green swords, molten armor, and cloven feet . . . the Doomguard.

As the dragon moved toward the front of the horde, Krasus identified the houndlike felbeasts, ever the precursors of the Legion. They seemed especially active; not only were their noses raised high to smell the air, but the sinister tentacles with which they absorbed magic darted forward eagerly.

And then the mage saw what the Legion hunted.

Refugees swarmed from the city's center, families and individuals creating a desperate flow through the narrow avenues. At their rear, trying to keep the demons at bay, were a small contingent of armored soldiers and a few robed figures that Krasus believed to be the legendary Moon Guard.

Even as the two neared, one of the Moon Guard in the forefront attempted to cast a spell. But by placing himself in the open, he only served to add to the list of victims. One of the felbeasts leapt forward, landing just before the sorcerer. Its tentacles shot forth with astonishing speed.

They adhered to the spellcaster's chest, physically lifting him into the air. Before anyone—even Krasus and Korialstrasz—could come to his aid, the thrashing Moon Guard sorcerer was drained of his magical forces . . . leaving a dead, dry husk in his place.

The red dragon roared. Had he even wanted to, Krasus could not have stopped his younger self from taking reprisals. In truth, his own memories of such horror kept the mage quiet. Too many had perished because of the Legion and even though by Krasus's interference Korialstrasz had come here, the former no longer cared. He had tried to keep from wreaking any more havoc on the time line, but enough was enough.

It was time for retribution.

As Korialstrasz swept past the front ranks of the demonic host, he let loose with a great blast of flame. The stream of fire engulfed not only the felbeast that had slain the sorcerer, but many of the pack following. Whining, the few survivors retreated, some singed badly.

Korialstrasz did not pause. He turned now to face the main horde, a second wave of fire enveloping the foremost demons.

Most perished instantly. A few of the more hardy Fel Guard struggled through the flames, only to collapse shortly after from their fiery wounds. One blazing Infernal sought to bat out the dragonfire and, when that did not work, ran headlong into a building, possibly in some vague hope that doing so would smother the flames. Seconds later, it, too, collapsed.

Even the Burning Legion could not stand the pure might of a dragon, but that did not make them defenseless. Up from their ranks suddenly flew a score of Doomguard. Krasus noticed them first and, though well aware of the risk, cast a quick spell.

Winds buffeted the foremost demons, throwing them back into the rest. The Doomguard became entangled with one another.

Korialstrasz let loose another breath.

Five of the winged terrors plummeted to the ground, fiery missiles that further inflicted damage on the horde below.

The rest of the Doomguard regrouped. Others shot up into the sky, doubling the numbers.

Korialstrasz clearly desired to face them, but Krasus abruptly felt the telltale warning signs of weakness. As Alexstrasza had said, together the two were nearly complete—but not quite. The added use of their strength depleted both quicker than normal. Already the dragon flew more slowly, less smoothly, even if he did not recognize that fact.

"We must leave!" Krasus insisted.

"Abandon the fight? Never!"

"The refugees have made good their escape thanks to us!" The delay had been just enough for the night elves to scatter into the lands beyond. Krasus had every confidence that they could keep ahead of the Legion at this point. "We must get word to those who can do more! We must continue on our original path!"

It pained Krasus to speak so, for in his heart he would

have wanted to burn to ash every demon in sight, but even now, more and more flew up to deal with the lone dragon.

With a roar of frustration, Korialstrasz unleashed one final blast that destroyed three of the Doomguard and sent the others fluttering back. The red behemoth then turned and flew off, easily outpacing the Legion despite his growing exhaustion.

As they soared past the palace again, Krasus saw with horror that more demons poured from its gates. Most disconcerting, however, were the night elven sentries that still stood guard on the battlements, warriors who seemed to have no regard at all for the desperate straits in which their fellow citizens found themselves.

Krasus had seen such blatant disregard in the face of horror before. There had been those during the second war who had acted in the same horrifyingly indifferent manner. *They are mesmerized by the demons' growing influence! If the lords of the Legion have not set foot on the mortal plane already, it cannot be long at all before they do!*

And when that happened, he feared that there would be no future for the world . . . nor, in this case, even a past.

There were dreadful noises disturbing her relaxation. Azshara had ordered music played for her in the hopes that it would drown out the objectionable noises, but the lyres and flutes had failed miserably. Finally, she rose and, with her new bodyguards surrounding her, gracefully wended her way through the palace.

It was not Lord Xavius but rather Captain Varo'then whom first she met. The captain fell down on one knee and clasped a fist against his heart.

"Your wondrous majesty . . ."

"My darling captain, what is the cause of such awful clamor?"

The scarred night elf looked up at her with a veiled expression. "Perhaps it'd be easier to show it to you."

"Very well."

He led her to a balcony overlooking the main area of the city. Azshara rarely came to this balcony save for public displays, much preferring the view of her extravagant gardens from her chambers or the glimpses of the Well of Eternity that her visits to the tower offered her.

But the sight before the queen was not the one to which she had grown so accustomed. Azshara's golden eyes drank in the images of her city, the ruined structures, the endless fires, and the bodies littering the streets. She glanced to her right, where the walled quarter of the Highborne still stood peacefully.

"Explain this to me, Captain Varo'then."

"It's been told to me by the counselor that these have proven unworthy. To fully prepare for a world of perfection, all the imperfect must be swept away."

"And those below were considered lacking in the judgment of Lord Xavius?"

"With the recommendation of the great one's most trusted servant, the celestial commander, Mannoroth."

Azshara had briefly met the imposing Mannoroth and, as with her counselor, she had been overwhelmed by the great one's high servant.

The queen nodded. "If Mannoroth says it must be so, it must be so. Sacrifices are always required in the name of glorious pursuits, I always think."

Varo'then bowed his head. "Your wisdom is boundless."

The queen accepted his compliment with the regal aplomb with which she took the *many* compliments she received on a daily basis. Still gazing at the carnage below, Azshara asked, "Will it be long, then? Will the great one soon come, too?"

"He will, my queen . . . and it's said that Mannoroth has called him *Sargeras.*"

"Sargeras . . ." Queen Azshara tasted the name, ran it across her lips. "Sargeras . . . truly a fit name for a god!" She put a hand to her breast. "I trust I will be given advance warning when he makes his entrance. I would be deeply disappointed if I could not be there to greet him myself."

"I shall see to it personally that all is done to give you fair warning," Varo'then said, then bowed. "Forgive me, my queen, duty demands my attention now."

She waved a negligent hand, still fascinated by both the scene below and the true name of the god. The captain left her alone with her bodyguards.

In her mind, Azshara began picturing the world that would replace what had been decimated. A more magnificent city, a true monument to her glory. It would no longer be called Zin-Azshari, as gracious as the people had been to name it that. No, next time it would simply be called *Azshara.* How much more appropriate a title that was for the home of the queen. *Azshara.* She said it twice, admiring the way it sounded. She should have requested the change long ago, but that did not matter now.

Then another, more intriguing thought entered her mind. True, she was the most perfect of her race, the icon of her people, but there was one who was even more glorious, more magnificent . . . and soon he would come.

His name was Sargeras.

"Sargeras . . ." she whispered. "Sargeras the god . . ." An almost childlike smile crossed her face. ". . . and his consort, Azshara . . ."

* * *

Messengers arrived at Black Rook Hold at the rate of one every few minutes. All demanded to see the master of the hold immediately, for each had news of import.

And every missive to Lord Ravencrest boiled down to the same dire news.

Sorcery had been all but stolen from the night elves. Even the most skilled could do little. In addition, other spells that constantly relied on drawing from the Well to keep them maintained had failed, in one or two places with catastrophic results. Everywhere, panic ensued and it was all officials could do to keep chaos from erupting.

From the most important place itself, from those regions near Zin-Azshari . . . there had been no word.

Until now.

The messenger brought in by the sentries could barely stand. His armor had been in part ripped from his body and bloody scars covered his flesh. He staggered before Lord Ravencrest, falling to one knee.

"Has he been given food and water?" the noble asked. When no one could answer, he growled out an order to one of the soldiers standing near the entrance. Within seconds, sustenance was brought for the newcomer.

Among those waiting impatiently were Rhonin and the others. They had gone from being prisoners to some undefinable status. Not allies, but not outsiders. The wizard had chosen to remain silent and in the back of the throng, the better to ensure that his status did not slip back to prisoner.

"Can you speak now?" Ravencrest rumbled to the messenger once the latter had eaten some fruit and drunken almost half a sack of water.

"Aye . . . forgive me, my lord . . . for not being able to do so earlier."

"Judging by your condition, I find it hard to believe you actually even made it here . . ."

The night elf kneeling before him looked around at the others assembled. Rhonin noted how hollow his eyes had become. "I find it hard to believe I'm here myself . . . my lord." He coughed several times. "My lord . . . I come to tell you . . . that I believe it . . . it is the end of our world."

The flat tone with which he said the last only served to add to its horrific impact. Dead silence filled the chamber. Rhonin recalled what Malfurion had said before. *It's begun.* Even Malfurion had not understood what he meant, only that he knew that something terrible was taking place.

"What do you mean?" persisted Ravencrest, leaning close. "Did you receive some terrible message from Zin-Azshari? Did they bid you to relay this monstrous announcement?"

"My lord . . . I come *from* Zin-Azshari."

"Impossible!" interjected Latosius. "By the best physical means it would take three to five nights and sorcery is not available—"

"I *know* what was available better than you!" snapped the soldier, disregarding the Moon Guard's high rank. To Lord Ravencrest, he said, "I was sent to plead for help! Those who *could* funneled what little power they could gather to send me here! They may be dead . . ." He swallowed. "I may be the only one to survive . . ."

"The city, lad! What of the city?"

"My lord . . . Zin-Azshari is in ruins, overrun by bloodthirsty fiends, creatures out of nightmare!"

The story flowed from the messenger like a wound beyond sealing. Like all other night elves, those of the capital had been stunned by the abrupt and inexplicable loss of nearly all their power. Many had gone to the palace to seek reassurances. The crowds had swelled to hundreds.

And then from the palace had poured out an endless multitude of monstrous warriors, some horned, some winged, all armed and eager to slaughter those in their midst. In seconds, people had died by the scores, no quarter given. Fear followed and others were trampled by those who sought to escape.

"We ran, my lord, all of us. I can only speak for those who fled in my direction, but even the most hardened warriors did not long stand."

But the demonic horde followed, catching those who could not keep up the pace. Scattered groups managed to flee out of the city, but even there the fiends hunted them.

No one interrupted his tale. No one argued that he suffered delusions. They all read the truth in his eyes and voice.

The messenger then described how he came to be here. A group of Moon Guard and officers had put their heads together, trying to come up with some defense or course of action. It had been determined that Black Rook Hold had to be informed and by lot that duty had fallen to the soldier present.

"They warned that the spell might not work as planned, that I could instead be sent to the bottom of the Well or even back to the c-city . . ." He shrugged. "I saw little choice . . ."

With tremendous strain, the spellcasters had begun their work. He had stood in the middle as they gathered up what little energy they could. The world had begun to fade around him—

And just as he had vanished, he had seen the monstrous hounds leaping upon the party.

"I landed some distance north of here, my lord, battered but alive. It took some time to reach an outpost where I could obtain a night saber . . . and then I headed to y-you as best I could."

A much subdued Ravencrest slumped back. "And the palace? The palace, too, is in ruins? All slaughtered there?"

The messenger hesitated, then said, "My lord, there were sentries atop the walls. They watched the people before the gates opened . . . and then they watched the monsters come out and butcher all of us!"

"The queen would never allow that!" spouted one of the noble's officers. Others nodded agreement, but many kept their opinions hidden.

Their commander had his own notion as to what such news meant. His expression already grim, he muttered, "It's as we believed, then. This must be the work of the Highborne."

"Surely even they would not be so insane!" Latosius argued. "True, their sorcerers think themselves superior even to the Moon Guard, but they are night elves just like us!"

"So we would believe, but their arrogance knows no bounds!" Ravencrest slammed his fist on the arm of his stone chair. "And let us not forget that the Highborne obey the dictates of the lord counselor . . . Xavius!"

Rhonin had heard the name mentioned prior, but now the venom with which it was repeated stunned him. He leaned by Malfurion, asking, "Who is this Xavius?"

Malfurion had much recovered, thanks in great part to his twin's aid. With some slight help from Brox, he now stood next to the others. "He who whispers in the queen's ear. Her most trusted advisor and a rival of Lord Ravencrest. I don't doubt myself that Xavius is involved, but he couldn't do this without Azshara's compliance! Even the Highborne worship her!"

"They'll never believe that," Illidan remarked. "Forget that for now! Let them think it's the counselor! Their choices will still be the same in the end!"

Although he did not exactly trust Illidan, Rhonin had to agree with the other night elf in this regard.

And it seemed that the choice of villains had already been made. Ravencrest stood, shouting to the others in attendance. His officers jammed their helmets on as if ready to go and ride out toward the capital immediately.

"All Moon Guard, all spellcasters of any reasonable ability, should be gathered as quickly as possible! Garo'thal! Send out messengers to every military post and commander! Resistance must be organized! This foul situation must be contained!"

Latosius confronted the noble. "Something must be done to regain the use of the Well! Force of arms alone will not stand against those monsters! You heard the messenger!"

The bearded noble thrust his face into that of the Moon Guard. "I hope to have some sorcery at hand, especially from your vaunted order, but, otherwise, force of arms is all we really have at the moment, isn't it?"

Illidan suddenly abandoned his brother and the rest. "My lord, I feel I may be of some aid! I still have some ability for casting spells!"

"Splendid! We'll need it! Zin-Azshari must be avenged, and the queen freed from the Highborne!"

Rhonin could not stand still. He had seen what the Burning Legion could do and, even though this was all in his past, he could not stand by as Krasus hoped. Within him he still sensed the ability to summon magic, use it as he willed. "My Lord Ravencrest!"

The noble looked him over, clearly not yet certain what to make of him. "What do you want?"

"You need someone who can cast spells. I offer myself."

Ravencrest looked doubtful.

In response, the wizard summoned a ball of blue light

over his left palm. It took him more effort than usual, but not enough that he showed that effort.

The commander's expression of doubt melted away. "Aye, you're welcome to our ranks—" Out of the corner of his eye, he must have noticed Latosius about to object. "Especially since little else has been offered to us."

"If whatever spell cuts us off from the Well's strength can be but removed—"

"Which would require sorcery of some magnitude in the first place . . . and if you could do that, Moon Guard, we wouldn't have a problem at all!"

As he listened to them argue, Malfurion's heart sank deeper. Such bickering served no good cause. Action was what was called for, but with little in the way of any sort of magic to back up Lord Ravencrest's intended military force, the future looked dark, indeed. If only—

His eyes widened. Perhaps he could do something.

As his brother and Rhonin had done before him, Malfurion stepped up to the noble. Ravencrest eyed him with some disbelief.

"And now you? You plan to offer sorcery such as Illidan here claims to still wield? I would welcome it if you have it, regardless of your past crimes."

"I offer not sorcery, Lord Ravencrest, but a magic of a different sort. I offer what has been taught to me by my shan'do, Cenarius."

Latosius laughed mockingly. "This is the worst jest yet! The teachings of a mythical demigod?"

But Ravencrest did not dismiss Malfurion out of hand. "You truly believe you can be of some aid?"

The younger night elf hesitated, then said, "Yes, but not from here. I need to go somewhere . . . quieter."

The noble's brow furrowed. "Quieter?"

Malfurion nodded. "I must go to the temple of Elune."

"The temple of the Mother Moon? I hadn't even thought of them. Their support is definitely needed in this time of crisis—but what do you hope to achieve there?"

Trying to keep his uncertainty hidden, Malfurion Stormrage answered, "The removal of the spell that keeps the Well of Eternity's power from our sorcerers, of course."

TWENTY

All was well in the world . . . for Lord Xavius, anyway. His dreams, his goals, were well within reach. Better yet, the great one was quite pleased with him. The shield spell that he and Mannoroth had set into motion had not only succeeded in sealing the Well's might from all but the Highborne, it had also enabled them to widen and solidify the portal. In the space of only a few scant hours, hundreds of the celestial host had poured through.

Mannoroth had immediately taken control of them, sending them out to purge the unfit. Once, Xavius might have found that idea horrific, but he now fully embraced the ways and methods of Sargeras. The god knew best how to achieve the perfect paradise the counselor sought. Had not the quarter reserved for the homes of the Highborne been completely spared? From those who served the palace would arise the new Golden Age of the night elf race, an era eclipsing any existing prior to it.

Lord Xavius had been granted the further honor of monitoring the work that made all this possible. He kept in delicate balance the spell that constantly regenerated the shield. The labor required had been more than even Mannoroth had planned and if the spell failed now, it would be near impossible to repeat without effectively sealing the portal first and using the combined might of all the Highborne sorcerers.

But Xavius had no intention of letting any disaster befall the precious shield. Not that he expected any trouble. What could happen here in the heart of the palace?

A brooding figure stalked into the chamber, peering around impatiently.

"Where isss Mannoroth?" hissed the Houndmaster.

"He commands the host, of course," responded the night elf. "He goes to clear Zin-Azshari of the unfit."

Something in Hakkar's expression momentarily disturbed Xavius. Almost it seemed that the counselor had said something that the Houndmaster found amusing. What that could be, though, the night elf could not possibly say.

Through the portal materialized four more of the Fel Guard. One of the even more menacing Doomguard stood nearby. He barked something in an unknown tongue to the newcomers, who immediately marched out of the chamber.

The celestial host moved with remarkable military precision, instantly obedient to orders and constantly aware of their duties. Even Captain Varo'then's elite Guard paled in comparison, at least in Lord Xavius's mind.

"How fare preparations for the hunt?" the counselor asked Hakkar.

The hint of mockery left the hulking figure's expression. "It goesss well, lord night elf. My houndsss and the Fel Guard who run with them have their explicit ordersss. Thossse that Mannoroth desssiresss captured will be."

He turned and stalked out of the room, leaving in his wake an oddly satisfied Lord Xavius. While he much respected the status of the Houndmaster, the night elf now saw himself closer in rank to the great one's commander.

The counselor looked once again at the spell of which he

had been an integral part. Only a few yards from the portal, the cluster of blue, flashing nodules over the diagram Mannoroth had drawn were the only physical signs of the shield spell. With his magical eyes, however, Xavius could make out other swirling patterns in orange, yellow, green, and more. A powerful cornucopia of magical forces of which he was now in control.

Just as he was now in control of the destiny of not only his own people . . . but the rest of the world as well.

The temple of Elune did not need to be warned of the catastrophe that had befallen the realm of the night elves. They had not personally been touched by the Well's loss, but they could still sense the sudden emptiness. When throngs came to the various temples to ask for guidance, the priestesses throughout the realm conversed with one another through methods utilized since the Mother Moon had first touched the heart of her initial convert, discussing what could be done. They chose to invite the people in for mass prayer, let Elune give them comfort. They also searched with their skills in the direction of the Well . . . but like the Moon Guard, they could not divine just what had happened.

Yet, even though they still retained the gifts granted them by their goddess, that did not mean the priestesses were safe from the horror unleashed soon afterward. When the Legion overran the temples in the capital, even those as far away as Suramar felt the deaths of their sisters there, felt their agonies as the horde slaughtered them without mercy.

"Sister," one of the other priestesses called to Tyrande, who had been pouring water for the faithful. "There is one at the front entrance who requests to see you."

"Thank you, sister." Tyrande handed the jug to another priestess, then hurried off. She could only assume that Illidan had come to see her again. Tyrande dreaded speaking with him, unsure what she would say if he brought up a possible match between them.

Yet, it was not Illidan, but rather another she had not thought to see for a very, very long time.

"Malfurion!" Without realizing what she did, Tyrande threw her arms around him, hugging Malfurion tightly.

His cheeks darkening, he whispered, "It's good to see you, Tyrande."

She released him. "How did you come to be here?" A sudden fear arose within her. "Broxigar? What have they done with—"

"He's with me." Malfurion pointed behind himself, where Tyrande saw that the orc waited in a dark corner near the entrance. The monstrous warrior looked quite uncomfortable as he eyed the many night elves.

She glanced around but saw no guards other than those of the temple. "Malfurion! What madness brings you here? Did the two of you sneak back into the city just to see me?"

"No . . . we were captured."

"But if—"

He gently put a finger to her lips, silencing her. "That story must wait. You know of the terror in Zin-Azshari?"

"Only some . . . and even that's too much! Malfurion, the *terror* we felt in the minds and souls of our sisters there! Something dreadful—"

"Listen to me! It spreads beyond the capital even as we speak. What's worse, now the Moon Guard are helpless against it! Some spell all but cuts off the Well's power from them!"

She nodded. "So we have surmised . . . but what does that have to do with your coming here?"

"Is the Chamber of the Moon in use now?"

She thought. "It was earlier, but so many have come for guidance that the high priestess had the main worship chamber opened instead. The Chamber of the Moon may be empty now."

"Good. We need to go there." He signaled Brox, who hurried over. To Tyrande's astonishment, the orc even carried an ax.

"You were captured . . ." she reminded Malfurion.

"Lord Ravencrest saw no more reason to detain us, providing Brox stayed with me."

"I owe you both," reminded the broad-shouldered warrior. "I owe my life."

"You owe us nothing," Illidan's brother returned. To Tyrande he said, "Please take us to the chamber."

With her in the lead, they headed into the temple. Despite Brox's attempt to stay as close to his companions as possible, he could not hide his appearance from those night elves gathered inside. Many looked in horror at him and some even screamed, pointing at the orc as if he was the one responsible for their turmoil.

Guards caught up to them just as they neared the Chamber of the Moon. The foremost was the one who had spoken with Tyrande about Illidan.

"Sister . . . it is the custom to allow any entry into the Mother Moon's temple, but that creature—"

"Elune says that he does not have the same right as any other believer?"

The sentries looked uncertainly at one another, the first finally replying, "It does not say exactly anything about other races in that regard, but—"

"But are not all the children of Elune? Does he not have the right to come to her for guidance, make use of all facets of the temple?"

There was no answer to this. Finally, the lead guard waved them by. "Just please keep him from sight as much as possible. There is already enough panic out there."

Tyrande nodded gratefully. "I understand."

As they entered, they found only two other acolytes in attendance. Tyrande immediately walked up to the pair and explained the need for privacy, pointing specifically at Brox. In truth, the orc's presence was all that was needed to encourage the other sisters to quickly retreat.

Returning to Malfurion, she asked, "What do you hope to do?"

"I intend to walk the Emerald Dream again, Tyrande."

She did not like the sound of that at all. "You plan to journey to Zin-Azshari!"

"Yes. There I hope to learn the truth about what has been done to the Well."

Tyrande knew him better. "You don't hope to simply learn the truth, Malfurion; I think you intend to *do* something about it . . ."

Instead of replying, he studied the center of the chamber. "That seems the most tranquil location."

"Malfurion—"

"I've got to hurry, Tyrande. Forgive me."

With Brox in tow, he walked to the place he had chosen, then seated himself on the ground. Legs folded in, Malfurion looked up into the moonlit sky.

The orc seated himself across from the night elf, but made room when Tyrande joined. Malfurion glanced questioningly at her. "You needn't stay."

"If in any way the Mother Moon can help me guide you, protect you from harm, I intend to do so."

Malfurion gave her a grateful smile, then grew grim again. "I must begin now."

For reasons beyond her, Tyrande suddenly seized his hand. He did not look at her, his eyes now shut, but briefly the smile returned.

And suddenly Tyrande felt him leaving her.

It had been a quickly devised, desperate plan, one from which Malfurion understood Lord Ravencrest actually expected little result. Yet, with the Moon Guard virtually powerless, he had seen no reason why the upstart young night elf could not at least try.

Now Malfurion only had to hope that he had not made empty promises.

Tyrande's hand on his own proved invaluable to wending his way into the sleeplike trance. Her touch had comforted Malfurion, eased the incredible tension the horrific events of the past few days had created.

Soothed, he reached out to the world around him, to the trees, river, stones, and more as he had with Cenarius.

Yet, this time he was met not by the tranquil elements of nature—but rather *turmoil*.

The world was no longer in balance. The forest knew it, the hills knew it, even the heavens felt the wrongness. Everywhere he focused, Malfurion sensed only disharmony. It struck with such force that for a moment the night elf nearly drowned in it.

Instead, he fixed again on Tyrande's light touch, drawing peaceful strength from her nearby presence. The discord faded, still there but unable to overwhelm him.

Once more steady, Malfurion reached out to the spirits of nature, touching each and letting them feel his own calm. He understood their turmoil and promised that he would act in their name. The night elf asked in turn that they be there if he needed their assistance, reminding the spirits that both he and they desired a return to the balance.

The sense of discord dwindled more. It would not go away so long as the Highborne meddled with the Well, but Malfurion had at least created some semblance of harmony again.

And with that done, he was able once again to enter the dreamscape safely.

Free from earthly confinement, he paused to gaze down at his friends, especially Tyrande. It was easier this time to summon the images, transpose the reality over the idyllic landscape. Both Brox and Tyrande immediately materialized . . . as did his own body, of course.

To his surprise, he noted a tear drifting down one of Tyrande's cheeks. Instinctively, Malfurion reached to wipe it away, only to have his finger pass through it. Yet, as if feeling his nearness, the young priestess reached up with her free hand and not only wiped away the tear, but also touched the area.

Forcing himself to turn away, Malfurion looked to the sky again. He focused on the direction of Zin-Azshari, then stepped up.

The familiar greenish tint permeated everything. Malfurion concentrated, again overlapping the shadow world with elements of reality. With what seemed a combination of half walking, half flying, he drifted over the now-covered dreamscape, sensing the myriad aspects of both the true and subconscious worlds.

But as he journeyed, an unexpected presence caught his attention. At first he doubted his senses, but a quick search verified his first suspicions.

Shan'do? he called.

Malfurion felt his mentor touch his thoughts, but only in an indistinct manner. However, the touch was enough to convey that Cenarius was well. The last of the felbeasts had been dealt with, but some other matter urgently demanded the demigod's attention. Malfurion realized that the forest lord had felt the presence of his student in the Emerald Dream and had quickly reached out to let the night elf know that all was not yet lost.

Comforted by Cenarius's unspoken message, Malfurion moved on. The green haze thinned further and soon he saw the world below almost as he would had he been truly able to fly like a bird. Hills and rivers passed swiftly by as he focused more on his destination.

And as he neared the capital, for the first time Malfurion beheld the horror.

As terrifying as the messenger's descriptions had been, they had not fully conveyed the monstrous cataclysm that had befallen the fabled city. Much of Zin-Azshari had been razed to the ground as if a great boulder had rolled over it time and again. No building on the outskirts had been left standing. Fire ruled everywhere, but not simply the crimson flames with which Malfurion was familiar. The capital was also awash in foul green or pitch black fire clearly of an otherworldly nature. As Malfurion passed over them, he could feel their evil heat despite being in the dream realm.

Then he caught his first glimpse of the demons.

The felbeasts had been monstrous enough, but the creatures following them sent new chills through him, the more so because they were clearly intelligent. Despite the huge horns, devilish faces, and horrific forms, they moved in concert, with terrible purpose. This was not some mindless horde, but an army dedicated to evil.

And more and more poured out of the gates of the palace even as he approached.

He was not surprised to see that the vast, beautiful structure was not touched in the slightest. As the messenger had said, sentries still lined the walls. Malfurion passed near a few and saw in their eyes a terrible pleasure at the horrific panorama below. Their silver orbs were tinted with red and some looked as if they desired to join the demons.

Revulsed, Malfurion quickly pulled away from them. He looked to the side of the palace and noted that the homes of the Highborne had also been left whole. Some of the queen's servants even journeyed from one building to another as if nothing of consequence was taking place around them.

His revulsion growing, the night elf pushed on toward the tower. As before, Malfurion sensed the incredible forces being drawn up haphazardly from the dark Well. If anything, the Highborne had more than doubled their efforts. Savage storms raged over the Well, touching even within the embattled city.

Last time, he had tried to enter the tower at the point where he had sensed the spellwork. For this attempt, however, Malfurion dove lower, finding a balcony near the bottom. Moving much the way he would have if he had been entering by physical means, the night elf hovered just above the balcony, then moved through the open entrance there.

To his surprise, his attempt worked. He almost laughed. None had thought to protect this interior entrance from such as him. The hubris of the Highborne had enabled him to penetrate the palace with ease.

Slowly Malfurion floated along the corridor, seeking the path up. Near the rear, he found the main stairway—and with it, more than a dozen of the huge, horned warriors he had seen outside.

Malfurion's first instinct was to pull back in the hopes that they would not see him. Unfortunately, there was nowhere to hide. He braced for their attack . . . then cursed himself for his stupidity when the first of the demonic band lumbered past him.

They could not see his dream form. He breathed a sigh of relief, watching as the last vanished down the hall. When it became clear that no more followed, Malfurion steeled himself and ascended the stairway.

He passed several chambers on the way up but did not pause for any of them. What Malfurion sought lay at the very top of the looming tower and the sooner he reached it, the sooner he could devise some plan.

Just what he intended, the night elf did not know. Despite having turned to druidism, Malfurion was almost as adept at sorcery as his brother and even in his present condition he believed that he could cast some sort of spell.

Some distance up, Malfurion suddenly encountered a barrier. He reached out, feeling the air. An invisible force blocked his way, perhaps the same force that had prevented him from entering on his previous attempt. Perhaps the Highborne had not been so negligent after all.

Still determined, the night elf thrust himself forward with all his might. He felt the barrier squeeze against him, almost as if Malfurion attempted to walk through a true wall. Yet, the more he pushed, the more it seemed the wall softened some, almost as if about to—

Malfurion fell through.

His entrance was so abrupt that he floated there, unsure that he had actually succeeded. Turning, he tried to touch the barrier, but felt only a vague, very weak force. Either his presence had disrupted the barrier or it had been designed only to prevent intrusion, not departure.

A short distance up, he found himself confronting two

guards and a thick door that had to lead to where the Highborne worked. Once satisfied that the guards did not see him, Malfurion put a hand to the door, testing it.

His fingers slipped through the door as if it were nothing. Bracing himself, the young night elf entered.

His first sensation was one of absolute disorientation, for the chamber where the Highborne performed their foul work was far more massive than the outside implied. Malfurion's own home was dwarfed by the vast room.

And the Highborne needed all that space, for what they did not fill themselves swarmed with ranks of grotesque warriors, all heading toward the very door through which Malfurion had passed. Up close their monstrous faces shook him more. There was no compassion, no mercy . . .

Forcing away such thoughts, he drifted toward where the Highborne worked, watching their efforts with a combination of fascination and disgust. The Highborne appeared driven beyond sanity. Most had a hungry look to them. Their once-elaborate garments hung from their bony bodies and a few strained to stand, but all stared intently, eagerly, at the product of their toil, a fierce, pulsating gap in reality.

Malfurion started to gaze into the center of that gap, but suddenly had to look away. His brief study had been enough to let him sense the monstrous evil deep within. It amazed him that the Highborne could not see what it was with which they dealt.

Trying to forget the fear that had almost now gripped him, Malfurion turned—and came face-to-face with who could only be the queen's counselor, Lord Xavius.

Malfurion floated only inches from the elder night elf's unsettling eyes. He had heard of the advisor's artificial orbs, the magical eyes with which Xavius had purposely replaced his own. Streaks of ruby darted across the ebony lenses,

lenses almost as black as the dark force Malfurion had sensed in the magical gap.

The counselor stood there with such an intense expression on his harsh visage that at first the younger night elf thought that he had been seen, but that, of course, was only his own fanciful notion. After a moment, Xavius stepped forward, walking through Malfurion and heading to where the Highborne relentlessly continued their efforts.

It took Malfurion a moment more to recover from the unexpected encounter. Lord Xavius more than anyone else was the one the Moon Guard and Ravencrest had blamed for the horror outside. Seeing him now, Malfurion could believe it. He still felt that the queen also knew what happened, but that was a fact that could be verified later.

With determination, Malfurion headed toward what had to be the array that controlled the shield. Three Highborne sorcerers stood around it, but they seemed to be monitoring its actions, not actively shaping it. He drifted past them, moving up to study the details.

It was a masterfully crafted display, some of it on a level far beyond that which Malfurion himself could cast. Still, it did not take him long to see how he could affect it, even cancel it.

Of course, that assumed that Malfurion could do *anything* in his dream form.

To test the possibility, he whispered to the air, asking of it a simple jest. Even as the request left his lips, a breeze tousled ever so slightly the hairs on the back of one sorcerer's head.

His success thrilled Malfurion. If he could do this much, he could do enough to disrupt the shield spell. That would be all the Moon Guard would need.

He stared at the heart of the magical matrix, focusing on its weakest link—

"A foolish, foolish thing to attempt," commented a cold voice.

Malfurion instinctively glanced over his shoulder.

Lord Xavius stared back at him.

At him.

The counselor held up a narrow white crystal. His eyes—eyes with which he could evidently see even a dream form—flared.

A tremendous force sucked Malfurion toward the crystal. He tried to pull back, but his efforts went for naught. The crystal filled his view . . . then became his world.

From within the tiny, impossible prison, he looked out at the huge, mocking visage of the elder night elf.

"An interesting thought occurs to me," Lord Xavius commented almost clinically. "How long do you think it will take your body to die without your spirit within?" When Malfurion did not answer, the counselor simply shrugged. "We shall just have to see, shall we?"

And with that, he pocketed the crystal and plunged Malfurion into darkness.

They had reached the outskirts of the area where Krasus hoped to find the elf in question. He did not comprehend how he knew that the one he sought lived near here, but suspected that Nozdormu had left that information in the back of his mind during the vision. Krasus silently thanked the Aspect for considering the difficulty of such a search. It also gave him hope that soon this catastrophe would be corrected, and that he and Rhonin would return home.

That assumed, of course, that he could *find* Rhonin.

His guilt at not immediately hunting for his former pupil was only partially assuaged by the fact that the one he pursued now had been identified by one of the five elemental powers as essential to both the past and the future. The moment he located this mysterious night elf, the dragon mage intended to look for Rhonin, to whom he owed much more than the human knew.

Korialstrasz suddenly slowed, dipping down toward the trees in the process. "I can bring you no nearer."

"I understand." Any closer to the night elven settlement and the inhabitants would notice the leviathan.

The red dragon alighted, then lowered his head to the ground so that Krasus could dismount. That done, Korialstrasz inspected the vicinity.

"We are not far. No more than an hour or two."

Krasus did not mention how much of a struggle those two hours would be once he left the company of his younger self. "You have done more than I could ask."

"I do not intend to abandon you now." Korialstrasz replied, folding his wings together. "Despite the form you wear, you may have forgotten that our kind can shift shape. I will transform into something more akin to those among whom we must mingle."

The dragon's huge frame suddenly shimmered. Korialstrasz started to shrink and his form took on a more humanoid appearance.

But a second later, he reverted to his natural shape, his eyes momentarily glassy and his breath ragged.

"What is it?" Krasus eyed his younger self helplessly.

"I—I cannot transform! To even attempt it fills me with agony!"

The mage recalled his own reaction when he had first attempted to resume his dragon form after arriving in this time. It did not surprise him that Korialstrasz suffered a similar difficulty. "Do not try again. I will have to go on my own."

"Are you certain? I note that when we are together, we both suffer less from whatever maladies afflict us . . ."

A mixture of anxiety and pride touched Krasus. Trust the younger version of himself to see the truth. Did Korialstrasz know *why*, though?

If he did, the dragon did not say so. Instead, Korialstrasz added, "No . . . I know you must go on."

"Will you remain here?"

"So long as I can. It does not appear that the night elves journey much to this region and the trees are tall and will hide me well. If you need me, though, I will come at your call."

"I know you will," responded Krasus because he knew himself well.

The mage bid the dragon farewell and started the arduous journey toward the night elven settlement. However, just before he would have been out of sight of Korialstrasz, the latter called quietly to him.

"Do you think you can find the one for which you search?"

"I can only hope . . ." He did not add that if he failed, then *everyone* would suffer because of it.

Korialstrasz nodded.

The closer he journeyed to the city—and the farther he moved from the dragon—the more ill and weary Krasus felt. Yet, despite his growing infirmity, the lanky figure continued on. Somewhere in there was the night elf in question. What he would do when he found him, Krasus did not yet know. He only hoped that Nozdormu had perhaps left that information locked away in his subconscious, to be released only when needed.

If not, it would be up to Krasus's own judgment.

It seemed to take forever, but at last he noticed the first signs of civilization. The distant torches likely marked a surrounding wall or even an entrance to the city itself.

Now would come the most difficult part. Although in this form he somewhat resembled a night elf, they would still recognize him as other than that. Perhaps if he pulled his cowl over his head and leaned forward—

Krasus suddenly realized that he was no longer alone in the forest.

They came from all sides, night elves clad in much the same armor as those who had captured him prior. Weapons resembling lances and swords pointed menacingly at the intruder.

A young, serious officer dismounted from a night saber, then approached him. "I am Captain Jarod Shadowsong! You are a prisoner of the Guard of Suramar! Surrender and you will be treated fairly."

With no other option, Krasus held out his hands so that they could be bound. Yet, deep inside, he felt some satisfaction about his capture. Now he had his way into the city.

And once there, all he had to do was try to escape . . .

TWENTY-ONE

The night saber hissed as Rhonin tried to mount it. He held the reins tightly, hoping that the beast would understand he was supposed to be where he was.

"Are you settled?" Illidan asked him.

Malfurion's brother had become the wizard's unofficial warder, a task which Illidan seemed not to mind at all. He constantly watched Rhonin as if trying to learn from his every movement. Whenever the human did anything at all remotely magical, the night elf paid the utmost intention.

It had not taken Rhonin long to understand why. Of all those present, he represented the most potent source of magic available. For all their arrogance, the night elves apparently had limited understanding of the forces they wielded. True, Rhonin found it more difficult to draw the power for his spells, but not so much that he was helpless as most of them were. Only young Illidan came anywhere near having Rhonin's ability.

I can help him, the wizard decided. *If he wants to learn, I'll help him learn.* Whatever his personal opinion of Malfurion's twin, Rhonin saw in Illidan much potential.

He only hoped that some of that potential would be available by the time they confronted the Burning Legion.

* * *

They rode out of Suramar, heading at the swiftest pace the panthers could set for Zin-Azshari. Rhonin felt some trepidation at leaving, for now he put more distance between himself and Krasus. More and more the wizard was certain that he was destined never to return to his own future. He could only hope that, whatever time had in store for Vereesa and their children, it would be a life worthy of them.

That assumed, of course, that there would be any future at all.

Lord Ravencrest kept his force riding for the rest of the night and into the day. Only when it was clear that many of the animals could go no farther did he reluctantly call for a stop.

Their ranks had grown, others joining them along the way thanks to advance riders sent out. They now numbered more than a thousand strong, with more arriving constantly. Lord Ravencrest wanted as huge an army as possible before they encountered the enemy, a desire matched by Rhonin, who knew well the terrible might of the demons.

Having settled on his own course of action, the wizard finally approached Lord Ravencrest, offering whatever information he could recall of their potential foes. As a way of explanation, he indicated that the Burning Legion had once invaded his "far-away land," ravaging everything—the last, at least, certainly the truth. Rhonin also described to the noble the course of the terrible war and how much devastation had been caused before the defenders were able to beat the demons back.

While it was not clear how much Lord Ravencrest believed, he at least took Rhonin's descriptions of the demons to heart, ordering his soldiers to adjust their tactics as necessary based on what he saw as their weaknesses. Latosius and the Moon Guard looked askance at the prospect of confronting the felbeasts in particular, but Ravencrest assured them that a contingent of his finest would surround them at all times. He also made certain that the fighters in question would know to strike first at the tentacles if they could, removing further the danger to the spellcasters.

The night elven commander obviously recognized that Rhonin had left much out, but did not press the latter further because of the valuable knowledge already gleaned. He also rightly assumed that Rhonin held his own life in enough regard to do what he could to see that defeat was out of the question.

Despite the massive growth of their force, they never slowed. One night became two, then three. Casting a minor spell that enabled him to see in the dark as well as his companions, Rhonin quickly adjusted to the nocturnal activity. However, he remained well aware that the demons cared not in the least whether the sun or the moon shone down and impressed this upon the noble. The monstrous warriors of the Burning Legion would fight until they could fight no more. The defenders had to be ready to face them even during the day.

As the night elves neared Zin-Azshari, they noticed an eerie green light illuminating the area ahead, a light that seemed to emanate not from the murky heavens, but from the city itself.

"By Elune!" muttered one soldier.

"Steady," commanded Lord Ravencrest. He stretched up, peering ahead. "Something is coming . . . and fast."

Rhonin did not have to ask what. "It's them. They already knew we were coming and plan to meet us as quickly as possible. They never waste time. The Legion lives only to fight."

The commander nodded. "I would've preferred a chance to scout the area and make judgments on the enemy. But if they wish to fight immediately, then by all means, we shall not disappoint them. Sound the call!"

Horns blared and the lines of the night elves spread out,

moving into battle formation. Now an army of several thousand, the armored riders and foot soldiers were a tremendous sight to behold. Rhonin recalled the might of the Alliance and how it had similarly awed him the first time he had seen it prepare to battle the demon's allies, the Scourge.

He also recalled how the lines that day had been shattered by the monstrous fury of the invaders.

It won't happen again! He looked to Illidan, who seemed far less confident now that he faced reality.

"Don't lose yourself in fear," the wizard remarked, having seen where it could lead. "You have a gift, Illidan. I've taught you some on how better to draw power. The Well may be cut off from us, but its essence permeates the land, the sky, and everything else. If you know how to sense it, you can do anything you did before the shield appeared."

"I follow your wisdom, shan'do," returned the young night elf somberly.

Rhonin had heard the word before, especially when Malfurion had referred to his teacher, the demigod, Cenarius. He wondered where the forest lord was now. Such an elemental being was needed at a time like this.

Then the first horrific figures marched into sight and Rhonin's thoughts turned only to survival.

Survival . . . and Vereesa.

The Burning Legion had laid waste to everything up to this point and yet they hungered for more destruction, more mayhem. The felbeasts bayed and the demon troops behind them roared in pleasure and anticipation upon seeing the row upon row of figures before them. Here were more lambs to the slaughter, more blood to be spilled.

With a single horrific battle cry, they charged.

Lord Ravencrest nodded.

"Archers stand ready!" shouted an officer.

More than a thousand curved bows aimed skyward.

The noble held his hand high, watching. The demon horde drew nearer . . . nearer . . .

He dropped his hand.

Like a flight of screaming banshees, the rain of arrows flew toward the enemy. Even knowing that death fell toward them, the Burning Legion did not slow. All they saw were those who must die.

The shafts descended.

Demons they might be, but they were demons with flesh. The first rank fell almost to the warrior, some with so many arrows in them that they could not lie flat on the ground. Felbeasts collapsed everywhere. One or two Doomguard dropped from the sky.

But the Burning Legion trampled over their own as if not even seeing them. Felbeasts ignored their dead brethren, howling and slavering as they neared the night elves' lines.

"Damn!" muttered Ravencrest. "One more volley! Quickly!"

With smooth precision, the archers readied. The bearded noble lost no time in signaling them to fire.

Again death rained down upon the horde, but this time with far less effect. Now the Legion raised shields, formed better ranks.

"These are not mere beasts," uttered an officer near Rhonin. "They learn too fast!"

Lord Ravencrest ignored him. "All archers to the rear! Position and be ready to fire on the inner ranks! Lancers! Prepare to charge!"

"My lord!" Rhonin called. "May I?"

"At this point, wizard, anything you wish to do is granted! Just do it!"

Rhonin stared at the area before the front ranks of the on-coming demons. He concentrated, drawing in the power. It took more effort than usual, but not enough to keep him from success.

His eyes narrowed.

The ground erupted before the Burning Legion, an ex-plosion of dirt and rock that assaulted the monstrous war-riors like a line of heavy catapults. Many Fel Guard flew in the air while others were buried under tons of earth. A huge boulder landed atop one felbeast, cracking its spine in two like a twig. The rushing mass halted, many colliding.

The archers took advantage, sending another volley into the packed horde. Scores more fell, adding to the chaos.

Cheers rose among the soldiers. The Moon Guard, on the other hand, looked somewhat jealously at Rhonin. Latosius snarled at his fellow sorcerers, urging them to action.

The efforts of the night elven spellcasters proved to be far less spectacular than Rhonin's. Rings of energy that fell upon warriors of the Burning Legion often faded without any ef-fect. A handful of demons dropped, but even some of those recovered.

"They're useless!" Illidan snapped.

"They're trying," the wizard corrected.

Instead of arguing, the young night elf suddenly pointed at the horde, muttering.

Serpentine tentacles of black energy snaked around the throats of several dozen of those in the Legion's forefront. The demons dropped their weapons and shields and tried to tear the tentacles free, but before they could do that, the ten-tacles burned through their necks, going through flesh and bone with little trouble . . . and eventually decapitating every one of Illidan's targets.

It was all Rhonin could do to hide his distaste. Something

about the night elf's choice of attack did not sit well with him, but when Illidan looked for approval, the wizard still managed to nod. He could not discourage the only other person who had any ability. If they survived, Rhonin would teach Illidan other, better ways to deal with a foe.

And if they did not survive . . .

Once again, the Burning Legion surged on. Under their feet they crushed the corpses of their comrades. They roared as they approached, their maces and other horrific weapons held high and ready.

"We have to close with them now," Ravencrest decided. "You two stay in the back and continue doing whatever you can! You're our best weapons for now . . . possibly forever!"

Illidan bowed his head to the noble. "Thank you, my lord."

" 'Tis the truth, young one . . . the terrible truth."

With that, the night elven commander urged his mount ahead of them, joining his warriors. Lord Ravencrest drew his weapon, raising it high.

The lancers tensed. Behind them, the foot soldiers stood poised to follow. At the rear, the archers prepared for another shot.

Ravencrest slashed downward with his sword.

Horns blared. The archers fired.

The night elven force charged to meet the enemy, their night sabers snarling challenge to the demons.

Just as the lancers neared, the arrows struck. Distracted by the charge, those demons in front were whittled down by the bolts. Disarray momentarily took hold of the foremost line, exactly as Lord Ravencrest had intended.

The swiftness of the night sabers enabled the lances to drive in deep. Despite their immense size, several Fel Guard were thrust into the air as the night elves' spears penetrated not only the armor but everything within.

The sheer force of the charge actually pushed back the Burning Legion for a moment. Night sabers did more damage, biting and tearing at those packed tight before them. Foot soldiers joined in from behind, filling in gaps and thrusting at anything that was not one of them.

Their lances all but useless now, the riders drew their own weapons and did battle. Far back, the archers continued to unleash volleys at the ranks beyond the fighting.

Another row of riders, Lord Ravencrest among them, still waited. The noble's gaze flicked back and forth, studying each individual struggle, seeking the weak areas.

Rhonin and Illidan were not idle, either. The wizard cast a spell that solidified air above one section of the horde, literally dropping the sky on them. Illidan, in the meantime, repeated his serpentine spell, throttling and beheading several demons at a time.

The Moon Guard did what they could, their efforts slight but still of some aid. They could not, despite their best efforts, overcome the lack of direct contact with the Well of Eternity and it showed in their increasingly frustrated expressions.

Then, one of the night elven sorcerers screamed and pitched backward, his skin sloughing off like water. By the time he hit the ground, he was little more than a skeleton in a pool of what had once been his flesh. The other Moon Guard stared at the corpse in consternation, only Latosius's berating voice driving them back to their task.

Rhonin quickly surveyed the Legion, seeking the spell's source. It did not take him long to spot the culprit, a sinister figure further back in the lines. The spellcaster resembled one of the Fel Guard, but with a long, reptilian tail and far more ornate armor. It also wore a black and bloodred robe over the armor and the eyes that watched over the battlefield revealed an intelligence far superior to those on the front line.

He had never faced one himself, but the wizard recognized from descriptions an Eredar warlock. Not only were they the sorcerers of the Burning Legion, but they also acted as its officers and strategists.

But the warlock had made the mistake in assuming that the Moon Guard were the ones responsible for the most devastating spells. That gave Rhonin the opportunity he needed.

He watched the warlock cast again, but as the latter let loose with his dark spell, Rhonin usurped it, turned it back on its creator.

The demon gaped as his skin slipped free of his body. His fanged mouth stretched in an inhuman cry and his gaze turned toward the wizard.

It was the last act by the warlock. The demon's mouth continued to stretch, but only because nothing now held the jaw bone tight. For the briefest of moments, the fleshless figure stood there . . . then the skeletal remains collapsed in a pile that disappeared beneath the endless wave of Fel Guard.

With no one to command them, that part of the Legion grew disoriented. The night elves pressed forward. The front ranks of the demons buckled . . .

"We are defeating them!" one young officer near Ravencrest proclaimed.

But as quickly as the demons had wavered, they now moved forward again with even more determination. In the back came Doomguard who drove them forward with whips. More felbeasts struggled to get through the defenders and reach the sorcerers.

Night elves screamed as two Infernals barreled their way into the riders, tossing animals and soldiers alike. A hole opened up and demons poured through.

"Advance!" Ravencrest shouted to those with him. "Don't let them cut up the lines!"

He and the other riders charged the monstrous warriors who had broken through. Ravencrest himself slashed off the tentacles of a felbeast, then drove his blade into its head. A night saber fell upon one of the demon soldiers, ripping apart the latter with its claws and long fangs.

The gap dwindled . . . then vanished. The night elven lines reformed.

But although they now had a solid front again, the defenders were still pushed back. For all the armored horrors that the night elves had slain, it seemed twice as many came to reinforce the swarm.

Rhonin swore as he cast yet another spell that inflicted the Burning Legion with a series of deadly lightning bolt attacks. As magnified as his power still was, he knew he could have done even more with the Well open to him. More important, he and Illidan still provided the vast bulk of magical support for the night elves, but neither could be everywhere. Illidan, for all his eagerness to use whatever spell he could to slaughter the demons, was tiring quickly and Rhonin felt little better. With the Well's power free to their use, both could have cast fewer times yet with much more satisfactory results.

More screams arose as the night elves continued to be pushed back. Fel Guard smashed in heads, caved in armored chests. Their hellish hounds ripped apart foot soldiers. Doomguard leapt above the fray, then dove into the elven throngs, swinging away with their weapons. Infernals began popping up everywhere, raining down upon the defenders much the way the night elves' arrows had done to them earlier.

Another of the Moon Guard cried out, but this time because a felbeast had slipped through. Four soldiers managed to sever its tentacles, then thrust their blades through its chest, but by then it was too late for the sorcerer.

Another volley went up from the archers . . . and then immediately arced around and flew back at them. Although many had the good sense to run, several stood transfixed by the astonishing reversal.

Those died swiftly as their own bolts pierced their throats and their chests.

Rhonin searched, but could not see the Eredar warlocks responsible. He cursed again that he could not be in more than one place and that the actions he took were not what he had hoped.

We're losing! For all their dedication, against the demons the soldiers needed the Moon Guard . . . and the Moon Guard needed the Well. Back at Black Rook Hold, Malfurion had said that he hoped to deal with the shield the Highborne had placed, but that had been days ago. Rhonin could only assume that the young night elf's spell had failed . . . either that, or Malfurion had died in the attempt.

"The line's buckling again!" someone called.

Rhonin forgot all about Malfurion. There existed now only the battle . . . the battle and Vereesa. With what perhaps might have been a last silent farewell to her, he focused once more on the endless ranks of demons, trying to devise yet another devastating spell and already knowing that, by itself, it would not be nearly enough.

But was there anything *anyone* could do that would be enough?

"Shaman, has there been any change?"

Tyrande shook her head. "Nothing. The body breathes but the spirit is absent."

The orc frowned. "Will he die?"

"I don't know." Would it be better if he did? She had no idea. For more than three nights, Tyrande had watched over Malfurion's body, first in the Chamber of the Moon, then in an untenanted room further inside the temple. The senior priestesses had been quite sympathetic, but they had clearly believed that nothing could be done for her friend.

"He may sleep forever," one had told her. "Or the body may wither and die from lack of sustenance."

Tyrande had tried to feed Malfurion, but the body was limp, unresponsive. She dared not trickle water down his throat for fear that he would choke to death.

Last night, Brox had cautiously made the suggestion that perhaps, if they knew there was no hope, it would be better to quickly end Malfurion's suffering. He had even offered himself as the one to do it. As horrifying as it had been to hear, the novice priestess understood that the orc had offered what he would have given a good comrade. He cared for Malfurion.

They had no notion what had happened to his dream form. For all they knew, it floated around them, unable for some reason to enter the body. Tyrande doubted that, however, and suspected that something had happened to him when he had tried to destroy the shield spell. Perhaps his spirit had been eradicated in the attempt.

The thought of losing Malfurion stressed Tyrande more than she could have ever thought possible. Even Illidan's precarious mission did not bother her as much. True, she worried about the latter twin, too, but not quite in the same way that she did the one whose body lay before her.

Putting a hand to his cheek, the priestess of the moon thought not for the first time, *Malfurion . . . come back to me.*

But once again, he did not.

Thick, green fingers gently touched her arm. Tyrande looked into the worried eyes of the orc. He seemed not at all ugly to her at this moment, simply a fellow soul in this hour of grief.

"Shaman, you've not slept, not been out of this room. Not good. Step out. Breathe the night air."

"I can't leave him—"

He would not hear her protest. "What'll you do? Nothing. He lies there. He'll be safe. He'd want you to do this."

The others saw the orc as a barbaric creature, but more and more Tyrande realized that the brutish figure was simply a being who had been born into a more basic society. He understood the needs of a living being and understood the dangers of losing track of those needs.

She could not help Malfurion if she herself grew weak or ill. As difficult as it was for her, Tyrande had to step away.

"All right . . . but only for a few minutes."

Brox helped her to her feet. The young priestess discovered then that her legs were stiff and almost insufficient to keep her standing. Her companion had been correct; she needed to refresh herself if she hoped to go on for Malfurion.

With the orc beside her, Tyrande journeyed through the temple to the entrance. As before, the outer halls were filled with frightened and confused citizens, all trying to gain reassurance from the servants of the Mother Moon.

She feared that they would have to fight their way outside, but the crowds moved quickly to avoid Brox. He took their continual repulsion of him in stride, but Tyrande felt embarrassed. Elune had always preached respect of all creatures, but few night elves cared for other races.

The two stepped into the square. A cool breeze touched her, reminding Tyrande of times as a child. She had always loved the wind and, had it not looked unseemly, would have stretched out her arms and tried to embrace it as she had when little.

For several minutes, Tyrande and Brox simply stood there. Then, guilt once more caught hold of the priestess, for her childhood memories began to include times with Malfurion. She finally apologized to the orc and insisted that they return inside. Brox merely nodded his understanding and followed.

Yet, they had not quite reached the steps of the temple when one of the Suramar Guard called out to her. Tyrande hesitated, uncertain if the soldier sought to bother her because of Brox.

But the officer apparently had another mission in mind. "Sister, forgive me. I am Captain Jarod Shadowsong."

She knew his face if not his name. He was only slightly older than she and with somewhat round features for a night elf. His eyes were slanted slightly more than average, too, giving him a probing expression even when he tried to be friendly and courteous, such as now.

"You wish something of me, captain?"

"A bit of your time, if I might be so bold. I have a prisoner who has need of aid."

At first Tyrande wanted to decline, her urge to return to Malfurion foremost in her thoughts, but her duties took priority. How could she turn from some unfortunate in need of her healing skills? "Very well."

As the orc started to follow, Captain Shadowsong looked askance. "Is *that* coming with us?"

"Would you rather he stand out in the square by himself, especially during these troublesome times?"

The officer reluctantly shook his head, ending the matter. He turned and quickly led the pair on.

Suramar had only a small facility for prisoners, most of any import ending up in Black Rook Hold. The structure that Captain Shadowsong led them to had been created out of the base of a long dead tree. The roots formed the skeleton of the building and workers had created the rest from stone. There was no more solid a building than this save Lord Ravencrest's hold and the Suramar Guard were proud of that.

Tyrande eyed the rather bland building with some trepidation, imagining from its monotone exterior that it could only house the worst of villains. However, she steeled herself and did not reveal any misgivings as the captain bid her to enter.

The outer chamber was devoid of any furnishings save a simple wooden desk where the officer on duty no doubt worked. With most of the armed might of Suramar gone, the rest of Captain Shadowsong's comrades were no doubt out trying in vain to keep the peace.

"We found him in the woods the very evening Lord Ravencrest and the expeditionary force departed. Many of our detection spells have failed, sister, but some do contain their own power. One of those alerted us to the intruder. With some escapes in the recent past—" He looked momentarily at the orc. Captain Shadowsong clearly knew of Brox's present status, else he would have immediately tried to arrest him. "—we took no chances and immediately went to investigate."

"And how does that pertain to me?"

"The—prisoner—we found was quite weary. After deciding it was not a ruse, we brought him back. He grows no better since then. Because of his *peculiar* nature, I want him alive if and when Lord Ravencrest returns. That's why I finally came to you."

"Then, by all means, please lead the way."

There were only a dozen cells in the chamber behind, although the officer was willing to tell Tyrande that he had more down below. She nodded politely, now a bit curious as to what sort of being lay inside the one. After Brox, she almost expected it to be another orc, but Captain Shadowsong's reaction to Brox made that assumption inaccurate.

"Here he is."

The priestess had expected something huge and warlike, but the figure within was no taller than the average night elf. He was also thinner than most. Underneath the hood of his rather plain robes she noted a gaunt face very much akin to one of her own, but pale, almost ghostly, and with eyes less pronounced. Judging by the shape of his hood, his ears were also smaller.

"He looks like one of us . . . but not," she remarked.

"Like a *ghost* of one of us," the captain corrected.

But Brox moved forward, almost seeming hypnotized by the unsettling figure. "Elf?"

"Perhaps . . ." remarked the prisoner in a voice much more deep and commanding than his appearance let on. He seemed equally interested in Brox. "And what is an orc doing here?"

He knew what her companion *was*. Tyrande found that extremely interesting, especially with so many strange visitors of late.

Then the prisoner coughed badly and her concern took over. She insisted that Captain Shadowsong open the door for her.

As she neared the mat on which he lay, the young priestess could not help but look into that face again. There was more to it than appearance alone indicated. She sensed a depth of wisdom and experience that literally shook her to the core. Somehow, Tyrande recognized that here was a very, very ancient being whose condition had nothing to do with his age.

"You are gifted," he whispered. "I had hoped for that."

"Wh-what ails you?"

He gave her a fatherly smile. "Nothing even your abilities

can cure. I convinced the captain to find one such as you because time is running scarce."

"You never told me to do any such thing!" Jarod Shadowsong protested. "I went by my own choice."

"As you say . . ." but the prisoner's eyes said otherwise to Tyrande. He then looked again at Brox. "Now *you* are something I did not calculate on, and that worries me. You should not be here."

The orc grunted. "Other said so, too."

"Other? What other?"

"The one with flame for hair, the one who said . . ." Here Brox paused and, after a surreptitious glance at the Guard captain, murmured, "The one who spoke of this as past."

To Tyrande's astonishment, the prisoner sat up. Captain Shadowsong started forward, his weapon already drawn, but the priestess waved him back.

"You saw Rhonin?"

"You know him?" asked Tyrande.

"We came here together . . . I thought him trapped . . . elsewhere."

"In the glade of Cenarius," she added.

He actually laughed. "Either chance, fate, or Nozdormu moves this matter forward, praise be! Yes, that place . . . but how do you know of it?"

"I've been there . . . with friends of mine."

"Have you?" The gaunt face moved closer. "With friends?"

Tyrande was uncertain now what to make of him. He knew many things that most ordinary night elves did not, of that she was certain. "Before we go on . . . I would have a name from you."

"Forgive my manners! You may call me . . . Krasus."

Now Brox reacted. "Krasus! Rhonin spoke of you!" The

orc actually went down on one knee. "Elder . . . I am Broxigar . . . this is the shaman, Tyrande."

Krasus frowned. "Perhaps Rhonin spoke too much . . . and likely has inferred more."

Her companion's reaction settled one matter for the novice priestess. Rising she turned to the captain. "I would like to take him with me to the temple. I believe he could be better cared for there."

"Out of the question! If he escapes—"

"You have my promise that he will not. Besides, you yourself said that it was essential he be well. After all, if he must face Lord Ravencrest—"

The Guard officer frowned. Tyrande smiled at him.

"Very well . . . but I'll have to escort you there myself."

"Of course."

She turned to help Krasus rise, Brox coming from the prisoner's other side. As Tyrande held him close, she noticed Krasus hide a satisfied smile.

"Something pleases you?"

"For the first time since my inopportune arrival, yes. There is hope, after all."

He did not clarify and she did not ask him to do so. With their aid, he left the Guard headquarters. Tyrande realized that Krasus played no game in one regard; he was seriously weak. Even still, she sensed the authority within him.

With Jarod Shadowsong behind them, they returned to the temple. Once again, it took only the appearance of the orc to create a path for them.

Tyrande feared that the guards and senior priestesses would be another problem, but, like her, they seemed to innately sense Krasus's prominence. The elder priestesses actually bowed toward him, although she suspected that they did not quite understand why.

"Elune has chosen well," Krasus remarked as they neared the living quarters. "But then, I knew that when I saw you."

His comment made her face darken, but not because of any attraction. Rather, Tyrande felt as if she had been given a compliment by one at least as significant as the high priestess herself.

She intended to bring him to a separate chamber, but without thinking instead walked into the one where she had been keeping Malfurion. At the last moment, Tyrande tried to halt.

"Is there trouble?" asked Krasus.

"No . . . only that this room is being used for a stricken friend of mine—"

But before she could get any farther, the cowled figure struggled away from her, pushing toward Malfurion's prone form.

"Chance, fate, or Nozdormu, indeed!" he spat. "What ails him? Quickly!"

"I—" How to explain?

"He walked the Emerald Dream," Brox responded. "He's not come back, elder."

"Not come back . . . where did he seek to go?"

The orc told him. Tyrande had thought Krasus's face pale enough, but now it literally whitened. "Of all the places . . . but it makes bitter sense. If I had only known before I left there!"

"You were in Zin-Azshari?" Tyrande gasped.

"I was in what *remained* of the city, but I came here in search of your very friend." He studied the still body. "And if, as you say, he has been like this for the past few nights, I may be much, much too late . . . for *all* of us."

TWENTY-TWO

A night elf cried out, his breast plate and chest cut open by a demon blade. Another near him had no chance to utter a sound, a Fel Guard mace crushing in his skull. Everywhere, the defenders were dying and nothing Rhonin had done so far had been sufficient to alter that horrific fact. Despite Lord Ravencrest's determined figure at the forefront, the night elves were slowly being slaughtered. The Burning Legion gave them no respite, constantly pummeling the lines.

But even knowing he and the rest would die, the wizard fought on.

He had no other recourse.

The news of the defending army's arrival had taken Lord Xavius by some surprise, but it had not made him any less confident of the final outcome. He saw how many of the great one's celestial host flooded through the portal and felt certain that no army arrayed against them could possibly stand long. Soon, the unfit would be cleansed from his world.

Mannoroth led the Legion against the fools and Hakkar was on the hunt, leaving all in the counselor's skilled hands. He peered briefly in the direction of a small alcove near the entrance, wherein he had stored his most recent prize. After news arrived that the defending forces had been decimated,

Xavius would take the time to see to his "guest." At the moment, he had far more important things to do.

He returned his attention to the portal, where yet another group of Fel Guard had materialized. They received their instructions from the towering Doomguard left by Mannoroth, then marched to join their bloodthirsty brethren. The scene had repeated itself some dozen times in just the past few minutes, the only difference being that each successive batch of arrivals was larger in number than the last. Now they almost took up the entire chamber.

As the latest troop of Fel Guard passed, Lord Xavius heard Sargeras's glorious voice in his head. *The pace increases . . . I am pleased.*

The night elf knelt. "I am honored."

There is resistance already.

"Merely some of the unfit delaying the inevitable."

The portal must be protected . . . it must not only remain open, but be strengthened more. Soon . . . very soon . . . I will come through . . .

The counselor's heart leapt. The momentous event neared!

Rising, he said, "I shall see that everything is done to prepare the way for you! I swear it!"

He felt a wave of satisfaction . . . then Sargeras departed his thoughts.

Lord Xavius immediately turned to the array that kept the shield spell functioning. He had inspected it after the intruder's attempt to destroy it and found it intact, but one could never take chances.

Yes, it was still in perfect order. Thinking of his "guest," Xavius mulled over some of the things he would do when Sargeras finally stepped forth from the portal. Surely the queen would have to be there and, of course, an honor guard had to be arranged. Captain Varo'then would deal with the last matter. The counselor himself intended to be the first to greet the celestial one. As a proper gift, Xavius decided that he would hand over the crystal and its contents to Sargeras. After all, this was one of the three that Mannoroth had felt significant enough to send the Houndmaster after again. How foolish Hakkar would look when he came back to discover that the advisor had so easily captured one already.

Lord Xavius could hardly wait to present his prisoner to the great Sargeras. It would be especially interesting to see just what the god did with the young fool . . .

His nightmare continued.

Malfurion drifted within the crystal, staring out at what little he could see of the chamber. He had been placed in a small nook in the alcove, the crystal set on an angle. The alcove gave him a glimpse of the area near the doorway, which meant that the captive watched a constant stream of demonic warriors lumbering by, death clearly on their minds. That, in turn, twisted his heart further, for he knew that they went out to slay every night elf they could find . . . and all because Malfurion had failed to destroy the shield.

Although his surroundings did not give any indication of the passage of time, Malfurion felt certain that at least two nights had gone by since his capture. In his dream form, he did not sleep, and that made those two or more nights even longer.

How stupid he had been! Malfurion had heard the tales of Lord Xavius's eyes, how people said they could even see the shadows of shadows, but he had taken those for fanciful stories. Little had he suspected that the same lenses that enabled the counselor to observe the natural forces of sorcery also let him take note of a spirit in his sanctum. How Lord Xavius had laughed!

Malfurion had tested his crystalline cage several times early on and found it too strong. Perhaps with more teaching the young night elf might have discovered some flaw, but that hardly mattered now. He had *failed*. He had failed himself, his friends, his race . . . his world.

Now, nothing but Lord Ravencrest's defenders likely stood in the way of the demons.

He had to do *something*.

Steeling himself, Malfurion once again tried to use what Cenarius had taught him. The crystal was a part of nature. It was susceptible to his spells. He ran his hands over the edges, seeking a weakness in the matrix that held it together. It was not quite a druidic spell he utilized, but close.

But still he found nothing.

Malfurion screamed out of frustration. Thousands would die because of his failure. Illidan would perish. Brox would perish. Tyrande—

Tyrande would perish.

He could picture her face, visualize it better than any other. Malfurion imagined her concern for him. He knew that she likely sat near his body, trying to summon him back. The imprisoned night elf could almost hear her calling to him.

Malfurion . . .

The night elf shook. Surely, he had begun to lose his mind. It astounded Malfurion that the process had started so quickly, but then, his situation was a most terrible one.

Malfurion . . . can you hear me?

Again it felt as if Tyrande's voice echoed in his thoughts. He peered out of his prison, trying to see if perhaps Lord Xavius had begun some sort of mental torture, but of the counselor Malfurion could see no sign.

With some trepidation, he finally thought, *Tyrande?*

Malfurion! I'd scarcely hoped!

He could hardly believe it himself. True, she was a priestess of Elune, but still, such an act should have been beyond her. *Tyrande . . . how did you reach me?*

Thanks to another . . . he's been searching for you, he says.

The only ones that Malfurion could think of were Brox and Rhonin. Tyrande had met the orc, though, and while a courageous warrior, Brox lacked any magical skills. Could it be Rhonin? Even that made little sense, the wizard having supposedly ridden off with Lord Ravencrest.

Who? he finally asked. *Who?*

My name is Krasus.

The sudden switch unsettled Malfurion. The voice was like none he had ever felt, although in some ways it hinted of Cenarius's. Whoever this Krasus was, he was not simply some night elf, but much, much more.

Do you sense us still? asked the new voice.

I do . . . Krasus.

I have shown Tyrande how we can work through her bond to you to reach out to your dream self. The trick is difficult, but we hope to do it only long enough to free you.

Free me? Glancing again at his prison, Malfurion doubted that it would be possible.

A cunning trap, yes, Krasus went on, surprising the night elf. Apparently the link enabled them to see just where Lord Xavius had imprisoned him. *But I have dealt with its like before.*

Now Malfurion's spirits rose further. *What must be done?*

Now that we have moved your body—

You've done what? Moved his body? The risk to it—

I am quite familiar with the risks. When Malfurion protested no more, Krasus continued, *It was necessary to bring it . . . closer to one of our party. Now you must listen, for we must do this quickly.*

The night elf waited tensely. If they could release him from the crystal, he would do anything they said.

I must see the crystal, see every facet of its nature. You are a druid. This you can show me.

Acknowledging his understanding, Malfurion surveyed the entire interior of his magical cell. He looked at every corner, every facet, showing the crystal's strengths and its possible weaknesses. Nothing he saw gave him any encouragement, but he suspected that Krasus knew far better than he what to look for.

There! The disembodied voice made him pause before one edge. Malfurion had studied it earlier, noticing a slight fault to it, but had not been able to make any use of the spot.

It is the key to your escape. Touch it with your mind. See how the flaw works?

For the first time, he did. The fault was minute, but still distinct. How had he failed to see that earlier?

With experience comes wisdom, they say, Krasus suddenly replied. *However, I am still working to prove that adage.*

He ordered Malfurion to use the skills the forest lord had taught him to feel the entire width and breadth of the flaw, to understand its ultimate nature. To know it as well as he knew himself.

You should be able to note its most vulnerable place, its key, so to speak.

I don't— Yes! He did! Malfurion sensed the location. He pressed against it, eager to be free . . . but it would not give way.

You are strong, but not yet fully trained. Open your thoughts further to us. Let us in, no matter how many of us there are. We shall be your added strength and knowledge.

Clearing his mind as much as he could, Malfurion left himself open to Tyrande and the mysterious Krasus. He immediately felt the distinction between the two of them. Tyrande's thoughts were caring but firm, Krasus's wise but frustrated. Curiously, the frustration had nothing to do with Malfurion's situation.

Now . . . try again.

The imprisoned night elf pictured his dream form as a physical one. He literally pushed against the flaw as he would have any weak barrier. Surely, it would give if he pushed hard enough . . .

It suddenly felt as if the other two pushed with him. Malfurion could almost envision Tyrande and the other at his side, straining.

The flaw began to give. A minute crack developed . . .

A tiny, tiny gap appeared as the fault opened ever so slightly.

It is your doorway! urged Krasus. *Go through it!*

And Malfurion's dream form *poured* through the slim opening.

He grew as he left the counselor's cell, expanding until he stood his normal height. The change was simply a change in his own perspective, but he much preferred it to the insect-like position in which he had been while imprisoned.

Now . . . before you are noticed . . . return to us!

But here Malfurion disagreed. He had come this far to do what needed to be done to save his people, his world. The shield spell *had* to fall.

Malfurion! Tyrande pleaded. *No!*

Ignoring both, he floated around the corner . . . and stopped. Lord Xavius stood at the other end of the chamber, attention riveted on the dark portal through which the demons constantly arrived. Almost it seemed the counselor communed with whatever lurked deep within. Malfurion shuddered, recalling the inherent evil of that entity.

Still, the present situation worked in his favor. If Xavius would just keep staring into the vortex a few moments more, Malfurion could accomplish his task and be away.

He drifted toward the array, already aware of how to destroy it. A few simple alterations and it would be no more.

Both Tyrande and Krasus had ceased speaking, which either meant that they intended to let him see this through or . . . or the link with him had been somehow severed. Whichever the case, he could not turn back now.

With one last glance at the lord counselor, Malfurion reached in with his power. He first altered one of the interior components of the spell, guaranteeing its eventual instability regardless of what he did next.

It was the strength of the world, of nature, that Malfurion summoned now. He used it to force the array into a new combination, a new form that would negate its purpose and ultimately cause it to dissipate.

The shield spell faltered . . .

Lord Xavius instantly sensed the wrongness. Something terrible was happening to the shield spell.

Within the portal, Sargeras, too, sensed something amiss. *Seek!* he commanded his pawn.

The counselor spun about. His dark, magical eyes fixed on the precious array—and the ghostly intruder whom he had captured before.

The imbecile was meddling with the spell!

"Stop him!" roared Lord Xavius.

The shout nearly upset everything Malfurion had set into motion. He managed to regain his control, then looked to where Xavius pointed furiously at him, screaming for the Highborne or the demons to seize him. However, neither seemed able to obey that command, for, unlike the counselor, they could not see Malfurion's dream form, much less touch it.

Lord Xavius, on the other hand, could do both.

When it became clear that the others were of no use to him, the queen's advisor threw himself toward Malfurion. His artificial eyes radiated dark energy and Malfurion sensed an attack of some sort coming. Instinctively he raised his hand, asking aid of the wind and air.

Bolts of crimson lightning darted toward him and, had they actually reached the younger night elf, would surely have obliterated him. However, mere inches from Malfurion, the bolts not only struck some invisible barrier—solid air, perhaps—but were diverted back by the wind that the ghostly figure had summoned.

With deadly accuracy, the bolts struck the huge warriors near the portal.

The demons were tossed about like leaves in a storm. Several crashed against the walls while two collided with the sorcerers who kept working on the portal. That, in turn, threw the latter's efforts into near chaos. The portal heaved as if breathing raggedly, opening and closing in mad fashion.

The Highborne sorcerers struggled to keep the portal under control. Several demons about to step through suddenly vanished back into the darkness within.

One of the larger, winged figures standing near the opening charged in the direction of Malfurion. The huge demon obviously could not see the night elf, but swung about with its weapon in the clear hope of striking something. Malfurion tried to avoid the weapon as best he could, not at all certain that he was immune to it.

Lord Xavius had ducked away from his reversed spell, but now the counselor returned to the fray. From a pouch at his side, he removed yet another crystal.

"From this one, you shall not escape . . ."

The magical eyes flared.

Moving quickly, Malfurion set the demon between himself and the counselor. Instead of his intended victim, the advisor drew in the startled demon. The brutish figure roared its rage at such trickery and grasped in vain in the general direction of Malfurion before being sucked into the crystal.

Xavius swore and tossed the crystal aside, caring little for the fate of its contents. All his attention remained focused on the ghostly form that only he could see.

"My lord!" cried one of the sorcerers. "Shall we—"

"Do nothing! Keep at the task at hand! The portal must remain open and the shield must keep intact! I *will* deal with our invisible intruder!"

That said, Xavius prepared to cast again. Malfurion, however, had no intention of waiting for him. He turned and darted from the chamber, passing through the outer door without so much as a glance from the wary sentries.

The furious counselor immediately rushed after him. "Open the door!"

The guards obeyed. Xavius rushed out of the chamber and down the steps in pursuit of his adversary.

But Malfurion had not fled downstairs, instead floating within an inner wall of the tower. There, unseen by the lord counselor, he waited until he was certain the trouble had passed.

Returning to the chamber, Malfurion immediately drifted to the array. He had to destroy it quickly, before the Highborne had the chance to reinforce it.

However, as he reached for it, a familiar dread returned to him. Malfurion shivered and, despite himself, looked toward the portal.

You will not touch the shield . . . the terrible presence within uttered in his mind. *You do not wish to. You wish only to serve me . . . to worship me . . .*

Malfurion fought the urge to give in to that voice. He

knew what would happen to everyone if the one who spoke had the chance to enter the world. All the evil unleashed by the demons so far paled in comparison to what commanded them.

I . . . will . . . not be one of your pawns! Almost screaming from effort, Malfurion tore his gaze from the vortex.

He could feel the dread figure's fury as he sought to recover. The evil within could not affect him directly other than to play with his thoughts. Malfurion had to ignore him, think only of those he cared about and what failure meant to them.

Just a few seconds more—

His dream form twisted, suddenly wracked by incredible pain. He spun around, falling to his knees.

"No more games . . ." muttered Lord Xavius, standing at the doorway. Near him, several perplexed guards searched in vain for the enemy with whom he spoke. "No more near disasters! I will rend your spirit form to shreds, scatter your essence over the world . . . and only then will I give you to the great one to do with as he pleases . . ."

He pointed at Malfurion.

More and more the Burning Legion crushed the lines of the night elves. Lord Ravencrest kept his followers from being ripped apart, but they continued to give ground.

A fierce battering ram created by Rhonin plowed into the demons, tossing several back and digging deep into the horde. It slowed them in that one place, but everywhere else the Legion continued to advance.

From somewhere, Rhonin heard Lord Ravencrest shouting orders. "Strengthen that right flank! Archers! Take out those winged furies! Latosius, get your Moon Guard back!"

It was hard to say if the senior sorcerer heard the noble's command, but, either way, the Moon Guard remained where they were. Latosius stood at the forefront, ordering this spellcaster or that to deal with various situations. Rhonin grimaced. The elder night elf had no concept of tactics. He wasted what little might his group had on several minuscule attacks rather than on one concerted effort.

Illidan saw this, too. "The damned old idiot's making no use of them at all! I could lead them better!"

"Forget them and concentrate on your own spells—"

But even as the wizard said this, Latosius suddenly reeled. He grabbed at his throat and slumped over, blood pouring from his mouth. His skin blackened and he collapsed, clearly dead already.

"No!" Rhonin surveyed the Legion, found the warlock, and pointed.

Using the trick unleashed earlier by perhaps this same demon, Rhonin seized several arrows in flight and sent them hurtling down upon the warlock. The robed figure glanced up, saw the bolts, and simply laughed. He gestured in a manner Rhonin assumed created a defensive shield around him.

The Eredar ceased laughing when each bolt not only penetrated his shield, but went *through* his torso.

"Not as strong as you think, are you?" muttered the wizard in grim satisfaction.

Rhonin turned again to Illidan—only to find the latter gone. He looked around, found the determined young night elf riding madly toward the Moon Guard, who seemed in complete disarray without their leader.

"What does he—?" But Rhonin had no time to worry about his would-be protégé, for incredible heat suddenly surrounded him. He felt as if his skin were about to melt.

The Eredar warlocks had finally identified him as a major threat. More than one certainly had to be attacking him. He managed to summon enough strength to momentarily ease the incredible heat, but no more. Slowly, they were cooking him alive.

So this was it. Here he would die, never knowing if his part in this battle would keep history more or less intact or destroy it utterly.

Then . . . the intense pressure on him all but ceased. Rhonin reacted instinctively, using his magic to completely counter the remaining danger. His eyes cleared and he finally managed a fix on the key spellcaster.

"You like fire? I'd like it a little cooler."

The wizard reversed the spell cast upon him, sending at its user an intense wave of cold.

Rhonin sensed the bitter chill overwhelm the warlock. The Eredar stiffened, turning a pale white. His expression contorted, freezing in mid-agony.

One of the Fel Guard bumped the warlock. The frozen figure toppled, striking the hard ground with a harsh crash and scattering bits of iced demon over the battlefield.

Trying to catch his breath, Rhonin looked to the Moon Guard, the direction from which he had felt aid come. His eyes widened as he saw Illidan at their head.

The young night elf smiled his way, then turned back to the struggle. He directed the veteran sorcerers as if born to it. Illidan had them aligning in arrays that magnified what little strength they had through *him*. He, in turn, drew forth their power, thereby increasing the intensity of his own spells.

An eruption in the midst of the Burning Legion destroyed scores of demons there. Illidan let out a triumphant cheer, unaware of the strain now on the faces of the other sorcerers. He had used their power to good effect, but if he repeated such steps too often, the Moon Guard would burn out one by one.

But there was nothing Rhonin could do to let Illidan

know that and, in truth, he was not all that certain he should try. If the defenders fell here, who else was there?

If only Malfurion had not failed . . .

Mannoroth looked upon the battlefield and was pleased. His host swept across the land—not just where they encountered no resistance, but even where the puny inhabitants of this world had quickly decided to meet the Legion in battle.

He appreciated their effort to bring this struggle to a close so soon. It meant paving the way sooner for his master, Sargeras. Sargeras would be pleased with all that had been accomplished in his name. He would reward Mannoroth well, for the demon had managed this feat without having had to ask for the aid of Archimonde.

Yes, Mannoroth would be rewarded well, receiving more favor, more power, among the Legion.

As for the night elves who had so far aided the demons in their endeavor to take this world, they would receive the only reward Sargeras ever gave to such . . .

Utter annihilation.

TWENTY-THREE

alfurion thought he had outfoxed Lord Xavius, but once again, it was the young night elf who had played the fool. What had made him think that the counselor would continue to hunt for him through the stairways and corridors when clearly Malfurion would want to return to the tower and complete his mission?

It would be his final mistake. Lord Xavius was a gifted sorcerer with the power of the Well upon which to draw. Malfurion had learned much from his shan'do, but not enough, it seemed, to stand up to such a deadly foe.

And Lord Xavius was aware of that as well.

Yet, in Malfurion's head suddenly came a voice . . . not the voice from within the portal, but rather that of the mysterious Krasus, who Malfurion had long thought had abandoned him.

Malfurion . . . our strength is your strength . . . as you did in the crystal, draw upon the love and friendship of those who know you . . . and draw from the determination of those like myself, who stand with them for you.

Not all of what he said made perfect sense to the night elf, but the essence of it was clear. He sensed not only Tyrande and Krasus, but also Brox now. The three opened up their minds, their souls to Malfurion, giving to him whatever strength he needed.

You are a druid, Malfurion, perhaps the first of your kind. You draw from the world, from nature . . . and are not we all a part of both? Draw from us as well . . .

Malfurion obeyed . . . and just barely in time.

Lord Xavius cast his spell.

It should have left little trace of Malfurion's dream self. The younger night elf raised his hand to ward off the evil attack, but he did not expect his powers to be sufficient even now. The counselor's previous assault had weakened him badly.

But the spell never struck. The attack was dismissed as easily as if Malfurion had brushed away a gnat from his face.

Rise up! Krasus urged. *Rise up and do what must be done!*

He did not mean that Malfurion should do battle with the counselor. That would be a dangerous waste of time. Instead, the night elf had to finish what he had started.

Malfurion struck at the shield spell.

The array shifted out of sequence. Two of the Highborne hurried to adjust it, but the floor beneath their feet suddenly gave way as the stones there acted on Malfurion's silent request to cease their natural tendency to be strong and hold things together. With a scream, the pair dropped from sight.

Lord Xavius struck angrily at Malfurion, enshrouding him in a vapor that clung to the latter's dream form and tried to eat away at it. Malfurion struggled at first, but the combined strength of Tyrande, Brox, and Krasus steeled him again. He quickly summoned a wind that assailed the vapor, scattering it.

But while Malfurion dealt with the vapor, Xavius took the opportunity to restore the shield spell to some order. He then turned toward his adversary, his next intent obvious.

Malfurion grew frustrated. This could not go on indefinitely. Eventually, he would either lose or be forced to flee. Something had to change . . . and quickly.

He spun, but not toward either the array or Lord Xavius.

Instead, Malfurion now faced the portal.

Again he called upon the wind, this time asking it to prove it was strong enough to push about more than simple vapor. Malfurion eyed the Highborne in particular, daring the wind to show what it could do.

And within their sanctum, the sorcerers suddenly found themselves assaulted by a gale. Three of their number were quickly thrown across the chamber, where they struck the opposing wall hard. As they fell, another stumbled away from the pattern, then tumbled over one of the still forms.

The rest bent low, seeking to keep from the wind's full wrath. Yet, despite no more falling prey, it was clear that the losses already suffered had put a strain on the survivors, for the portal shimmered and twisted dangerously. The sense of evil that Malfurion had felt lessened.

Fiery hands suddenly seized him by the the back of the neck, throttling Malfurion. They burned into Malfurion's dream form as if into his own flesh, causing him to unleash a scream that, despite its intensity, only his attacker could hear.

"The power of the great one is with me!" roared the queen's advisor with much satisfaction. "You are no match for us both!"

Indeed, Malfurion felt the evil reaching out again from the shifting portal. While still not as potent as when it had sought to turn him to the Highborne's side, it added much to the counselor's already fearsome might. Against it, even the strength Malfurion received from the three proved insufficient.

Tyrande . . . He did not try to summon the priestess, only feared in his mind that he might never see her again, never be near her.

The voice of Krasus suddenly filled his head again. *Courage, druid . . . there is another of us who has been waiting for just this moment.*

A fourth presence intruded, immediately adding itself to those strengthening Malfurion. Like Krasus, it was a being far superior to a mere night elf. He sensed a weakness in it, but compared to any of Malfurion's own kind, such weakness was minute, laughable. Oddly, it almost felt as if the new presence was the twin of Krasus, for they were so much alike in feel that at first he had some trouble differentiating between the pair.

Even the new voice in his head reminded him much of Krasus. *I am Korialstrasz . . . and I freely give what I have.*

Their gifts were those with which life, nature, had endowed them. The added presence of Korialstrasz multiplied Malfurion's will a hundredfold, giving him hope such as he had never had.

You are a druid . . . Krasus reminded him yet again. *The world is your strength.*

Malfurion felt invigorated. Now he sensed not only his distant companions, but the stones, the wind, the clouds, the earth, the trees . . . *everything.* Malfurion was nearly overwhelmed by the fury the world radiated now. The evil thus far perpetrated by the Highborne and the demons offended the elements as nothing ever had before.

I promised I would do what I could, he said to them. *Grant me your strength as well and it will be done!*

To Malfurion, this took place over what felt like an eternity, but when he at last glanced at Lord Xavius, he saw that only a second at most had perhaps passed. The counselor stood almost as if frozen, his expression sluggishly altering as he prepared, with the power of his master behind him, to finally destroy his ghostly adversary.

Malfurion smiled at the other night elf's folly. He raised his hands to the hidden sky and called upon its might.

Outside, thunder roared. The Highborne around the portal and the array faltered again, aware that this was not a part of their work. Even Lord Xavius frowned.

And suddenly the palace tower shook—then *exploded*.

Captain Varo'then knelt before Azshara, his helmet carried in the crook of his arm. "You summoned me, my glorious queen?"

Two of Azshara's servants brushed her luxurious hair, something she had them do several times a day to keep it fluffed and perfect. While they performed this task, she amused herself with sampling the exotic scents brought to her recently by traders.

"Yes, captain. I wondered what that noise was coming from above. It sounded as if it originated from the tower. Is there some trouble of which I have not been informed?"

The male night elf shrugged. "None that I am aware of, Light of a Thousand Moons. Perhaps it is the prelude to the great Sargeras's entrance."

"You think so?" Her eyes lit up. "How wonderful!" She waved him off. "In that case, I should be prepared! Surely we are in for a wonderful event!"

"As you say, Glory of Our People. As you say." The captain rose, replacing his helmet on his head. He hesitated. "Would you like me to investigate, just to be certain?"

"No, I am certain you are correct! By all means do *not* bother Lord Xavius!" Azshara sniffed another vial. The scent made her blood race in ways she enjoyed. Perhaps she would wear *this* one when she met the god. "After all, I am certain the good counselor has everything in hand."

* * *

The top half of the tower chamber had been sheared off, the lightning bolts sent by the heavens ripping it away and sending the roof and more hurtling into the black Well below.

Several large chunks of stone had collapsed into the room, killing two of the Highborne and scattering most of the rest. The shield array and the portal still stood . . . but both had been badly weakened.

Shrieking winds tore at those within. One sorcerer thrown near the edge by the blasts made the mistake of rising. The winds caught his robed form, carrying him backward.

With a pathetic shriek, he followed the top of the tower down into the Well.

An intense downpour battered at the survivors. Still struggling to keep their spells intact, the Highborne fell to their knees. This did little to preserve them, though, so severe was the storm.

Only two figures remained untouched by the elements. One was Malfurion, his dream form allowing the wind and rain to pass through harmlessly. The other was Lord Xavius, protected not only by the power he drew from the Well, but by the evil still managing to leak through from the dark vortex.

"Impressive!" shouted the counselor. "If, in the end, futile, my young friend! You have but the power of the Well upon which to draw . . . while I also have the might of a god!"

His remarks made Malfurion smile. The lord counselor did not yet realize what he now fought. He assumed that he still simply faced another adept sorcerer.

"No, my lord," the younger night elf called back. "You have it turned around! For you, there's only the Well and the supposed might of a demon that *claims* godhood! For me . . . there's the power of the world itself as my ally!"

Xavius sneered. "I've no more use for your babbling . . ."

Malfurion felt him summon from the Well such power as

surely none before ever had. It jarred the druid for a moment, but then the strength that served Malfurion reassured him.

"You must be stopped," he declared to the counselor. "You and the thing you serve must be stopped."

Whatever spell Lord Xavius intended to cast, Malfurion would never know. Before the counselor could complete it, the elements themselves assailed him. Lightning struck again and again at Xavius, burning him from within and without. His skin blackened and peeled, yet he did not fall.

The rain became a torrent that poured all its might down on Malfurion's foe. Xavius seemed to melt before the younger night elf's eyes, flesh and muscle sloughing off— and yet the counselor still strained to reach him.

Then, thunder cracked, thunder so loud that what remained of the tower shook, sending another of the Highborne into the dark waters of the Well. Thunder so loud it shook Malfurion himself to his very being.

Thunder so loud that Lord Xavius, counselor to the queen and highest of the Highborne—*shattered*.

He howled like one of the hellish felbeasts as he exploded, a howl that continued even as the pieces scattered in the air. The cloud of dust that had once been the advisor spun around and around, tossed about by an angry, fearsome wind.

The remaining Highborne finally abandoned their posts, fleeing from the wrath of the one who had bested their feared leader. Malfurion let them depart, knowing that he had depleted himself beyond measure but still needing to deal with one final matter.

With Lord Xavius no longer there to protect it, the shield array collapsed easily. A simple gesture from the young druid finally dismissed the evil spell, removing at last the possible impediment to his people's survival. He only prayed that it was not already too late.

At last, he returned his attention to the portal.

It was but a faint shadow of itself, a mere hole in reality. Malfurion glared at it, knowing that he could not permanently seal off his world from the evil within . . . but he could at least give it some respite.

You delay the inevitable . . . came the voice he dreaded. *I will devour your world . . . just as I have so many others . . .*

"You'll find us a sour treat," Malfurion retorted.

Once again he unleashed the elements.

The rain washed away the precious pattern over which the portal floated. Bolt after bolt of lightning struck the very center of the hole, forcing that within to retreat further. The wind swirled around the weakened spell, tearing away at it with the intensity of a fierce twister.

And the earth . . . the earth shook, finally succeeding in breaking up the last bits of foundation left to the high tower.

With no corporeal form, Malfurion had nothing to fear from the collapsing structure. Despite his growing weariness, he watched it all happen, determined to see for himself that there would be no last reprieve.

The floor tipped. Instruments of dark sorcery and pieces of what remained of the walls clattered toward the lower end. A tremendous groan accompanied the collapse.

The tower fell.

As it did, the portal closed in on itself, rapidly shrinking.

A sudden suction caught Malfurion off guard. He felt his dream form pulled by a powerful force toward the vanishing hole.

I will still have you . . . came the faint yet baleful voice.

The night elf struggled, urging his dream form away from the gap. Dust flowed through him and into the shrinking portal. Other refuse followed.

The strain became unbearable. He was dragged closer and closer . . .

Malfurion! Tyrande called. *Malfurion!*

He clung to her call, trying to use it as a tether. Below him, the last of the tower joined the rest in the dark abyss of the Well of Eternity. Only Malfurion and the tiny but malevolent hole remained.

Tyrande! he silently called. He shut his eyes, trying to picture her, trying to come to her.

I have you . . . said a voice he could not identify.

The world turned upside down.

Mannoroth felt the loss. Mannoroth felt the emptiness even before it happened.

The huge, bestial commander paused in the rear of the horde, turning his ugly, tusked head in the direction of the tower.

The tower that was no longer there.

"Noooooooo!" he roared.

Rhonin felt it. He felt the sudden surge of power, the surge of strength. He suddenly imagined himself able to build worlds, take the stars from the heavens and rearrange them to his desire. He was invincible, omnipotent.

The spell sealing off the Well of Eternity had been destroyed.

Immediately he looked to Illidan, to see if the young night elf had sensed the same. Rhonin need not have feared, though, for Illidan clearly had experienced the same rush of strength as he had. In fact, not only did the Moon Guard all look strong and ready, but so did the *rest* of the defenders as well.

The Well and the night elves are one, the wizard realized.

Even those who could not cast spells were still tied to it to some extent. Its loss had stripped them in ways that they could never realize. Now, though, Rhonin saw in every figure, from Lord Ravencrest down to the lowliest soldier, a renewed confidence and determination. Truly they now thought themselves unbeatable by any force.

Even the Burning Legion.

Horns blared. The night elves gave a collective roar well matching anything emitted prior by the demons. The front lines of the Legion faltered, not at all certain what this abrupt change meant.

"Have at them!" shouted Ravencrest.

The defenders surged forward. Demons suddenly found themselves harried as never before. Felbeasts were slaughtered before they could make their way back to the horde. Tusked warriors dropped one after another as each time the night elves' blades sank true. The encroaching Legion was stopped dead in its tracks.

Illidan led the Moon Guard against the invaders, continuing to guide their efforts through his own spells. The land itself rippled beneath the Burning Legion's feet, tossing demons about as if they were nothing. Several of the winged Doomguard burst into flames as they darted overhead, becoming instead fiery missiles that added further mayhem to their own ranks.

Rhonin did not stay out of the battle, either. With the memories of all those who had died this day and all those who would perish in the future war in mind, he struck again and again at the ones responsible. An Eredar warlock who foolishly sought to match him was enveloped by his own robes, which twisted tightly until they snapped the demon in twain. From the wizard then came a punishing series of blue lightning bolts that methodically hunted down other spellcasters among the Legion, leaving behind only slight piles of ash to mark the former foes.

For the first time, true pandemonium broke out among the fearsome warriors. This was not the battle expected, the bloodshed desired. There was nothing here now save their own deaths, a prospect even the demons found daunting.

Their lines buckled. The night elves pushed forward.

"We have them now!" shouted Lord Ravencrest. "Give them no quarter!"

The defenders rallied further around his cry. Despite the imposing size of the invaders, the night elves advanced undaunted.

And Rhonin and Illidan continued to pave the way to victory. The wizard looked up, spying several of the savage Infernals plummeting toward the defenders. As ever, the fiery demons were rolled up into balls, dropping like boulders to create the most disastrous results.

For once, Rhonin made some use of Illidan's tactics. With the Well from which to draw, he created a huge golden barrier in the sky, one which the Infernals could not avoid. The barrier was not simply a wall, however, for Rhonin had another purpose in mind. He shaped it according to those desires, curving it and forcing those demons who crashed into it to bounce instead in the direction he chose.

The very midst of their own army. .

Even the bolts he had cast down upon the demons earlier could not have done as much devastation as the fearsome behemoths did now. More than two dozen Infernals struck the Legion's center at various points, decimating the ranks and creating huge, smoking craters. The bodies of the enemy flew everywhere, crashing down upon others and multiplying the damage tenfold.

From far to his side, the wizard heard triumphant laughter. Illidan clapped his hands in honor of the human's successful effort, then pointed at the harried enemy.

A part of the Burning Legion's left flank suddenly floundered, many immediately sinking to their knees. The solid earth below them had become as soup and the heavy, armored forms of the demons could do nothing but plunge beneath its surface like stones. A few struggled, but, in the end, any who had the misfortune of being where Illidan had cast vanished.

With a wave of his hand, the young night elf resolidified the earth, erasing all trace of his victims. He then turned back to Rhonin and, with a grand flourish, bowed to the wizard.

Rhonin kept his expression set, only nodding again. If nothing else, Illidan surely kept the demons at bay.

At last, under such brutal assault, the Burning Legion did the only thing it could do—retreat en masse.

There was no horn, no call. The demons simply began to back away. They kept a semblance of order, but clearly it was all their commanders could do to maintain that much. Even still, they did not move fast enough to suit the defenders, who took full advantage of the victory.

The Moon Guard in particular savored the turn of events. They hunted the felbeasts especially, turning some into gnarled bits of wood, others into rodents. Several simply burst into flames as they ran—their tails between their legs— for the questionable safety of the Legion ranks.

Here and there, pockets of resistance remained, but those were quickly whittled down by the eager soldiers. Fel Guard lay everywhere. Rhonin had no doubt that each night elf thought about the countless dead the Burning Legion had already left in its wake. There had to have been many friends and loved ones among Zin-Azshari's victims.

However, one cause for which the night elves continued

to fight concerned the wizard. Even now, Ravencrest shouted her name, using it to further rally the troops.

"For Azshara! For the queen! We ride to her rescue!"

Rhonin had heard Malfurion's suggestion that the queen was likely as complicit in the slaughter as most believed her counselor and the Highborne were and he suspected that to be the truth. The wizard could only keep telling himself that the truth would come out if and when they reached the palace.

Back and back the Burning Legion went, edging into the very borders of the ruined capital. They died in droves, they died by weapon or wizardry, but they *died*. The battle raged unceasingly through the darkness, the ground buried under the corpses of the fiendish invaders.

Perhaps it would have gone on, perhaps they could have taken the fight into Zin-Azshari itself and even reached the palace, but as day forced its will upon night, the defenders at last flagged. They had given their all in an effort well worth praise, but even Lord Ravencrest saw that to go on would put the night elves at more risk than they could afford. His expression reluctant, he nonetheless signaled the horns to sound the halt.

As the horns called, Illidan's expression grew cross. He tried to make the Moon Guard follow him forward, but while some seemed eager enough, all clearly had spent themselves of their physical energy.

Rhonin, too, was exhausted. True, he could still cast spells of great destruction, but his body was covered in sweat and he felt faintness in his head if he moved too quickly. His concentration slipped more and more . . .

Illidan aside, the rest of the night elves knew that they could go no further—not in the daylight—but that did not take away from what they had accomplished. True, the threat had not been removed, but they now saw that the demons were limited. They could be slain. They could be driven back.

The commander quickly sought volunteers to ride out through the various parts of the night elf realm, their mission of two purposes. They were to rally those they found in order to create yet a vaster force, a multipronged defense with which to meet the next assault of the Burning Legion—for surely there would be one—and also to see the extent of the devastation elsewhere.

In addition to that effort, the noble also immediately set his personal sorcerer—Illidan—in charge of the Moon Guard already with them. There was some mild protest from those most senior among the survivors, but a simple show of power in the form of one last harsh explosion among the retreating demons quickly silenced the young spellcaster's critics.

Pleased with his new status, Illidan sought out Rhonin to tell him. The wizard nodded politely, on the one hand wondering if he had ever been so enthusiastic when younger, and on the other worried about how Illidan's new status would affect his personality. Illidan had greater potential yet than what had so far been revealed, but his recklessness was a trap that could create of him a danger in its own way as deadly as the Burning Legion. Rhonin vowed to keep an eye on his counterpart.

Left alone again, the one human among the night elves slowly surveyed the force that had been arrayed against the demons. Sunlight made their armor glitter, giving the host an epic appearance. They looked and acted as if they could defeat any enemy. Despite that, however, Rhonin remained aware that they needed a far greater force if they hoped to win the final struggle. History said that victory was ensured, but too many factors—himself included—now muddied the outcome. Worse, the Burning Legion was well aware of the magical might against them; they would be seeking the wizard and Illidan more now.

Rhonin had been the target of the demons and their allies in his own time. He did not look forward to repeating that situation.

And what of the one most responsible for this night's success? Not Rhonin. Not Illidan. Not all the Moon Guard or Lord Ravencrest and his legions. None of them was the real reason for victory.

What, the weary wizard thought as he gazed out at dark Zin-Azshari and the disorganized horde, *what has happened to Malfurion?*

TWENTY-FOUR

He lay as still as death, that image made all the worse by the fact that none of them could sense any trace of the link they had once had with him. Tyrande nestled Malfurion's head in her lap, the soft grass underneath acting as the rest of his bed.

"Is he lost to us?" asked a perplexed Jarod Shadowsong. The captain had accompanied the group out to this location far in the woods, ostensibly to keep an eye on his prisoner, Krasus. He had not played a role in their spellwork, but had instead ended up acting as guard when the situation had changed. He had grown from reluctant addition to concerned companion even though he still understood little of what had taken place.

"No!" Tyrande snapped. In a more apologetic tone, she added, "He can't be . . ."

"He does not smell dead," rumbled Korialstrasz.

Jarod Shadowsong looked askance each time Korialstrasz spoke. He had yet to grow used to the presence of the red dragon. It might have amused Tyrande at one time, but not under the present circumstances. She herself had quickly come to accept the behemoth, especially since she sensed some hidden relationship between Korialstrasz and Krasus. They seemed almost like brothers or twins.

Thinking of twins made her gaze down at Malfurion again.

Krasus paced the area. He seemed much healthier now and the young priestess had noted that the effect had magnified when he had come within sight of the dragon. Unfortunately, that health did not help the pale figure now, for he appeared as worried as she did about Malfurion—even though Krasus had clearly never met him before seeing the night elf in the temple.

Brox knelt across from Tyrande, his ax placed next to his stricken friend. The orc's head was buried in his chest and she could hear him muttering what sounded like a prayer.

"The area was charged with powerful magical forces," murmured Krasus to himself. "It could have dispersed parts of his dream self to every corner of the world. He might be able to regather himself . . . but the odds of that . . ."

Captain Shadowsong looked around at the others. "Forgive this impertinent question, but did he at least accomplish what he hoped to?"

The cowled figure turned to him, expression flat. "He did do that at least. I pray it is enough."

"Stop talking like that . . ." Tyrande insisted. She wiped a tear from her eye, then gazed up at the sunlit sky. Despite the brightness, Tyrande refused to look away. "Elune, Mother Moon, forgive this servant for disturbing your rest! I do not dare ask for him to be returned . . . but at least give us an answer as to his fate!"

But no glorious light shone down on Malfurion. The moon did not suddenly appear and speak to them.

"Perhaps it would be better if we brought him back to the temple," suggested the Guard captain. "Maybe she can hear him better there . . ."

Tyrande did not bother to answer him.

Krasus paused in his pacing. He stared to the south, where the woods thickened. His eyes narrowed and he pursed his lips in frustration. "I know you are there."

"And I now know what you are," returned a booming voice.

The nearest trees suddenly melded together, forming a figure with a lower torso akin to that of a huge stag and a chest, arms, and face more like those of Tyrande and Jarod Shadowsong.

Fists tight, Cenarius moved slowly toward the band. He and Krasus matched gazes for a time, then both nodded in respect.

The forest lord walked over to where Tyrande held Malfurion. Brox respectfully stepped out of the way while the Guard captain stared open-mouthed from where he stood.

"Daughter of my dear Elune, your tears touch the heaven and the earth."

"I cry for him, my lord . . . one you also loved."

Cenarius nodded. His forelegs bent in a kneeling motion and he touched Malfurion's forehead ever so gently. "He is a son to me . . . and so I am pleased that he has one like you who also holds him so near . . ."

"I—we've been friends since childhood."

The forest lord chuckled, a sound that brought songbirds near and made a cool, refreshing breeze caress the cheeks of each in the party. "Yes, I heard your pleas to dear Elune, both the spoken and unspoken ones."

Tyrande did not hide her embarrassment. "But all my entreaties have been for nothing."

His expression turned to one of honest puzzlement. "Did you think that? Why would I come, then?"

The others froze. The novice priestess shook her head. "I don't understand!"

"Because you are young still. Wait until you reach my age . . ." With that, Cenarius opened his left hand.

An emerald light rose from his open palm. It floated a few inches above as if orienting itself.

Rising, the demigod stepped back to observe his student. "I walked the Emerald Dream, seeking answers to our many terrible questions. I hunted through there looking for what could be done about these followers of death . . ." A gentle smile crossed his bearded visage. ". . . and imagine my surprise when I found one I knew drifting in the Emerald Dream . . . but in a very dazed and much confused state. Why, he didn't even *know* himself, much less me!"

And as Cenarius finished, the light drifted over to Malfurion, sinking harmlessly into his head.

The night elf's eyes opened.

"Malfurion!"

Tyrande's voice was the first thing that registered with Malfurion and he quickly seized upon it, using it as a tether, a lifeline. He pulled himself from the abyss of unconsciousness toward a bright but comforting light.

And when he opened his eyes, it was to see Tyrande under the morning sun. Surprisingly, the daylight did not bother him and he even thought that it revealed to him a Tyrande so beautiful he could not at first believe it.

He almost told her, but then the presence of the others made him shut his feelings inside again. He settled for touching her hand, then acknowledging the others.

"The—the shield—" His voice sounded like that of a frog. "Is it—"

"Gone," replied a figure who was and was not a night elf. To Malfurion, surely this had to be Krasus. "For now, the

Burning Legion has been held in check . . . at least in one place."

Malfurion nodded. He knew that the war was not over, that his people still faced annihilation. Yet, that did not take away from the night's triumph. If nothing else, there was still hope.

"We will fight them," Tyrande promised. "We will save our world."

"They can be beaten," agreed Brox, brandishing proudly the weapon that the young druid had helped create. "This I know."

Krasus remained pragmatic. "They can . . . but we will need more help. We will need the dragons."

"You'll need more than the dragons!" Cenarius bellowed. "And I go now to see to that!" He stepped from the others, but gave Malfurion one last smile. "You've made me proud, my *thero'shan* . . . my honored student."

"Thank you, shan'do." He watched as the demigod melted back into the trees.

"Do we return to Suramar now?" asked a figure in a Guard officer's uniform. Malfurion could not place him, but assumed the others had a reason for him being here.

"Yes," said Krasus. "We return to Suramar."

With Tyrande's help, Malfurion rose. "But only for a short time. The portal through which the demons flowed was destroyed, but, unlike the shield, the Highborne can re-make it easily. More will come, I'm afraid."

Despite his wish otherwise, no one disagreed. Malfurion looked to the direction of Zin-Azshari. A terrible evil had come to his land, one that had to be stopped before it could raze all in its path. Malfurion had helped in great part to stop the Burning Legion's initial advance and, for reasons he could not himself explain, he did not doubt that it would somehow fall to him again to assist in keeping the invading demons from destroying his beloved Kalimdor.

Malfurion only prayed that when that time came he would be found ready to face them . . . or else not only Kalimdor but the *entire* world risked obliteration.

CONTINUED IN
WAR OF THE ANCIENTS
BOOK TWO
THE DEMON SOUL

ABOUT THE AUTHOR

Richard A. Knaak is *The New York Times* bestselling fantasy author of 26 novels and over a dozen short pieces, including THE LEGEND OF HUMA and NIGHT OF BLOOD for *Dragonlance* and DAY OF THE DRAGON for *WarCraft*. He has also written the popular *Dragonrealm* series and several independent pieces. His works have been published in several languages, most recently Russian, Turkish, Chinese, Czech, German, and Spanish. He has also adapted the Korean Manga, RAGNAROK, published by Tokyopop, for American audiences and will be overseeing the new *WarCraft* Manga, the first volume of which will be out about the same time as WELL OF ETERNITY. In addtion to the second volume of WAR OF THE ANCIENTS—THE DEMON SOUL, the author is at work on EMPIRE OF BLOOD, the final book in his epic *Dragonlance* trilogy, THE MINOTAUR WARS.

Future works include THE BURNING LEGION—the conclusion to the *WarCraft* trilogy—and a third *Diablo* novel. His most recent hardcover, TIDES OF BLOOD, the sequel to NIGHT, was just released by Wizards of the Coast.